EDGEWOOD ACADEMY ELITE BOOK 3

BEAUTIFUL
Ascension

P.H. NIX

Copyright © 2024 by P. H. Nix

All rights reserved.

No part of this book may be reproduced in any form or by any electronic or mechanical means, including information storage and retrieval systems, without written permission from the author, except for the use of brief quotations in a book review.

BLURB

Are you ready for the exciting end of the Edgewood Academy Elite? There are so many questions left to answer. Can the Heirs get their girl back or has too much damage been done?

Edgewood thinks it's destroyed me, but I'm coming back swinging.

I let them in, and they broke my heart. Now, it's time for the Heirs and the town of Edgewood to pay. Wyatt, Owen, Lev, Sebastian, Wes, the Fraternitas, and Samantha thought they won. I'm going to strip them of the one thing they whole dear–power.

As I dig for answers, more questions arise. An organization more powerful than Fraternitas promises me answers, but it will come with a cost. One that will shake Edgewood to its core, but I'll do anything to protect what's mine, even if it costs me the ones I love. It's time they all pay. Starting with Samantha Davenport. Her world is about to be spun on its axis. Then I'll step on the neck of the Heirs and spit in the face of the organization they hold so dearly.

The Queen is back, and my Ascension will be beautiful.

Beautiful Ascension is the final book in the Edgewood Academy Elite Series. It is a slow burn why choose dark college romance. This means the main character ends up with more than one love interest. As the series progresses, so will the level of darkness. It is an 18+ series with profanity, a feisty heroine, bullying, and obsessive and possessive themes.

Content Warning: This might not be the series for you if you have triggers. Please remember self-care. I never want my readers to put themselves into a place where the world they disappear into causes harm. Please don't go into this story blind if dark romance is new to you. Please visit https://linktr.ee/authorphnix for a more detailed list of triggers.

GLOSSARY

To help with some of the Jamaican Patois in this series, I've provided a glossary of terms.
Box: slap
Bwoy: boy
Cyaan: can't
Deh: there/they
Dem: them
Dem don't righted: they're not okay
Di: the
Eediots: idiots
Fi: to
Fuckery: bullshit
Gal: Girl
Haffi: Have to
Har: her
Irie: cool/good
Mi den yah: I'm okay
Nevah: never
Not ah bumbo: Not a fucking chance
No suh: no sir

Pussyholes: assholes/fuckers
Suh: So
Tump: punch
Unnuh: one or more people
Wah gwan: Hello/What's up
Wha di ras: what the hell/fuck
Whine: A form of dancing

PLAYLIST

Listen on Spotify: Beautiful Ascension: Edgewood Academy Elite Series Book III
Jar of Hearts- Christina Perri
Traitor- Olivia Rodrigo
The Apology I'll Never Receive- Rory
Only Love Can Hurt Like This- Paloma Faith
Lose You to Love Me- Selena Gomez
You've Created a Monster- Bohnes
Exile- Taylor Swift
Little Girl Gone- CHINCHILLA
You Broke Me First- Tate McRae
Unsteady- X Ambassadors
Dynasty- Miia
Paint the Town Red- Doja Cat
Cut You Off- CHINCHILLA
Wake Me Up When September Ends- Green Day
The Heart Wants What It Wants- Selena Gomez
Take This Pain- Jake Banefield
Without Me- Halsey
Mount Everest- Labrinth

Coming Home- Skylar Grey
I See Red- Everybody Loves an Outlaw
Apologize- One Republic ft. Timberland
If I Would Have Known- Kyle Hume
Lose Control- Teddy Swims
Jericho- Iniko
Put It On the Floor- Latto
Greedy- Tate McRae
Falling in Love with Who I Am- Aqyila
Bathroom- Montell Fish
In This Moment- Whore
Fuck You- Silent Child
Monsters- Shinedown
Dragula- Rob Zombie
My Chick Bad- Ludacris ft. Nicki Minaj
Your Love is Gone- SLANDER & Dylan Matthew
Forget Me (Cover)- Celina Sharma
War of Hearts- Ruelle
What Was I Made For- Billie Eilish
You Are The Reason- Calum Scott
Control- Zoe Wees
Get You the Moon- Kina & Snow
Breakfast- Dove Cameron
Sex and Candy- Alexander Jean
Flames- Donzell Taggart
I Guess- Saint Levant & Playyard
Make Me Feel- Elvis Drew
Blow- Ed Sheeran ft. Chris Stapleton & Bruno Mars
Bongos- Cardi B ft. Megan Thee Stallion
Jiggy Woogie Baby Lawd & DLegend
Rodeo- Lah Pat
Attention- Doja Cat
I Know- Big Sean ft. Jhené Aiko
Bleed For You- Elvis Drew ft. Nazaki
Always Been You- Jessie Murph
Psycho Crazy- Halestorm

Karma's a Bitch- Sophia Rayne
Rise Above it All- UNSECRET & Mike Mains
Brother- Kodaline
Venom- Eminem
See You Again- Wiz Khalifa ft. Charlie Puth
Lift Me Up- Rihanna
Until I Found You- Stephen Sanchez
Don't Blame Me- Taylor Swift

AUTHOR NOTE

While Samantha Davenport is a vile character created from the depths of my imagination, some of what she and Owen endured happens in real life, daily. 1 in 9 girls and 1 in every 20 boys have experienced some form of sexual abuse before the age of 18.

Willing or unwilling, Samantha was knowingly groomed, repeatedly sexually assaulted and manipulated by the adults around her. This doesn't take away from her deplorable actions, but victims' voices should be raised. We can still hold her accountable for her part throughout this series and also call out the horrible things that happened to her.

Please read responsibly, as this series contains content not suitable for minors and is for an 18+ audience. For a full list of content and trigger warnings, visit: https://linktr.ee/authorphnix.

*Any statical data referred to in this book was obtained from the Rape, Abuse & Incest National Network (RAINN). For more information on RAINN or the data provided, visit: https://www.rain.org/.

ARIAH

"I didn't want to come to this stupid fucking engagement party in the first place," I grumble to myself.

This damn thing feels so restricting, and my feet freaking hurt. Everything just feels off.

"We can sneak out the back. No one will ever know," Shay whispers, sensing my growing frustration.

"I wish. If I leave, all the plans I've been working on will fall through. I need the Fraternitas to believe I'm a docile, willing participant."

Shay snorts. "Docile? Do you know who you are? If they think for a minute you're anything but—" She's cut off.

"Oh look, it's the reject," Brittany slurs.

Someone's hammered.

"Did you say that in the mirror to yourself?" I challenge, and her nose scrunches as she curls her lip in anger.

She takes a step forward, but Reign blocks her. "I wouldn't do that if I were you."

Brittany looks momentarily stunned, but she quickly recovers. "Whatever. I'm over this whole thing. Owen sent me to find you."

Rolling my eyes, I retort, "Right, because Owen sending you to deliver a message to me is ever going to be believable."

"Whatever. Suit yourself. Don't say I never tried to do you any favors." Brittany spins, almost taking out a passing waiter and his tray of hors d'oeuvres. "Stupid bitch Sam better be happy," I swear she mutters before skulking away.

Another twenty minutes go by, and I need out of these clothes or at least a quiet spot to have a moment to myself.

Shay's talking with her mother, and Reign steps away to find Elias, so I slip away. I want to be alone.

Huffing, I make my way down another long-ass hallway, seeking out a room to have a moment to catch my breath.

Who the fuck wants to be at the engagement party of the men you swore cared about you?

"Fucking contract, and its goddamn rules," I mutter as I try each door handle and find each one locked.

It was bad enough coming back and finding out that there was no mistake. Those assholes really did choose the vile cunt and strung me along so that they could crush me. *Well fuck her and fuck them too!*

Pausing, I rest my hand against the wall, taking off these godforsaken heels. No one should have to wear death traps. Heels, like thongs, should be considered crimes against the state, punishable by death.

I rub my aching foot and try to process the last three months since I stepped back into this bullshit town. The bullying and constant reminders I was always someone they were using. Tears build in my eyes.

Cut it the fuck out, Riah. You're built stronger than this!

Damn the mantra today. Today, I'm not built strong. Today, I want to find a corner and crumble.

Sighing, I rest my foot back on the floor and try the last door in this wing. *If this one is locked, I'm picking the motherfucker.*

I test the knob and sigh in relief when I'm met with no resistance. I'm so excited that I finally found a room that I'm not aware that someone—no, someones—are in here.

My head jerks at the sound of a female moan, ready to apologize, when the sight that greets me freezes me to my spot.

I'd recognize the back of that head anywhere. *Owen.* His back might be to me, but his tattooed neck is unmistakable.

Samantha's on top of him, riding him as she holds a knife to the spot where my "A" is carved in his chest.

I must let out a gasp because both their attentions turn to me.

"Can't you see we're fucking busy?" Owen snaps. "Get the fuck out of here!"

"No, stay and watch as I carve the last of you from them, and then you'll finally recognize your place, you gutter troll," Sam sneers. A combination of pleasure, victory, and menace fills her usually stiff face.

I will my feet to move, but it's like my brain is trying to process the sight of Owen, *my Owen,* underneath her and refuses to cooperate.

"Get the fuck out," Owen growls, and a pain I've never felt before shoots through me, spurring my feet into action as I escape. I don't stop running until the unbearable pain racking my body causes me to collapse.

My soul is cracked so wide open I don't realize someone's arms are wrapped around me. I hear the faint murmurs telling me it's okay, and they have me before I let grief suck me into its darkest depths. As my grip on reality blinks in and out, I know one thing without a doubt.

I'm going to burn this town to the motherfucking ground.

1

ARIAH

FIVE MONTHS EARLIER...

I step into the room, noticing I'm the last girl to arrive. The Council and Wyatt, Wes, Lev, and Sebastian are here, but I don't see Owen.

What the hell is going on?

Confusion knits my brows as I stand next to Wes. "What's going on? Why are we meeting here?"

Before he can answer, Mr. Edgewood fills in the blanks, but it still makes no sense.

"Why are we doing this now instead of next weekend?" I ask Wes.

"We know who we want, and it doesn't make sense to prolong the process another week. The event will just be a formality. We want to stop having to go out and string girls along who'll never be Fraternitasm wife material. Why should we pretend when the person we want has been right here all along? The rest of you are worthless, and only one of you was ever worthy of becoming our Chosen," he replies. The brashness in his tone is off-putting, but his eyes are trained on Sam as he imparts them.

My gut roils with apprehension and nervousness as I stand in line with the remaining Selected, perplexed at the change of plans, a question on the tip of my lips when Mr. Edgewood speaks.

"To fulfill the last rite into the Fraternitas, the original male Heir must select a bride when they come of age. But five original bloodline male Heirs must come together every five generations to choose one wife, ensuring the continuation of a strong original bloodline."

Staring around the room, I take in the look of excitement on Lev's, Wyatt's, and Sebastian's faces. Owen's noticeable absence sets off every alarm bell in my head.

Where's Owen? They wouldn't do this without him?

When my gaze land on Wes, the tightness in his face is the only warning that something fucked is about to happen.

I watch as Wes steps forward with a ring-sized box in his hands, barely hearing his father announce that Wes will announce who they've made their Chosen.

The pulse in my neck is beating so loud. I nearly miss it when Wes states, "We, the Heirs of Edgewood, in our last act before becoming full members of the Fraternitas, select," he opens the box to the sparkling princess-cut four-carat diamond centered on a platinum band lined with four two-carat stones. "Samantha—"

Sharp pain and nausea hit me as his words strike a blow I'm not prepared for. I don't need to hear the rest of his words and skirt around the room that has broken into chaos and race from the living nightmare.

"We're here," my grandmother says, squeezing my knee and snapping me from the scene playing on a loop in my mind.

I've been so lost in my thoughts I don't remember the trip here. Not the drive to the airport or the flight to Colorado.

After returning to the house and deciding that it was time to leave, now that I was no longer contractually obligated to stay in Edgewood, numbness saturated my pores. I know people have tried to talk to me at points throughout the trip, but I shut them out. I didn't want to deal with the question of, *'How are you?'* or the encouraging, *'Things will get better.'*

Fuck that shit.

I know I'll eventually keep going. I just don't want to right now.

Pulling the door handle, I exit the car, joining Jamie and the twins.

"Riah," Kellan wraps his arms around my waist.

"It will be okay, Ry. Next time we see them, we'll kick 'em in the shins," Kylan adds, squeezing me from behind.

I snort as a tear leaks from my eye. I quickly swipe it away and bask in their love and sense of loyalty while I choke back a sob. The assholes didn't just impact my life. They impacted theirs, as well.

The twins loved the time they spent with the guys, and as much as Wyatt was their first favorite, Wes quickly became their second.

Sighing, I close my eyes, attempting to stave off the memories of all the time the twins spent with my guys. *Fuck they aren't mine anymore.* Wyatt would teach them how to sleuth around the house undetected. Lev played video games and taught them code. Sebastian showed them the difference between Windsor and Pratt knots. Wes, he'd spend endless hours going on imaginary missions to destroy evil invaders. And Owen bought them their own knives so he could teach them the places on the body to aim for to cause the most pain.

How could all of it have been pretending?

All of the dates, the moments shared, and the words said. *How the fuck could they have all been fake?*

"You're the best protectors any sister could ask for," I whisper, bending to finally return their embrace before they bolt toward Jamie.

Tears leak in rivulets down my face, and I can feel the panic grip me, crawling over my body as all of my senses attack me at once, with tightness wrapping around my chest, the nausea rising in my throat, the whirring in my ears, and the overpowering smell of dread.

I let them in, and they destroyed me. Them and the whole goddamn town. I didn't want to play their twisted game. They forced my hand. And for what? To chew me up and spit me out?

Rage melts away my sadness. All the Loves, Angels, and Doves were as bullshit as the counting and dirty sluts. I feel my pussy clench at the memory of Wyatt and Owen taking my virginity or Wes pushing me to my knees.

So many firsts with them.

I groan, questioning every moment and interaction over and over again. I freaking hate being this conflicted.

Was it real? Was it not real?

I want to pick up my phone and get answers so badly, but how much clearer could they have been? The declaration solidified with a ring. I was not theirs. I was only good enough to be a toy. For the first time in my life, the sting of betrayal surfaces every insecurity that even my mother's lies couldn't garner.

The will to give up is calling me. I can almost see it off in the distance. Like a mirage, it uses my greatest fantasies to compel me to succumb to the peace by quitting.

A hand clasps my shoulder, forcing my eyes to snap open and suck in a lung full of air before meeting the warm gaze of my grandmother's knowing stare. "Breathe. It won't stop the pain, but it will remind you that you survived and are still here to fight."

"What if I'm tired of fighting?" I challenge because I am that. Tired.

Tired of being strong, tired of being the adult, tired of the bullshit, tired of hurting, and most of all, tired of being deceived by the people who are supposed to love me. I'm just fucking tired of it all.

"Then you rest, gathering your strength, until you're ready again. Because while we can be here to fight alongside you, this battle is yours to lead, my dear." With that, she squeezes my shoulder again before corralling the twins and heading up the stairs of a mansion that rivals the Edgewood Estate. The ranch-style estate sits on what feels like endless acres of land on the Colorado mountainside.

"This is where Thomas's associate organized for us to live in the few hours we were on the plane?" I ask.

"Oh no, Sweetheart. This is the Bradford Estate. Thomas had to say that just in case someone was listening," my grandmother explains.

A summer breeze blows my hair from my face, and I lift my chin to the sky as it envelops me.

Today, I'll give into despair, allowing myself time to mourn, but tomorrow... tomorrow, I'll begin to gather my strength. For now, I'll do what my grandmother instructed.

Breathe.

2
ARIAH

The pounding in my skull is a reminder never to cry this much ever a-freaking-gain. Thank fuck for the blackout curtains in my room because, otherwise, the ache when I try to open my eyes would probably be unbearable.

Groaning, I rise from the bed and head for my en-suite bathroom, careful not to bump into or trip over anything. The expansive room has a different setup than the one back in Edgewood, and I can't remember where the couch and desk are.

I make it to the sink unscathed but don't dare to turn on any lights. The longer I can avoid any brightness, the happier my aching head will be. I grab my toothbrush and start trying to revive myself before going downstairs. I'm supposed to officially meet some members of the Bradford family today.

Once finished in the bathroom, I throw on shorts and a band tee before shuffling my way down the steps. As my feet hit the landing, I overhear hushed voices in a heated argument.

"Aaron, this is getting out of hand. The goddamn Novus Ordo Seclorum paid a personal visit to the Fraternitas," an unknown male voice states.

The Novus Ordo who now?

Trying to hear more, I inch closer, hoping they'll divulge anything that explains more.

"We weren't expecting Elise to fuck this up so badly. We thought we had a handle on her before things went to shit," my father grits, his exasperation with this situation evident by the bite in his tone.

At the mention of Elise, my stomach roils at the memory of her vile confessions before I sliced her throat. I wonder if that's why the guys strung me along. Revenge would be high on my list if it were me.

"You've all played it fast and loose. That's why Owen was—"

Owen was what?

The words of the mystery man are drowned out by Jamie flying down the stairs away from the giggling twins chasing her. Their timing couldn't have been worse.

"Be careful," I instruct as they pass me by, still shrieking and announcing to the world people are close by.

"We will," one of the twins shouts back, never stopping their pursuit of our sister.

Once they've disappeared down the hallway, I hear footsteps approach and turn in time to see my dad and a man who is his mirror image but older. He's about half an inch shorter than Dad, but they have the same athletic build, tall and lean. However, where my dad still has some strawberry blond mixed in with his now salted gray hair, this man has a full head of white hair and a matching beard. His silver eyes widen in shock before warmth sets in, but he stays rooted a few steps behind my dad.

"How are you feeling, Ry?" Dad asks.

"As best as one can be after they found out they were being used in a stupid game they didn't want any part of but were foolish enough to allow themselves to be vulnerable, like an idiot, and get hurt," I mutter.

Dad pulls me into a hug. "I'm sorry, Ry. This will all be over soon, I promise," he offers as he releases me.

"It is over for me. Whatever's going on is no longer my concern. I met my part of the contract," I retort.

My father grimaces.

"What?" I question.

Isn't this over?

They made their choice, and it wasn't me. No, I was only strung along for long enough to lower my guard so they could rip my heart out and stomp all over it.

Dad clears his throat, pulling me from the looming downward spiral. My attention refocuses in time to see that the man who was standing in the background is now right next to my dad.

"Ariah," the man's tenor voice whispers as if he's in disbelief that I'm standing before him.

I give an awkward wave. "That's me."

"It is you." He smiles. The crinkle at the corners of his eyes and laugh lines around his mouth make me slightly more at ease. However, an easy smile isn't enough to prove anything.

I clench my teeth to ward off the images flitting through my mind. Hundreds of easy smiles each of my . . . *the* guys gave me, and they all meant nothing.

Growling, I correct myself. *They aren't mine. They never were.* I was just a pawn in their fucking game. Someone to use for payback. Every interaction was a bullshit ploy for revenge.

"This is Tobias Bradford, your grandfather," Dad explains, and it's my turn to look surprised.

I really freaking have a grandfather.

It's not that I doubted my grandmother, but when you've lived your whole life being told by your parents that you have no other family, and then you go from a missing parent and a traitorous mother, who's now dead, to the return of not only your father but his once non-existent family, you're allowed to be somewhat shocked.

Pausing, I look between them, trying to wrap my brain around this moment and everything that's led me here. . . the years of deception and hiding. The twisted games they've been playing for power have made me a casualty of war. Anger simmers beneath my skin.

They've all been fucking lying. He's going to have to earn the title of grandfather.

My thoughts volley between understanding and losing it, but I'm too tired to rage. Exhaustion still racks my body. I need more time to lick my proverbial wounds.

"May I hug you?" Tobias inquires, reminding me I'm not alone and I need to be more vigilant. I hesitate, wanting to rebuff one of the men responsible for my current state, but I eventually nod, the part of me that wants to hug my grandfather winning over. Barely a breath passes before he has me wrapped in his arms.

Tobias Bradford's hug is strong and comforting. "I've dreamt of this day since the day you were born," he murmurs into my hair, his spiced woodsy scent filling my nose as I pull from his embrace.

His statement is like a bucket of ice water being dumped over my head, quickly reminding me of their betrayal.

"So, you all knew we were out there, and you left my sister and brothers to what? Just hope for the best?" I accuse, needing to lash out. The rational side of me knows it's bigger than just us, and the Bradfords are in danger. My grandparents did what was necessary for their family to survive. *I get it.* That doesn't mean I can't be pissed about the fallout of their actions.

"Is everything okay out here," a voice booms.

I turn in the direction of the sound to a tall, muscular man with chestnut brown hair and his face set into a scowl.

Tobias looks up and says, "Yes, Conner. Everything is fine." Then he gazes at me. "Ariah, this is Conner, one of our heads of security."

I study the broody man standing in the entryway. He scrutinizes me a moment longer before whirling around and leaving.

"Let's go into the kitchen and get you something to eat while we talk," Dad suggests, recapturing my attention. I grumble but follow anyway.

I'm starving. Maybe a little food will help me see a little less red every time an image of my time with the assholes who hurt me flits through my mind.

By the time my grandfather speaks again, I've eaten, and we're all sitting around the dining room table.

"I won't pretend to know the hurt and anger you're feeling right now," he begins, staring at me with his matching silver eyes, ensuring he has my attention. "But I know the pain of losing years with my family and sacrificing firsts and sitting on the sideline while your child and grandchild have to fight."

There's pain etched into his every word. I deflate. My rage dwindles to a simmer. As much as I want to take all of my frustrations out on them, I recognize how they were also used.

"Why didn't any of you fight back? Why did you let the Selection continue once you were at the helm?" I probe, asking the question plaguing me since I discovered the Bradfords' role in this clusterfuck.

Tobias sighs. "Because deals were made long before I was born, and going back on the agreement would lead to greater problems than we've already faced."

"What could possibly be worse than finding out your mother was a backstabbing, manipulative, power-hungry bitch?" I growl.

The tightness in both their faces conveys the severity is greater than Elise's betrayal.

"We can't say anything else, Ry," my father laments, and just like that, the fuse lights, and my anger is renewed.

"Can't or won't?" I challenge. My frustration with this entire situation churns in my gut, causing my breakfast to sit heavily in my stomach and threatening to empty on the table in front of us.

Rubbing at the creases in his forehead, my father replies, "You know there are things we can't tell you. At least not yet."

"You need to sing a different song because you're stuck on repeat," I snap.

Always the damn smoke and mirrors.

Tobias speaks this time. "Please try to understand. There are things we can't share before the proper time, or it will do more harm. Just be patient a little longer."

"I'm tired of all the secrets," I huff, crossing my arms. I think I've been more than patient with the trickles of information I've been receiving, much of which has come after I've already been dealt a massive blow.

"Ry." My dad starts, but I cut him off.

"No, Dad! You both need to give me something. Anything. I've followed *every* rule. Showed up to *every* stupid event and allowed myself to be humiliated for the sake of some dead men's instructions. I deserve answers," I seethe, meeting both of their eyes.

"That's all we can say for now," Dad replies, both of them having the decency to at least look remorseful, but it isn't enough.

Sick of their evasion tactics, I stand from the table. "Well, until you have something you *can* tell me, I'm going back upstairs."

I exit the kitchen, ignoring my father's attempts to gain my attention. I know I'm being childish, but I'm over all the secrets. If they won't tell me what I need to know, I'm going to figure it out myself. It's time for Edgewood to leave its archaic bullshit where it belongs, in the past.

As I rest my head on my pillow, I make a decision. I'm going to bring the Fraternitas and its Heirs to its knees.

3
ARIAH

"It's time to get your shit together," I mumble to myself, but there's no conviction in my tone. The girl staring back at me is unrecognizable. Dark circles encompass my eyes like a bad attempt at a smokey eye, displaying my lack of sleep. My collarbone is more prominent, a testament to my lack of appetite. It's not that I'm refusing to eat. It's that any attempt has been mostly unsuccessful.

Leaning over, I splash water on my face, hoping the cold temperature will put some color back on my cheeks and make me appear less sluggish. My gaze narrows in the mirror.

Yeah, I don't believe the bullshit I'm slinging to myself, either.

Sighing, I close my eyes, mentally preparing myself before going downstairs. I know if I look like death run over by an eighteen-wheeler twice, Dad will make me see the doctor. He threatened to do so last week. Luckily, I was able to use the *"adjusting to time zones"* excuse. I know that won't go over today. We've been here for two weeks, and I've spent most of that time hiding in my room, quelling my mounting anger and nursing my bruised heart. Some of which I've made known.

Amid my rage, I may or may not have left Owen a voicemail

that relayed my feelings about how the fuckwads treated me. I would've preferred to say it to them, but I quickly learned I was blocked by all of them, further fueling my anger. I still can't wrap my head around what happened.

I finish in the bathroom and then head downstairs, my senses on alert for the helicopter parenting that's about to take place.

As if my thoughts summoned him, Dad rounds the corner just as I'm about to enter the kitchen. Our gazes lock. *Prepare for worrying parent in three. . . two. . . on—*

"You're seeing the doctor today, Ry. It's been two weeks, and you look worse than last week."

"Gee, Dad. Way to make a girl feel good about herself," I quip, but he dismisses my sass, recognizing it for what it is. . . deflection.

"Dr. Jaffri will be here in fifteen minutes. Get yourself something to eat," he instructs.

He freaking preemptively called her.

I dig my nails into my palms to keep myself calm. I expected him to call. I just didn't think he'd do it without speaking to me first.

Do I know that this is from a place of love? *Yes.* However, this isn't the way it should've been handled. I should have been consulted. I'm of sound mind, capable of deciding a plan of action surrounding my health.

"Don't look surprised. I told you I was calling if you weren't getting better, and you aren't." His gaze narrows, and he lifts a finger, preparing to list all his reasons for overstepping. "You're withdrawn to the point that you hide in your room about ninety-five percent of the day." I roll my eyes at his "measurements of time" as his middle finger joins the index one. "You aren't eating." Then comes his ring finger. "And you barely sleep."

I'd argue with him, but after he ticks off his points, I know he's right. I'm barely holding it together.

"Fine," I mutter. Now it's his turn to look shocked. He wasn't expecting me to acquiesce so easily. *Maybe I should've made him sweat.* That makes me smile as I pose my question. "Were you expecting a fight?"

His brow quirks. "Remember, I know you."

I snort. "While I don't appreciate you overstepping and making the appointment behind my back, I also know it's time for me to be seen."

Dad sighs. "You left me little recourse. I tried to give you time to come around, but you continued to put it off and make excuses. However, I am sorry for not having a conversation with you before calling Dr. Jaffri."

I nod. "You're right, and thank you."

He pulls me in for a hug, kissing the top of my head. "Go grab some breakfast. Dr. Jaffri will examine you in the medical wing."

"Medical wing?" I ask, squeezing him before I pull from his embrace. He nods, and I roll my eyes. "Of course, there's a medical wing. Because those are standard in all homes," I mutter, and he laughs as I head to the kitchen.

The cook prepares my breakfast, and ten minutes later, I'm giving myself an internal high five for finishing my smoothie and bowl of oatmeal before heading for the medical wing.

I'm poked, weighed, and instructed to take deep breaths before she prompts me to explain the reason for her visit.

In the last hour, Dr. Janan Jaffri has drawn blood, prescribed medication, and agreed to get my records from my previous visit to the doctor. In short, she's amazing.

The barely five-foot woman is a force. She scolded Dad for making the appointment without my consent and eased some of my worries. Not only do I admire her tenacity, but I also admire her fashion sense. She's wearing a stone-blue linen suit with a white camisole and a matching hijab adorned with light gray and white flowers, which looks beautiful against her tawny skin.

"Take one tablet every night before bed, and you should sleep soundly through the night," Dr. Jaffri explains, handing me the prescription bottle.

"And is this safe?" I inquire, taking the pill bottle from her outstretched hand.

I have to ask because things didn't go as planned the last time a doctor prescribed me medication.

That's an understatement of epic proportions.

I'll add it to the long list of grievances the Fraternitas will be made to account for.

"Ariah." Dr. Jaffri's raised voice garnered my attention. I must've zoned out admiring her gold and sapphire-encrusted nose ring while I contemplated getting my own piercing.

"Sorry. What did you say? I was distracted by how pretty your nose ring is."

A warm smile fills her face. "Thank you, and yes, the medication is safe. I will be back to check on you in a month, but if you find that any of the medicine I've prescribed isn't working, please don't hesitate to call."

I nod my agreement and thank her before going back to my room.

"Do you think he's going to look like Dad?" Jamie whispers in my ear.

"Maybe." I shrug. "We'll find out soon. He should be arriving any minute now."

I scan the dining room table. The twins look five seconds away from being over it. They're fidgeting and pulling at their suits. They really hate wearing them, and I can't say I blame them. My focus shifts to where my grandparents sit, and the way our grandfather looks at our grandmother makes my heart squeeze.

My eyes close as images of Owen and Wyatt bombard me. We've been in Colorado for three weeks, and it has been radio silent. Not a word from any of the guys. So, I'm making peace with the fact that I was truly played.

Inhaling, I open my eyes in time to see Dad walk in with a man and woman. I immediately know the man is our uncle. He has the signature Bradford gray eyes, but his hair is more fiery red than strawberry blond. He's also taller and broader than Dad. But my uncle isn't the one who captivates me. It's the raven-haired woman with eyes so ice blue they almost look white. When her gaze locks on mine, she smiles, and I know instantly that she's as deadly as she is beautiful, and the deadly may edge out the beauty.

"Holy shit," I blurt before I can stop myself. Her smile grows even bigger.

"Hello. You must be Ariah." Her sultry voice caresses my ear like fingers trailing up a spine. Goosebumps race across my skin. *I think I have a lady crush.*

I nod, unable to get my brain to signal my mouth to speak.

"Kids," Dad booms, breaking the connection and forcing my attention to where he stands. "This is your Uncle Liam."

I watch as Liam and the mystery woman take a seat, waiting for Dad to introduce her as well, but the introduction never comes. My lips part, ready to question her lack of introduction, when my grandmother subtly shakes her head just as the mystery woman speaks.

"It's okay, Miss Tabby. I'll help Ariah master the art of getting answers from the most unlikely sources soon enough."

Her sultry voice is so captivating it takes me a moment to register her words. "What do you mean?"

"This is your new trainer," Dad chimes in.

"And you don't think I should know my trainer's name?"

The nameless woman snickers. "So much to learn. I can't wait to begin."

I'm tempted to ask more questions and to challenge another instance of secrets being kept from me, but my uncle cuts in, and the conversation moves on to business meetings lined up for the summer that require my father and grandfather's attention as dinner is served.

"Well, this is uneventful," Jamie whispers, leaning in so no one can hear.

Amused, icy eyes meet mine, signaling she can hear even over the banter.

How the fuck did she hear that?

Noticing the attention on us, Jamie sits ramrod straight in her seat and begins to eat her food.

As soon as she's finished, she asks if she and the boys may be excused. The 'yes' barely passes Dad's lips before she shoots from the table, shouting for the twins to hurry up.

"Now that the kids are gone, we can discuss the other reason for this dinner," my grandfather announces, garnering my full attention. Maybe this dinner won't be a bust after all.

"And what is that?" I ask.

I wait for him to answer, but my uncle does instead.

"How we're going to get you to become the head of the Fraternitas."

My eyes widen in surprise as I blurt, "I'm not interested in being the head of anything."

"Since the Fraternitas's inception, there has been a shadow organization working to destroy what was built," my grandfather explains. "We discovered that the Filiae Bellonae isn't the only group who want to see us gone or replaced."

No longer interested in the dessert on my plate, I drop my fork and listen intently, eager to learn more.

"Over the last fifty years, there has been an active movement to eliminate the Bradford line in the hopes of forcing a shift in power," my uncle adds.

The reminder of what Elise did sickens me. My anger at her betrayal still festers beneath my skin.

Clearing his throat, my father states, "The only way to end our hiding and keep our family safe is to change the way the Fraternitas works."

Needing a moment to process, I grab my glass of water and take a sip before placing it back on the table.

I think back over this last year. . . over the past few years. My family has been irrevocably changed by the actions of the Fraternitas and the Filiae Bellonae, and for that, both organizations must pay.

Inhaling, I pull my shoulders back, meet my family's gazes head-on, and exclaim, "Tell me what needs to be done."

4
ARIAH

"Come on, Ry," Kellan whines as he and Kylan pull my hands toward the backyard.

They've both been begging me for the last hour to take them outside to swim.

"Jamie's already outside, but Dad said we can't go unless an adult is out there, and you're the only adult around," Ky explains.

"Okay, I'm coming. You both don't have to drag me," I snort.

They drop my hands and turn to give me the 'we weren't born yesterday' look in unison before running for the door.

Freaking twin shit.

By the time I stepped outside, Jamie is jumping off the diving board, Ky has his shirt stripped off, and Kell has kicked off his shoes. The twins look to see if they have the okay, and before I can give a complete nod, they're running.

"Hey, no running," I shout, peeling off my shorts. They immediately switch to "walking briskly."

They yell, "Sorry," just as they cannonball into the water. *Yeah right.*

I shake my head, then yank my tank off. Kellan is standing at the side of the pool, preparing to belly flop when I slide into the heated water.

Jamie swims across the deep end as I watch the twins take turns, seeing who can create the biggest splash.

"Let's play Marco Polo," Jamie suggests once she reaches me.

"Oh, we haven't played that in years. See if the boys want to," I instruct, and she disappears under the water.

A smile crests my face, a foreign feeling since we arrived here last month. But in moments like this, where my siblings are laughing instead of worrying, I can momentarily forget the sting of betrayal that caused me to move across the country.

Jamie and the twins are swimming toward me when I hear footsteps approaching. I shield my eyes from the sun in time to see my grandmother. Her warm gaze connects with mine. "Having fun?" she asks.

"Get in and play with us," Ky demands, making her laugh.

She dips her head. "How can I refuse such an offer?" That has the twins and Jamie yipping in excitement. My earlier smile returns, growing tenfold.

Our grandmother never misses an opportunity to love us. She's ever-present, steadfast in how I always imagined a grandmother would be. It still surprises me that she took on the role of our house manager, risking her life to ensure we had family watching over us.

I'm jolted from my thoughts when water splashes me in the face. Wiping the water out of my eyes, I see the twins giggling at Jamie, whose arms are now crossed.

Shrugging, she unapologetically states, "Glad to have you back with us. Now, since you were daydreaming, you're it."

I hear our grandmother trying to cover up her amusement with a cough.

"Traitor," I mumble but turn around and count to thirty.

We're on our third round of the game when Dad comes outside. I'm not as angry with him today. He's still not telling me anything, but I'm okay with not knowing for now. Once I calmed down, I recognized that my approach was all wrong.

"Ry, can you come inside for a bit? I have a few people I want you to meet."

"Booooo," Kell shouts from across the pool. "We're playing a game, Dad."

Dad's lip quirks. "Sorry, Buddy. I promise she'll be back in a bit."

Kellan doesn't look at all appeased by his response.

"Promise I'll come right back," I assure him as I climb out of the pool. I grab my towel, wrap it around me, then wring out the excess water in my hair. As droplets fall to the concrete, I examine my blue-black strands. *It might be time for a change.*

"Why don't you grab something from the pool house to put on and then meet me in my office," Dad instructs.

I nod, slipping on my sandals, and we part ways.

Once I'm dressed, I head inside, managing only to get lost once this time.

"Stupid freaking big-ass house with too many damn hallways," I mumble.

I'm still learning where everything is, but the laughter coming from the room is a clear indicator I might be in the correct spot. Dad's shout as I pass the room confirms it.

"We're in here, Ry," Dad announces, and I turn around, pushing the slightly ajar door open.

Entering the room, I see Tobias, who I'm starting to warm up to, Dad, Reign, and two other men I don't recognize.

"Hey, Ariah," Reign greets.

I give him a quick wave as I take my seat around the table. "Colorado is far from Edgewood. What are you doing out this way?" I ask Reign.

A throat clears. "I've invited Reign, Elias, and Fernando here," Dad begins. My eyebrows arch, silently questioning why. I don't have to wait long for an explanation. "They're going to be the lead team on your security detail."

Security detail? My nose scrunches in confusion. "Why do I need a security detail? I thought all that ended once I wasn't—" I don't finish my sentence. The reminder of what happened last month is like a knife to the chest. I rub at the spot where hope used to sit. Clenching my teeth, I blink away the building tears.

So much for not thinking about them today.

"Unfortunately, the threat is still high. Until we've found all the members of the Filiae Bellonae, we can't leave you unprotected," Tobias explains.

I'd argue, but it makes sense. They made it clear the other night. Someone out there wants us dead. What doesn't make sense is why. Elise was clear that her objective was to ensure I solidified my spot by joining the two organizations. I can't do that if I'm dead. I know something bigger is happening. I just don't have all the pieces to put it together.

"Okay," I sigh. Both Tobias and Dad look shocked. "What, did you think I was going to argue? I might be stubborn, but I'm not stupid. There's too much at stake for me to act like I'm a one-woman army. I'm not freaking Natasha Romanoff."

"Who?" Tobias questions. I huff a laugh at the puzzled look on his face.

"The Black Widow," Elias answers. "She's a badass spy from Marvel."

As Elias explains who Natasha is, I study him and Fernando. Both men look nearly identical. However, where Fernando has white-blond wavy hair, emerald eyes, and olive skin with bronze undertones, Elias has straight, dirty-blond hair, bluish-gray eyes, and olive skin with a more golden brown hue. And like Reign, they look like they never skip a day at the gym. Their postures give off military, and knowing Mikhael, they have extensive combat training if they're here with Reign.

"So you guys are basically going to be my shadow for the foreseeable future?" It's more of a statement than a question, but Reign answers.

"Like a second skin."

Snorting, I retort, "More like an unknown antibiotic-resistant rash." The room erupts into laughter.

Dad stands. "Since you took this better than I expected, why don't I show the guys to their rooms and give them a tour of the security room."

I roll my eyes as they exit. "I'm not even going to justify that comment with a response," I mutter, and my grandfather coughs, trying to cover up his snickers.

Turning, I fully take in my grandfather. His eyes sparkle with mirth as a bright smile sits on his tan face. *He's enjoying this.*

"Your dad means well," he states.

Crossing my arms, I grumble, "So well, he's keeping secrets." I know I sound like a petulant child, essentially proving his earlier notion that he had a reason to worry that I wouldn't take the news of having guards well.

The smile falls from his face, the jovial look quickly replaced by a pensive one. "Let me tell you a story."

Eager to hear anything that might give me more insight into what's going on, I blurt out, "Okay," with so much enthusiasm, Tobias's lip quirks.

His eyes bore into mine when he begins. "Nearly forty years ago to the day, your grandmother found out she was pregnant with your father, and what was supposed to be a joyous time for a young couple was instead rife with worry. My father and mother were poisoned. My brother's and his wife's throats were slit open in their sleep. All in the span of one night."

I want to say something, but I'm afraid he'll stop if I utter a sound.

"Anyone with Bradford blood in their veins was at risk. I hadn't been head of the Council for a full year when whoever was left of my family was killed off."

Tobias stands, walks to the bar, and pours himself two fingers of scotch.

Leaning against the bar, he takes a gulp and sighs, like he's trying to find the words before he continues. "We had a meeting, the newly established Council. We sat down and organized a long-term solution. My family's bodies weren't even cold before it was decided to hide."

I can see the pain etched into his face. There is a mixture of regret and anger in the set of his clenched jaw.

Remembering some of what I've been told, I state, "That's when you decided to give Dad up?"

He shakes his head. "We wanted to keep him at first. We thought just hiding would be enough, but two months before your father was born, someone broke into the home we were living in and attempted to kill your grandmother."

A gasp bursts from my throat when he lowers the collar of his light blue polo and reveals a jagged scar that disappears under his shirt.

"I killed the asshole who did this, but he left his mark, and it also made me realize the only way to ensure the Bradford line would live on was to make people believe the Bradford line had died."

They staged all their deaths.

As if he can see the wheel turning in my head, he nods. "Yes. That night, the killer successfully killed your grandmother, father, and me before succumbing to his injuries and dying."

"So, why did our grandmother risk her life to come back?"

He smiles. "Because you all needed family watching over you, and it was time to take a stand. Your mo-Elise had one thing correct. It's time for the Bradfords to take their rightful seat at the head of the table and join the families together. But to do that, you'll need to be patient, especially right now. We know you want answers, and you'll get them in time."

"How—"

Tobias holds his hand to silence my question. "When the time is right, you'll be told. Until then, you need to be ready."

My shoulders slump. *More evasive answers.*

"What does that even mean?"

"It means, dear child, that you train." Then he drains the remainder of his drink and exits the room, leaving me to stew on his words.

5
ARIAH

"Fuck, you always take me so good, Love. Look at this tight pussy taking my dick. Barbell by barbell." Wyatt groans as he rolls his hips, seating himself deeper inside me with each stroke.

"More," I beg. My wanton plea is barely audible between moans.

Hazel eyes bore into mine, darkening with lust as he grips my ass, angling my body up to meet his thrusts.

But I want more. I need more. I want the darkness I know to linger beneath the jokester. The one that gripped my throat until I came so hard I nearly passed out.

Licking my swollen lips, I return his lust-filled gaze with my own. "More. Please, Wy."

A smile creeps onto his face as he registers precisely what I'm asking for. His right hand slides up my stomach, gliding over my heated skin. My body shivers at the touch, my nipples tightening in anticipation. I sink my teeth into my lips when his hands wrap around my throat, pulling me to him.

"Is this what you want, Love?"

"Yes." I blissfully sigh before his mouth crashes to mine, and he eases me back down on the bed, his hand still firmly gripping my neck.

I watch as he stares down where we're joined. His focus fixates on his cock pumping in and out of me before his gaze returns to mine.

"Such a greedy pussy," he growls, slipping out of me.

I whimper at the loss of him.

His hand tightens around my throat, his eyes never leaving mine. He watches me, his pupils dilating more as ecstasy is etched on my face. Then, he lines himself up with my entrance and leans over, pressing his lips to my ear. "Wanting my cock," he croons as he slams back, squeezing my neck until I see spots dance in my vision. The loss of air heightens my sensation, making my walls spasm around him as he buries himself deeper than ever.

I want to scream my release, but he's using his hold as leverage to piston his hips. My eyes roll until I'm sure only the whites are visible.

"Holy fucking shit," Wyatt roars, and I feel him filling me as my vision blacks out.

My eyes shoot open, adjusting to the darkness. I look around, sure I'll find Wy in bed with me. I swear I can almost smell him.

It was just a dream.

The wetness between my legs indicates how real of a dream it was. I guess it's better to wake up turned on than crying. *Perspective.*

I climb out of my bed and strip to take a shower. I make it to the door when my phone rings. I ignore it but only make it a few steps into the bathroom when it rings again.

Huffing, I rush to grab it and see it's Shay.

"Bitch." Her smiling face pops on the screen. "Why do I have to call you more than once? Didn't we have this talk already? If you don't want me to—"

Cutting her off, I mimic her sassy tone, "Leave my hospital bed and walk to Colorado, you better answer my calls."

"Well, if you know better, then do better," she teases. "You don't want me to interrupt my healing process because you know I will."

I roll my eyes. "The guilt is strong in this one."

Shay laughs before she narrows her scrutinizing brown eyes on me. "How are you?"

Rubbing at the brim of my nose, I survey myself. It's been a little over two months, and while some days are hard, it gets a little easier to breathe each day. Today is one of those days. I'm not plagued by sadness or anger. "I'm good," I answer honestly.

Satisfied with my answer, Shay's smile doubles in size. "That's what I like to hear. Now let me look at your hair."

I turn my head, allowing her a better view. I just got it done yesterday, and it's still weird to see my natural hair color when it falls into my face. "I'm still getting used to it."

"It looks amazing. Don't get me wrong, I loved your hair when it was blue, but I love this more," she states.

"Well, it was this or a tattoo. And since getting a tattoo isn't an option, back to strawberry-blonde I went," I reply.

If I'm honest with myself, I'm glad I decided to return to my natural color. It's symbolic. I'm taking my power back. The reason I dyed my hair in the first place was to hide, and I'm done hiding.

"Save the tattoos for college," Shay jokes. "Speaking of college. Have you looked at any schools out there yet?"

I groan. She's been pestering me about what school I'm attending, and I refuse to answer her. Because I'll be at Lincoln-Wood University this fall. I just haven't told anyone about my plans. "I still have time to decide," I lie. I don't like lying to her, but I know she'd try to convince me to stay. She's been pushing the 'anywhere but Edgewood' angle for weeks now. Finally, when I confronted her about it, she said it was not worth returning and seeing the guys fawning over Samantha. I cried for days after that revelation.

Somewhere in the back of my mind, I was holding out hope that it was some ploy. Every time I dissect that day in Mr. Edgewood's office, I swear I see the confused looks of shock on everyone but Wes's and Samantha's faces. I beat myself up for days after we arrived, questioning whether I should reach out and get answers. Only, when I finally did, I discovered everyone but Owen had me blocked, and that fucker didn't pick up. So, I was devastated when Shay dropped that bomb after I finally built up enough confidence to ask. It takes a lot to swallow your pride, but I'm glad I did because the "what ifs" would have eaten me alive.

"Ry," she calls, and by how loud she is, I know she's been trying to get my attention.

"Sorry, I spaced. What did you say?"

"I said, what about Groveton?"

Sighing, I reply, "I have no interest in going to Texas for school, even if Eva's going to be there."

Shay's lips thin before she responds, "Well, just remember it's an option."

"Don't you go home today?" I inquire, hoping to change the subject. I don't want to lie any more than I already am. Luckily, she takes the bait.

Nodding, she says, "My parents should be here soon. I just wanted to check in on you before I head home. They have some big welcome home cookout brewing."

My heart aches. I should be there for that. I open my mouth to apologize, but it's like she knows what I'm about to say, and it's her turn to cut me off.

"None of that. You need to take care of yourself. I'll be okay."

"Fine," I concede. "Have you heard anything from Brendan?" I know this is a sore subject for her. He disappeared after she was shot, but I need to see if I have to hunt him down and kill him for breaking my best friend's heart.

She shakes her head, and I can see the hurt in her eyes, but she doesn't say anything. I'm about to tell her it's his loss when her room door opens, and Mrs. Warren walks in. "Ariah, Baby, is dat yuh?" she greets, her accent more pronounced than usual.

I wave to her, happy my phone is angled so you can only see me from the neck up. There's no need to give her mom a free show. "Hi, Mrs. Warren." I wave. "Take care of our girl for me."

"Yuh dun know. I would have it no other way," Shay's mom says, walking over to her and fussing.

Shay rolls her eyes before we say our goodbyes, promising to send me pictures later.

I drop my phone on my bed and finally hop in the shower.

●

"You should never leave home without a weapon," she instructs, holding the fake weapon to my throat, and I groan.

We've been at this for hours, and I'm hungry and sore.

This woman has outmaneuvered me at every turn, and I don't even know her name. When we met a month ago at dinner, I asked her once I was able to get a moment alone with her, and her exact words were, *'Names give people power over you, Ariah. Never give anyone power over you. It could be the difference between life and death.'* Then she proceeded to hand me my ass as she trained me. If I weren't learning some new techniques, I'd fight my grandfather for making me do this shit.

As I try to suck in a lung full of air, I plant myself on the floor. "I need a timeout. Better yet, I need replacement lungs," I wheeze.

"What you need is to keep conditioning. Who's been training you? They've been taking it easy on you."

Sitting up, I reply, "You'll have to excuse me. I'm a bit rusty."

She quirks her lip as she sizes me up. "You don't strike me as the rusty type."

She's got me there. I've been training even on the days I wanted to cry. *Especially* on those days. There's nothing like picturing your exes' faces on a punching bag to motivate you.

"Let's go again," she demands.

My heart is still thudding in my chest, so I stall. "Have you heard about the latest murder?"

She arches her perfectly shaped black brow. "Murder?" she questions.

"Yeah, it's like the third one since I've been here. This time it was some rich asshole's rapist son."

"Well, I hope whoever did it made it hurt. Now, let's go. I'm going to show you how to use these," she commands, pulling out a pair of metal hair sticks.

Intrigued, I stand. "I've always wanted a pair of these."

"Once you learn how to use them, I'll have custom ones made

for you. Now get to work," she states, training me until the door opens.

My father and grandmother step inside.

"Good to see you again, dear girl," my grandmother greets her.

The tough exterior of the woman who's been training me for weeks melts away, replaced by a warm smile. "Miss Tabby. How are you?"

As they talk, my dad calls me over, and I can tell from the look on his face this is what I've been waiting for.

"It's time, Ry."

6
ARIAH

Today feels heavier than any day has since I arrived. Something is brewing in the air, but I can't pinpoint what it is. At first, I thought the uneasiness was because my dreams were filled with glimpses of my time with them before they ripped out my heart. It felt so real.

When my eyes snapped open this morning, I swore I could feel the lingering presence of someone in my room hovering over my bed, but much like last time, no one was there. Now, I'm starting to wonder if my sleeping meds are making me hallucinate or if my subconscious mind hasn't caught up to the fact the guys are no longer mine.

Shaking myself of my earlier dread, I tilt my head up and bask in the August sun. Who knows how long it will be before I can do this again. With summer coming to a close, the mounting pressure of what I need to do presses hard against my solar plexus.

"We're here," Jamie squeaks in excitement, pulling me from my thoughts. A place in which I feel like I've been trapped more often than not.

Lowering my gaze, I see the clearing ahead where Dad and the twins are set up. Yesterday, Dad mentioned having one last trip up the mountain. This time, we're having a late lunch before we hike back down.

I smile, watching them. Dad instructs them where to put the cooler, and they're goofing off. Kellan and Kylan are in true form.

Colorado has been good for them. *For us.* We've had time to mourn the loss of the mother we once knew and come to terms with the evil woman I killed. We're not entirely healed, and we don't pretend to be. We'll always mourn the person she was before she showed her true colors.

Now I need to do the same with them.

My smile melts from my face, tears building in my eyes. I squeeze them shut, trying and losing the battle to prevent them from falling.

Needing more time, I quickly wipe them and tell Jamie, "Go on. Tell Dad I'll be there soon."

She looks at me, confused. "You're not coming?

I force a smile, hoping she won't notice my mounting sadness. "I'm going to walk for a little longer," I explain.

Her emerald eyes narrow, studying me for a moment. I watch as she processes what she's seeing. She must observe something because she doesn't question me further.

I watch, ensuring she makes it to Dad before turning down one of the trails. Not wanting to venture too far from safety, I walk another five minutes. Even with Reign only steps behind me, I wouldn't put it past someone to sneak onto our property with everything going on. The wooden bench and river I've visited a handful of times since arriving at our family home appear on my left.

"I'm going to sit here for a bit," I inform Reign. He's been with me out here each time I decide to visit.

The only acknowledgment that he heard me is the dip of his head. It's all I need to walk down the path.

A warm breeze blows the wisps of my hair out of my face as I sit down and watch the water flow by. Purple Lewisias line the embankment, growing amid the rocky terrain. There is something magical about this place. It's the only space I can truly clear my mind, and I desperately need a clear one to make this decision.

Am I finally ready to face them?

While the past eight and half weeks have been precisely what I needed, knowing the stakes, I can't hide anymore. I've trained, spent time learning about the Bradford role in the Fraternitas, and started healing. It's time to go back. I won't allow what happened to me to be the fate of anyone else again. The Fraternitas needs change, and neither the Council nor those assholes who somehow still make my heart ache are capable of doing it. I've wallowed enough. It's time to end the Fraternitas' archaic system.

After the conversation I had at dinner that night nearly two months ago and the one I had with just my grandfather when I was introduced to my protection detail, I know there's a power struggle. No one believes the Filiae Bellonae is done trying to stage a hostile takeover, but we all agree that if the mission were to merge organizations under the Bradford line, then killing me wouldn't be their plan. The question is, are the Heirs in on it?

The more time I've had to think about everything that's happened, too many signs point to a hostile takeover with their help. Selection girls were murdered until Samantha was able to become a pick. The rapid rate at which Wes went from hating me to doing everything in his power to earn my trust was partially why I made him work so hard. He hated me and was vocal about how beneath him I was. Yet somehow, I slowly fell for him. Then, Lev, who can't stand to be touched, allowed me, of all people, to touch him like I'm some anomaly. The quintessential "not like other girls." I should've recognized their game.

My guess is that they quickly learned bullying me into submission wasn't an option. I should've prepared myself for the emotional tactics. But how could I? There was so much vulnerability and sincerity in their actions. I'm usually a great bullshit detector. I mean, like being able to sniff gaslighting from across the globe, but I didn't see this coming until it was too late.

I think the added bonus to the plan we've devised is that I get the opportunity to make each Heir regret the day their dads decided to nut inside their moms instead of on their faces.

"Ariah," Reign's gravelly timber shouts.

I twist to where he stands. "Fifteen more minutes," I reply to his unspoken command.

"We can't. Your dad wants to be back at the house before it's dark, and you know he wants you all together for this one," he explains.

He's right. Dad brought jumbo Jenga and Tic-Tac-Toe for us to play. "Okay, five minutes then," I sigh. I'd stay in this spot forever if I could.

I hear his muttered curse before he presses the com in his ear to relay our ETA.

Twisting back to the river, I watch the way the water beats against the rocks in its path and think how metaphorically perfect this scene is. Water is a force that wears the most jagged pieces smooth, given enough opportunity. It has the ability to both destroy life and rebirth it, much like fire. And while water is not entirely undefeatable, it's one of the most vital elements.

So, do I burn their world down or beat it into submission?

"Okay, we've got to go," Reign instructs, leaving no room wiggle room for negotiations. It's like having an annoying know-it-all big brother.

Peering out, I take in the beauty of the landscape around me for the last time and stand. Once again, this spot has been just what I needed. I have my answer.

It's time to go back.

7
ARIAH

"Why aren't you coming back with us, Grandpa?" Kellan whines as we sit outside under the Colorado evening sky.

I watch the orange, red, yellow, and purple hues line the scattering clouds as the sun sets off in the distant mountains. Part of me wishes I could stay here in the bubble of calm, but a greater part of me recognizes changes must be made.

A shriek of laughter before a large-sounding splash garners my attention. Turning to the pool, I see a very wet Nando and Eli rising from the water. Their scowling faces lasered on Reign, who's bent over cackling. He's so distracted he doesn't notice when Jamie and Kylan sneak up behind him. Both give each other a knowing look and smirk before shoving Reign into the pool.

"That's what you get," I shout once Reign's head pops up from the water before he flips me the finger and grins.

Our grandparents decided to throw a small graduation and going away party. High school seems so long ago, and I honestly forgot about graduation in all the mayhem. *Yet another thing they robbed me of.* The list of their transgressions is mounting.

Gazing around the intimate gathering, I recognize some of the people I've met since being in Colorado mixed amongst a crowd of unfamiliar faces. One, in particular, grabs my attention. I feel like I've seen her before, but I can't be sure. I study her for a moment. Her brunette hair is highlighted auburn and falls just past her tanned, slender shoulders. Her head turns slightly as if she can feel my eyes, and honey-brown eyes connect with mine. A catlike grin curls her lips before she winks, then returns her attention to the man she is watching.

"Who is that?" I lean over and whisper to my grandmother.

She follows my line of sight and smiles. "That's Brea, Dear."

"She looks familiar. Have I met her before?"

"I'm sure you'll meet her at some point this evening," my grandmother replies.

Way to not really answer my question.

Sighing at her non-answer, I ask, "And who's that?" nodding to the man across the pool who Brea's been watching.

"Caden Danvers, sole heir to the Danvers Group Incorporated. Your grandfather is a silent investor, but once we come out of hiding, he will join their board of trustees," she explains.

Watching Caden, I can see why Brea might be ogling him. He's a handsome man. Tall and in his mid to late twenties. He has curly charcoal-colored hair that's been loosely styled, striking hazel eyes that are more blue-green than brown, and an athletic build that would be obvious even if he wasn't in shorts and a polo.

"I will be along shortly, Kellan. Granddad needs to wrap up a few things before I can join you all."

My head whips back to the table at our grandfather's words. All interest in Brea and Caden forgotten.

"You're coming back? Is it safe?" I blurt out.

My grandparents have worked so hard to keep our family out of harm's way, going as far as relinquishing the leadership of the Fraternitas to the Edgewoods, faking their deaths, and going into hiding.

"It's time. Much like you, my time for hiding is over. If we're going to put the rightful Heir back at the helm, all hands must be on deck," he states.

Unease fills me. They've sacrificed so much already. I was apprehensive and angry when I first met my grandfather, but we've gotten closer over the past nine and a half weeks. While I may not agree with all the secrets they still keep from me, I understand some of the whys behind it.

I don't want anything to happen to him or to them.

Sensing my worry, my grandmother's hand rubs my back. "We need to keep you safe. You're the future of this family, Ariah. All paths to change will be made through you."

Well, that's not pressure or anything.

I open my mouth to object, but my grandfather silences my rebuttal with his next words.

"We've been on defense for too long. Now, it's their turn, and we won't stop until they're all dead."

I could've sworn I left the photo on my dresser. I need that damn picture. I knew I should've packed it away, but seeing it each morning fortified my need to stay focused and to work harder.

"You ready to go, Ry?" I look up to see Dad standing in the doorway and smile.

Bronston has pushed the limits of our relationship. It's been frustrating, especially when he and Granddad would pull their *'we'll tell you when it's time'* bullshit. I chuckle at the memory of some of my outbursts. It wasn't until after a few heart-to-hearts with my grandmother that I realized that just because I didn't like their answers didn't mean they were treating me like a child.

His throat clears, and I know I've been lost in my head and have yet to answer his question.

"Almost, but I can't find the photo. I swore I left it on the nightstand for me to pack last, but it's not here." I sigh.

"Maybe you or one of the packers boxed it up with the other stuff," he suggests.

Rubbing my forehead, I try to remember whether I saw it before bed last night. He's probably right. With all the stress of the move and my nervousness about heading back, the picture is probably with the others.

I take one last look around before heading to the car. When I step outside, I see five identical SUVs.

"Is the president here or something?" I ask Reign, stepping up beside him.

He says something in his earpiece before turning to me. He's wearing his no-nonsense face. I guess that should be expected. We rarely left the estate, but whenever we did, the jokester persona he regaled us with at home was nonexistent.

"Necessary precaution," is his only response before he walks off to bark orders to the security team.

"There's been a threat," Dad states, opening the car door.

This gets my attention, but I slide inside and wait for everyone to settle before I rattle my questions. Gram, Jamie, and the twins climb in next and buckle up before Dad finally joins us.

"I can't wait to get back home," Kylan says.

"Yeah. Theo and Zavah said they caught the biggest frogs, and we're going to find bigger ones," Kellan adds. Their matching looks of excitement keep us all entertained on the drive.

We're pulling out on the stretch of road leading to the airstrip when an explosion rattles the vehicle.

"What the fuck was that?" I shout, looking out the window and seeing smoke billowing into the sky from what looks miles away.

When I don't hear anyone answer, I turn in time to see Dad and Gram shake their heads. It's then I notice the fear etched on my siblings' faces. Gone is the banter and fun atmosphere in the car.

We ride in silence. No one says anything until we're safely escorted onto the plane.

Once we've taken off, Gram leads the kids to the bedroom in the back. As soon as I see them walk through the door, I whirl on Dad. I don't get a chance to bombard him with questions because he's holding up his hand.

"We sent four decoy SUVs on different routes after we got wind of a possible assassination attempt," he begins.

The hairs on the back of my neck prickle. "Was anyone on our team hurt?"

"No. All decoys were self-driven. But it wasn't one of our cars that was taken out."

I arch my brow and scrunch my face in confusion. "But the explosion?"

"Was an enemy who was dealt with. Your trainer is not someone you ever want to have hunting you," he states, and for the umpteenth time since I met my lethal trainer, I wonder who the fuck she is.

Knowing Dad won't tell me her name. I focus on pressing matters. "Do we know who was after us?"

"The only thing I can tell you at this point is that it's not the Filiae Bellonae."

I massage my temples, exhausted from the excitement of the day. If it wasn't Elise's organization, who the hell else wants us dead?

"Like you said. Your mother—Elise didn't want you dead. She wanted you married to the Heirs so that both organizations would be unified under your rule. Which means there are more players on the board," he further explains, sensing my inner thoughts.

"Let me guess. You know the players, but '*I can't tell you anything else right now*'," I say, mimicking his favorite phrase.

"I don't sound anything like that, Ry," he jokes, and I roll my eyes.

My eyes droop, weariness setting in now that the adrenaline has worn off.

"Go get some rest. It'll be another three hours before we arrive," Dad encourages.

Yawning, I stand and walk to the back of the plane, peek in on my siblings' sleeping forms, and then open the door to the other room. The minute my head hits the pillow, I'm out.

I don't know how long I've been sleeping when I hear my grandmother's voice attempting to coax me out of sleep.

"There she is. It's time to wake up, sleepy head," she murmurs. Her words finally register.

I sit up, stretching before I respond, "How long have you been trying to wake me?"

"Not too long."

Rubbing my eyes, I stand. "Thank you," I whisper, reaching out and embracing her.

"You don't have to thank me," my grandmother replies, kissing the top of my head.

Releasing her, I exit the room and make my way to the front of the plane, where my father is lost in something on his laptop screen.

"Everything okay?" I probe, sitting next to him and buckling my seatbelt.

He looks up. "All good. Just reading over a few plans from the Council. I'm catching up on what I missed."

"Do they have any information on who's behind all this?"

Dad shakes his head. "Nothing concrete. Strategies have been deployed, and contingencies are in place."

I'd ask what they are, but I know he won't answer. I'm surprised he said that much.

"We'll be landing in New Haven, Connecticut, in ten minutes," the pilot announces over the intercom, sobering me.

Butterflies flutter in my stomach, making me queasy. "We're really back," I whisper. So many emotions run through me simultaneously, like excitement, sadness, anger, and fear. As much as I want to pretend I'm fearless, I'm not. The thought that I'll start LWU in a week and have to see *them* with *her* has my stomach in knots.

"You can do this, Ry," Dad encourages, lifting my chin. I didn't even recognize my head was bowed. "You're one of the strongest people I know, and you won't be alone." Then, he stands and presses a kiss on the top of my head before giving me some much needed space.

Leaning back, I close my eyes, waiting for the plane's wheels to hit the tarmac, signaling the close of one chapter and the beginning of a metamorphosis.

My eyes pop open as we touch land, with Granddad's words playing on a loop. 'We've been on defense for too long. Now, it's their turn, and we won't stop until they're all dead.'

Edgewood won't know what hit them.

8

SEBASTIAN

"*There's been another reported death in the Bronston area, bringing the total number of victims killed in recent months to eight. Maxfield Rothberg was discovered early this morning, nailed to his front door.*"

I shake my head as I put my Porsche 911 into park in front of the house the guys are staying in on campus. The murders in the Colorado city have been all over the national news.

Shutting off the engine, I open my door and step outside. Then, I make my way up the front stairs.

I'm here to check on Owen. The rest of the guys are out. When Owen didn't respond to any of the group text messages, I knew I needed to stop by before heading to Le Toucher to meet with Matthieu.

As I enter the house, all I can think is how the entire summer has been shit. Senator Baker has given power to one of the most vindictive bitches I know. Samantha Davenport makes all my issues with Vivian seem like minor disagreements. And the person struggling the most with our current circumstances is Owen.

Not only was he kidnapped and tortured for weeks, but he was also dropped off on the side of the road with an explosive in his arm, barely alive.

Climbing the steps, I ruminate on how devastated he was once he discovered Ariah was gone. Part of me is glad he wasn't around to see the utter heartbreak on her face when Wes chose Samantha.

It's an image burned into my memory, haunting me in my daydreams and nightmares. Ariah opened me to the possibilities of life after heartbreak—to pouring love into someone who doesn't take advantage, instead returning it in spades.

I'm about to knock on Owen's door when I hear her voice.

"You broke me. Each of you stole pieces of my heart and carelessly discarded them."

I wait for his reply, but I'm greeted with an anguished cry.

"How could I have been so foolish to believe that any of you were ever genuine? H-h-how?" Ariah chokes out. "This is my fault. I lowered my guard with the whispered promises of forever, and we all know that a promise is a comfort to a fool. And guess what? I'm that fool."

My eyes snap shut at the hurt in every word as I wait for Owen to rebuff her—to chastise her for the asinine thought that she's foolish. *It never comes.*

"This is the last time I'll ever reach out to any of you. It's time for me to make peace with how stupid I am for ever believing, for ever trusting the sweet poison that was your I love yous."

Her words slice through me.

"I need you to hear this and pass the message on to the rest of your cowardly friends."

My breath hitches, resting my palm against the wall, waiting for the fatal blow.

"I may be down, but I'm far from out. You and your *fiancée* can have this moment because it'll be the last one I ever give any of you. You're all dead to me."

My eyes spring open, and I fight the urge to drop to my knees. The finality in her tone spears me through my chest, sending chills down my spine.

"Nooooo," Owen shouts, his broken screams the perfect representation of the torment coursing through me. "No. . . no. . . no! You don't mean that, Angel. I'll fix this—we'll fix it. I promise. Owen mutters almost incoherently.

I burst through the door. "Ariah," I growl as I take in the scene before me.

"Press one to delete this message. Press two to save this message. Press three to replay this message. Press four to return to the main menu."

It's a voicemail.

Owen's so lost in his phone that he doesn't acknowledge my presence, and the message begins to play again.

"No. . . no. . . no. You have to forgive us. Don't lose faith," he exclaims before turning his tear-streaked face at me. "She's going to forgive us, right? She has to, doesn't she?"

Searching for the right thing to say, my lips part, but no words come out.

"Bash, we have to fix this—we have to," he trails off, standing and pacing the room as the voicemail plays again.

My nostrils flare as I dart forward, snatching the phone from his hold and pressing one.

"Message deleted," the computerized voice announces.

"What the fuck did you do?" Owen roars, charging at me. I wrap him in my arms, squeezing until he stills.

"She's ours, O. She'll never be able to be anyone else's—we won't allow it," I declare.

Twisting, he works to free himself, but I only tighten my hold.

"Do you hear me," I bark, gripping his arms and shaking him. "Ariah Bradford is ours, and we'll fight every obstacle, known and unknown, trying to keep us apart."

He pauses as if only just registering what I've said. Nodding, he mutters, "She'll forgive us—she has to."

"Damn fucking right, she will," I insist. "She's coming home, Owen. Senator Baker and Samantha don't get to win."

I release him, and his arms hang limply at his side before he looks up. Fire blazes in his hazel eyes.

There he is—my brother who doesn't know the word surrender.

With each deep breath Owen takes, his determination sets in, fueling my resolve.

Meeting his stare, I proclaim, "We'll work on freeing you and ending Baker, then we'll bring our girl home."

9
WYATT

"You stupid fucking bitch! We had a deal," Wes snaps, charging at Sam, but Sebastian's arm shoots out, halting his forward progress. He's not fast enough to stop Owen, though.

Owen's knife is pressed firmly against her carotid artery. "You fucking tried to kill her. What's stopping me from *actually* killing you?" he seethes.

I watch in revulsion as she tries to grind into Owen, and her eyes pool with lust. "If you wanted to play, Owen, baby, all you had to do was ask," Samantha moans. At the sight of our disgust, her lips curl into a snarl. "The bitch was only safe if she stayed the fuck away. Now she's back. All bets are off."

Tilting my head, I study her, narrowing my gaze until she feels my attention boring into the side of her face. She turns, and at the simmering rage in my eyes, some of her bravado slips from her demeanor.

Good. She's finally realizing she's not the biggest beast in the room.

"It's funny you think you can change the rules, Sam," I hiss, stalking toward her. She tries to turn her head, but I grip her face. "This deal only works if she's alive. We'd end ourselves before we ever let you kill her. So don't be stupid," I command and drop my hand in time for Owen to pat her cheek with his blade and back away.

She huffs as she rights herself, fixing her clothes and schooling her features. "Fine, if you want her and Owen to live, you'll stay the fuck away from her and make her believe none of what you had with her was real."

"I'm not fucking doing that," Owen barks. "Kill me now because I won't ever lie to her."

Samantha whirls in his direction. "I'll kill her and you. I honestly don't give a fuck. I only need one of you for this to work anyway." She points to the watch that controls our fate. "One press of this button, and it's bye-bye Owen," she singsongs.

Owen snorts. "You're still not listening, are you?" he taunts, raising his knife to his own throat. "I'll kill myself, and then nothing will stop them from killing you."

"You see," Sebastian chimes in, stepping forward. "You've overplayed your hand. While you might be able to control us now, if Owen or Ariah die, all bets are off. So we have you by your pussy as much as you have us by the balls. So, my suggestion is, don't overestimate your power here."

Gritting her teeth, Samantha surveys the room. She must finally recognize she's not entirely in control. Fisting her hands at her sides, she shrieks, "You better make her believe this is true because if she goes poking around, I won't give a fuck if you all die. I'll kill her." Then she storms from the room.

None of us speak until we see her car peel out of the driveway on the monitor mounted on the wall.

"Why did she come back?" Wes asks.

Lev holds his finger to his lips, silencing us as he walks the room, only stopping each time he hears a beep from the device in his hand. Once he's finished, he faces us. "She planted three devices in this room."

"How the fuck does she keep sneaking spyware in here?" I demand.

"Since we're no longer allowing her entry to the Fraternitas or our houses, the country club offices aren't as secure, making it easier to bypass security. But I have an idea," Lev states.

"What is it?" Wes grumbles.

Lev motions for us to follow him and stay silent. We walk down the hall to the private elevators. He scans his handprint and enters his code. Once we're safely inside, he speaks. "We play along and give Sam what she wants."

His statement is met with a chorus of vitriol from all of us at once.

"Fuck no!"

"Absolutely the fuck not!"

"Have you lost your goddamn mind?"

"What the hell is wrong with you?"

Lev holds his palms up. "Hold on to your nuts. Give me a second to explain."

"This better be fucking life-altering," I mutter as the elevator door slides open, and we step out, heading for the SCIF. We only use this room when we have extremely sensitive documents or conversations that need to happen, and the Fraternitas isn't an option.

We enter our entry codes and scan our pupils for entry one by one. This room doesn't allow any visitors—*Heirs only*.

"Out with it. What's this plan?" Sebastian inquires once we're all seated.

Lev explains his earlier statement in more detail, and for the first time in weeks, we feel like there's hope. So, for the next three hours, we devise a plan.

"I'll do it. It'll be the most believable if it's me. She expects this from me," Wes volunteers, and I feel bad because his part in this will be one of the hardest. But the truth is we'll all have hell to pay once this is over—once we can safely claim her as ours.

Once plans are outlined, and tasks have been assigned, I voice the unspoken question stifling the air in the room. "Will she forgive us for what we have to do?"

It hangs like an oppressive weight on a fraying rope before Wes answers, "We'll have to fight like hell to ensure she does."

"Is everything in place?"

"Yeah, man," Colt sighs. "Between your girl and the guys, your ass is going to be handed to you once they find out how much shit you've been doing behind their backs."

I smirk, picturing the fight Ariah will give me once she finds out the lengths I've gone to keep an eye on her. "You let me worry about that. Just make sure her house by LWU is set, too."

"Why isn't Lev doing this?" Cooper asks.

Rolling my eyes, I retort, "Because, Asshole. They can't know until it's time for them to know."

"Right," Coop snorts.

"Don't you have your own *girl* to worry about?"

"Fuck off," they both shout before the line goes dead. I can't help but feel a little sorry for the hell Eva is going to face this year at Groveton.

Well, when you play stupid games, you win stupid prizes—and Eva played the most foolish game of all.

Shrugging, I slide my phone into my back pocket as I stride over to the side of Ariah's bed. Eva's the Jacobis' problem. I have more important matters to focus on. One being the delectable girl before me.

Something falls into place at the sight of Ariah sleeping soundly in her bed. She's back, and I'm torn on how I should feel. I want—no, I need her to be safe, and being here will not do that. But the peace that settles over me now that she's home stomps all over that.

We can keep her safe. If I think about it enough, I can make it true. We already have plans in motion to ensure we can end this farce of an engagement. For now, we're trapped. But that's a tomorrow problem.

Tomorrow, I will have to be someone she's never known before—we all will be. Tonight. Tonight, I can pretend everything is as it once was—time has rolled back to after we got rid of her mother, and we were preparing to announce her as our Chosen.

"Hello, Love," I whisper in her ear as I slide behind her and groan. It's been too long since I've last felt her pressed against me.

My hand glides up the expanse of her exposed skin while I press a kiss to the top of her left shoulder, where I know four tiny freckles are.

I slide my hand across her stomach and rest my lips in the crook of her neck as I close my eyes and count her breaths. Each inhale and exhale is a reassurance she's really here, and I'm not dreaming her into existence.

A soft sigh escapes her mouth as she sinks into me. "Even in sleep, you know where you belong," I hum against the thrumming pulse of her throat.

I'm nuzzling deeper, enjoying the feel of my stubble against her soft skin, when I feel my phone buzz in my back pocket.

Ignoring it, I continue to pepper kisses along her back, inhaling the scent that is uniquely hers. Ariah unconsciously grinds into me, and my semi grows fully erect. "You're killing me, Love. I'm trying to be good tonight," I mumble.

"Please," she murmurs sleepily, and I pause.

Is she awake?

Tonight would be far more interesting if she were. However, the steady rise and fall of her chest indicates she's just sleep-talking.

"Wy, please," she begs, and I watch in awe as her hand slips between her legs.

Fuck it.

I lose my battle with self-control and slide my hand up and cup her breast. My thumb lightly grazes her nipple until it's erect.

A groan escapes me at the smell of her arousal. I'm tempted to replace her fingers with mine, but the sight of her pleasing herself to thoughts of me is far too intoxicating to interrupt. So, instead, I pinch her nipple and nip and suck the back of her neck, knowing it will leave a mark, but she won't see it.

Ariah's breaths increase as she climbs closer to her release, and I stop to watch her fingers work rapidly, pumping in and out of her pussy before swirling against her clit.

It's fucking breathtaking.

I slide back as she turns to her back, her legs falling open, giving me a perfect view of Ariah playing with her pussy.

Closing my eyes, I bask in her whimpers. *She's close.* I lower my head, preparing to feast and catapult her over the edge when her cries of ecstasy turn into keening sounds of pain.

"Why did you leave me?" Ariah demands, her hand stilling. All of my earlier lustful thoughts evaporate as her dreams of pleasure morph into nightmares.

"What did I do?" Her question is a whisper, but it reverberates in my skull like it's coming through a megaphone placed right against my ear.

Ariah curls in on herself, her hand no longer beneath her sleep shorts. Instead, they wrap around her body as if she's consoling herself. The sob that escapes her cracks my chest open, and I lean in to wipe the rivulets of tears streaming down her face.

"Please don't leave me," she implores repeatedly.

"Never. We'll *never* let you go," I promise emphatically. Then I settle behind her, pulling her flush against me until her cries slow into staccato breaths before evening out, and I don't move until I know she's calm.

The sound of birds chirping signals that dawn is approaching, and I reluctantly let her go and rise from the bed before heading for the door and exiting the house.

I pull my phone from my back pocket before climbing into my car. I start the engine and check my notifications and see I have missed text messages, and they're all from the same person. *Lip-Filled Troll Barbie.*

> LFTB
>
> someone's being a naughty boy
>
> consider this your last warning
>
> see her again and there will be consequences
>
> so I hope she was worth it.

I bang my hands on my steering wheel. *Fucking Sam.* I can't wait until we can end this bitch.

Starting the engine, I take one last look up at Ariah's window and try to make peace with what will happen today.

I massage the bridge of my nose, then put the car in drive. Then, with my resolve firmly in place, I say, "She's always worth it."

10
ARIAH

"It's move-in day, Bitch!"

"It's about time you got here. I thought you changed your mind about living with me," I tease as she climbs the last step outside our house.

We both move aside as the movers begin to unload Shay's things.

She checks her watch. "I'm only thirty-ish minutes late. I'm so glad you refrained from sending out a search party."

"Whatever, Ho, I'm just happy to see you up and moving around," I say before embracing her while warding off the immense guilt crushing me for being the reason she was shot. Nausea roils in my gut at the memory of my best friend falling to the ground, and I hold my breath, hoping I won't need to run to the bathroom.

Shay pulls back from the hug like she can sense the shift in me. "You better not cry, dammit. I'm okay, and the fuckers who were responsible are dead."

"But—"

"But yuh bumbo," She interjects. "You will not blame yourself for the fuckery behavior of others."

The vehemence in her tone makes me wonder if she isn't only referring to her being shot.

"This means those fucking idiots. I may love them like brothers, but their stupid decisions are theirs to own," she continues, confirming my suspicion.

The tenuous hold on my emotions breaks, and warm tears trickle down my face. Lifting my arms, I quickly wipe the evidence of the emotional disaster I've become.

"I know," I resignedly huff. "But it's easier said than done. I keep assessing where I missed the signs I was being played."

"You two ever going to actually come inside?" Nando inquires.

Shay arches a brow.

"Security detail. That's Fernando," I reply to her unuttered question.

"And just how many *Fernandos* are there?"

Rolling my eyes, I tug her inside before answering, "A team will shadow me on campus. Reign, Elias, and Fernando will be my primary guards since they'll also be enrolled as students."

"You mean there's more fine-ass men inside?" She quips, making me snort.

"Let's do a tour, and then I'll introduce you."

We walk around the expansive eight-bedroom house aptly named Bradford Manor. It's usually used when high-ranking officials and famous people visit campus. However, one call from Dad and this place has become home for the next four years, fully decked out in the latest technology and amenities we might ever need.

"Is that an indoor pool?" Shay aptly questions.

"Yup. Apparently, the one in the back isn't sufficient," I quip, passing the glass-enclosed heated space.

Shay bumps my shoulder. "Glad to see Colorado hasn't zapped you of your sarcasm," she teases, making me laugh.

"Not a chance. Sarcasm is one of the primary food groups required to meet my daily nutritional value goals. It's doctor-recommended and approved," I joke and lead her down the hallway to the gym, equipped with a sparring ring for my training. Now that I'm back in Edgewood, Mikhael will once again be tasked with keeping my skills sharp, and I can't wait to show him what I've learned while away.

"Not that I haven't missed your ass, but are you sure you're ready to be back?" Shay inquires after we step back into the hallway and head for the game room.

I wait until we're inside to reply, "You know this had to be done."

"That's not what I asked," she retorts, halting my steps with a hand on my shoulder. "Are you sure this is the only way? You still have time to go to UConn, Yale, or FIT and focus on your fashion designs. Shit, you could even go to Groveton and get far the fuck away from this bullshit altogether. Eva would love the company."

She's right. It would be so easy to tuck tail and run. No one would blame me, but to do so would mean looking over my shoulder for the rest of my life, and I won't do that. Not with what's at stake.

Turning, I meet Shay's gaze so she can see the determined set of my jaw.

She needs to recognize the conviction in my gray eyes to understand that running away might appear to be the best solution for most. In this instance, it's not. Because the road most traveled isn't always the right path. It's just the one with the least resistance.

"I have to do this. If I don't, this shit will continue forever, and it's about more than just me now. I need to protect my family," I explain, and for a shadow of a second, I think she's going to argue, but instead, she nods her understanding.

"So, who else will be our wardens in our time here?" Shay says in an effort to shift the energy in the room.

I give her the rundown on who will be with us and team rotations just as we stop outside of a hidden door.

Staring up, I wait for the panel on the wall to appear for me to place my palm on the scanner. The door slides open, and inside, Reign, Eli, and Nando are watching the wall-to-wall monitors while Davi and Bodhi seem to be discussing plans for the first day of classes tomorrow.

"This is the security room," I inform Shay, causing everyone to stop and finally acknowledge us.

I introduce Shay to each person on the team.

"Conner and Markus are going over the routes to your classes," Reign announces. "Once they're back, we'll meet to go over the expectations for you to remain living on campus."

"Like I could ever forget what I agreed to in order to be here," I mutter.

Before Reign can lecture me again on the importance of following protocol, I drag Shay out of the room and down the hall.

"You're not a fan of the security detail, I take it," Shay astutely points out.

"No. The security detail makes sense."

Shay's brows scrunch when I glance at her as we walk. "Then what's with the pout?"

Not wanting to sound like a brat, I change the subject. "Let's go get something to eat. Then you can tell me how you're doing now that you're up and about again, and I can tell you all about my time in Colorado."

"Fine. I'll let it slide for now, but we're going to talk about what your issue is at some point."

I wring my hands around my wrist until I feel the bite of pain that soothes me. My anxiety is mounting, and I question whether I should be doing any of this for the millionth time because the protection detail isn't the problem. Shit, Dad's requirements for me to live on campus aren't the actual issue here, either. *It's them.* It's knowing that I'll undoubtedly see them, and then they'll know.

We stop in the state-of-the-art kitchen, run by some world-renowned chef and her staff, to grab some snacks before finally making it to Shay's room.

"A chef? Really?" Shay snickers. "I guess you're finally accepting you're now firmly doing rich people shit." Her joke lightens the tension building as my thoughts spiral.

My lips curl at the truth in her statement. "Fuck. I am, aren't I?"

We both laugh as we flop down on her king-sized bed. All her things have been delivered, and a team is already beginning to unpack. We spend the first hour catching up on her recovery and the lack of Brendan's presence.

"So, he what? Fell off the face of the Earth?" I probe, wishing I could find the asshole and knock some sense into him.

"It seems that way. All of his social media accounts have disappeared, and any number I had to reach him has been disconnected. I've tried everything short of hiring a private investigator to find him," she confesses.

I grit my teeth and try to reign in my temper before speaking again. How fucking dare he ghost her after she was shot when she left the party early to spend time with him. "Well, the dumb fuck doesn't deserve you if you ask me. Now you get to focus on yourself, and when you're ready, get back out there."

Another two hours pass as we discuss our class schedules for tomorrow. I missed orientation, and she fills me in on what was covered. The light in the room begins to dim as dusk arrives. I look at my watch and see it's almost time for dinner. I begin to stand when Shay's hand lands on my leg, signaling me not to move. I know what's coming before she even says it.

"Seriously, Ry, are you ready for this?"

Sighing, I answer, "No." I can feel the tears building, but I dig my nails into my palms and swallow them down before I continue. "Is one ever ready to have the people you love rip your proverbial heart out and stomp all over it before turning their backs on you to be with the vilest human to exist?"

Shay pulls me into her arms. "You're going to get through this. The first time will be the hardest, but I'll be with you every step of the way. Just know mi cyaan promise I won't tump Samantha in har face or box di idiot bwoy dem inna dem face."

"It's fine, Shay. In the end, it will all be fine. I'm not back here for them. I'm back here for me and what has to happen to protect my family," I say, hoping my tone conveys the confidence I don't wholly possess at the moment. But you know what they say. *Fake it 'til you make it.* And I'm going to fake it all the way to the helm of Fraternitas.

11
WES

"Remember if you—"

"Shut the fuck up already," I growl, cutting off Samantha's eighteen-hundredth reminder of what has to happen.

She whirls to a stop in front of me. "Listen, Wesley, I've been nice enough to leave your little trash toy alone. That deal is only good if you do your part." She angles her head at Lev and Wyatt. "If you *all* do your part."

Sebastian is back at Edgewood Academy, the lucky bastard, and Owen won't be seen anywhere in public near the bitch—threats to his life be damned. The rest of us don't have that option. Sam literally holds his life in her hands, and if we don't do what she wants, he'll die. While he has no qualms about playing Russian roulette with his life, we won't take the chance.

"Don't you worry, we'll play your stupid game," Wy snickers. His lips quirk, and I arch my dark brow in his direction.

He's up to something.

The look of mischievousness is painted all over his freckled face. He's been like this all summer, but it's gotten more blatant the closer to the start of school.

We're standing in front of the F. A. Bradford School of Social Sciences and Humanities building—one of the four departments located in the Bradford Quad, which is aptly named since every building in this area is named after a Bradford. Owen is supposed to meet us here once his class is over. He's going to flip his shit when he sees Sam.

It's the first day of classes, and we all agreed to meet here for lunch. Unfortunately, Samantha thought that included her. One of the annoying stipulations to her being our Chosen is that she has access to our schedules, and she wasted no time ensuring she had breaks whenever we did. I'd send him a message to warn him if this vapid bitch would give me room to breathe.

"How much longer do we have to wait for him?" Sam whines, and as if on cue, the doors to the humanities building slide open, and students begin to file out.

"As long as it fucking takes. No one wants you here, so if you don't want to wait, no one is begging you to be here," Lev seethes. He's finally starting to look a bit more like himself. There was a period over the summer I swore we would have to stage some sort of intervention after he scratched the shit out of his neck. Luckily, our new plan has provided an outlet. Between trying to locate Eshe Solomon or another hacker to deactivate the bomb in Owen's arm, he's a man on a mission.

Five more minutes pass before Owen exits the building. He still has a slight limp, but the bruises on his face have all healed. Physically, he's almost one hundred percent—emotionally, it is a different story. We all have been on heightened alert after Lev told us about the incident at his house.

"What the fuck is *she* doing here?" Owen snarls. His face reddens in anger, and his fists clench at his side.

"We're going to lunch, my love," Samantha snips back.

Wyatt throws his arm around Owen and whispers in his ear, pulling him away from the plastic girl with a death wish. It's a move made to look like a greeting as people walk by.

"You should stop pushing him if you hope to last the week," I warn. It's a warning she doesn't deserve, but it's more for Owen's life than hers.

Samantha slides her arm through mine before following in the direction Owen and Wyatt went. "And you should know that I'm the one making the rules. Not any of you. So, get him in line, or he'll be eliminated," she orders and places her disgusting lips against my cheek. I have to fight not to push her off of me.

"You kill Owen, and there'll be nothing left for you to leverage against us," Lev states. "So, *Samantha*, remember your control isn't endless, nor is your power absolute." Then he walks past to catch up to Owen and Wyatt, leaving me to deal with the girl who's like an infection that penicillin can't fix.

As we walk across campus, other students stop and greet us, offering their congratulations on our upcoming wedding. I have to fight not to gag each time Samantha runs her clawed nails along my exposed arm or leans in to kiss me. It's the longest ten-minute walk to the dining hall ever.

Once inside, I extricate myself from her hold, ignoring her muttered protest of what it will look like if we don't walk in looking like a loving couple. "No one's going to think anything. We're here to eat—not be joined like Siamese twins." I grumble, then leave her standing by the entrance to find the guys.

I find them close to the window, opting not to sit at our reserved table in the center of the room. My face scrunches in confusion as I sit next to Lev.

"We won't sit there. That's reserved for the Heirs and their Chosen—not some power-hungry wench," Lev states, and I nod in agreement.

I groan when I see Samantha heading for our table, but she's stopped when a group of cheerleaders intercepts her. I'm not sure what they're saying, but it's enough for Sam to smile and go to their table.

"Thank fuck," Wyatt exclaims, relief etched on his face.

I think we all collectively sigh once Sam officially sits and begins animatedly talking. Her hands move with each word she makes, but that's about the only thing on her that moves.

"Have any of you seen her?" Owen asks, causing our attention to focus back on our table.

Her. He means Ariah.

I've been trying to catch glimpses of her, but we don't have any classes together until later this week. Lev worked our schedules so that at least one of us would be in each of her classes. Wyatt has English with her later today, so she'll be on campus today. My lips curl up into a smile at that thought.

"Not yet," Lev answers, while Wy and I give a quick no with a shake of our heads.

Owen fidgets at that response—absentmindedly rolling a razor between his knuckles.

"Put that shit away," I whisper as Lev holds Owen's hand still. Owen's nicked his skin with each pass of the razor's edge.

Blinking back into awareness, Owen looks down, his head slanted, and watches the blood trickle from the superficial cuts.

"Come on, O. You can't let our girl see you like this," Lev pleads.

"But she's not *ours* anymore. Is she?" Owen murmurs without looking away from his hands.

Wyatt's fist hits the table. Not loud enough for anyone to notice but enough to rouse Owen from his trance. "She's *ours*. No stupid bitch can change that."

Owen snorts, but it lacks any real emotion. I watch as his sullen eyes look around the lunch table before landing on the group of cheerleaders Samantha's sitting with. "*That* stupid bitch has though, hasn't she?"

Scratching at the scruff along my jaw, I say, "He has a point. Sam holds all the cards. Even if we bullshit her that she doesn't have the upper hand. Right now, she and Senator Baker are calling the shots. We can only mitigate the severity of everything by playing along."

We go silent when our food is delivered, waiting for the staff to be out of earshot.

"Listen, I won't have you assholes giving up. We have plans in the works," Wyatt snaps. "And Wes, you'll do your part. Samantha isn't dumb, so she knows it's a ruse, but it's one she wants to play. So, let's play until we hear back from Teagan." Then he picks up his burger, and right before he takes a bite, I hear him mumble, "Because we have more than ourselves to fight for now."

Just as I'm about to ask him what the fuck he's talking about, the hairs on the back of my neck rise. I watch as a smile lights Wyatt's face, Lev's mouth drops open, and Owen's hazel eyes dilate, and I know she's finally here.

I turn just in time to see Ariah walk through the door with Shay and three other guys—guys that are standing way too damn close. One has his hand on the small of her back.

"Who the fuck are those assholes?" I bark.

"One's Reign," Lev offers. "But I'm not sure about the other two."

Owen hops from his chair. "That's dead and deader if they don't put at least ten feet between them and my angel."

Wyatt cackles. "It's good to have you back finally. I thought you were going to turn into a morose fucker for sure."

Before I can fully take in Ariah's now reddish-blonde hair, a shriek that we've all become familiar with rises above all the chatter in the room.

Samantha is on her feet and charging in Ariah's direction. Owen is the first to take off, but we all follow a nanosecond behind him.

A wall forms in front of Ariah before Sam can get within fifteen feet of her.

Maybe I won't end them just yet.

"Do it if yuh tink yuh bad," Shay seethes, stepping around Reign and the two other guys guarding Ariah.

Ariah's hands push at the bodies blocking her. "Is this really necessary? I'm not some damn damsel in distress. Move," she commands.

My heart stops when Ariah steps into view. I survey her, taking in the blush of her skin and the fullness of her lips. *Have her breasts gotten bigger?* I continue my perusal and stop when my eyes take in her—

"You stupid bitch. How the fuck did you get pregnant? It was supposed to be me," Sam shouts, and everyone's gaze whips in her direction.

"What the fuck do you mean it was supposed to be you?" Lev hisses. "What did you do?"

Ignoring Lev's question, Samantha slides her arm through mine, and I'm tempted to shove her away, but she taps at the watch around her wrist—a reminder to fall in line. But how the fuck are we supposed to fall in line when Ariah's pregnant? She's goddamn pregnant.

We need to reassess. My nostrils flare at the sight of the guys touching her. Like they're staking their claim. I have to work hard to keep my face blank.

Assessing the situation, I move quickly. Samantha needs to be states away from Ariah. I'm mad she's breathing our girl's air at all.

"Let's go, Samantha. You have nothing to worry about. It's probably some rando's baby. Ariah was never too selective with who she let between her legs. Look how easy it was for her to spread them for all of us," I choke out and force myself to turn away. Ignoring the gasp of shock, I put one foot in front of the other, hoping to get Samantha away before she does something stupid.

Once we're outside of the cafe, I breathe for the first time in ten minutes. Sam's whining about something, but I could give two shits what it is. I'm too focused on Wyatt's mumbled words earlier.

'Because we have more than ourselves to fight for now.'

12

ARIAH

"*Let's go, Samantha. You have nothing to worry about. It's probably some rando's baby. Ariah was never too selective with who she let between her legs.*"

Wes's words are a dagger to the heart. He caught me flat-footed. I couldn't find the words to flay him for his bullshit ass statement. But I shouldn't have been surprised. That's who Wes has always been. I was just the fool who believed he changed.

Stupid fucker.

The cafeteria moves out of focus as tears blur my vision. I can't fight the exasperated huff that escapes me as the distorted image of them walking away assaults me.

I think I see Owen reach for me for a moment, but by the time my eyes close to prevent the tears from falling, all four of their backs are to me. Wes is linked arm-in-arm with Sam, and as they exit the cafe, she turns around and smirks. Well, she attempts one anyway. Her face is still as frozen by Botox as I remember.

"Come on, Ry, let's get you out of here. We can eat back at the house," Shay whispers in my ear as she tugs me free from my trance.

"Those are the assholes you used to be with?" Elias growls, but I still can't find the will to speak.

"Fucking pussyholes is what they are. Wait 'til I see them later," Shay snaps.

I walk aimlessly behind her, not uttering a sound.

It's not like I expected them to fall at my feet with endless apologies or for them to say their choice was a mistake and I was really their Chosen. I just wasn't expecting them to find out about my pregnancy and dismiss it like it's not one of theirs.

"Ariah," Reign sighs exasperatedly, which means he's been trying to get my attention for a long time.

"Sorry. How long were you calling me?"

Reign's mouth curves into a sympathetic smile, and I want to punch him. I don't need him or anyone else feeling sorry for me. I'm one sad smile away from screaming.

"Not long. I wanted to know if you still wanted to attend class later?" Reign states.

His question only fuels my rage. I didn't do anything wrong. Why should I have to walk around despondently while they are unaffected?

"Yes," I snap, stomping up the stairs and into the house.

No one calls me on my bratty-ass attitude, and it's for the best. I'll apologize later. I know I'm being petulant, but I can't seem to find the fucks to give at the moment.

They all let me escape to my room without another word.

"How fucking dare they," I shout, slamming my door.

Plopping down on my bed, I snatch the ultrasound photos off my nightstand. My anger abates at the sight of them. The photo from my first appointment that went missing the day we moved back is still unaccounted for.

Memories of my first visit to the doctor's office flood my mind as I lay down. Dr. Jaffri confirmed what I already knew to be true. I was pregnant, but I couldn't understand how. I had the implant and religiously made sure they all used condoms. Are there statistical anomalies? *Sure.* But there'd need to be a perfect storm to be that protected and still get knocked up. Dr. Jaffri answered one part of the question during that visit. I had no implant in my arm. But it wasn't until the second appointment that I gained clarity on how truly fucked my situation was.

We'd been in Bronston for almost five weeks, and the ache in my chest hadn't dulled. I was still questioning my abrupt departure from Edgewood. It was necessary. However, it didn't change the turmoil that raged inside me since leaving.

Dad was so worried, constantly reminding me that I could talk to him and reassuring me it would all be okay in the end. The earnest plea in his eyes almost made me cave that day. I knew I could talk to him. He'd always been my safe place, but at that time, it felt like a journey I needed to do alone. I needed to process and come to terms with all the changes in my life over the last two years.

Dread filled my stomach as I climbed out of the backseat of the SUV that day. I was so conflicted. Anger and betrayal fought against joy and hope. I was too damn young to have anyone's baby, but part of one of the guys was growing inside me.

"We can always do this at the house," Dad offers.

I inhale a centering breath before I respond. "No, I'm not being forced to stay in the house when you said the threat is low here." Then, we enter the building of the upscale office complex.

Reign and Elias step from the elevator, making eye contact with Dad and Fernando. "Everything's clear, Mr. Bradford," Reign states, and I roll my eyes. It's like having annoying-ass older brothers.

"Thanks, guys," Dad says as we step into the elevator they just vacated.

"Kiss asses," I mumble under my breath, earning a chuckle from Dad.

Reign leans forward just as the door chimes, signaling we've reached our destination. "You're just jealous," he teases, and I elbow him.

"Of your ugly mug? Never," I giggle, appreciating the momentary reprieve from my intrusive thoughts.

However, the arrival at the office door harshly reminds me how real this fucking is.

"Miss Bradford. Welcome," the woman at the front desk greets, standing and motioning for me to head for the back. "She's ready for you."

Dad grabs my hand, halting me. "Do you want me to come with you?"

"I'll be okay," I reassure him with a soft smile, then turn and follow the receptionist to the back.

She's all teeth and cheers as we walk down the corridor. "This must be such an exciting time! So much planning and getting things in order."

I listen as she yammers on, and I want to be annoyed with her happiness for me, but she's not aware of how difficult being here is. So I nod along until she seats me and tells me I'll be seen shortly.

Once the door closes, I slump back in the chair and try to massage away the stress. "It's not even nine in the morning, and I already want this day to be fucking over," I grumble as the door opens.

"Ah, Miss Bradford, a pleasure to see you again. Are you ready to discuss a few things?" Dr. Janan Jaffri asks as she sits across from me.

I shift in my seat and square my shoulders. "Were you able to find out how this happened?"

Concern lines her face, and I can feel the panic growing like a creeper vine up my legs. The confidence I felt moments ago evaporates, and I start rubbing at the skin of my inner wrist.

"It's as I suspected," she states.

It's one thing to suspect someone did this on purpose. It's a whole different level to have those suspicions confirmed. My panic turns to ash as fury blazes in its place. "So, I was never given the birth control implant?" I ask for clarity. Part of me is hoping if I ask, her response will be different.

"There is no record of it," she reiterates, and I grind my molars.

"Then what did that doctor put in my arm?" I ask through clenched teeth, trying to remember that Dr. Jaffri isn't the cause of this.

She opens the folder on her desk and turns it to face me. "It was a fertility boost cocktail." She points to my lab work and continues, "You see this line here? This is essentially a prenatal vitamin on steroids. You were given a super dose of Folic Acid, B12, and B6, as well as Vitamins C and D. That alone would be perplexing to give a healthy teenage girl. But the injection of Gonadotropins confirmed that there was no way they would give you a fertility drug to boost egg production with an implant. It's counterintuitive."

My stomach churns at that revelation, and I'm not sure if it's because of the news she's just relayed or because I'm fucking pregnant. I spring from my seat and bolt through the door for the bathroom down the hall. I barely reach the toilet before whatever smoothie I drank this morning empties into the porcelain bowl. All the while, one word is on repeat in my brain. Pregnant. Pregnant. Pregnant. It's playing on a loop like an annoying nursery rhyme.

The bathroom door bursts open, but I don't look to see who's joined me. I already know. "I'm okay, Dad. Just give me a second."

I hear his footsteps click against the tiled floor and the sound of a faucet turning on before he's back at my side, helping me stand and wiping my face. "Ry, I know you're strong and want to do this alone, but you don't have to."

The tears that were building in my eyes rolled down my face. Their salty taste makes my stomach lurch, but luckily, nothing threatens to come up.

"Why would someone do this, Dad?" I sob, and he pulls me into his chest. The familiar woodsy scent reminds me of him when I was little, and I would run to him when I was upset.

"I'm sorry, Ry. I wish I could've protected you more," he whispers into my hair, and the trickle of tears turns into a steady stream.

The question is protected from who? My brain works overtime at the thought that my father and the other Council members had a hand in this.

Pushing from his embrace, I levy my accusation. "Was it you? Did you and this fucked up organization do this to me?"

Guilt gnaws at me at the sight of hurt in his face before he masks it. "No," he sighed. "I won't pretend we don't have plans and that by choosing Samantha, the boys have fucked them up."

An invisible dagger slices through my heart, right to the core of me, at the mention of that goddamn day. I've spent weeks replaying every situation. . . every moment spent with them, analyzed. How could I have been so fucking blind?

Sensing the change, my dad curses, recognizing his mistake immediately. "Dammit, Ry. I'm sorry. I feel like a goddamn broken record, but I don't think I have the right words."

A light knock at the door reminds me that we're still at Dr. Jaffri's office, and I need to finish this appointment. "Miss Bradford. The doctor sent me to check on you," the receptionist's voice sounds through the door.

"We can talk more later. Let's get you seen," Dad says, coaxing me from the stall.

Once my mouth is rinsed and I have a piece of gum, I'm brought to the examining room. An ultrasound machine sits next to the exam table. I climb up and wait while my father sits in one of the chairs. Our eyes connect, and I mouth 'thank you' as Dr. Jaffri walks in.

"How are you feeling?" she asks.

"Much better, thanks," I reply as she begins her initial examination.

"I know this is overwhelming, but it's going to be important for you and the baby's health that you manage your stress. Has the sleep aid I prescribed you been helping?"

Sucking air through my nose, I take a deep breath as she listens to my lungs before responding, "Yes. I've been sleeping so soundly that someone could creep in my window and sleep next to me, and I wouldn't notice."

A choking sound turns our gazes in my father's direction, and he's five shades redder than he was when we first arrived.

"Are you alright?" Dr. Jaffri inquires, stepping in his direction.

He holds his hands up, halting her. "I'll be okay. I just choked on spit," Dad wheezes.

Dr. Jaffri guides me down on the table, instructing me to lift my shirt before she turns on the ultrasound machine and washes her hands.

I watch with interest as she applies gel to the probe and then places it against my abdomen. She points to the monitor, and at the same time, a whooshing sound fills the room, followed by what can only be described as the galloping of hoofs. "This is Baby Bradford," she announces.

My eyes lock on my baby. Perfection. Even at this stage, utter perfection. Did I want to be a teenage mother? Fuck no! But this is—

A gasp interrupts my thoughts. "Well, this is unexpected," Dr. Jaffri mumbles loud enough for me to hear.

"Is everything okay, Janan?" My dad jumps from his spot in the corner, reaching my side before Dr. Jaffri can respond. If I weren't so concerned with what she's seeing, I'd have questions about their familiarity.

"There are two heartbeats," Dr. Jaffri says almost inaudibly.

Did this bitch just say two?

"As in, the baby's heart is beating twice, or are two total?" I screech out. My earlier panic returns a hundredfold.

Clearing her throat, she replies, "Twins."

Once the oxygen returns to my brain, I shout, "Which super sperm motherfucker did this to me?"

As the last of my memory from that day fades, something Samantha said in the cafe sparks into awareness.

'You stupid bitch. How the fuck did you get pregnant? It was supposed to be me.'

She wanted to get pregnant. So, how did it end up being me instead? Did that cunt plan something, and the doctor screwed up?

Picking my phone up, I dial Dad.

"Hey, Ry. Everything good?" he greets.

Too focused on this new information, and I get directly to the point. "We need to find the doctor that put in the implants. She either made a mistake or didn't implant me on purpose."

13
LEV

"She's pregnant?" Sebastian questions. His blue eyes grow three times their original size as shock sets in from Wes's words.

We're seated around the Council's table in their private chambers at the Fraternitas as Wes informs Sebastian and the Council of the shocking news.

"How's that possible?" Sebastian mutters, more to himself, but it's still loud enough for us to hear.

Never missing a moment to be a wiseass, Wyatt explains, "Well, you see when a man and woman have sex, the man's sperm fight each other to fertilize—"

"You know what I fucking mean," Sebastian spits. His jaw tenses as he grits his teeth. "Ariah, like all the other Selected girls, was given a birth control implant, and she was adamant about using condoms." He turns to face Wyatt. "So, again. How is that possible?"

Pulling out my phone, I do a quick search before responding, "It's possible, just highly unlikely. The combination of the implant and a condom reduces the likelihood of conceiving to less than one percent."

"Thank you, Captain Brainiac," Owen chimes, his sarcasm

evident. "The more important question here is, what are we going to do? We can't leave her to go through this pregnancy alone or think we don't want her."

A throat clears. "Nothing changes," Mr. Edgewood states. "It's even more important we continue to play along. We can't risk any harm to Ariah. She's carrying the future of the Fraternitas."

"I don't give a shit about the future of this organization," Owen snaps.

Before his father can respond, Wes asks, "Did you have something to do with this?"

Donald Edgewood's face scrunches in outrage. "Absolutely not. We wanted you to choose Ariah, but we wouldn't go this far."

"I distinctly remember you urging me to sleep with her," Wes retorts.

Owen's nostrils flare. "Is that true?"

"I merely suggested that if you all were going to sleep with any of the Selected, Miss Bradford would be the best choice," Wes's father replies dryly.

Wyatt is out of his seat and grabs Wes by the collar of his navy blue polo before we can react. "Is that why you were on a mission to get her to forgive you? Because Daddy said so?"

"We don't have time for this," Sebastian shouts.

"Let him go, Wyatt," I order.

Wyatt's wild eyes snap in my direction. "Not until he answers."

"I'm quite curious to hear his response as well," Owen adds, twirling a knife between his knuckles.

"Fuck you both for thinking I'd do that," Wes growls, pushing Wyatt until he drops his hold. "I can admit I was a major dick when she first arrived."

"That's putting it mildly," Sebastian snorts, making Wes glare in his direction.

"Says the guy who ran so hot and cold you gave her whiplash," Owen murmurs.

Sighing, I say, "We don't have time for this. We've all done something that we need to apologize for. So, let's stop with the blame game bullshit and focus."

Wyatt takes his seat, but Owen doesn't stop glaring at Wes. "I still want an answer."

Wes goes rigid—his face flushing red with anger before his heated gaze meets Owen's matching one. "No. I just said I wouldn't do that. I fucking love her. It took me all year to realize it, but I'd never do that to her. I've been trying to do everything so we can get her back."

"Enough," my father commands. "Your trivial shit isn't the concern here. You can have your group therapy session later. Right now, we're going to discuss the next steps."

Chastised, Owen and Wes huff but keep quiet.

"We're going to up security around her. Increasing her discreet detail and you five will make Samantha believe she's in control until we can get that damn chip out of my son," Owen's father orders.

"You can't expect us to ignore our pregnant girlfriend. It was bad enough we had to treat her the way we did today," Owen confesses.

Sebastian massages the bridge of his nose. "What did you do?"

Slumping in his seat, Owen deflates as he remembers our encounter with Ariah earlier.

I open my mouth to explain, but Mr. Edgewood holds his hand up, signaling me to stay silent. "They can fill you in on that later. Just know the plan hasn't changed. We expect you all to continue following orders. Stay away from Ariah Bradford until further notice."

•

I slam my laptop close. "Why can't I find anything?" I grumble, pushing away from my desk and standing.

It's been four hours since the meeting at the Fraternitas, and I'm no closer to finding a way to deactivate the chip. I can't find Eshe. There's no trace of her anywhere. Which means she's either in hiding, being held, or dead. I'm desperately hoping it's the former rather than the latter because if she's dead, we're fucked.

Groaning, I pull out my phone and dial Thomas.

"What's up?" He says, not wasting time with any greeting.

"Are we secure?" I inquire, not wanting to say anything if we're being tapped.

He grunts twice and hangs up. *Not secure, then.*

A minute later, a text appears.

> T
>
> Teagan... ten minutes...

I know not to reply, and the text vanishes, like it was never sent, once it shows I've read it.

Striding to my desk, I sit back in my chair, then push the button on the left side, and my wall opens up to two rows of monitors. Then, I place my thumb over the sensor and level my eye to the scanner. The drawer pops open. I pull out my encrypted wireless keyboard and token, then connect it to the encrypted server. The screens come online, and I enter the newest code and wait.

The screen comes to life, and Teagan is on the other end.

"Long time no see Levi," she greets.

"I wish it was under better circumstances."

She grunts her agreement. "I've been updated. Eshe is dead. She was found two days ago with her throat slit."

"Fuck," I exclaim.

"Fuck is right. With her went any real hope of deactivating that chip. Short of getting a hold of the man who inserted it in Owen, there are very few other options."

My hands ball into fists at my side. There has to be another way. Owen would sooner kill himself than let Samantha force us to marry her. There's an expiration date on his willingness to cooperate.

"You said 'few options.' What else is on the table?"

She smiles. "You know how much I like solving the unsolvable. I'm working on hacking the chip."

My eyebrows arch in surprise. "Is that possible?"

We might be able to get out of this after all.

I always held out hope, but despair grew as each day passed, and I was greeted with only dead ends.

"It's going to take some time, but I'm sure I can build a code to hack either the chip or the device that vindictive bitch is using to control you all," she explains.

"Do you think you can do it before this dumbass engagement party that's happening in a little over a month from now?"

"I'm running round-the-clock code. You'll be the first to know as soon as I have an answer."

Nodding, I ask, "Is there anything I can do?"

"If you can find a way to clone the device Samantha is using, that can speed this process up exponentially."

"You'll have it before the end of the week," I state.

She dips her head, and then the screen goes black.

Spinning in my chair, I fist-pump into the air. This is the biggest break we've had in months.

I turn back to the monitors as my fingers fly across the keyboard.

A genuine smile curls my lips at the sight in front of me. Ariah's lying on her bed, fast asleep—her hand resting on her baby bump.

Wyatt thought he was slick, enlisting the Jacobis to help him put cameras in her room. He should know. Not much gets past Q.

"We'll all make this up to you, Dove. Just hold on a little longer."

14
ARIAH

"Twins," Shay exclaims, staring at the sonogram. "I still can't believe I'm going to be an auntie!"

Even after it was confirmed, I still couldn't wrap my brain around the fact that two lives were growing inside me. "You and me both," I quip as Reign parks the car in the student lot on campus.

He and Elias will be my guards today while Fernando works on some secret project with my dad. Everyone was tightlipped, outside of saying it was a personal matter when I questioned what he would be doing. My guess is that it has something to do with his family in Polanco.

Shay and I both have classes. She has chemistry, and I have sociology. I'm still miffed that we don't have even one class together this semester.

"Were you able to find out what you're having?" She asks as we unbuckle and gather our bags.

My sixteen-week appointment is next week, and Dr. Jaffri said if I wanted to and the twins weren't being shy, I could find out the sex of the babies.

"Not yet, and to be perfectly honest, I'm not sure I want to. The only thing I care about is having a safe and healthy pregnancy. Everything else is pretty much white noise."

Shay waits until we're on the sidewalk before speaking again. "Sigh. Fine. Out the window goes my gender reveal idea," she laments in quite a dramatic fashion, placing the back of her hand on her forehead and throwing her head back like a damsel in distress.

I snort, "You really need to be a drama major instead of a science one. I think you'd have a more lucrative acting career than one in forensic science."

"You wound me further," she gasps. "Have you not heard of Henry Chang-Yu Lee?" My face scrunches, and when she notices my confusion, she continues. "He's only, like, one of the fathers of forensic science. He's helped solve numerous cases through crime scene investigation and reconstruction."

Her excitement is palpable, making me smile. She knows I was only joking, but her joy makes me grateful that she's still here with me. I shudder at the thought of how close I came to losing her.

"You could play a forensic scientist on television like they do on *CSI* or *Dexter*," I joke.

She rolls her eyes. "I know at your last appointment you mentioned Dr. Jaffri looking into what could've happened with your implant. Did anything come of that?" Shay steers the conversation back to the original topic.

I shrug. "We have some ideas, but until we find the doctor who was supposed to put in the implant and didn't, we won't know who was responsible."

"But you used condoms as well. Shouldn't that have helped mitigate the probability of you becoming pregnant if the implant failed? I mean, I know condoms aren't one hundred percent, but they should've helped some, right?" Shay inquires, handing me back the ultrasound pictures as we walked across campus.

I nod. "It should've, but as you said, they aren't foolproof, and without knowing why the doctor didn't insert the implant, choosing instead to give me a fertility shot, I won't know the extent of why this happened."

We're approaching the Quad, where we'll separate when she asks, "Are you sure you're ready for this?"

"Nope. I'm absolutely not sure, but I know when all options were presented to me, the path I chose felt the most right."

I'm too young to be a mother to one child, much less two, but I knew the instant I heard their heartbeats, I'd burn the whole fucking world to the ground before I let anything or anyone harm them.

Shay hugs me. "And I'll be here with you every step of the way. Even if those ras eediots can't pull their heads out of their asses."

I squeeze her back but don't respond. Any mention of them still feels too raw after what happened earlier this week. Since then, I've seen one of them in each of my classes, but they don't speak or acknowledge me. So, I'll do the same.

The onus is on them to reach out, and if they never do, I might be a single parent, but I'll have a village supporting me. It will also fuel my desire to bring the Fraternitas to heel.

Releasing each other, we agree to meet here after classes are over before saying goodbye.

Reign and Elias position themselves on each side of me. We walk in silence as we approach the Humanities building. It's not until we're outside of my sociology class door that Reign speaks. "Wyatt will be in there."

My throat tightens at the mention of his name. The one who claimed me so boldly that I believed him despite my reluctance to trust. *Some good that did me.*

Inhaling, I ease the air past the lump in my throat and stiffen my spine. I knew it wouldn't be long before I encountered him. I've been dreading seeing them in my classes. I quickly curse the registrar's office. Only my luck would make it so they'd each be in one of my classes.

"It's fine," I lie. "Which one of you will be inside with me today?"

They both study my face, quickly reading that I'm full of shit, but neither calls me on it.

"Both of us," Elias answers.

I arch a brow, conveying my silent question.

"Two guards will be outside during classes from now on, and there will always be at least two of us inside with you," Reign explains.

"What aren't you telling me?" I grumble, knowing there's been some new development I'm not privy to.

Reign's eyes soften at my obvious annoyance. "There's no big conspiracy on this one. After the incident in the cafe and discovering you'll have the Heirs in your classes, we've revised your detail."

"Fine," I sigh, then pull the door open. I'm the first to arrive, so we find seats in the back of the class. Since day one, they've insisted that this provides the best vantage point.

We're situated in our seats before people start to trickle in. I'm scrolling through Summer's social media accounts when I feel his presence. *Wyatt.* He's here, and I have to force myself to keep my eyes on my phone, reading through Summer's posts about her first year at uni.

Admittedly, I should be satisfied that she's still alive, but I'm not. Especially now that I know someone's trying to overthrow the Fraternitas by any means necessary. I've briefly even considered Sam's involvement, but I can't imagine she'd kill her friends, even with her being malicious and self-centered. I don't think she'd go that far. Plus, they chose her in the end anyway. A plan I'm sure they had all along.

Wyatt's spiced, smokey scent that is uniquely his alone wafts through the air as he walks by. My nostrils flare as the memory of the nights I was weak and slid my hands between my legs, thinking of how it felt to nestle my nose in the crook of his neck while he'd piston inside of me.

I shake my head, trying to force the visual from my mind as I feel my nipples pucker. I sigh in relief when the instructor calls everyone's attention to the front.

"Good afternoon. For those of you who missed class week, I'm Dr. Liliana Monroe," she states.

Professor Monroe can't be more than twenty-eight. Her auburn hair sits in an asymmetrical bob that fits her pixie-like face that looks swallowed by her circular-framed glasses. They suit her, though. I listen as she does a quick synopsis of what we covered last week. Discussing the syllabus, outlining her expectations, and the term research paper required on top of weekly assignments.

I'm about to zone out when I hear a slew of phones going off at the same time the course guide, once displayed on the smartboard, is replaced by a video that automatically plays.

A room that is so familiar comes into view as moans erupt from devices and the screen. I watch in momentary horror as I realize it's me in the video. My head is thrown back in ecstasy, and my legs are spread wide for all to see a clear view of me playing with my pussy.

What the actual fuck?

Professor Monroe works tirelessly to turn off the video to no avail. Elias storms to the front of the class and unplugs the damn thing. The professor then demands everyone stop playing the video unless they want to be expelled from school for conduct unbecoming of a student at LWU.

"Miss Bradford, I'm——" the professor attempts to apologize, but I halt her words with a raise of my hand.

Fury floods my veins, and I turn my glacial gray eyes on Wyatt, whose jaw is clenched like he's upset that whatever scheme they've cooked up to embarrass me has been thwarted.

"There's nothing wrong with a woman exploring her own body and taking pleasure when and how she fucking sees fit. I'm not ashamed to masturbate. The person who recorded this private moment, unbeknownst to me, is the only one who should feel fucking remorse," I exclaim. "Now, Professor Monroe, please continue with your class. Hopefully, the immature fucks who did this will recognize the error of their ways, but I highly doubt any of them have the sense to feel anything from their self-entitled pedestals."

A proud smile forms on the professor's tan face as she nods, then refocuses the class's attention, making them concentrate on their syllabi.

"Do you want to go?" Reign growls in my ear. I turn to see his teeth clenched so hard I'm sure he'll crack his pristine teeth as his vitriolic stare is aimed past me in Wyatt's direction.

"Not a fucking chance," I retort. "No assholes are running me from the room with their childish bullshit," I say that part loud enough, ensuring Wyatt can hear, and I mean every word I've said, even as my heart cracks at the lengths men I swore cared for me are willing to go.

Closing my eyes, I renew my resolve to break them before they can break me.

15
WYATT

I'm going to filet Samantha!
I wonder if I throw her dismembered body in a fire if her plastic parts will melt?
I don't think I've ever hated someone so much in my entire life. She's a fucking poison that, unless handled properly, will kill you. I need her gone like last year. Worse than any rat infestation or global-like pandemic. She festers until you annihilate her.
Pulling out my cell phone, I text Lev.

> ME
> Any progress?

I messaged him in class to deal with the situation. I had to wait until Ariah was distracted to ensure she didn't see me. But at this point, even if she did, she'd probably believe I was reporting on how she reacted to the video.

When it played, I had to dig my nails into my palms and grit my teeth so as not to react. I was so pissed—*I am so pissed*. I knew immediately this was the work of Samantha and her minions. The question is how the hell she tapped into a feed that no one knew about except the Jacobis and myself.

My phone buzzes as I walk through the doors of our campus house. If we weren't trying to keep Samantha from having any contact with Ariah, I would've complained that we decided to live in the Edgewood house, clear across campus from the Bradford house.

> **LEV**
> upstairs.

That's it?
Sighing, I scratch my stubbled jaw and climb the stairs.
I hear them before I see them.
"No, Owen. Ariah would be devastated if you allowed yourself to be killed. Stop trying to be a fucking martyr and work with us instead of giving up," Sebastian snaps.
He's been a moody fucker the longer he has to stomach interactions with the viper. *Shit, we all have.*
"I only offered to carve her face up for this fucking stunt," Owen huffs, tossing a knife I've never seen him with before into the air.
Sebastian rubs the bridge of his nose as if trying to find the patience required to deal with Owen. He's been a testy fucker with an even shorter fuse than me.
"Which would lead to Samantha setting off the chip and killing you," Wes says, trying to reason with him.
I take my seat as they continue to bicker.
"Okay, everyone's here now, so shut the fuck up," Lev demands before turning to me. "Were you ever going to tell us that you set cameras up in her room in Colorado and here?"
Quirking my lip, I tilt my head and arch my copper brow. "Nope. This was on a need-to-know basis, and none of you needed to know," I quip.
Lev's hands fist at his sides. "Well, smartass, thanks to your selfish behavior, Samantha was able to have someone backdoor the system."
I close my eyes, flexing the muscles in my jaw to reign in my anger. It's the only thing I feel remorse for. I knew Lev would have the best tech to protect Ariah from something like this. But I was so

angry with them—with myself. None of us deserve her, but I won't let her go.

"This also means you knew she was pregnant?" Sebastian infers.

I nod. There's no use hiding that.

"What the fuck, Wyatt? Why would you keep something so pivotal to yourself? We're supposed to be a unified unit on this," Wes growls, making me turn and see all the hurt and disappointment on all their faces.

"We are," I shout. "But I'll always put her self-interest first. Like I told you last September—until I'm convinced you idiots won't fuck this up royally, I'll keep the shit I deem necessary from you and do so unapologetically."

No one speaks for what feels like a solid five minutes, and I'm okay with that. I'll never apologize for keeping Ariah safe. Fuck anyone who doesn't support that.

Owen's the one to speak finally. "While I'm pissed at you for keeping her pregnancy a secret, I respect and understand why you did," he offers.

He gets it—he always does.

"You would cosign this bullshit behavior," Wes snaps. And as usual, Wes's pissy attitude rears its ugly head.

"Pot meet kettle," Sebastian fake coughs, making me chuckle.

Owen's arctic glare pivots from me to Wes. "Let's not act like you don't do the same shit. We all have for one reason or another. So, instead of griping at each other, let's focus on how we will get back at the cantankerous bitch responsible for this."

Feeling chastised, Wes huffs as he leans back in his seat and crosses his arms.

Big fucking baby.

"I had Q send out a virus to anyone who received the video," Lev explains.

"How do you know it'll work?" I ask.

Lev turns and pulls up an invitation. "Because we're throwing a party, and the only way to get in is with a code unique to each person. Which can only be accessed by downloading the invite."

"Fucking genius," Owen cheers. "Though, I'm not looking forward to partying without Ariah."

Sebastian squeezes his shoulder. "Same, but we'll get her back soon."

"Oh. We won't be partying. We're just hosting the event," Lev divulges.

"Then where the hell will we be?" Wes questions.

Lev pulls up another screen displaying his email. "We'll be meeting with Mrs. Davenport."

Fucking finally!

"How did you get her to agree?" I inquire.

"Teagan," Lev answers. Seeing that none of us are picking up what he's putting down with his one-word response, he continues. "She set up an untraceable video conference so Samantha's mother can contact us while her daughter parties."

"Fuck yeah," Owen shouts. "She can finally explain her outburst during the Chosen ceremony."

I grimace at the reminder of that night. Each time someone congratulated us, I wanted to rip out their larynx and shove it down Samantha's and the Senator's throats. The only good things to come out of that night were capturing Jameson, a feat I'm still curious to get all the details about, and discovering Samantha's mother was not colluding with her daughter and stepson.

We've been trying to arrange a way to speak with Mrs. Davenport for weeks. Our intel has revealed that Samantha has her parents under house arrest with round-the-clock guards ensuring they never leave the house. The vindictive brat has no loyalty except for maybe to Senator Baker. But I guess since she's fucking him and he gave her who and what she's always wanted—*Wes* and elevating her status—it's not surprising that she'd be loyal to him.

"You know at least one of us is going to need to be at the party," Sebastian states. "Samantha is going to want to preen like a proud peacock."

"More like a green anaconda, squeezing the life from us before attempting to swallow us whole," Wes mutters.

"That's a more accurate depiction of Samantha," I jest.

I see the moment resignation sets in because Wes's shoulders slump, and his face pinches. "It has to be me, doesn't it?"

Lev nods. "Unfortunately. She's made it known that she'd get rid of everyone except you in a heartbeat on many occasions."

"The lecherous viper has been vocal about killing you if she can't have you," Owen adds.

Wes massages his temples as if he can rub this entire situation away. "It's fine," he sighs. "As long as we can get the necessary information from Sam's mom, I can put up with her shit for one night."

Now that we have that settled, I need to ensure all traces of that video will be wiped. "What happens to anyone who doesn't download the invitation?"

"An email from the school Bursar's office has also been sent out," Lev replies. "And before you ask, I have code scanning for anyone who tries to upload the video to any site."

Satisfied with that answer, Sebastian stands. "If you'd all excuse me. I need to meet Matthieu at the club. He finally has the information we've been waiting for."

A Cheshire Cat smile pastes on my face. "Step one in Operation Destroy Sam can finally commence."

16

SEBASTIAN

"Is it set?" I ask Matthieu, confirming the accuracy of his earlier text message.

Matthieu lifts his glass, swirling the amber liquid—the clinking of ice sounding ten times louder in the silent room. His piercing, jeweled eyes meet mine as he brings the drink to his mouth and sips. There's a level of challenge in his gaze, and I know the favor I've asked of him is one that tests the limits of our friendship, but for Ariah—I'd risk it all.

I wait, not uttering a word or displaying my growing impatience. We've made a gentleman's agreement, and I'd say we're even for what he's getting in return. He finally lowers the glass, never looking away—two alphas silently feeling each other out. To look away would alter the dynamic of who is on higher footing—neither of us willing to lose ground.

"Everything is in place," he finally answers.

Another moment of silence passes before we dip our heads—an acknowledgment of our mutual respect for one another's steadfastness.

I clear my throat, preparing to move this conversation along. "How long before we get what we need?"

"Senator Baker has committed to the annual VIP membership at our exclusive Los Angeles location. He's already made a reservation for our Pitch Black room," Matthieu replies.

My eyebrows feel like they've hit my hairline at this information. "As in *the Pitch Black room?*"

He nods, "The very same. It seems our Senator has unique tastes. I'm actually surprised he wasn't a member already—his requests for special additions to what the room already includes had R'chelle asking for approval."

My heart rate kicks up. I wouldn't be surprised if Matthieu could see the veins in my neck pulsating.

This is precisely what we were hoping for.

"Has he already confirmed his guest?" I probe.

No one can enter any of Le Toucher's locations without being thoroughly vetted. They must also provide some form of leverage—a secret no one can know. It helps prevent anyone from releasing details about what happens behind the doors of any of Matthieu's clubs.

What guests aren't aware of is that every location is monitored. Each playroom is outfitted with cameras—an extra level of insurance if you will. It's part of the contract they sign—it's just written in invisible ink that doesn't appear until a black light or other UV source is applied.

"Guests," he corrects, and I arch a brow, signaling him to continue. "The Senator will have two women and three men in attendance."

Interesting.

"Making it a party then?"

He huffs a laugh. "Of sorts."

"Well, don't keep me waiting. Who will be celebrating with our dear senator?"

"The president's daughter." His jaw clenches at the mention of Isabella, but he continues, "Two other members of the senate, Samantha Davenport." My lips curl into a smirk once he says her name. "And Brian Porter."

"And the surprises just keep coming, don't they?" I offer at the mention of Brian's name. "Who'll be in charge of the room?"

In order to help play out a member's fantasy, a room attendant is present, either participating or facilitating.

"The Senator has requested two attendants, Amélie and Henri."

They really are going for the full experience.

Amélie and Henri are two of the most sadistic attendants. Only guests who want to explore their darkest sides—the ones they hide from respectable society—ask for them. I've only heard of one instance where both were requested, which ended up with bodies Matthieu had to dispose of.

"What nights has he requested? We're eager to get out from under Senator Baker's thumb," I confess.

Matthieu turns to his computer, shaking the mouse to bring his monitor to life. Angling the screen in my direction, he says, "Saturday, October 14th. They've reserved the entire club for the night. They're playing some twisted game of Capture the Flag."

"With Amélie and Henri involved, I'm sure twisted is not the right word," I quip, making him chuckle.

My phone buzzes, garnering my attention. I hold up my finger, signaling for him to wait as I pull it from my breast pocket.

> **PARASITE**
>
> What are you doing at a sex club, Sebastian?
>
> You wouldn't want me to push a little button and end Owen's life, would you?

I growl at the sight of her threats.

"Samantha?" Matthieu guesses.

"The one and only leech," I mutter, sliding my phone back into my suit pocket. "Another reason why we want to move things along. She's getting increasingly demanding. Constant threats toward people I love. To put it simply, she must go."

He rubs at his newly grown beard. "I could just have her killed. Why go to these lengths?"

I wish it were that simple. I'd have killed her months ago.

"Unfortunately, she holds the power at this time."

His eyes narrow in confusion. "Explain."

"When Owen was taken, a chip was implanted in his arm, and Samantha has the device controlling it," I explain.

Matthieu grimaces, "I see now why it's so important you get the information you need."

My cellphone vibrates again. The steady hum lets me know it's a call this time and not a text. Matthieu nods his head when I request another moment.

Pulling the device from my pocket, I see that Samantha is now calling me. I hit ignore, but the phone rings almost immediately after I rejected her call.

Annoyed, I answer, "What the fuck do you want?"

She tsks. "Is that any way to treat your fiancée?" Her voice grates my nerves.

"In title alone because, like Vivian, you just don't know when to let go. With any luck, you'll meet the same fate. So, I'll ask you again, what the fuck do you want, *Samantha?*"

"Fine, get your ass back here. We have a meeting with the wedding planner, and you *all* need to be in attendance," she demands.

I snort. "We haven't been involved with planning any part of this sham, and I'm busy at the moment."

"It's almost like none of you care about Owen. You're all always testing the limits of my patience," she shrieks, and I can almost see her stomping her foot like a toddler in full tantrum mode. "You'll get back here now and take the dick that belongs to me out of any—"

I end the call, wasting no time, turning my phone on do not disturb.

"Was that wise?" Matthieu questions.

"As much as Samantha believes she's in control, she's not. If she ever did activate the chip, killing Owen, she'd die."

Matthieu's office phone rings, and I wait while he answers it. "What do you mean Miss Davenport is on the line for me?"

My jaw clenches at the level of audacity and stupidity this girl possesses.

"Fine, put her through," he instructs before hitting the button for speakerphone. "What can I do for you, Miss Davenport? Senator Baker's appointment isn't until October, and only he can call in and request any addendums." Matthieu's aloof tone expresses his annoyance.

"Well, if you let my fiancé into your club to fuck some random girl, I'll ruin—"

"If," Matthieu barks, silencing her. "*If* I did let your fiancé in my club, it wouldn't be any of your fucking business, little girl. Don't call my office threatening me. You don't want to experience what happens to those who do. Now, I suggest you go sulk over the perceived infidelity of your *fiancé* and get the fuck off my phone."

He doesn't wait for a response before he ends the call.

"Charming, isn't she," I jest.

His hands run through his wheat-colored hair as he regains his composure. "Anything you need from here out, consider it done. Samantha Davenport has made an enemy, and if by chance she survives you, I promise she won't survive me."

I grin. The stupid girl always puts her over-priced stiletto in her collagen-injected mouth.

"Isabella will be delivered to you the morning after she leaves your club."

Now it's his turn to smile. His tongue glides over his canines, showcasing the evil that simmers just beneath the surface.

Standing, I fix my suit jacket and then stretch my arm out. Matthieu takes my proffered hand, and the deal is sealed.

I check to see if I feel an ounce of remorse for the devil I just placed in Isabella's path, but there's none.

I'd bloody the world to ensure Ariah is safely back in our arms.

17
ARIAH

The first week of school has flown by. I've been able to avoid any interaction with the guys or Samantha. Even on days like today, when all of us are in the same Thursday afternoon history class.

After the incident in the food court on the first day and the dumbass video of me flicking my bean, it's been radio silent. My dad was livid once Reign gave his daily report. He immediately called Teagan to wipe the internet of all traces and had her come to install a new security system. I've only heard mentions of the infamous Teagan. She's supposed to be one of the best coders in the world.

"You know the routine," Reign begins while parking the car in what I've discovered is our designated spot. But it's not just this parking space. Apparently, no other vehicles can park in the first row in any of the lots around campus unless they're a Bradford or on the Bradford payroll. "You're with us—"

"At all times. No matter what," I mimic, rolling my eyes.

"Be a wiseass all you want, Ry—just don't be a stupid ass," Elias chimes in.

Reign turns off the engine and then cranes his neck enough for me to understand the severity of the situation. His hard eyes and stern jaw illustrate that playtime is over.

"I'm not being a wiseass. I'm just showing you that I get it. You don't have to do the same speech every time we go anywhere," I complain, crossing my arms. The sharp pain that jolts through my tender breast makes me drop them faster than I crossed them.

Fucking pregnancy bullshit. I swear I'm putting in a complaint with management about all the side effects of carrying children.

"I'm sure Samantha Davenport has already informed Senator Baker and whoever they're working for about your pregnancy," Nando explains.

Groaning at that fact, I grab my bag and exit the car. "Fine," I huff, genuinely sounding like a petulant child.

Ever since the infamous leaked video, they've been hypervigilant, never allowing me to go anywhere alone. Now, Reign, Elias, and Nando always accompany me to this class. Scratch that. *All* my classes. I want to be more annoyed, but I'm not. I appreciate everything they're doing to keep me safe.

There is the added bonus of pissing off the guys.

Anytime Reign, Eli, or Nando touches me in a way that can be perceived as intimate, and I swear I can feel daggers being pointed in our direction. It's like they expected me to wallow in misery while they get to move on.

Well, fuck that and fuck them.

I won't let their bullshit dampen my earlier good mood. I have my sixteen-week appointment later today. So, I just have to make it through this three-hour class without stabbing anyone in the eye.

That should be doable.

With my bag positioned on my shoulder, my hands move instinctually to the metal hair sticks in my messy bun, adjusting them. It's like my trainer said, *'You should never leave home without a weapon.'*

Once we step onto the sidewalk, Reign grabs my bag and slings it over his shoulder, placing his hand on the small of my back while Nando takes point and Elias positions himself at our backs.

We're walking across campus toward the history building.

"You excited for your appointment?" Reign asks.

I nod, "Might find out what I'm having today."

"Might? You don't want to know?" he volleys back.

I shrug. "The babies might not be in the showing mood, and I'm not sure I want to know. It doesn't matter what I have. They'll be mine, and I'll love them."

"So gangbangs are what you live for now? Did we bust you wide open, or were you always gagging for it?"

I don't have to turn to see who's speaking. I'd know Wes's condescending voice from anywhere.

My lips curl in disgust when I turn to see his hand wrapped around Samantha's shoulder as she pets his chest, and both of them glare at me.

"Oh look, if it isn't the future miserable CEO and his coked-out wife," I retort, not slowing my stride.

Samantha breaks from Wes's hold, attempting to storm in my direction.

Elias and Fernando have already positioned themselves to ward off her attack, but Wes yanks her back by her hair so hard that when she crashes back into him, some of her extensions are wrapped in his fist.

Throwing my head back, I burst into laughter.

"What the fuck, Wesley?" Samantha snarls.

I'm tempted to stay and watch them bicker, but I notice Wyatt, Lev, and Owen approaching, and I can't face all of them together right now. It's already bad enough that I have to endure a whole damn afternoon breathing their same air.

"I can't believe those are the same dudes I met earlier this year," Reign says.

The fissure grows in my chest at the reminder of what was, and my shoulders slump. "You and me both," I mumble.

We continue in silence after that.

As much as I try to tell myself nothing they're doing affects me, it's so far from the truth. It hurts. Each time I see them with her, or they look past me like I never existed, another part of me cracks. It's getting harder not to say something and to not ask why or demand answers. I have so many 'why' questions.

I'm so lost in my thoughts that I don't realize we've made it to the lecture hall or that Reign's been trying to get my attention until he squeezes my shoulder.

"Earth to Ry. We're here."

I look around, taking in the room. I've managed to miss the entire walk.

Sighing, I take my seat, and Reign hands me my bag before sitting next to me.

He brushes an errant strand of hair out of my face before tipping my chin up until I meet his light brown eyes. "They're fucking idiots, Ry, and if they can't get out of their own way, then they never deserved you in the first place."

A growl sounds from the front of the room, and I look up in time to see Owen standing just inside the door, gritting his teeth while he stares daggers in our direction. More specifically, where Reign's hand still lingers on my cheek.

I narrow my gaze and swear I see hurt in his hazel eyes.

Why the fuck would he care? None of them have shown an ounce of feelings besides disdain and aloofness since my return.

Owen runs his hands down his face, rubbing the scruff of his jaw. He looks like he hasn't slept in weeks. My heart skitters at that possibility. So many demons plague him. No matter how angry I am with them, I'd never want him to succumb to what haunts him. He was already teetering on a precipice.

He breaks our stare down first, storming out of the room. I spring from my seat, ready to follow him, before a gentle hand stops me.

Turning, I narrow my gaze on where Elias is holding me.

"It's for the best," he offers, and I want to scream.

I can feel Owen. He needs me. I'm about to argue that very point when Samantha walks in holding Owen's hand. "I've got you," she gloats, a smug grin on her face as she looks in my direction.

A soft caress slowly pulls my attention away. Reign leans and whispers into my ear, "Never let them see how much they hurt you. People will use your love for them to destroy you and then use what's left of you as a step ladder."

His words pierce me, but I know they ring true.

"But it hurts. Today. . . today, it hurts," I confess, and I feel the tear fall before I can stop it.

Reign thumbs it away. "I know it's difficult, and this entire situation sucks giant donkey dick dipped in shit, but you'll get through."

I snort, making him smile.

"There she is." Elias cheers and then adds, "Don't let anyone withdraw more than they deposit into your life, Ry. You can't do anything with insufficient funds."

"What are you two, fortune cookies?" Fernando jokes. "Mija, listen. These two are going to give you parables. Just say the word, and I'll stitch them new mouths."

Elias punches Nando's shoulder. "You can't go threatening to Glasgow people so loudly in public."

Fernando has the nerve to look affronted. "I was protecting her honor. Those assholes wouldn't survive a week if they were dating one of my sisters. Their balls would be earrings, and their dicks would be made into straws to sip their mojitos."

I almost choke on my spit, gasping at his words. "When can I meet your sisters?"

Nando shakes his head and mumbles something in Spanish about loca gringas asking for trouble, but I can't be sure.

Our conversation is cut off once the professor walks in and requests we pass forward last week's homework, then begins his lecture.

I can feel their attention on me throughout the class. I'm unsure which one it is, but Elias and Reign are right. They don't deserve me.

So, once the professor dismisses us for the day, I'm up and out of my seat, brushing past them with Reign, Nando, and Elias in the same formation we arrived in. My resolve renewed, and I say, "Let's go see my babies."

18
OWEN

My angel's carrying our baby, and we're being forced to pretend she's nothing to us. That alone is reason enough for me to jam a metal rod through Samantha's frontal lobe.

Her pregnancy is partially why I'm willing to play nice for now. I can't afford for anything to happen to her, and I won't let our kid grow up without all of us. But each moment without her is a slice down a vein—I'm bleeding out.

"This is the appointment she could find out what she's having," Wyatt shares. "Our baby is the size of an avocado."

"Or a grenade," I offer, and he chortles.

Wyatt shakes his head. "Only you'd think of weapons to compare the size of our baby in utero."

Shrugging, I retort, "You can have your fruit basket—I'll have my weapon arsenal." My words give me an idea. "I think I'm going to start assembling one, so once they're old enough, we can teach them how to use everything."

I wait for the rebuff, but it never comes. Wyatt hums in agreement. "I like it—even more if we have a girl. She needs to be badass and fully capable of protecting herself."

"Will you two idiots focus? We're almost in," Lev commands from the comms in our ears.

Tsking, I taunt, "Aww, are you still salty you didn't get to come? Don't worry, Levi bear. You can teach them to hack into any asshole that dares to fuck with them."

He growls, and I swear I can picture the sneer on his face.

"You're coming up to a door on the left," he states, ignoring my jibes. "Punch in 722091."

Wyatt punches in the numbers, then the red light on the door flips green, and the lock clicks.

"Now take the stairs up four flights," Lev instructs.

As we climb the stairs, I begin to worry. *Will our being here put her in more danger? Are we being selfish for wanting to be here for her appointments?*

"Are you sure Sam doesn't know where we are?" I inquire, voicing my concern.

Lev sighs. "Yes, for the hundredth time. Wes is distracting her."

Poor guy. He always seems to draw the short straw, having to take one for the team when it comes to Samantha—*still better him than me.*

"How exactly is he *distracting* her?" Wy asks.

"He took her shopping," Lev answers, and Wyatt and I groan.

I wouldn't have volunteered to do that for any amount of money.

"Unlucky bastard," Wyatt murmurs, and I nod in agreement.

We climb the last flight of stairs and come to another locked door.

"I don't know if I should be annoyed or glad that Dr. Jaffri is taking Ariah's safety seriously. How many goddamn security measures do we have to go through? We're going to miss the whole damn appointment at this rate," I whisper shout.

I hear Lev's fingers flying over his keyboard. "Quit your whining. There are not nearly enough measures in place. Once you two leave there, I'm going to work with Teagan and the Jacobis to fortify their security. It was far too easy to bypass all their systems."

The lock disengages as he gives us our next round of instructions. Ariah is on the tenth floor behind three security layers, which doesn't include her personal guards outside her exam room. My nostrils flare at the memory of how Reign touched her. *I hope that's not his jerking hand because he won't have it much longer.* Then, there are also six armed men positioned at the entrance of Dr. Jaffri's office and four more in the waiting room.

"Okay, the vents you're looking for should be coming up on your left. Unscrew the bottom two screws. This will allow you to crawl through without any suspicion," Lev instructs.

Wyatt pulls tools from his pocket and then opens the vent. We both silently discuss which one will climb in first before he squats down for me to stand on his shoulders.

"What the hell have you been eating, Owen—bricks?"

Lev bursts into laughter in our ears as Wyatt pushes up, and I slide in head first, leaving my legs out for Wyatt to use as leverage.

Once we're both successfully in, we army crawl.

"What room is she in again?" I ask after what feels like hours.

"Shhh. You fuckheads need to be quiet. I'll let you know when to stop," Lev reprimands.

Rolling my eyes, I continue in silence, mainly because he's right. We know the entire building has been emptied for this visit, but Ariah's security detail is also stationed on other floors and could hear us. *Reign might not be as stupid as I thought—he's still a dead man.*

I hear her before Lev can even say anything. My heart thumps out of my chest at being in such close proximity to her. Inhaling, I can faintly pick up her scent. She's wearing something soft and floral.

"Everything has been fine," Ariah says. I miss her doctor's first question but catch the next one as I move into position for Wyatt and me to both be able to see.

Dr. Jaffri sits on a stool by a computer, facing Ariah. "Your lab work came back, and it looks like your calcium and iron levels are running a bit low, as well as your vitamin D. Have you been taking your prenatal vitamins and getting enough rest?"

"Yes to the vitamins. No to the sleep. Some nights I'm just restless, and others, I'm knocked out," Ariah replies, chewing on her plump bottom lip, and I have to fight a groan and pray my dick behaves.

The doctor's hand swirls on a device that I didn't notice in her hands. "How many nights would you say you've been restless in the last week?"

"Three," she and Wyatt answer at the same time.

Of course, he'd know.

"Shut the fuck up, or you'll both get caught," Lev barks.

Dr. Jaffri clears her throat. "I know the answer to this question, but I'll ask it anyway. How is your stress level?"

Ariah snorts, "Well, considering the guys who helped make this happen. . ." She points to her growing stomach. "They are outwardly campaigning to try and embarrass me as they make my life hell and rub it in my face any chance they get that I'm not good enough for them. . . I'm freaking fantastic. On top of the world even, Doc. Oh, and let's not forget there's someone out there trying to kill me, and the only reason I'm even knocked up is because the doctor never put the implant in."

"We're going to have to try and work on reducing your stress levels. You're already a higher-risk pregnancy." *Higher risk? What the fuck?* "Due to carrying twins."

Twins? As in two?

"Did she just say twins?" Lev blurts out, knowing we can't answer him.

I want to jump down from this vent and pull her in my arms. Ariah should be resting and pampered. She shouldn't be warding off the likes of Samantha's wrath with our forced assistance. With all that's happening, I'm not sure how she'll forgive us when the time comes.

"I won't say I understand what you're going through, Ariah, because your situation is so unique for someone so young, and it's compounded by being pregnant with twins and figuring out single parenthood."

My fist clenches at that statement. I want to shout that she'll never be alone. Even when she feels that way, we're always watching. I grind my molars, trying to calm my rage—half tempted to gut the Senator and Samantha, but I know that wouldn't end this, and we *need* this to end.

Dr. Jaffri goes through more questions before she examines Ariah. I have to fight not to want to stab her for touching my Angel. Do I know this is necessary—*yes*. Do I care—*no*.

Turning on a machine by the exam table, Dr. Jaffri smiles and asks, "Okay, are you ready to see them?"

Then, for the first time during this entire visit, our girl beams—full-on grins, teeth and all, as she eagerly bobs her head in excitement.

"Now, this is the same warm gel we used last time. I'm going to squirt some on your abdomen, and then we'll work our way up to see where the twins are hiding out."

I watch, my eyes transfixed on the monitor. Two sets of thumping noises fill the room like they're already arguing with each other. It takes a minute, but then the first one appears in 3-D. I can see the face. I listen intently as the doctor points out the head, stomach, and various other body parts before moving to find baby two.

My focus flits from the screen when I hear Ariah gasp. Tears fill her beautiful gray eyes, looking far less haunted than when she arrived.

"It looks like they're both behaving. Do you want to know what you're having?" Dr. Jaffri asks.

Ariah quickly wipes the tears from her eyes before responding, "Yes, please."

"Baby A." The doctor moves the probe over to the left part of her stomach. "Is a boy."

"Holy fucking shit! We're having a boy," I hear Sebastian yip in the background. I almost forgot he was there. He's been so quiet this entire time.

I wait, never moving my focus from where the doctor moves the probe, fearing I might miss something.

"And Baby B is a girl. Congratulations, Miss Bradford. You're having a boy and a girl."

I don't realize I'm crying until something cold and wet lands on my hand. I can't remember the last time my tears were for anything but sadness or anger.

We're going to be fathers. Seeing them makes it that much more real.

We don't say anything or move until Ariah and the doctor have left the room. Reign and Fernando sweep the room to ensure no one somehow snuck inside. We're almost free and clear when they both head for the door. Reign instructs Fernando to accompany Elias to bring Ariah to the waiting room. Once they're gone, Reign steps back inside and looks right at us in the vents.

"You need to hurry up and end this because you best believe we won't hesitate to make her ours if we don't think you can give her what she needs." He whirls around, slamming the door closed, and I move his death up on my list.

19
ARIAH

"Shay, is it really necessary to start buying them all these clothes? I haven't even hit the halfway point," I argue, remembering how I had to stack yet another corner of my walk-in closet with boxes from SSENSE.

For the last week, I've walked into my room to see it filled with boxes upon boxes of baby clothes and stuffed fruits with a basket to put them all in. Today's delivery included two giant stuffed pears.

"Um, it wasn't me this time," Shay exclaims. "I promised I would lay off buying for a week."

Turning, I look back to where Reign stands with Eli and Nando in the foyer. "Which one of you did it?

Elias pretends to zip his lips while Nando shrugs his shoulders, and Reign smirks.

"Jerks," I mutter loud enough for them to hear, making them snicker.

"Let us spoil you, girl," Shay admonishes, handing me a giant bottle of water. "Everything I've heard and seen says women tend to feel ignored once babies are born, and I refuse to let you feel that way at any point during and after your pregnancy."

I bite the inside of my cheek to stop myself from crying. I've felt like a big ole baby recently. Any and everything elicits some emotion out of me that ends with me in freaking tears.

Heat flushes my skin, and I rub the back of my neck, trying to accept my friend's words. It's hard to accept help or care from anyone when each time you make yourself vulnerable, someone proves you should never let down your walls. You can't hurt me if I have little to no expectations of you.

Shay wraps her arms around me and then stoops to speak to my belly. "Your mom is one of the strongest people I've ever met, and you're both lucky to have her, but sometimes she'll forget that, and I have to remind her to fix her crown because that's what ride-or-die bitches do."

"Shay," I shout, gawking at her as I try to smother my laugh. "You don't swear at them in utero."

"With the mouth on you, they were doomed from the start. One thousand bucks say their first word will be *fuck* or *bitch*," Shay jokes as she jumps up and dodges my punch before running for the door. "Let's go get some lunch before we have class."

I grab my bag, and we're out the door. We talk and rib each other on the drive to campus. Shay and Eli battle back and forth with 'yo momma' jokes while we egg them on.

"When did we travel back to the nineties?" Reign quips.

"The same time your fashion sense did," Shay retorts without skipping a beat.

I laugh so hard I nearly piss my pants. Reign decided to go with an ode to Zack Morris from Saved by the Bell. His hair is gelled to the gods. I don't think a sledgehammer could ruin it.

"Who are you trying to be cute for?" I tease as he opens the cafe door.

Reign's face scrunches in confusion. "I don't look any different than I do every other day."

"Bullshit," Nando says. "You even added an extra spray of cologne before we left."

That earns him a scowl. "The fuck I did," Reign argues, but his cologne is definitely more prominent than usual.

"Who is she or he?" I probe, arching a brow in challenge.

We taunt him until we're seated at our table. I'm so distracted by our fun that I don't notice that we're sitting three tables away from Lev, Wes, Sebastian, Owen, and Wyatt until a shrill voice announces their presence.

"Eww! Who let the trash in?" Samantha sneers.

Shay opens her mouth to say something, but I pinch her side. "Ignore her. You know she thrives on chaos."

Shay's lips curl, but thankfully, she lets it go.

After a few weeks of Samantha's shit, I've officially decided to treat them like the guys are treating me. They don't fucking exist.

Our food arrives, and I notice my lunch has extra servings of veggies to go with my steak.

My eyes narrow to slits. "Okay, which one of you changed up my meal plan?"

Everyone throws their hands up, signaling it isn't them. The first time it happened, I thought it was a fluke, but every time we eat here, my order has extra dark leafy greens accompanied by the smoothie I used to drink in Colorado—chock-full of vitamins.

I make a mental note to call my dad later to see if this is his or my grandmother's doing.

"Someone probably thinks you need to be on a diet, you fat cow," Sam hisses.

Lifting my hand, I massage the bridge of my nose. *Why must this cunt always try me?*

"Oh look, it's Sam," I announce dryly.

"You should've stayed gone before you end up like your other family members. The Bradfords don't have a place here anymore. Your entire existence is irrelevant."

Her words replay in my head. She's got my attention now. Too bad for her—that's never a good thing.

Nando stands up, and Samantha takes three steps backward when she notices none of the guys followed her over here. "You might want to take that shit somewhere else, Barbie, because *all* threats are met with the full force of our protection. My hands don't discriminate when I'm protecting *our* girl."

Samantha yammers something else, but I can feel someone's gaze boring into the side of my face. I turn and see Wes's jaw locked tightly in a sneer. Lev is halfway out of his seat, and Owen has his knife in his hands. However, Wyatt is leaning back in his chair with the biggest shit-eating grin, like this is the entertainment he's been waiting his whole life for. None of them come to her aid, though.

"Huh. That's interesting," I mumble to myself. *Why aren't they over here protecting her?*

Before I can ponder the question longer, Samantha's screech pulls my focus back on her.

"What is it with this girl? Does she have a magic pussy? I don't know why anyone would try to claim her. She's nothing, a nobody that thinks—"

I move with a level of speed my pregnant ass probably shouldn't be able to. It's fast enough that Samantha doesn't see it coming until she's on the floor grabbing her bleeding nose. Her skirt's flipped up, and everyone has a prime view of her pussy spread wide open.

The cafe is silent. The only noise is the pounding in my ears and the devil on my shoulder telling me to stomp on her face.

I ignore that messy bitch. She's always trying to get me locked up.

Tilting my head, I scrutinize her, wondering once again how they could choose someone so vapid.

"That was my nose, you dumb bitch—"

I don't allow her to finish. I snatch my smoothie from the table and dump it on her face, relishing in her screams.

"Why does this feel like déjà vu?" I tap my chin, pretending to think. "Oh yes, it's because you tried this last year, and I rocked your shit then, too."

Samantha attempts to get to her feet three times and falls before one of the cheerleaders sitting next to us helps her.

"You'll pay for this," she snarls and begins to storm away, only to slip and hit her elbow as she braces herself. *Bet she wishes she didn't wear heels today.* I try to hold in my laugh when she slips her stilettos off and stands on the first try. She glares before she screams and leaves the lunch room.

"Tell your plastic surgeon I said hello," I shout at her retreating form.

20
WES

"Holy shit, that was fucking hot," Wyatt groans, and I don't have to look to know he's squeezing his dick. The fucker is always turned on when Ariah puts Samantha in her place.

"What the fuck is he doing?" Owen growls.

I follow Owen's line of sight and see Reign has Ariah in his lap and his fucking palm resting on her stomach where our kids reside. Our eyes connect as he leans to whisper something in her ear. Then he winks. He fucking *winks* at me! My hands grip the table until the wood feels like it will splinter.

This motherfucker is dead!

Whatever he's saying has *our* girl blushing and laughing as she turns to push his shoulder before he lifts her, depositing her safely in between him and Elias.

"He's goading us," Sebastian calmly states. His steady lilt pulls my attention away from the men who continue to test the limits of our patience. "Ignore them," he continues, feigning disinterest—his aloof demeanor giving nothing away except the imperceptible twitch that makes the vein on his right temple pulsate. He's here to meet with one of the professors in the sociology department. He said something about student teaching or being a teaching assistant.

"I'm going to use a cheese grater on Elias's face," Lev hisses.

My head snaps back to Ariah's table at Lev's venomous tone in time to see Elias pick up a strawberry from his plate and brush the loose strands of Ariah's hair out of her face.

I forget to breathe as he brings the fruit to her mouth and nestles it between her waiting lips. Elias's thumb catches the excess juice trickling down her face as she bites down. Then he lifts his stoney gaze to mine in challenge as he licks his thumb.

Death would be too easy for them. At least one hundred ways to prolong these arrogant fucks' suffering. They're supposed to be guarding her, not seducing her.

"What the fuck?" I spit.

Owen whips out a switchblade and hops up. His intentions are written all over his face. Before he can even take a step in their direction, Sebastian's hand shoots out and grips his forearm.

"Don't," is Sebastian's only command.

Blazing hazel eyes that would terrify even the most fearless man sneer at Seb's hold as if his touch offends him before leveling him with a glare. "Let. The. Fuck. Go," Owen snarls. His lips curl, exposing his teeth and the tightness of his jaw. "Or I'll slice you into a jigsaw puzzle."

"O. You gotta sit down," Lev reasons. "We can't risk it. There are too many eyes in here."

Owen's face contorts, his eyes close as if an internal battle rages within. His nostrils flare—sucking in air before mumbling something unintelligible. Then, the tightness in his body slowly relaxes—the rigidity in his posture uncoils, allowing him to finally relent and take his seat.

A cackle comes from the other side of our table. Wyatt is in stitches, his face splotchy as tears leak down his cheeks. He's laughing so hard that he can barely get the words out. "You should see all your faces." He stands, hiking his shoulders up and hunching over as he beats his chest. "Me, Tarzan. She, Jane. Me take Jane. No one have Jane but Tarzan."

"Why aren't you more upset about this? What do you know, Wyatt?" I seethe. He's always keeping fucking secrets, and I, for one, am running out of patience.

Ignoring my question, Wyatt stands, leveling us all with a glare before he smirks, turns, and walks away.

"Well, that was enlightening," Lev mutters, and I share his sentiment. It always feels like he knows more than he shares, and I, for one, am sick of it.

Cracking my knuckles, I glance back to their table. Ariah's laughing, enraptured in whatever it is Reign's saying. *Stupid fucker.* I want to strangle all of them for the smiles she's giving them—break every limb that's touched her—-and gouge out their eyes for even looking at her. Even more aggravated than I was before, I return my attention to our table. Something needs to be done. "One of us needs to strap that fucker down and interrogate his ass. Wyatt knows too much and never shares a thing before he deems it time," I demand. "I'm sick of that shit."

The table's quiet before Lev breaks the silence. "Wy wouldn't say a damn word."

"He'd die before he confessed anything," Owen adds. "And I respect him even more for it. We're fuck ups. We're stubborn, selfish, and arrogant. At this point, we're all talk and no action."

My hackles rise. "What do you call what we're doing now? This is all for her," I argue.

Sebastian sighs, "It's still for us. The end results are still self-serving. Even if our intentions are good—they're still to benefit our wants regardless of her needs."

Owen smiles. "What he said. We have to earn the right to be with her."

"Which means our decisions should put her first," Lev chimes in.

I mull over their words. *Has this all been about us?*

"Our decisions have put her first," I exclaim, staring each of them down. "She's our forever. I don't care how long she's mad—as long as she knows she'll be mad by our sides.

Before lunch becomes a group therapy session, Samantha

appears in the cafe doorway, her entry as dramatic as her exit. I stifle my laugh when I see the tape around her extremely swollen nose. Owen is not so inclined. He full-on points and snickers when she sits at our table.

"Laugh it up now," she croaks. "Just know her stunt will cost you. Then we'll see who's laughing last."

I roll my eyes, but Owen tilts his head, studying her. "Your threats are getting old."

Samantha's mouth twists, and she gasps in pain. *Guess she forgot her nose was broken.* "The wedding has been moved up. We'll be married in December, and the engagement party is in two months." She stands, preparing to walk away. She pauses mid-turn. "Oh, and your *girl's* invitation will be hand-delivered with explicit instructions that her attendance is mandatory."

My fists clench under the table. *We're running out of fucking time.*

"Who's laughing now?" Samantha mocks, turning on her stilettos and storming out.

I secretly pray her heel snaps, piercing her nonexistent heart when she falls backward on it.

"We need this to be over. Not for our sake," I exclaim once I'm sure Samantha's gone.

They all nod in agreement, and no other words need to be exchanged.

For her—for our babies—for our futures.

21
ARIAH

"The look on Wes's face," Shay squeals, bouncing on my bed. "Priceless. Freaking epic!"

She hasn't stopped grinning as she gives me a play-by-play of the guys' reactions to what Reign and Elias did.

I can't lie. It's great to know they reacted so strongly. Hearing the recounting of Owen springing from his seat to Wes looking like he sucked on a lemon made my day. Not because I want them back. *Okay, part of me does.* But because they're experiencing a sliver of the hurt I feel daily. However, at this moment, between their reactions and feeling Samantha's nose crunch against my fist, I'm riding the high.

"Serves those fuckers right," Shay giggles before changing the subject. "Have you had any progress with finding that doctor?"

Shaking my head, I reply, "No. Her practice 'mysteriously' closed, and Dr. Lambert, along with anyone else who worked there, have all somehow disappeared. At least that's what my dad told me."

Shay's russet brow arches. "Are we not believing your dad?"

I shrug, "He's back on the Council, and while I know he'd never do anything to put me in danger purposefully, I also know that no one is divulging pertinent information under the guise of keeping me safe."

She points to my stomach. "Umm, can you blame them?"

"I'm pregnant, not helpless," I retort, narrowing my eyes. "I'm not asking to go in guns blazing. I'd just like more honesty and clarity about what's happening."

I'd also like to know why guys who've supposedly moved on and never wanted me in the first place are reacting like they have some claim over me. Why do they even fucking care?

I don't voice any of these concerns to her, fearing she'll tell me not to hold out any hope.

Shay's never said to move on, but it's the way she and everyone else looks at me, with fucking pity. She's never judged me, but I feel like my character has been weighed and found wanting.

I'm a pregnant girl, fresh out of high school, not sure who her children's father is because she was passed around like a toy by boys who like to share. I know what I thought I had with the guys was unconventional, at best, and scandalous, at worst, based on societal norms. But fuck society and its puritanical culture. The obsession with propriety has only ever fostered polarity and complacency. Anyone who has a problem can shove their judgments down their throats and choke on them.

"What can I do to help?" Shay asks, pulling me from my internal musings. "I can go—"

I cut her off. "Nope. Absolutely not. I will not put you in harm's way ever again. Especially not intentionally!"

It's her turn to look affronted. "So, I'm supposed to sit and look pretty while my pregnant best friend tries to fight the world? Not ah bumbo."

"Shay, the last time you were with me, I watched in horror as you were shot. Then, I had to explain to your mother why her daughter was fighting for her life. I won't do that shit again. Not a bumber," I attempt to mimic her patois, and by the look on her face, I failed.

"It's bum-bo," she snorts. "Let's leave the horrible accents to Miss Cleo, please, and tanks."

I squint in confusion. "Who the hell is Miss Cleo?"

"A television psychic," she begins, then shakes her head. "You know what, never mind. It's irrelevant to this conversation." Shay reaches out, clasping my hands in hers. "You didn't shoot me, nor were you responsible for me being shot."

I tug, preparing to refute her claims. It was my fault. Elise used her to get to me, then tried to kill her. She was. . . shit, still *is* in danger.

"Ariah, I've lived in Edgewood since elementary school. Do you think I don't have some insight into how things work around here? Don't you think I know more is happening and that my family also has a role in it? No family in Edgewood is without its skeletons or bloody hands. There's no such thing as an ethically earned billionaire. And every family in Edgewood's net worth starts with the letter B."

"None of that means I should ask you to put yourself in danger for me," I snap, tears building in my eyes. "I won't do it, Shay. I'll never ask that of you," I profess, my tone softening, my gray eyes meeting her brown ones, imploring her to understand. I don't care if her family's hands are dirty. I won't ever be the reason why she's hurt again.

Her head tilts and a warm smile appears on her freckled face. "You won't have to because whether you ask it or not, I'm going to help."

A tear falls, and I close my eyes, wanting to shake some sense into this crazy bitch.

Shay lets go of my hand, and then I feel her warm finger catching it before it drips on me. "I won't do anything dangerous, but I can help. I want to help."

All I can see is her body dropping on the ground on a loop in my head. My lips part to argue, but a knock forces my attention toward my room door, where Conner stands.

"Someone is waiting for you downstairs with a package," he explains. He must notice my confusion because he continues. "It's been scanned, but according to the delivery instructions, it must be hand-delivered to you. No exceptions."

Huffing, I brush away any remnants of evidence of my crying and stand. "Okay. I'll be down in a minute."

Conner nods, and there's a look I can't decipher on his face before he disappears from my doorway.

"What do you think it could be?" Shay inquires.

"There's only one way to find out," I say, rising from the bed.

We both descend the stairs and see a finely dressed man standing in the foyer. His suit and demeanor are reminiscent of the Selection process. Dread fills my belly, and I know what this must be before he speaks.

"Miss Bradford?" the man's gravely voice questions.

Unable to speak, I quickly dip my chin in confirmation.

He opens a scroll. *A real-life scroll, like a royal decree is about to be announced.* Clearing his throat, he begins to read. "Ariah Elaine Bradford, your presence is hereby formally requested to be in attendance on Saturday, November eighteenth, two thousand and twenty-three, at the Edgewood Country Club at seven o'clock post-meridiem."

I want him to shut up, but he just keeps going.

"For the celebration of Wesley Benjamin Edgewood's, Wyatt Alexander Grant's, Sebastian Blake Grant's, Levi Nathaniel Washington's, and Owen Preston Jefferson's engagement to Samantha Marie Davenport."

Bile rises in the back of my throat, and I force it down. This is to humiliate me. I know without needing an explanation. I embarrassed their *fiancée*, and they're making me pay for it.

"I won't go," I shout, interrupting his long-winded announcement. Those assholes can get fucked if they think I'll step foot in that country club to celebrate.

The man looks perplexed by my outburst. His shock immediately turns to disdain, and his lips curl in disgust as he barks, "Attendance is mandatory per the contract you signed. Failure to attend will put you in breach of contract, and the full force of the Fraternitas will be brought down on you."

A blur moves in my periphery. Reign grabs the man by his throat, hoisting him in the air as he flails, struggling to find purchase. The scroll, along with the box, drops at Reign's feet.

"You will treat her with the respect she's due and not just because she deserves it but as a Bradford... the rightful Heir to your prehistoric pathetic boys' club. Do we have an understanding?" Reign snarls, glaring daggers at the man, whose face flushes red before turning almost purple, grunts his agreement. "Perfect. I'm glad we're in agreement."

Reign's grip slackens, dropping the man, and his body crumples to the floor. I watch as he sucks in much-needed air.

"Was that necessary," I mouth when Reign's gaze meets mine.

"People need to understand that all disrespect will be met with unapologetic force," Reign asserts, then kicks the man's side. "Get up and finish this bullshit speech, and then get the fuck out!"

The man gathers the contents, places them back in the box, and scrambles to his feet as if his ass was on fire. He massages his throat before he continues. "You will find all—"

Elias cuts him off. "Apologize!"

"What?" The man asks.

"Don't make him repeat himself. You won't like the outcome," Nando adds.

The man's once-red face drains of its color. "I-I-I. . . I'm s-sorry," he finally gets out. "I was out of place, and it won't happen again."

I almost feel bad for him.

"You will find more details within this box," he croaks, attempting to hand it to me. My hands don't move to accept it. "Miss Bradford." He tries again. "Miss. I can't leave without you accepting the box.

Groaning, I resignedly take the box. He turns and dashes from the house the moment it's in my hands.

I stare down at the gold box, and I don't mean plated gold. The stupid thing looks like it's made of solid gold. *Who the fuck does this shit?* It's ostentatious packaging in poor taste.

"That's ridiculous," Shay mutters, pointing at the gaudy invitation.

I hum in agreement as I walk toward the kitchen.

"Where are you going?" Elias questions.

"I'm putting this where it belongs," I answer, striding past him. I don't stop until I reach my intended destination.

Shay gasps when she sees where I'm headed.

"Do it," she encourages.

Turning, I smirk, appreciating her support. But in this instance, I would've done it even without it. Pulling the handle, I open the trash compactor and dump the box, and all it contains precisely where it belongs. Down the fucking chute with the rest of the garbage.

I slam it closed, then wheel around and head to my room.

22
OWEN

My eyes droop as I fight to stay awake in the back of my math class. This professor needs to put some inflection in his monotone voice. I don't even know why I bother coming. Outside of the classes I have with my angel, college can suck my left nutsack.

What I want is to get my hands on one of her guards. Those fuckers' days on this earth are numbered, but all the damn Dudley Do Rights have thwarted every attempt to catch one of them.

My head dips, jolting me from my doze. *I gotta get the fuck out of here.*

Sighing, I stand, grab my belongings, and then descend the stairs. I need to get some damn air. If I sit here another minute, there'll be drool on my desk.

"Mr. Jefferson, the class has not ended," the stuffy instructor in the god-awful oversized muddy-brown tweed suit states.

Thank you, Captain Obvious.

I roll my eyes, not bothering to dignify his astute observation with a response, then turn the knob, exiting his room into the hallway. I don't stop walking until I'm standing in the quad outside the math and sciences buildings and feel the cool fall breeze on my face.

The leaves have started changing colors—vibrant reds, oranges, and purples announcing autumn is here.

This is exactly what I needed.

Increasing my stride, I pass groups of students lounging at benches along the sidewalk. I ignore the lust-filled stares from girls who don't give a fuck that I'm *"engaged."* Bile churns in my gut at the reminder.

Samantha Davenport is a bitch who couldn't handle rejection and has taken the term spoiled rich girl throwing a tantrum to a new level. If the blood in my veins didn't pump for only one girl, I'd take up their offers and fuck them into oblivion in front of the leech we're being forced to marry.

My fingers graze over the imperceptible bump on my arm—the invisible collar around all our necks, forcing us to heel at the feet of a twisted girl and her crazy brother, the Senator.

Growling, I double my speed. I need quiet, and too many cheerful students are ambling around for me to think here.

I'm barely out of the quad when I hear my name being called.

"Owen," someone shouts, but I keep walking, praying they'll take the hint. "Owen." They try again. "Hey, man, hold up!" The sound of feet pounding against the pavement, getting closer, makes me reluctantly stop.

Turning, I spot Jordan. *Or is Justin? Maybe Jasper?* Whatever the fuck his name is, he's about to get a knife to the throat for bothering me.

"Hey," he greets, bending over and resting his hands on his thighs to catch his breath. "Almost thought you were ignoring me, figured with all the people roaming about, you didn't hear me."

I quirk a brow, preparing to tell him I was ignoring him, and he should've taken the hint, but he rambles on.

"Are you finally cleared to play?" He questions, reminding me of yet another reason this shit with Senator Baker and Samantha has to end.

Due to the extensive injuries I endured during my time in captivity, I was forced to be benched for the first six games of my college career. Football isn't as big of a deal to me as it is for Lev, but it still annoys me that I'm sidelined.

"Not until our homecoming game in two weeks," I reply.

"Fuck yeah, in time for the Groveton game," he exclaims, and I share his excitement.

Groveton is a big game, and not just because they're our division rivals. Each year, the winning team gets bragging rights and hosts the annual masquerade party. Groveton has won the last few years—something that hasn't gone unnoticed.

"With you and the rest of the Heirs on the field this year, Groveton doesn't stand a chance. The stands are going to be packed."

My mood instantly sours. *She won't be there.*

I grunt, pissed that Ariah won't be amongst the crowd cheering us on. I need out of this conversation before I lay this no-name asshat to the ground. I know it's not his fault we're in the bullshit predicament, but I also know my knives don't care.

"Are you heading down there to see the trainer?" James inquires, pulling me from my thoughts of cutting him a new smile.

Surveying him, I take in his hulking frame, sandy-brown hair, and amber eyes. He's about an inch or two shorter than me, but his muscles are double mine—he's definitely on our offensive line.

Nah, he doesn't look like a James. Whatever his name is, he'd see the predator under my skin, lying in wait.

I shrug, clenching my jaw, trying to hold the beast back. The stiff set of my shoulders and scowl should be warning enough to shut him up. But Johnny here can't take the hint.

Nope, Johnny's not right, either. What the hell is this dude's freaking name?

Oblivious to my death stare, he continues. "It's just that we know this week is when you're being examined, and I know how eager I am—we all are—to have you back on the field with us."

This is worse than an ex who refuses to take the hint.

He'd definitely die first in a horror movie.

Not bothered by my silence, he yammers, "We're having a

kickass start—no losses, and if you're back, Groveton won't have a shot, and the party is ours next year."

Needing this conversation to be over so I can finally get some quiet, I start walking away, heading for the gym. His earlier question about seeing the trainer spurs me toward the field house. A thirty-minute session with the punching bag in the gym should help temper some of my rage.

I sigh when he follows me. "Is there something else you need? I'm kinda in a time crunch here," I state. Proud of the lack of edginess in my response.

Before he can answer, someone shouts. "Hey, Justin, we're over here."

Justin. I knew it was some J name.

"You should go with your friends," I encourage, but it's more of a demand than a suggestion.

Justin nods, any inquiry forgotten, and runs for the group of our teammates playing ultimate frisbee.

The walk to Rubi is quick. I'm behind the wheel and outside the athletic building in five minutes flat.

I hit the locker room, change, and wrap my hands before I lay into the bag in front of me. Months of frustration, guilt, and loathing boil to the surface. Each strike is a proverbial blow at all of our enemies. Brittany Livingston—*jab.* Brian Porter—*right hook...jab...jab.* Senator Matthew Baker—*jab...jab...uppercut...roundhouse kick to the throat.* At the thought of Samantha, I pull out a blade and slice the bag down the middle, watching in satisfaction as I pretend it's her bleeding out.

Someone could say violence against women is wrong, and I'd agree without hesitation, but there comes a time when the person in front of you has no gender, name, or face—they're just evil. Those people should be gutted where they stand. I feel no sympathy for the bitch who conspired with the enemy to put an explosive in my arm so she could force us to marry her.

Fuck her and anyone who doesn't believe she's earned a gruesome end.

Breathless and spent, I drop my hands to my side and see that the sun has set and night has fallen.

How long have I been in here? It only felt like twenty minutes.

Grabbing my phone, I see it's after nine o'clock. I have missed calls and messages. Once I ensure none are urgent, I head to the locker room, shower, dress, and return to campus.

I'm passing one of the girls' dorms when I hear muffled moans and smirk. Someone's having an outdoor session.

"Fuck, that's it, lick my pussy good. You useless bitch," a familiar whiny voice demands, stopping me in my tracks.

I can't be this lucky.

Creeping in the direction of the very obvious sexual cries, I confirm that the nasally sound is indeed the cunt, Samantha. What I'm not expecting is to see Brittany Livingston's face buried between her spread thighs. My stomach churns at the sight.

I'm about to walk away when Sam's shrill cry, stating that she's coming, echoes in the air, followed by an oof and a body hitting the ground.

"What the fuck are you doing here, Brittany? Pull up your damn pants already," Samantha seethes.

"You weren't worried about what I was doing here fifteen minutes ago when your face was in my pussy," Brittany snaps, pulling up her leggings before she continues. "Or while you rode my fingers as I sucked your clit so good you didn't even remember to call out Wes's name," Brittany retorts. I can't see her face, but I'm sure a smug smile is plastered on it.

I duck behind the bushes when I see Samantha peruse the landscape around her, ensuring they're alone before she speaks. "Do you know how long it's been since I've been properly fucked?"

"Didn't you just have sex with Matthew and Brian earlier this week?" Brittany asks.

Sammy's been a busy bird.

"Matthew couldn't satisfy me with an instruction manual on how to screw, and Brian has a hard-on for Ariah. I'm tired of fucking people who call that bitch's name out as they come,"

Samantha spits, and I have to bite my cheek to refrain from growling.

Brian's now number one on the list. How fucking dare he think that he can pretend to have sex with Ariah—*my angel*. He's dead.

I must have missed part of the conversation in my rage because they're no longer discussing sex.

"How the hell did Ariah get pregnant, anyway? Didn't you arrange for the doctor to give everyone the implant but you?" Brittany inquires.

"I did," Samantha snaps. "That bitch double-crossed me. Then, I poked holes in every single one of Wes's condoms he had stashed in his room."

Fucking cunt.

I continue to listen and check what dorm I'm near before shooting off a quick text to our group chat.

ME
> Sam's the one who fucked with Ry's birth control. Also. . . Lev grab the camera footage from behind Brewster Hall.

WY
> That fucking bitch

WES
> How do you know this?

ME
> Currently listening to her confess it to Brittany outside the girls' dorm after Sam let Brittany bury her face between her legs.

LEV
> I need to wash my brain with bleach.

BASH
> We didn't need that play-by-play, Asshole.

ME
> If I have to suffer with that image burned in my head. . . so do you dickheads.

"So what are you going to do now? Ariah's pregnant. The Filiae Bellonae's mission is nearly complete. I bet your mom's happy," Brittany sorts. That earns her a slap across the face.

"Nothing is nearly complete. I didn't kill friends and fuck my brother just so that bitch could take what's mine," she shrieks.

Holy shit!

I will her to keep talking. I know she's guilty of more.

"Now get the fuck out of here and don't come back," Samantha commands, and like the pleb she is, Brittany scurries off.

Dammit!

Sighing, I wait until Samantha is about to turn the corner before my hand snaps out and grips her by her neck.

"You always were a cocky shit, weren't you?" I grit, slamming her against the brick wall of her dorm. I pull Mary from my hip holster and flip her open, pressing the sharp tip against Samantha's cheek until I see a trickle of red. "Always overplaying your hand," I mutter, basking in the sight of her blood as I drag the blade down her face.

"I've always wondered what it was like to play with you, Owen. Now that I know, I can't wait to have your knives on me," she groans. The scent of her arousal turns my stomach.

Pulling my hand back, I aim my knife at her cunt. "I don't think you'd enjoy playing with me very much. I'd fuck you, blade side out, until you bled out," I spit.

She lets out another grotesque squeal of pleasure as a gasp sounds behind me. I drop Samantha and turn in time to Ariah with her guards—hurt evident in her eyes, even in the dark.

I open my mouth, preparing to tell her it's not what she thinks it is when Samantha leans in my ear and whispers, "Uh uh uhh, lover boy. Not a word."

My shoulders sag, and I watch in horror as my angel walks away from me.

Whipping my head around, I grip Samantha's throat, squeezing until she realizes this isn't a game. Her clawed nails scratch against my skin, but I feel nothing—numbness has taken hold. I watch as her skin goes from pale to red to blue. Her legs dangle, no longer kicking to get free.

"I could snap your neck right now and die a happy man knowing my angel is safely in my brothers' arms. Stop fucking testing me, Samantha. The guys may fight to keep me alive, but I'd die for her. Do you fucking understand?" I bark.

She feebly nods, and then I drop her to the ground.

I spin around, holding my breath and running until I'm outside our house. I don't inhale, even when my lungs scream at me. *I don't deserve to breathe.*

Without Ariah, does it even make sense to try?

I drop on the step, finally gulping in a lungful of air. The feeling so euphoric, I momentarily smile.

"You know you'll need to fight the demons riding your back?"

I jolt at the sound of Sebastian's voice.

"What are you doing here?"

"Moving in. The Council has decided I'm better served here as a grad student," he replies.

I grunt. "What are they up to?"

"We can discuss their plans later. For now, though, I'm going to need you to work on wanting to be here for yourself," Sebastian instructs.

"Don't go all guidance counselor on me now, Bash," I argue.

He holds out his hand, helping me up. "You need to be whole and not just for her or the twins she's carrying—for you. Because you deserve it."

Sebastian turns, striding for the front door, and as I follow him, his words play on repeat. He's right.

I need to be whole.

23
LEV

"What the fuck do you mean she poked holes in my goddamn condoms in my room?" Wes shouts.

Owen gives a play-by-play of everything he overheard Samantha and Brittany discussing.

"That's what she said," Owen shrugs.

Wes's eyes light with awareness. "Fuck! That night she snuck into my room and sprawled her naked ass across the bed. That's when she did it."

Sebastian and Wes share a look.

"What is it?" Wyatt asks.

Clearing his throat, Wes mutters, "The condom Sebastian used at the pig farm was one of the ones from my room."

Wyatt rolls his eyes, "Oh, is that all?"

"What do you mean, is that all?" I question.

He stands and grabs a beer from the fridge before returning to his seat. "Do any of you care who the biological father of our babies are?"

"Of course not!"

"Fuck no!"

"Why would we?"

"Hell no."

We each retort with varying levels of vitriol.

"None of that matters. Any kids we have are ours. All of them will have part of her embedded in their DNA. Who the other part comes from doesn't concern any of us," I add.

Wyatt smiles. "Then what's next on the agenda? Because the way I see it, Samantha's fuck up is absolutely our gain."

"He has a point," Owen agrees.

"It also puts an even larger target on Ariah's back," I begrudgingly state.

They each focus their attention on me. "Explain," Wes demands.

I massage my temples in an attempt to stave off the growing headache pulsating through my skull before I answer. "Even if we are forced to marry Samantha," I pause, waiting for their outbursts to die down. "Even *if*, and that's a gigantic if with a negative zero probability of occurring. Any kids," I hold up my hand, signaling for them to spare me the dramatics so I can get this out. "Any kids Samantha had wouldn't be Heirs."

I watch in real-time as my words sink in. Sebastian is the first to say something. "Samantha would need to get rid of the twins for any children she had to be legitimate Heirs."

"Samantha's fucked either way," Owen exclaims. "If she hurts a hair on Ariah's or the twins' heads, she'll lose hers, and none of us would touch her with a borrowed dick, so we'd never consummate the fraudulent arrangement."

"Still, we need to bump up security around her. As annoying as they are, her guards protect her at all costs," Wes grumbles.

Turning, I shoot Thomas a text. He might be Samantha's "official" guard, but he's been running Ariah's security team from here. He immediately replies, informing me that he'll take point on Ariah's detail beginning next week. "Fuck yeah," I cheer. "Thomas is back on Ariah's team."

Wyatt snorts, "I can't wait to see the meltdown Samantha has when she hears this."

"What else happened tonight?" Sebastian inquires, facing Owen.

Owen's lip curls into a devious, self-satisfying smirk. "I may or may not have left her with a superficial scratch on her face. I'm quite surprised she didn't deflate when Mary poked her."

The room fills with raucous laughter. "You didn't?" I blurt between trying to catch my breath.

"Damn, I wish I was there to see that. I always miss the good shit," Wyatt harrumphs.

Suddenly, all remnants of Owen's jovial demeanor vanish. "That would've been the highlight of my night if it weren't for Samantha getting off on it and Ariah witnessing her do it."

"Shit," Wes barks. "That's not good."

Grimacing, Owen mumbles, "Not even remotely. The look on her face when she saw my knife—it broke a piece of me."

It's breaking pieces of all of us—especially Wes.

I look over to Wes, watching as he stares off into space. This has been hard on all of us in different ways. But I can't imagine what it's like having to go back to pretending you hate the girl you love after you fought so hard to gain her trust.

"She'll understand. We'll have a lot to make up for, but it won't be the incidents she sees that have us groveling. It will be all the secrets we've had to withhold," Wyatt declares. I gaze in their direction to see him squeezing Owen's shoulder. "That and, um, our spying," he grins.

The crazy fuck has been waiting on this showdown. I don't have it in my heart to burst his bubble that Ariah will kick all of our asses once she finds out about *all* of the ways we've been keeping tabs on her.

Owen composes himself and then continues. "There's the fact that I overheard Samantha confessing to killing her friends to get into the Selection."

I spring from my seat. "What?"

"You should've led with this," Sebastian shouts, and I'm inclined to agree.

We've been looking for who was responsible for the deaths of former selected girls for months. After both Vivian and Madeline were killed, we assumed the murders were the work of Elise. However, after Owen was taken, we took a closer look and discovered it was none of them.

"Do you really think Samantha would do this?" Wes questions. "I wouldn't put past her to manipulate one of her lackeys to kill for her, but Samantha doing it herself?"

Sighing, I open my laptop and pull up my files on all the murders, including the body parts sent to Ariah. Based on what we have on file. It's not a stretch to think Samantha hired someone. She was around when some packages were delivered, but I put nothing past her—her evil knows no bounds.

"You also wouldn't suspect she'd fuck her own brother," Owen begins. "Scratch that. Yes, you would."

"For fuck's sake," Sebastian snaps. "Is there anything the conniving skank won't do?"

"No," we all bellow in unison.

I bring up the last known murder, Meagan. She was Sam's most trusted ass-licker. "Why would she kill Meagan?"

"Wasn't her last date with you, Lev?" Wyatt asks, and I confirm with a quick nod. "What happened on that date?"

Thinking back to that night, I remember Meagan making a scene before storming out of the diner. "She was going on about how we had what was coming to us, and she couldn't wait until we were put in our places," I explain.

"That doesn't sound out of character for Meagan," Wes states.

I think harder, placing who was in the diner and her words before she left. "She said, 'I hope you assholes and that stupid bitch get everything coming to you. You all fucking deserve the hell that's about to rain down on this town.' Then disappeared through the door. Brian was there that night. I remember him staring so hard I was tempted to ask what the fuck he was looking at. Then I got a call, and Meagan was dead."

"Not just any kind of dead. She was baked alive, and her lips were sewn shut," Sebastian adds.

"Snitches get stitches or some shit like that," I mumble.

Owen's fingers drum on the table. "What if it was Brian? He's been behind a lot of shit and has gladly positioned himself at Sam's side."

This feels like a more plausible scenario. I wouldn't put it past Samantha to order the death and dismemberment of people, but she doesn't strike me as the get-her-hands-dirty type of girl—she's too fucking prissy for that shit.

"Still no luck on locating Brian?" Wyatt probes.

I shake my head, "No. At this rate, I wouldn't be surprised if he was dead."

"He wasn't last week, at least," Owen quips. "He and Senator Baker were both apparently giving Samantha the lamest fuck of her life."

My lips draw tight at the image. *Yuck.* "Not something I needed to know. In fact, I could've gone my entire life without knowing that," I quip.

"And I could've gone my whole life without seeing Brittany's face buried between Sam's legs," Owen retorts, and I have to fight not to lose my dinner.

Whirling my computer around, I change the subject. "I'll look into the murders again and see if there's a link to Samantha. Sebastian, can you and Wes work to find the damn gynecologist that was supposed to put the implant in Ariah's arm? We need to figure out why she didn't follow Sam's plan." Finally, I turn to Owen and Wyatt, who are already grinning from ear to ear. "I need you two to—"

"Double-check with Thomas and ensure Ariah's security is up to par," Wyatt blurts, completing my sentence.

"Fucking smartasses," I mutter.

They both chuckle. "Yet you love us anyway," Owen jests.

Refusing to entertain their bullshit, I stand and head upstairs. Once I'm settled, I turn on my monitors and do what I've done every night since she's been on campus—watch.

Ariah's in bed, her hand on her growing belly as she reads.

I turn on the sound only to find she's not reading, just talking.

"You two will be loved so abundantly. I only hope your dads will get their shit together. Even if they never want to be with me again, neither of you deserves to ever be shunned. And I'm going to let you both in on a secret—I know they love you both already. They're all just too thick-headed to realize it."

She's too fucking good for us.

A lump clogs my throat, threatening to cause a panic attack.

"I'm going to tell you about each of your dads—they're all uniquely special and will always hold a place in my heart. Your daddy Wyatt knew before I did that we were meant to be together. He believed enough for the both of us." Her voice cracks, but she continues. "Lev is a quiet force. He's the strong, silent type, tempering the boisterous personalities. I know he thinks I'm not paying attention, but I see him." She whispers the last part, looking up as if she knows I'm watching.

I listen as she ticks off the reasons she loves us, using her words to push down my rising panic. Instead, I allow her words to urge me to work harder so we can get her back.

24
ARIAH

"We never loved you. You were just too stupid to see that," Wyatt sneers, and the tears pooling in my eyes fall.

Obnoxious, loud laughter fills the room. "Did you really think someone like you could ever be who we wanted?" Owen seethes. "Look at you. You're pathetic."

"But the babies," I try to reason.

"Those abominations aren't ours, and you know it. Stop trying to pretend otherwise. We all know you would spread eagle to anything with a dick hanging between their legs," Sebastian snaps.

This can't be happening. Why are they doing this? I wrestle with the memory of who I thought they were and who they're showing me they genuinely are.

"No," I yell, standing from my chair. "You're lying. All of you are lying. There's no way you all pretended that well. I would've known."

"The only thing you know is how to be a dirty ho," Wes utters. "Now sit back and let us show you how we love our woman."

Samantha walks into the room naked and climbs on the table.

My hand shoots out, grabbing Lev's arm, hoping he'll see reason. "Please don't do this—don't destroy what we have together."

"There's nothing to destroy—you meant nothing to us," Lev scolds, yanking from my hold.

I watch in horror as they undress, and Sebastian positions himself at Samantha's entrance before slamming home. With each thrust of his hips, a part of me dies inside.

A sharp stabbing pain shoots across my stomach, and I cry out, but no one helps me. They're all too busy fucking her. Wyatt pumps his pierced cock in and out of her mouth just as a crippling cramp slams into my side, knocking the breath from my lungs. Samantha's moans of pleasure drown out my groans of dismay as I hit the ground.

Something's wrong. I'm not supposed to feel like this. Another blinding cramp shoots across my midsection, and I feel a trickle of fluid between my legs.

"No. . . no. . . nooo. This can't be happening. It's too soon," I mumble to myself.

I brace myself against the wall as I lower my hand between my legs.

"Fuck me harder," Samantha shrieks.

Lifting my hand, I see the red. "Help me, please. Something's wrong. Please. I don't want to lose my babies."

Owen takes his place between Samantha's legs, pistoning his hips. His cold stare meets mine. "They're better off dead."

Samantha's smug grin is the last thing I see before my vision blinks out.

I catapult up into the sitting position in my bed. My hands instinctively land on my stomach, feeling around as my heart races a hundred miles per second.

You're okay. It was just a dream.

My door bursts open, and my light flickers on. "Ariah," Shay shouts. "Is everything okay?"

Tears run down my face. I can't seem to find my voice to tell her no, but somehow she knows. Shay crosses the room and climbs in bed next to me, wrapping me into her arms.

"It's okay. Everything's going to be okay. Let it all out," she murmurs into my hair.

I try to speak, but nothing comes out between my staccato breaths but soft whimpers.

"Shhh. Don't try to speak. Let it all out first. I'm not going anywhere. Once you've calmed down, then you can tell me what's going on."

And for the next hour, I cry. No words are said. Shay holds me to her chest, and I soak her sleep shirt with my tears.

I'm unsure when I dozed off, but the morning light beams through my window as birds chirp the next time my eyes open, and I'm still wrapped in my best friend's arms.

"Light is the devil," I croak from dried lips.

Humming her agreement, Shay hands me a bottle of water, and I gladly quench my thirst, soothing my extremely sore throat.

Once I'm sufficiently hydrated, Shay speaks, "Are you ready to tell me what happened?"

The irrational part of me fears that if I utter a word of my nightmare, it will become my reality, but I kick that bitch in the head. Now that I'm up, that ho can take a seat.

"It was some fuck shit of a nightmare," I grumble before recounting everything from last night. "I think it's just my subconscious trying to process seeing Owen getting Sam off last night," I confess.

"Are you sure that's what he was doing?" Shay questions. Her brows furrow in confusion.

Shrugging, I say, "What else could it have been? They've made it abundantly clear that I'm not their choice. It's been hard to accept, but that dream felt so real last night. I don't know if I could survive something like that. It would break me if something they did were a catalyst for losing our babies."

Shay looks pensive momentarily before she shouts, "I would kill them before I ever let some fuckery like that happen, Ry. Trust and believe their dicks would be stuffed and mounted to my walls before they'd ever get to do anything like that to you."

I giggle at the image of Wyatt's pierced cock stuffed and hanging on a wall like hunters mount their kills.

"Laugh if you want to, but they'd be gutted. They're on thin ice as it is. Dem cyan touch a button if dem tink seh dem bahd. I wouldn't recommend it, dough," Shay's icy tone brokers no arguments, and for the first time, I notice the darkness behind her eyes.

Pausing, I study my friend, really take her in. "We're going to need to discuss this," I say, waving my finger over the expanse of her body. "This whole silent killer vibe you've got going on here."

It's her turn to snort. "One day, but not tuhday."

I watch as she looks lost in memory for a moment longer before she hops from the bed.

"Now, let's get up and go eat, and then do some shopping—nothing like retail therapy to compartmentalize the shit we don't want to deal with," Shay orders, pulling the covers off me.

●

Groaning, I place the sonograms on the nightstand beside my bed before heading to the bathroom. I swear the further along I am, the more my bladder thinks it should empty every three seconds.

The weekend flew by. After shopping with Shay on Friday, I had Dr. Jaffri make a home visit to ease my mind that all was well. She instructed me to keep my stress levels down because stress isn't good for the babies or their momma. So, I spent the rest of the weekend relaxing. Shay had a massage therapist specializing in pregnancy massages come to the house. We were pampered, had dinner, and then watched action movies.

Once showered and dressed for the day, I head downstairs to eat breakfast. Shay's already sitting at the table with Reign, Elias, and Fernando. My smoothie and pancakes with bacon and eggs are already on the table where I sit. Steam still wafts from the plate of food, and my mouth waters.

Another part of pregnancy I'm taking up with management—cravings. I've had the same breakfast with no deviations for the last three weeks. I won't even address the time I cried when sausage was on my plate instead of bacon.

"Morning Ry," Shay greets from her spot at the table, prompting everyone to lift their head in my direction and say hello.

Smiling, I sit down and reply, "Morning, all."

"Morning, Ry." My heart nearly jumps out of my chest when I see Thomas round the corner.

"Thomas," I shriek, jumping from my seat. All thoughts of breakfast are momentarily forgotten. "What are you doing here? I thought you were guarding *her*?"

A throat clears. "What, no love for dear old me?"

"Or me?"

My jaw nearly hits the floor. "Dad? Granddad? What are you all doing here?" I ask, rushing over and hugging them.

"Let's have a seat so you can eat while we update you on some important developments," my dad instructs.

Wasting no time, I sit and dig into my breakfast, excited to finally get some news.

They talk amongst themselves while I finish the last of my food. Reign is updating Thomas on security measures currently in place, and my granddad is talking to Shay, telling her stories about her mother before she was born.

"No way! Not Sandra Elaine Warren. There's no freaking way," Shay exclaims. "Not my overly serious mother."

"She was in trouble at least twice a week. There wasn't a limit she was scared to test—Sandra is far from timid," Granddad added, making Shay burst into hysterical laughter to the point she was snorting.

Sipping the last of my smoothie, I place the now empty Mason jar on the table. "Okay, now spill it."

"You never were one to mince words," Dad huffs with a smile. "A few things have come to light, and with the discovery of this new information, your protection is of the utmost importance."

The twins are also apparently impatient to hear the news. I can feel them rolling around in my stomach. It's the weirdest feeling, almost like butterflies on steroids.

"Do you need me to go for this part?" Shay offered, but I could see the hope in her eyes that she'd be able to get the scoop as well.

My dad shakes his head, "No. You're fine. But anything said here can never be discussed with anyone outside this room. Do you understand, girls?"

We both quickly agree, and Dad continues.

"It was brought to the Council's attention over the weekend that the doctor that was supposed to give you your birth control implant was murdered."

I gasp. "What the hell? Why?"

"From what we've uncovered so far, she didn't follow instructions," Thomas replies. "Leading us to believe one of two things, either Dr. Lambert was a double agent, pretending to work for whoever tried to hire her, or she refused to be bought and was murdered once she failed to do what was asked of her."

The day at the doctor's office replays in my mind. It was so long ago I can't recall much of what transpired other than her telling me the implant was in. "Are you saying she intentionally didn't give me the implant?" This was the same conclusion Dr. Jaffri came to, but it's still too wild to believe.

"All evidence points to Dr. Lambert purposefully not giving you the implant. She kept detailed records. My guess was for insurance purposes should she need to save her own ass," Dad explains.

Hanging my head, I rub the bridge of my nose. *This shit can't be life.* If I wasn't living it, I'd swear this shit is fiction. Between secret organizations vying for power, stupid patriarchal traditions, and endless backstabbing, this was the perfect recipe for daytime soap opera.

Once I lift my gaze, Dad continues, "We know in the end, she decided to work for Elise and Filiae Bellonae in the hopes of you getting pregnant. However, it's still unclear if she doubled-crossed the mystery person, going to Elise for a better payout, or if she was always working for Elise and used the scheme to suss out the mystery person."

"So what does this all mean?" I inquire, needing to get to the bottom line. Why was Granddad here, and how did Thomas become my guard again?

"I'll take this one, gentleman," my grandfather says. "It means the Council is aware of your pregnancy, and with the danger of a mystery organization, the Fraternitas will not risk the next Heirs' lives. So, Thomas is now in charge of your security. Elias, Reign, and Fernando will remain your main guards, but Thomas must always be with you whenever you leave this house."

I mull over his words. "How did the banshee, I mean Samantha, take the news?"

"Quite frankly, the Council doesn't care how she will react once informed. She may be the future wife of the current Heirs, but you're carrying the first set of Heirs with the original family bloodlines," my father retorts.

"My children will not be pawns," I snap. "I'm happy to have you here, Thomas. You've been missed, but if having you here is some silent contract of my acquiescence, you can just go now."

A proud smile crests their faces, but it's my grandfather who addresses me. "That's why I'm here, Dear. What did I tell you before you left Colorado?"

Recollecting his words, I repeat them verbatim. "We've been on defense for too long. Now, it's their turn, and we won't stop until they're all dead."

My grandfather beams with pride. "The offense has finally begun."

25
SEBASTIAN

I fix the collar of my shirt before adjusting my watch. I can't remember the last time I wasn't donning a suit. I almost feel like a fish out of water.

Turning, I make one last adjustment to my belt and then slide on my shoes. I sneer at the sneakers in my closet—putting those on is a step too far.

"Bash! What the fuck are you doing up there, man? We need to get going," Wyatt barks from the bottom of the stairs.

Rolling my eyes, I check my watch. We still have another two hours before class even begins. "Hold your fucking horses. I'm on my way down now."

I hear Wyatt growl in frustration. "I'm trying to get there earlier so I can sit near Ariah before her guards cockblock. Don't fuck this up for me, or you'll have to sleep with one eye open."

By the time I make it downstairs, Wyatt's already outside. Before heading to the car, I grab my coffee, bacon, egg, and cheese on a croissant, and some grapes.

"Took you long enough," Wyatt whines.

"I'd tell you that you sound like a baby, but I think you already know how bratty you sound," I mutter, starting my car.

Narrowing his gaze, Wyatt snatches my sandwich and licks the entire top of it. "Call me a brat again and see what happens."

"What crawled up your ass and lodged itself?"

He snorts, "Gee, I don't know. How about Riri's been back for over a month, and we're missing being part of her pregnancy? Let's also not forget she thinks we hate her to the point she's having nightmares that require in-home visits, and, oh, we still have to continue to breathe the same air as Samantha."

I can't argue with him. Everything's been shit since the night Wes was forced to select Samantha as our Chosen. We haven't had a moment's reprieve. Now Ariah's carrying our babies, and we have to pretend she's less than pig shit.

The anguish I felt watching her beautiful face twist, tormented in her sleep because she dreamed that we thought the twins were better off dead—it will haunt me for the rest of my life. I'll spend forever making it up to her. *We all will.* It feels selfish to want her to hold on, but there isn't a scenario where Ariah doesn't end up in our arms, where she belongs.

"You're right," I say, putting the car in reverse and backing out of the garage. "There's a fuck-ton of shit happening, but we're close now. It won't be too long before we divest ourselves of the parasite and her brother." I maneuver the wheel and shift into drive, pulling onto the street before I continue. "Then we can love on our girl so hard. After she kicks us in our dicks, of course."

Wyatt laughs. A genuine Wyatt laugh. It's been months since I've heard one.

I quickly peer at him before my gaze focuses back on the road. There's more traffic than usual on campus. His face straightens as if remembering there's no reason to be happy at the moment.

"Do you think we'll be able to pull this off?" he inquires.

"Huh?" His doubt surprises me, making me ponder the possibilities of our failure.

Nope, none of these are an option.

A nanosecond barely passes, and I am upset with myself for it taking me that long. We're getting her back. "There is no plan B.

There's only one outcome—get our girl back, even if life as we've known it implodes," I decree.

Nodding, Wyatt flexes his jaw. His hazel eyes refocus as resilience sets back in. "Until then, we continue to shower her with gifts. "

"How do you think she'll react when she finds out we're the ones sending her everything?"

He huffs a laugh. "I think it's best we keep her in the dark on this. You saw what she did to the invitation. Not that I blame her. That trash is exactly where it belongs."

Smiling, I pull into our designated spot in the campus parking lot. "My freaking spitfire. I never know if it's her submission or fight that gets my cock harder."

"Both. Why choose?" Wyatt retorts.

I dip my head, agreeing with his assessment. *Why choose, indeed?* "You good getting back to the house?"

"Yeah. I'll catch a ride with Lev. He's supposed to be meeting with Teag about, you know what."

Teagan is a fucking genius. I wouldn't want her as my enemy, her coding skills are light years ahead of any of the best I've seen in the business.

"Keep me posted," I request, grabbing my satchel and locking the car.

Wyatt stares out over the campus green before he peers at me. "Are you going to be able to get the guys switched into Dr. Monroe's Sociology class since their professor is out for the remainder of the semester?"

It's early enough in the semester that the switch won't be flagged by admissions, especially with the approval of the head of the Sociology department.

"Yup," I'll speak with her and make it happen," I reply. Then Wyatt takes off toward the cafe, and I increase my stride, heading for the humanities department.

I need to meet with Dr. Monroe, the sociology professor I'm assisting for the year, before her lectures begin.

A thrill shoots straight to my cock at the idea of being able to see my spitfire. I'm already figuring out ways to force her to my office hours. When the Council instructed me to enroll in graduate school to ensure eyes were on Ariah and prevent any more schemes from Sam, I hopped at the chance.

"Good morning, Mr. Grant. Welcome to the Sociology Department. May I get you anything while you wait?" The woman asked from behind her desk.

"You have me at a disadvantage. It seems you know who I am, but I don't know you," I reply, ignoring her initial question.

Her cheeks flame red. "Apologies. My name is Becky, Becky O'Donnell. I'm one of the graduate assistants for the humanities department. Dr. Monroe had me organize your office and set up your bio online."

So, not a stalker, then.

I can't handle any more crazy women in this lifetime or the next. "Ah, okay. Hello Becky, nice to formally meet you," I say, extending my hand and sighing in relief.

She shakes it, then asks me to follow her to my office. "You'll find everything you need in here. I've organized your files on your computer, added Dr. Monroe's calendar to yours, and set your office hours. Your password is your last name and your birthday. You'll need to update that."

"Thank you. Is Dr. Monroe ready to meet yet?"

Becky offers me a small smile, still beet red. *I guess I make her nervous.* "She's in a faculty meeting for another thirty minutes. She'll meet with you once she returns. Until then, get situated and welcome to the team."

She scurries out of the office as fast as her legs will allow. I almost sniff myself to see if I smell. I nearly call her back in here to explain why she's so skittish, but it's for the best. I'd rather her be leery of me than infatuated.

Walking across the room, I place my bag on the oak desk. I'm nearly around the desk when my phone vibrates, and I pull it from my breast pocket. *Matthieu's calling.*

I swipe to answer. "Tout va bien?"

"Oui. Everything is on schedule. I was calling to let you know the Senator and Miss Davenport spent Friday night at the club. I know this isn't the footage you asked for, but I have the video for you anyway."

"Ont-ils révélé quelque chose?" I continue to ask him questions in French to ensure some level of privacy in case someone walks by.

"Yes, they revealed a lot. Those two are sick fucks."

I chortle. "That says a lot coming from you."

"Well, considering Baker was using severed fingers in her ass while he tries to impregnate her, I'd say my disgust is warranted," Matthieu details. "I thought he was going to backhand Samantha when she demanded him to shove two fingers of some girl they killed earlier in her ass. Instead, two seconds after his hand was around her throat, she moaned, and he was visibly hard."

My eyebrows nearly hit my hairline. "Tell me you got it all," I rush out. This is exactly what we need for phase one of our plan.

"I just told you I did. I wanted to gouge out my eyeballs and rupture my ear drums. The entire fucking time, he kept saying, 'Does my dirty whore of a sister like taking my big, fat, long cock?' Which was hilarious because his dick was far from big, fat, or long. I almost feel bad for the poor bastard."

And now I need my memory wiped.

"Thank you for the horrid visual. Send the file directly to Lev. He can suffer through it." I pause when there's a knock on the door, and Dr. Monroe steps inside. "Listen, send it, and thanks again. I have to run," I explain before ending the call.

Looking at my watch, I see it's only been fifteen minutes since Becky left my office.

"It ended early," she states.

"I see. Hello, Dr. Monroe," I greet, introducing myself.

Adjusting her glasses, she replies, "Liliana." When she notices the puzzled look on my face, she continues, "Since we'll be working closely together this year, I figured it made sense for you to call me by my first name and leave the formalities behind."

"Okay, works for me. Is there anything we need to go over before class today?"

"I'm sure Becky filled you in on the basics, and I emailed you this week's lesson plan already. After class, we can arrange the days you'll lead the lesson."

I smile, genuinely excited. I've always been interested in continuing my studies and possibly becoming a professor. We cover a few more items before it's time for class. Seeing my in, I continue. "I'd also like to discuss three student transfers into your class."

Liliana studies me, remaining silent long enough to make me think I overstepped and I won't be able to get the guys into her class. "Do these transfers happen to be the other three Heirs currently in Intro to Sociology with Professor Blaine?"

"Yes, but he's out due to an emergency surgery," I respond directly, seeing no reason to beat around the bush.

She smiles. "Yes, of course. We can discuss the process once we return to my office. For now, let's head to the lecture hall."

I return her grin with one of my own. "Thank you," I exclaim. "I'm excited to see what it's like to instruct college-level courses."

"My partners are beyond excited that I'll have someone assisting with my lectures this year. They think I'm overworked and underpaid," she confesses, tucking her copper hair behind her ears.

I'm shocked at how open she is about her personal life. I already knew she was in a polyamorous relationship. One of her partners is the Dean of the university, and the others—the Dean's stepdaughter from his first marriage, two other professors here on campus, and billionaire CEO, Landon Philips. Their story—a bigger clusterfuck than ours and they've made it work.

Misinterpreting my hesitation, she asserts, "I don't hide who I am, Sebastian. It's important that anyone I work with understands from the beginning I accept no one's bullshit."

"There is no judgment from me. You just caught me off guard. I wasn't expecting you to divulge such personal information."

"Good. Now let's get to class, and you and your cousin try to keep the ogling of Miss Bradford to a minimum." I open my mouth to refute the claim, but she holds her hand up. "What did I just say? No bullshit."

Massaging the bridge of my nose, I run my fingers through my hair. "How did you know?

"Just because Ariah is too hurt to see the truth in front of her doesn't mean the rest of us are fooled. You'd take heed of how obvious you're all being if you're planning anything," she suggests, then turns, pausing in the doorway. "I'll see you in class."

26
ARIAH

"What is he doing here?" Fernando mutters, and I turn in time to see Sebastian as he walks in behind Dr. Monroe.

His navy button-up shirt and dark wash denim jeans appear painted on against his sculpted physique. He surveys the room until his gaze locks on me as if I'm who he's looking for.

Sebastian stiffens, his pristine white teeth clenching, highlighting one of my favorite features. . . his jawline. Even covered in stubble, the sharp, angular set of Sebastian's cheekbones is something I could ogle for hours.

"If I had to guess, he's probably weaseled his way into being a teacher's assistant or something. He's been on campus a lot more in the last couple of weeks," Reign states. "I'll look into it after this, but I'm sure we'll get our answers soon enough."

Reign, Elias, and Fernando talk amongst themselves. I'm, however, frozen in place. I can feel my skin heat as Sebastian's undivided attention grips me, burrowing through my defenses. Months of fortifications are obliterated by one look.

My pulse thrums as my breath hitches. *Do I dare to hope?*

Sebastian's azure eyes study me for a moment longer before his nostrils flare, his lips curl, and his attention shifts.

You're a fucking idiot. They hate you.

I want to kick myself for allowing myself to be vulnerable. To wish for men who almost broke me with the falsities. All it took was one heated gaze, and I was ready to present like a bitch in heat.

My shoulders slump. I thought he was seeking me out to greet me with a smile. Instead, it was another reminder that they've moved on. The look of disgust before he looked away was like a kick to the ribs.

"If I can get everyone's attention to the front of the class, please." Dr. Monroe waits for the room to grow quiet before she continues. "I want to introduce my TA for the year, Sebastian Grant. He'll lead lectures twice a month and handle my office hours. If you have an issue that only I can address, please email me, and we'll work out the best date and time to meet." Dr. Monroe turns to him. "Sebastian, please introduce yourself."

He clears his throat, "Good afternoon. As you've all heard, I'm Sebastian Grant. I'm glad I'll have the opportunity to work with you over the semester."

"That's one gorgeous man," a guy in the row in front of me stage whispers. Titters fill the room, and the back of the guy's neck turns beet red as he sinks in his seat, realizing the entire class heard his outburst.

Looking up, I see Sebastian's dangerous Colgate smile. The one that wields the power to make even the strongest-willed person melt. Something I know from personal experience. I know precisely what that mouth is capable of.

"Are you okay?" Reign leans in to ask.

Without turning, I reply, "Yeah. Why wouldn't I be?"

"The very flushed look on your face. You look a little flustered," he jests, and I'm half tempted to punch him in the shoulder.

Schooling my features, I retort, "It's hot in here. I just need something to drink, is all." But even I doubt the crap spewing from my mouth. I can't imagine anyone who'd blame me. Sebastian is fucking hot. My pussy clenches at the memory of him making me count and the time he took me on the hood of a car while his cunt of an ex-girlfriend was tied to a chair and forced to watch.

I'm so lost in the vivid scenes playing out in my head I don't hear my name being called.

"You really need to stop daydreaming. Your thoughts are screaming at me," Elias teases, and Nando and Reign join in.

I flip the three of them the finger.

"Miss Bradford, would you care to share?" Sebastian asks. It's more of a command than a question."

Pausing, I weigh my options. Should I be a brat and test his limits publicly, or do I bury my pettiness?

Sebastian arches his wheat brow in a challenge, making my decision obvious.

"Nothing that concerns you, Sir," I quip, quirking my brow.

I quickly glance at Dr. Monroe, preparing for my reprimand, but it never comes. Instead, she surprises me with a nod of what looks like pride.

"Is that so, spitfi—Miss Bradford?" Sebastian counters. The gravelly bass in his voice causes goosebumps to trail up my spine and my pussy to clench.

"Yes, Sir," I retort, then I internally high-five myself when the muscles in Sebastian's jaw tick.

He struggles to hide his reaction to my words, and I wonder if he remembers the times he had me at his feet.

A burst of laughter echoes off the walls, and I turn to the corner of the room where Wyatt sits, a Cheshire grin plastered on his face. His attention is already on me. Wyatt's lips curl into a smirk when our gazes connect, and he winks at me.

My nose scrunches in confusion. I expected disdain, not amusement.

Don't they hate me?

What if something else is at play?

I wonder, not for the first time, if I'm missing something. However, I don't get the opportunity to process what this means before Dr. Monroe begins class.

"Open your books to page two hundred and thirty-seven. Today, we'll be focusing on the interactionist theory," she orders.

I open my text and try to follow along, but I'm distracted. My thoughts flit from interaction to interaction with the guys, hoping to glimpse anything I've missed. I'm so lost in my memories that I hear nothing about the tenets of the micro-sociology theory and don't recognize that class has ended until I feel a tap on my shoulder.

"Time to go, Daydreamer," Elias teases with a knowing grin.

Glancing around the room, I confirm the lecture has ended, and we're one of the last to leave. I also don't miss that Wyatt and Sebastian are whispering in the front of the room, and with each stolen glance, it's safe to assume the conversation pertains to me.

I'm tempted to stay and see what I can glean from their body language, but my phone vibrates. A calendar notification displays on the screen, reminding me I have a crucial meeting I can't miss.

●

"Thank you for your time. I look forward to the next time we meet," I offer, standing and shaking each hand seated at the table.

"The pleasure is all ours, Miss Bradford. Should the situation in Edgewood not be handled, you'll hear from us," the woman explains.

Nodding, I bid one last farewell and turn to exit the room. Thomas opens the door to a waiting Reign and Elias stationed outside.

"How did it go?" Reign inquires.

"Not here," Thomas commands. "We need to get Ariah safely back home first."

I smile. "I missed your bossy ass, T."

He shakes his head. "And I missed your stubborn one."

Once we're safely in the SUV, the ride home is short. My grandfather and dad were able to help coordinate this meeting near Lincolnville, about thirty minutes outside the city in North Brentwood. Far enough to be off the Fraternitas radar.

I'm barely through the door when my phone rings.

"Hey, Dad. We just got back."

"Good. I was just checking on you. Your grandfather and I will be by tomorrow. Have the chef set the table for ten," he instructs.

I bite the inside of my cheek, swallowing the protest building in my chest. I desperately want to discuss the outcome of the meeting, but we can't risk anyone tapping the line and overhearing.

Inhaling, I finally respond. "Okay. I'll see you all tomorrow, then."

When a few seconds pass without a response, I pull the phone from my ear and check to see if the call is still connected.

My lips part, preparing to ask if everything's okay when he finally speaks. "I'm proud of you, Ry. We're closer to the end."

"Thanks, Dad," I reply, appreciating his encouragement. We say our goodbyes and then disconnect the call.

Kicking off my shoes, I contemplate if I want to go to the kitchen and grab a snack or fall into bed. I decide to head upstairs and shower before I find Shay. But locating her isn't a problem. By the time I'm dressed in my matching black sleep shorts and tank, she's already on my bed waiting.

"I know you can't say much, but blink twice if everything worked out," she requests.

"What are we in? A spy novel?" I joke.

She rolls her eyes. "You couldn't humor me, even just a little bit?"

Snorting, I blink twice, and her eyes bulge before she schools her features.

"You'd be a terrible spy. Don't quit your day job," I quip.

Shay launches a pillow from my bed at my face. "You wound me."

"Yet somehow your flare for the dramatic is always spot on," I giggle, tossing the pillow back at her.

"Did you hear about the party the guys are throwing next weekend?" She asks.

Sighing, I dip my chin. "Yes, that's all anyone can talk about."

"I know we're not going to that, for obvious reasons," she flicks her head to my stomach, which grows more prominent by the week.

"But we can go to the football game in two weeks. It's for homecoming week."

Focusing my gaze, I stare her in the eyes, ready to protest, but she continues.

"Come on, Ry. You can't let them rob you of every college experience. Plus, all the alumni will be here, and it's tradition to watch the game."

At the reminder that alums will be here, I remember my dad discussing attending a few events this month at LWU.

"Fine," I groan. I'm excited about football, just not some of the players. Specifically, four of them and the one who will undoubtedly be in the audience with the hag cheering them on. "This is going to be a disaster."

"Nope, not even Samantha will act up. With all the alumni here, she'll be forced to be a person for once."

I cross my arms. "Because adults have ever been a deterrent for her," I mutter.

Shay concedes the point, and our conversation shifts to our week at school. I confess the moment of idiocy I had during sociology.

"You're not an idiot," she exclaims. "Did you have a moment of weakness? Absolutely. But that's to be expected. Feelings don't shut off overnight. They're the only dumbasses I see."

I allow her words to sink in. I'm not allowing myself any grace. I had... *have* genuine feelings for them.

Shay's right.

It's not a switch that flips off and on. I'm allowed to be hurt. All of this is easier said than done. The part of me that has been an impenetrable force out of necessity argues with the side that encourages me to be vulnerable.

They had so many of my firsts, and when I gave them my heart, they crushed it.

Like I didn't matter.
Like my feelings were theirs to play with.
Like I'm worthless.

My ire grows and is on the precipice of boiling over.

"Out of your head, Ry, and let's watch a movie," Shay coaxes.

Agreeing, I pack my intrusive thoughts into a box and shove it into the back of my mind.

The guys have had too much of my headspace for one day.

27
WES

September 28, 2023

> *Ariah,*
> *Weeks since I last held you: 16*
> *Weeks Pregnant: 20*
> *Baby size: Banana*
> *Today, I had to allow a venomous bitch to press her lips to my cheek while she pawed her hands all over me in front of you while I called your pussy ozone waste. It chipped another part of my heart away.*
> *The words are never for you—they're for her. Anything I've said to hurt you since the horrible day I had to announce her as our Chosen has been for her.*

"Wes. You in here, man?" Owen shouts, rapping his knuckles against my bedroom door. He doesn't wait for an answer before he turns the knob, and I slam my journal shut. All my words are only for her. They convey what I can't say out loud.

It started a week after she was gone. I could still smell her on my pillow. I stare at the drawer where the ziplock bag holds the pillowcase.

"Didn't you hear me calling you?" Owen asks, standing in the doorway.

I pull my eyes from the brown leather-bound journal, turning to peer at him. "Sorry, I was focused on something. I didn't hear you. What's up?"

He doesn't attempt to see what I'm doing. He already knows —*they all do*. "Lev wants to meet before the party starts."

"I'll be down in fifteen."

Owen nods, then closes my door.

Spinning back around, I open to the page bookmarked and pick up where I left off.

> *Every part of me aches for you—wanting nothing more than to fist your hair and make you a beautiful mess. My perfect dirty slut.*
>
> *I don't know if I'll ever share this with you, but I needed a place to show you that my heart beats only for you. Every decision since that day has been to get back to you. Every hurtful word—every scornful look—all of it is to get back to you. It was my decision to choose Samantha. And even if it's a choice I'd make every time, I'm destroyed knowing I have to hurt you.*
>
> *Always yours,*
Wes

Song: Sad Beautiful Tragic- Taylor Swift

Inhaling, I place my pen down and close my eyes. I try to make peace with who I've had to be to Ariah, knowing she may never forgive me. Even when she discovers it was all to keep her safe and save Owen, I don't see how she'll ever look at me the same.

My dreams are haunted by the pained look on her face each

time one of us does something. I only find solace in the fact it's almost over. Teagan has found a way into the device. Now, she's working tirelessly to develop a code to override the chip in Owen's arm. We're so close I can almost taste Ariah's skin.

Standing, I open my wall safe and place the journal back inside. The lock engages, sealing my private thoughts behind biometric security features. Then I walk over to my bed, tempted to pull out the pillowcase, but I know I'm short on time. Instead, I leave my room and head for Lev's.

Once I'm seated, he begins. "We'll all start off here tonight. We need Samantha to remember seeing all of us. Once the party gets crowded, Sebastian, Owen, and I will go to the Fraternitas and meet with Mrs. Davenport."

"Why don't I get to stay here," Owen inquires, sulking.

Lev doesn't skip a beat. "You'll kill Samantha if you're here. There's no way she'll behave with an audience this big, knowing we're being forced to make it appear as if she's our actual fiancée."

When I look, Owen's guilt is written all over his devilish grin.

"Exhibit A," Sebastian jests.

Huffing, Owen mumbles but agrees.

"I'll have a feed of the party up the whole time. All rooms upstairs will be locked, and we'll have security guarding the basement and stairway," Lev explains.

"Can't let anyone in your torture room," Wyatt snorts.

"Weren't you and Owen both down there just this morning adding knives, bodily fluids, and random monster dildos?" Lev quips.

Wyatt shrugs. "All the monster-romance girlies swear by monster peen, but something tells me being railed by a fourteen-inch centaur cock will not be the highlight of any person we deploy our zesty interrogation tactics on."

I shake my head. "You two are fucking idiots and need to stay off social media."

Wyatt and Owen grin conspiratorially, and I don't want to imagine what bodily fluids they have down there.

"We'll have a thirty-minute window with Samantha's mother.

During that time, the plan is to have her answer as many questions as possible. Then we'll be back in time for it to look like we never left," Lev explains.

We grunt our agreements, all of us understanding our roles tonight. As we stand, Sebastian declares, "Okay, gentlemen, let's get to work!"

●

LEV
Just arrived at the Fraternitas. Party still looks good. . . minus Sam trying to tongue you down.

ME
Copy and 😂🤮. . . 🙏 for me.

WYATT
I vote we kill her

OWEN
I second. We need at least one more to move this motion forward.

"Wesley," Samantha whines for the umpteenth time tonight. "You're not paying me any attention. You or Wyatt."

Wyatt's lip curls in disgust at her attempt to pretend to be sloshed. She's had one drink since she arrived—Diet Coke.

I subtly shake my head when his mouth opens. We need her to think we believe her bullshit.

He grits his teeth and spins away from us, surveying the crowd. The entire first floor is packed with people.

"Fine. I'll be right back. I'm going to get some drinks," Samantha pouts, stomping away.

"Can I just hang her like a piñata? I've got a bat covered in barbed wire in my room," Wyatt grumbles.

I laugh, "Add it to the list. You know Lev has a growing one."

"It's cathartic to add to it each time she breathes," Wyatt replies.

My cell phone buzzes.

> **LEV**
>
> Don't drink whatever she brings back. I just saw her slip something in your drinks.
>
> **OWEN**
>
> Can we kill her now?
>
> **BASH**
>
> No. . . much to my growing disappointment.

"Here you are. I got you both a drink," Samantha says, holding cups for us to grab.

We each take one and place it on the table behind us.

"Aren't you going to drink it?" She frowns.

"Why don't we dance instead," I suggest, and her eyes light up.

I take her cup and put it with ours, not missing her eyeing where hers is situated. As I pull her toward the center of the room, I signal Wyatt, but he's already two steps ahead of me, switching out her punch for one of ours.

Once we're at the center of the dance floor, Samantha immediately begins to grind on me.

"Don't you miss us?" She whispers when she whirls around, pressing her tits against my chest.

I push her away when she tries to grab my dick. "Sure I do," I lie. We need her to believe this part for what happens next.

Samantha smiles up at me, studying my face, searching for deceit. She won't find any. My mask is firmly in place. Her eyes fill with lust, and I have to bite the inside of my cheek to prevent myself from pushing her away. "I knew you'd eventually come around. You could only resist me for so long." Lifting her hands, she drags her claws down my chest. "I know that bitch couldn't hold a candle to what we have. She can't feed the beast inside of you that yearns for depravity. But I'll be your cum slut."

I have to fight the bile churning in my gut and smile. "Why don't we grab our drinks and head for the basement."

Beaming with satisfaction, she tugs me back to where Wyatt

stands. He holds out her cup as we approach and readily accepts it, guzzling its contents while I pretend to sip mine. You can never be too sure with Samantha. Knowing her, she'd spike all the drinks to ensure she was victorious.

Wyatt can't hide his glee.

Gotcha bitch.

I don't know what dosage she used, but she's wobbling on her feet by the time we reach the basement. Her words are slurred, and I'm tempted to let her fall down the stairs and crack her head open. Unfortunately, that would lead to Owen's demise. So, instead, I throw her over my shoulder and make my descent.

"Throw her ass in the back room. I'm going to grab a few things," Wyatt states, striding down the hall toward Lev's room.

Thoughts of our earlier conversation run through my mind as I toss her on the bed and secure her arms and legs with zip ties to the bedpost. She's wearing a dress and is pantyless, if I go by the vag slip I just got, making me nearly vomit.

Footsteps sound down the hall, and I turn, seeing Wyatt holding an automatic sex machine with the centaur dildo attached to it and a jar filled with a milky-white substance with hints of gray in it.

"Do I want to know what the fuck is in that?" I point to the glass container he just placed on the table in the room.

The question is barely out of my mouth before he answers, "Horse nut."

I rub my hand over my face. "And how exactly did you and Owen come by horse sperm? More importantly, why did you both even try to acquire it?"

"You never know when you might need it, and look." He points to Sam, passed out on the bed. "It didn't take very long for a situation to arise for it to be utilized," he states smugly.

Sighing, I ask the question I'm not sure I want the answer to. "What exactly are your plans for all of. . ." I wave my hands in the general direction of the table. "That?"

Wyatt adjusts the dildo. "She's been building up to demanding sex from you. Hence, the roofies in the drink bit. I say we let her believe that happened—Heir style."

It's brutal but fucking genius, and it's everything Samantha Davenport deserves. She planned to rape me or both of us tonight.

Well, uno reverse, bitch.

"Set this shit up," I instruct, pulling out my phone and texting the group chat to ensure Lev turns on the camera. This video is the perfect payback for the one she leaked of Ariah and will go a long way in bringing about the destruction of Edgewood's self-proclaimed queen. "Who's touching her to insert it?"

"Not it," Wyatt blurts before I can fully ask the question, and I growl. "Hey, you're the only one out of us who has willingly touched her pussy," he deadpans.

Flaring my nostrils, I huff, "Fine. Hand me some gloves and prop her ass up with pillows."

We both quickly get to work. Once she's positioned and the dildo is inserted. I turn the device on, and we both step out of the frame.

Using the remote, I start the machine. Slowly at first, ensuring it won't slip out. It's set to shallow thrusts because I'm sure fourteen is too many inches, not to mention the damn thing was so thick I barely could wrap my hand around the shaft.

"Make it go faster and harder. I know from Samantha's detailed retellings you two were rough. She needs to feel it once she wakes," Wyatt instructs.

I nod and increase the speed. She's taking about eleven inches, and the thrusts are hard. She begins to moan, and Wyatt makes a gagging sound.

"Wes," she groans before falling silent as her face twists in pleasure. "More," she begs, and I oblige, turning it up two notches, increasing the pace of the thrusts but not the depth.

She should be happy she can't die because death by dildo would be a fucked but hilarious way to go. However, she doesn't deserve that ending—her death must be slow and methodical.

Maybe there should be some level of guilt about taking advantage of a drugged Samantha, but I feel nothing—none of us do. She had every intention to drug us tonight. It would be the only way she'd ever get any of us to fuck her.

I want to claw my ears off when she screams my name during her release. I've always hated the sound of her voice, especially during sex. That's why I always gagged the cunt.

Wyatt steps over to the table, picks up the jar, and uncaps it as he strides toward the bed. I watch as he drizzles the horse cum all over her. Starting on her face, he ensures a good amount lands on her lips. He trails down her black dress, pulling the top down and exposing her fake giant tits. Her nipples are rock hard, her breaths are stuttered, and she's about to come again. Wyatt continues down her abdomen, stopping where the machine is pistoning in and out of her, and pours the remainder of the contents over the shaft of the dildo.

He turns. "Does this count as bestiality?"

No longer able to hold back my amusement at the situation, I burst into laughter before I reply. "I don't know, but I damn sure will call her a horse fucker."

"Seems fitting. Matches her 'brother fucker' moniker," he quips, and I hum my agreement.

Once she comes a third time, and I'm sure she's been screwed enough times, I turn off the machine. I snicker. The dumb bitch will feel it as soon as she wakes.

"This thing needs to be burned," I state, picking up a knife and cutting the zip ties. I smirk at the raw skin on her wrists and ankles. This will further cement her belief she had sex.

When I hear nothing, I crane my neck, looking at the vacant spot where Wyatt once stood. I'm about to shout his name when the asshole comes back in the room decked out in full hazmat gear. "I'll take that."

I part my lips to ask why, but he's already exiting the room with the device in a sealed bag.

Shaking my head, I turn back to the evil, lying cunt on the bed. A small part of me wonders what could've made the girl who was once our friend grow into the vindictive, jealous bitch she is today. None of that matters now, however.

Samantha Rose Davenport made her bed, and now she gets to die in it.

28
LEV

After the text from Wes asking for the cameras to record, I knew some fucked up shit was about to go down.

Samantha trying to drug Wyatt and Wes was beyond ridiculous but very like her. She was going to rape one or both of them, and I'm sure she would've recorded it as another way to throw salt in an already gaping wound.

"Five more minutes," Teagan announces.

I double- and triple-check our connections while we wait. Tonight's conversation could be exactly what we need to turn the tide. Each of us has been collecting evidence of all of Samantha's transgressions, and based on what's been discovered thus far, they're aplenty.

"How much do you believe she'll reveal?" Sebastian asks from where he stands. He's leaning against the wall with his arms folded across his chest and his left leg crossed over the right ankle. He's wearing dark wash denim jeans, a crisp white collared button-down shirt with the sleeves rolled to the elbow, and a pair of some fancy-ass brand of brown dress shoes.

It's always weird to see him in anything other than a suit. I can actually count on two hands the number of times that's happened since he graduated high school. Sebastian was a pretentious shit, but with a father like his, it was necessary.

"My hope is everything she knows, but I expect she'll give enough to keep her options open," I reply.

"It is the Davenport way. The opportunist, power-hungry, social climbing snakes they are," Owen hisses. He sits to my right, flipping a razor blade between his knuckles.

I nod in agreement. "True, but if she wants a chance to make it out of this alive, she'll provide as much intel as possible."

"Okay, boys. Go time in three," Teagan states, appearing on the monitor to my left. Her honey-brown eyes light with excitement, and a smile grows on her face.

"Teag. What style are we rocking this month?" Owen inquires.

She lifts the long purple, pink, and blue ombre strands. "Havana Twists. Forty-two inches," she exclaims. Then Teagan swivels her neck to display the intricate designs tattooed into her rich, brown skin on the shaved side of her head.

"New ink to top it off. Badass Teag," I say.

Posing, she responds—in a terrible fake Southern accent, "Why thank you ever so kindly."

"That was terrible," Owen snorts, and she laughs.

"I never claimed to be a thespian," Teagan quips.

A notification chimes on her end, shifting her focus to the left. Teagan's pierced brow arches before the sound of her fingers flying across a keyboard fills the room.

"Everything okay?" I probe.

Another moment passes before she replies, "Yup. Momentary setback. At some point in the last twenty-four hours, an extra layer of security was added to the Davenports' system. But we're good, and Mrs. Davenport is ready."

Sebastian strides toward the table and sits as Blair Davenport materializes on screen.

"Boys," she singsongs. "So lovely to see you. I wish it were under better circumstances, but alas, here we are nonetheless."

Samantha's mother is a glimpse into the future of what

Samantha might look like if she weren't going to suffer a timely end. Decades of plastic surgery, lip fillers, and Botox have made it impossible to see some of their genetic similarities. Aside from their piercing crystal-blue eyes, both mother and daughter have had so many procedures one could make the argument Samantha was adopted.

"Let's cut the small talk. Time is limited, and you have the information we want," Owen snaps.

Wait, I lied. They both make the same expression when they feel passed over or slighted in some way—the flare of their nostrils and curling of their lips as their faces attempt to scrunch. *Definitely not adopted.*

Blair schools her features, a smile returning to her face as if she remembers she needs our help. "Right. Well then, ask away," she mutters.

"What role has your daughter played in the Filiae Bellonae's efforts to overthrow the Fraternitas?" I demand.

She sighs. "Samantha was an integral part of the plan. She was our way into your lives without being overt. She was being used long before she agreed to be a co-conspirator."

My eyes widen at that information as I think back to when we were younger. There was a time when we'd all been thick as thieves —inseparable before the day she betrayed us.

"Her locket," Blair answers my unspoken question. "It was a recording device."

Owen gasps. "I remember that fucking thing. She'd never take it off."

"She couldn't even if she wanted to. The clasp could only be opened with the key fashioned solely for the necklace, and I had the only copy."

"So, you, what? Listened to us while we played?" I growl.

Blair smirks. "No one ever suspects young children. So many conversations were overheard. Your fathers spoke so freely, and none of you paid attention or understood what was transpiring. You were too young."

"But I wasn't," Sebastian chimes, and she rolls her eyes.

"Your father was in our pockets long before you were even born. He was so bitter about being passed over that it took nothing to get him to agree," she gloats, and Sebastian's lips thin.

Theodore Grant was a whiny dick. It shouldn't have been as shocking when it was discovered he was a turncoat.

Lifting her hand, Samantha's mother held up a finger at a time, ticking off what they discovered. "We knew the plan for Ariah to come back once she was near eighteen. We knew the Council had plans to rig the Selection so she'd become the Chosen, and we knew they planned to use your union to birth five sons—Heirs connected through the original bloodline."

If the Council hadn't already informed us of their ultimate plan over the summer, Blair's news would've left me speechless.

It was satisfying to watch the smugness melt from her face with our lack of surprise.

"Oh, I'm sorry. Did you think you revealed some bombshell?" Owen mocks. "If you want our help, you'll need to deliver more than shit we already know."

Needing to move things along before we run out of time, I jump to a time we believe Samantha agreed to help willingly. I ask the question we suspected we already knew the answer to, "Did your daughter purposely lure Owen and me out of school that day?"

Before she can answer, a woman in a maid's uniform brings her a blue cocktail, and Blair thanks her before she exits.

Owen leans forward, his eyes narrowing to slits. "We don't have all day. Answer the fucking question!"

Blair smirks, bringing the drink to her mouth and downing nearly half of the glass's contents before placing it off to the side.

"I'd tread carefully if I were you, Blair. We're your only chance to get out from under your daughter's thumb," Sebastian warns.

Unfazed, her shoulders push back, and she sits taller, pride evident in whatever she's about to reveal. "Of course she did. The minute she heard she wouldn't be your chosen and that some girl she'd never heard of was, her hackles rose. Jealousy is a powerful motivator. Sometimes too powerful." She pauses, and then a faraway look settles in her eyes before she continues. "From that day forward, she did any- and everything necessary to ensure she was your end game."

"What exactly does '*everything necessary*' mean?" I seethe.

Blair clenches her teeth. "I don't know when we lost control of her. I had her on such a tight leash. She shouldn't have had the time or the resources to orchestrate what she has."

If her daughter wasn't a grade-A cunt, I might feel sorry for her. Having a mother who manipulates you for their own personal gain does something to your trust. But every member of the Council is guilty of this. The more I think about it, Ariah and Samantha have similar situations. Both their moms used them instead of loving them. Only Ariah doesn't think the world owes her everything and should bow at her feet in worship.

"We're almost out of time, and you still haven't given us anything we don't already know," I state.

"Samantha was originally supposed to be one of the girls Selected. We'd planned to use her to ensure Ariah was the one Chosen in the end. But after the kidnapping and her bratty behavior over the years, we knew there was little chance of that. Some hope had returned when Wes started sleeping with her, but we quickly ascertained that was just a ploy."

A feeling in my gut begins to stir—something I've contemplated since Samantha's big reveal.

"She was told to do whatever was required to become one of the Selected. So, she killed her friends. One by one until you had no other choice but to choose her. What we didn't count on was for her to betray us and work for Senator Baker," she scowls in disgust at the mention of her stepson's name.

"You're a heartless bitch," Sebastian shouts.

Ignoring his outburst, Blair continues. "We didn't know everything she was up to until it was too late. Samantha and Matthew had masterfully positioned themselves to take over. They undermined every step we executed—the threatening messages sent to scare Ariah out of town. The orchestrated kidnapping from the school locker room where Ariah would be assaulted and then killed. Samantha staging her own kidnapping and rape, hoping you'd comfort her."

With each confession, my body coils tighter—desperate for release. The lack of an outlet for my rage causes heat to creep up the back of my neck, and my hands curl into fists on the table in front of me. If Blair or her daughter were in this room, they'd be ripped apart—neither deserve anything but gruesome deaths.

"Even with Elise's untimely demise, we were still on course. Ariah was in love with all of you, and we knew each of you already reciprocated the feeling, or you were well on your way there. However, our plans went up in smoke the night of the announcement," she snarls.

I watch as anger emanates from Blair, and I wish again that a screen didn't separate us.

Blair's jaw ticks, and she inhales, attempting to reign in her emotions. "When the announcement was officially made, I realized how fucked we were. As smart as my daughter may think she is, she's not. Because any daughter of mine would know to ensure they're the biggest bad on the table, and neither Samantha nor her idiot half-brother did that. Having Owen kidnapped to force your hand pissed all over the Novus Ordo Seclorum's plans."

My ears perk at the mention of their name.

"What do they have to do with any of this?" Owen questions.

I sneak a glance at the disguised calm in his tone. Owen's face is devoid of emotions, and the razor blade he had earlier has been replaced with a hunting knife.

"Silly boys," she chortles. "You must know by now the Fraternitas answers to powers greater than themselves. Did you honestly think they were in charge?"

"Just answer the fucking question," Sebastian barks.

Blair crosses her arms and sits back in her chair. "There isn't enough time to discuss all the Novus Ordo Seclorum entails. Just know nothing planned wasn't ordered, and the wrath they unleash can not be countered when an order isn't fulfilled. Even with our combined forces, we'd be nothing more than a gnat."

Thinking back to the day the Council met with them and the fear on our fathers' faces, everything clicks into place. Samantha and the Senator forcing our hand has put us all in the crosshairs of an entity we have yet to scratch the surface of their reach.

"What you're saying is, if we don't find a way to stop whatever plan Samantha and Senator Baker have put into motion, we're all fucked," I clarify, scrubbing my hand along my stubbled jaw.

Blair nods, then grabs her cocktail from earlier and drinks before responding. "Precisely, they have to be——."

A gagging sound fills the room as Blair claws at her throat. Her skin grows red before quickly turning blue.

"What the fuck is happening?" I shout.

Blair's body jerks, her face contorting in pain.

"Can we get someone to her?" Sebastian asks, pulling his phone from his pocket.

Owen grabs his wrist, halting him.

"O, what are you doing, man? Let me go. We need to call for help," Sebastian demands.

A glint appears in Owen's hazel depths. "No one can save her. She's lucky I couldn't get to her before now. She didn't have any further information she could provide, and she's part of the reason this shit happened," he spits, lifting the hunting knife to his mouth and licking it. "My only regret is I couldn't run her through with Quinn."

Throwing my head back, I laugh. "You crazy fucker, what did you give her?"

"Strychnine," Owen grins and stands, rubbing his hands together in excitement.

Teagan clears her throat, and our gazes shift to her. "There's never a dull moment when I work with you fools. I'm out. Until next time." She gives us a two-finger salute before disconnecting.

Peering at my phone, I notice it's nearly two in the morning. The party should be winding down. Then I check the files of Blair Davenport's confessions and save them to various drives.

Tonight seems to have been an all-around win for us if the pictures Wyatt sent to the group chat are any indication.

P. H. NIX

    I stand, and as we pack up our things, I can't help but wonder if maybe the tide is finally turning in our favor.

29
WYATT

"So let me get this straight. You infiltrated the Davenports' staff, convinced one of them to poison her, and then, while questioning her, you killed her?" I ask through my laughter.

Fucking Owen is worse than me when left to his own devices.

"She more than earned it. I'm only pissed I didn't get to savor it," Owen retorts, and I can't argue with that.

They arrived back at the house about two hours ago. We let the party continue for another hour before kicking motherfuckers out. Now we're sitting around the den in our basement. A live feed of Samantha is on the screen, so we don't miss the moment the hag wakes up.

Wes groans. "What if she didn't answer all the questions in time?"

Owen shrugs. "It takes up to thirty minutes before strychnine causes any lasting damage, according to Lev's very detailed notes."

"And you used to think I was being overzealous. My meticulous notes helped you time a murder perfectly," Lev gloats.

"You can meet Quinn since Blair didn't get the honor," Owen quips.

Peering around the room, I grin, enjoying the banter and lightheartedness. I can almost feel the shift. Where despair once resided, now determination thrums like the drums of war.

Sebastian claps his hands, garnering our attention. "Okay, we need to discuss what we learned before and determine what we're doing with the leech."

"We could use the smelling salts," I offer. "Or," I pause because I'm nothing if not dramatic. "We can just leave her to stew. The cameras are on, and we'll know as soon as she wakes."

Drumming his fingers on the arm of the recliner, Lev inquires, "Are we sure she's not wearing some device?"

"Unless it's embedded in her skin, there's no way," Wes states.

"She wasn't wearing a locket or any other jewelry?" Sebastian presses.

I shake my head. "Outside of her earrings, there was nothing else. Why?"

Owen leans forward and recounts Blair's admittance to sending an unknowing Samantha to our houses with a listening device.

"Should we wait then?" I inquire, but that thought makes me want to go in there and turn the mattress over. The jolt she'd get from her face smacking the floor should wake her. However, her waking up covered in horse jizz has a greater benefit. Plus, it's far more amusing.

"The room she's in is soundproof, and I'm sure Lev has some signal blocker running," Wes notes.

Once Lev confirms a jammer is on, they divulge what they learned.

"She faked her rape?" I yell, and Sebastian nods.

I open my mouth to express my shock until I remember all Samantha's done to this point. Faking her own kidnapping and rape is sadly not her worst offense.

The temptation to smother Samantha with a pillow now and fuck the consequences is strong, but losing Owen when I know we're close to being free from the cunt's claws is stronger.

"How high was that dose?" Sebastian inquires. "Shouldn't the effects be wearing off by now?"

"I have no idea. Wyatt switched her drink with one of ours," Wes explains. "Let's give her another hour to wake on her own."

We all grunt our agreement, then rehash our plan, going through what evidence we have and what we still need.

Forty minutes later, we're discussing the status of where Teagan is with deactivating the chip in Owen's arms when a squawky whine bleeds my ear drums.

"Wesley," Samantha croaks, and I turn in time to see her sit up in the bed and stretch.

My eyes light with anticipation when it appears she's finally registered she's covered in something. Then, everything that transpires happens as if time is moving in slow motion.

Samantha's mouth tips up into a shit-eating grin as her tongue swipes across her lips. She leans back and groans. "I knew he couldn't resist me."

"She didn't just—" Sebastian's blue irises bulge.

"She did," Owen exclaims, bouncing like a kid in a candy store.

Samantha's hands roam down her dress as she spreads her legs, and I have to force my head not to turn and my eyes not to close.

"He didn't use a condom," she squeaks in triumph. "Wesley Edgewood is finally mine!"

I snort. "Someone's being presumptuous."

Wes hums his agreement. "That's her default setting."

"Yup, that and being a bitch with an endless supply of audacity," Lev adds.

Another brain-shattering moan cuts off our conversation, bringing our attention back to the TV.

"Damn Wes, you fucked me so good," Samantha mutters, scooping cum from her chest and shoving her fingers in her pussy.

My stomach churns, but like rubbernecking as you pass an accident, I can't look away. "We're going to need to burn down the whole house after this," I grumble.

"Please, fuck me harder, Daddy," she whimpers.

I whip my head in Wes's direction. *"Daddy?"*

Wes rolls his eyes and shrugs but doesn't respond.

"Listen, the girl fucks her brother. Maybe her Daddy kink is real," Owen quips.

Dry heaving, Sebastian's hand covers his mouth, and all I can think is *same, buddy, same.*

"Blood and guts don't make you the least bit squeamish, but this does?" Owen jests.

Arching a brow, Sebastian counters, "Everything involving Samantha makes me violently ill." We all laugh.

Samantha is vile—rotten from the inside out. Her soul is black, but not in the same way ours are. We all have blood on our hands, stained from the responsibilities that come with being from money.

There is no such thing as an ethical billionaire, and every family in this town has a net worth that begins with at least a B. We all lie, cheat, and steal in some capacity to either maintain power or increase it. But the lengths to which Samantha was willing to go far surpasses even the greediest among us.

"Truer words have never been spoken," I mumble.

The screen goes black. "That's enough of that shit," Lev grunts.

"Did she just lick horse nut off her lips and then shove some—" Owen starts.

"Don't finish that sentence. I've suffered enough, thank you very much. As it is, I'm not sure a brain transplant would rid me of what I just witnessed," Sebastian blurts, cutting him off.

Owen, being Owen, cackles. "Fine, but please tell me we recorded that it's horse cum she's finger-banging herself with?"

Grinning, Wes stands, pulls his phone from his back pocket, and texts the group chat. As our phones go off, he says, "Every single fucking second of it."

A smile creeps on my face. We're one step closer to having what we need to ruin everything Samantha Davenport holds dear—her position as *"queen,"* her physical appearance, her public persona, and her quest for supremacy. I could add Wes to the list of things she'll lose, but the skank never had him.

Needless to say, the day her world crumbles, I'll be there to choke the life out of her and then piss on her wherever she lands with no remorse.

The downside to making Samantha think Wes fucked her is that it has made her more feral. Once she was done with her early morning flicking the bean session, she stormed out of the room in search of him. Unsuccessfully, of course.

We had security stationed outside her door, and when she tried to barrel up the stairs, she was lifted and deposited outside. She wouldn't be Samantha Davenport if she didn't make a scene. She screamed about her fiancée status and how she would have their heads once she informed her fiancés about their treatment of her.

Blistering text messages followed. All of which have gone unanswered.

"Explain to me again why you killed Blair Davenport?" Mr. Edgewood demands, forcing me to focus on the inquisition taking place.

I'd been asleep for maybe two hours before we were summoned by the Council. Once word of Blair's death reached them, our presence was required.

I'm actually surprised it took as long as it did.

"She needed to pay. Blair Davenport was one of the many catalysts for the clusterfuck we're in now," Owen declares.

Mr. Edgewood levels Owen with an icy glare. "That wasn't your fucking decision to make," he growls, slamming his palms against the table.

Owen meets his gaze, and without any fear, he rebuts, "You're welcome for cleaning up another one of this council's many fuck ups. Fuck ups so monumental that the Novus Ordo Seclorum made a personal visit."

The shades of red Wes's father turns in the span of ten seconds has to be a world record. Mr. Edgewood works his jaw, the muscles flexing before he responds. "All the more reason to stop going off half-cocked. Edgewood—the Fraternitas are under immense scrutiny. Any more *fuck ups*, as you've so nicely mentioned, and this entire town, Ariah included, will be eliminated."

"What the fuck do you mean, Ariah included?" I snap.

"I'm glad we finally have your attention," Mr. Edgewood hisses before continuing. "The Novus Ordo Seclorum is unforgiving and unyielding. They rule with an iron fist and will wipe out anything and anyone that presents as a problem. They are the *big bad* in the world. Nothing happens without their approval."

I stew on his words, remembering the warning levied when they visited.

Did we just make things worse?

"I see you're registering the severity of the situation," my father chimes. "You all need to tread carefully moving forward."

"We need to get this back in order now. We can't afford another visit before the Tribunal. Do you all understand what I'm saying?" Mr. Edgewood snarls.

One by one, we each agree.

"Good. Now, tell us what you learned from your meeting with Blair," Wes's father commands.

30
ARIAH

"Again," Reign commands, and I strike the bag in rapid succession. Chop to the throat, elbow to the stomach, and fist to the groin.

We are in the final circuit of today's training session, and I want to throat-chop Reign for making me do this at all. I'm hot and feel extra swollen today. My back hurts, and one of the babies has decided they should tap dance on my spine.

"I know where you sleep at night," I warn, and he chuckles. "Sleep with one eye open."

Reign's laughter grows. "Come on, Ry, we're almost done. If you were back in Colorado with your other trainer, you wouldn't make a peep. Now, combos."

Groaning, I shake out my legs, straighten my posture, and get into the neutral position, facing the punching bag. At Reign's command, I shift into a fighting position. My wrapped hands are up, protecting my face as I slightly bend my knees, evenly dispersing my weight on the balls of my feet. I quickly move through my first and second sets. . . right hook, left hook, and front kick.

I'm drinking water during my rest period when Elias walks in. "We should test your training against a person. A bag doesn't hit back, and there may come a time when you'll have to defend yourself. An assailant won't care that you're pregnant. In fact, that will probably make them bolder."

"Are you stepping in the ring then?" I challenge, pulling my curved daggers from their sheaths.

"Not if I actually want to keep my head," he quips and glances over his shoulder as Thomas walks in.

Thomas's massive frame eats up the doorway. "Means you're smarter than you look, Prescott," he quips.

I watch as he clears the threshold and enters the gym. I smile as he approaches. I'm so grateful to have him. I missed him, not because he's back to protect me, but because he's family. "It's been too long, T," I complain, sheathing my knives before hugging him.

A warm smile appears on his golden, tanned face. "I wasn't gone that long, Ariah, and I've been back."

Pulling from his embrace, I poke his muscular chest, and there must be a steel plate underneath because my finger hurts more than my poke. "You know what I mean, T."

Thomas nods. "I missed you too, Ariah. I'm glad to be back. I wish it were under better circumstances."

"Me too," I add before turning to grab my water. My head starts to spin as I approach the bench. Spots dance before me. My eyes blur in and out of focus. I make it another two steps. My legs turn to jelly, and I stumble, reaching out and praying I catch the wall, but the distance is still too great. The room begins swirling around me. *I'm going to faint.*

"Ariah!"

I hear someone shout, but I'm underwater. I lose my balance, pitching forward. . . my *babies.* Mustering my last bit of strength, I twist my body and prepare to fall. But as my legs give way, strong arms catch me before I hit the floor.

My name on someone's lips is the last thing I hear.

●

"She will need to keep her stress to a minimum and scale back on her training for the remainder of her pregnancy. Her body is working to nourish two babies. I need you all to take that into account."

"But, she's okay?"

I slowly come to, blinking into focus the people in the room. Familiar voices key me in on who's here.

"What else can we do to help, Dr. Jaffri?"

That's Dad, and obviously, he's speaking to my doctor. Thomas is at the foot of my bed, and Reign is hovering to my left.

"Make sure she stays hydrated, eating nutritional meals, and as I said before, reduce her stress," Dr. Jaffri explains.

I didn't think I was overdoing it. However, asking me to reduce my stress under current conditions is like asking Samantha not to be cunt. It's a math equation that no one can compute.

"Ry." I slowly turn at the sound of my grandfather's voice. "Hey there, Sweetheart. How are you feeling?" he asks, and everyone's attention zeros in on me.

Dad rushes to my side. "Ry! You scared ten years off my life."

I snort, "Way to be dramatic, Dad."

Dr. Jaffri comes over and shoos everyone away. "I need to do another check of her vitals and speak to my patient. Out with all of you."

"I'm not leaving," Dad declares as everyone else files out.

Thomas winks before closing the door, and I return my attention to the mini showdown.

Dr. Jaffri's eyes narrow. "You will if that's what she wants."

My gaze volleys between them. Dad's nostrils flare as my doctor crosses her arms.

What do we have here?

"Back to your designated corners," I joke, grinning at the sparks between them before continuing, "It's fine. He can stay."

"Very well," Dr. Jaffri concedes, breaking their stare off to grab a blood pressure cuff. She wraps my arm, starting the machine.

I hate these stupid things. They always hurt.

At the sound of the beep, Dr. Jaffri tsks. "Lower than before but still too high."

My eyes widen at the number. One-forty-five over ninety-five. Maybe I do need to relax more.

Sighing, I massage my temples. There's so much that needs to be done. I still need to change how the Fraternitas works or overthrow it altogether. As daunting a task as it'll be, it pales in comparison to finding a way to co-parent with any of the Heirs. That shit feels insurmountable.

"Breathe," Dad whispers, clasping my hand. "We'll find a way."

I look into his matching gray eyes and see the determination in them. He reads me like a book. "I'm so tired, Dad," I whimper through stuttered breaths.

My dad lifts his hand to my face, thumbing away my errant tears. Then he leans forward, pressing his forehead to mine. "We're asking too much of you, Ry. We'll find another way," he promises, sitting back. But even as he says the words, I know there isn't another way. Not after the meeting I had the other day. It's me, or Edgewood will be wiped out.

Inhaling, I center myself, calming my racing heart and slowing my scattered thoughts before I speak. "I can do this. I just. . . I just needed a moment."

"You'll need more than a moment," Dr. Jaffri scolds, reminding us she's in the room. "You're on bed rest for the next three days, and if your blood pressure isn't back within normal range by my next visit, it will be extended to two weeks."

My eyes bulge at the thought of being bedridden for two weeks. "But—"

"Don't you 'but' me. Rest. Whatever war you're waging will have to wait until Thursday," she commands.

The rebuff is on the tip of my tongue before I swallow it down. She's right. A few days' rest to ensure the babies' health and, most importantly, my own is warranted.

Arching a brow, Dr. Jaffri waits for my acknowledgment of her orders.

I nod. "I understand. I won't do anything but rest until our appointment on Thursday."

Satisfied with my answer, she replies, "Good. Now, continue to stay hydrated, take your multivitamins, get lots of rest, and eat. You'll be back to taking over the world soon enough."

My dad grabs my hand. "I love you, Ry."

I smile. "I love you too, Dad."

He gently squeezes my hand as he leans in to kiss my forehead. "I'm going to walk Dr. Jaffri out, and then I'll bring you some dinner."

Humming my agreement, I watch as they both leave the room. Before the door fully closes, my eyelids get heavy, and the idea of resting becomes increasingly appealing.

I'll take over the world next week.

31
WES

"Yes, I'm sure. I want three dozen—a dozen white lilies, a dozen red magnolias, and a dozen lewisia flowers. And instead of baby's breath, use the wild carrot flowers, the white ones."

I pace the length of my room as I finish instructing my personal shopper. "Yes, the carrot onesie. The one that says, 'I don't carrot at all.' Two of them."

Once I heard Ariah was put on bed rest due to stress, I punched a hole in the wall outside the lecture hall. It was made even worse by Samantha's gloating. It took Lev and Sebastian to pull me off her. I would've choked the life out of the skank otherwise. I didn't care who saw me, but luckily, there wasn't anyone in the hallway at the time.

After that, I stormed out of the building and ran all the way back to the house. Once I calmed down, I got on the phone with Julie, our personal shopper.

If we can't be there in person, we'll be there in spirit—with the help of a few gifts.

"What was that?" I ask, sitting on my bed before I wear a hole in the floor. My knee bounces as she reads everything off the list, confirming she hasn't missed anything. "That's right. A charm bracelet with each of the fruits I've mentioned," I confirm.

My room door opens. Lev steps inside and closes the door behind him. "Is that Julie?" He mouths, and I nod. "Tell her to add carrot cake cheesecake, no nuts or raisins, and red velvet cupcakes with cream cheese frosting."

I relay his request to Julie. "No, don't put who it's from. Just do it like we've done the last few times. We don't need the credit. We just want to make sure she's cared for."

Lev walks across the room and then sits at my desk as I finalize the last of our purchases before ending the call.

"Any updates?" I inquire. I stormed out of the building before I heard the full report. There wasn't a chance I could remain there with my fuse as short as it was.

"Owen almost sliced Sam's throat open when she refused to leave. Then Wyatt basically dragged her outside when she threatened to set off Owen's chip because we aren't treating her like fiancés should."

My lips thin. "She's pushing us. I almost think she's trying to goad us into activating the damn thing."

Lev shrugs. "It's that, or she really gets off on us manhandling her."

"It's the manhandling," we both say simultaneously.

I snort, "It's definitely more that. She's the definition of a masochist."

"The problem is that Samantha's also a sadist," Lev states.

Standing, I shake my head. "No, I don't think so. She yearns to be degraded, even more so when pain is inflicted. Outside of sex, she's a power-hungry opportunist cunt."

Lev pauses, assessing my words. "So, you don't think it's you she's after? She's been obsessed with you for years."

"No. She thinks she wants me, but it's the power I represent that she truly wants. I'm an Edgewood. My family name is everywhere, and my father is the head of the Council. Samantha knows attaching herself to me would open more doors than she's ever dreamed of."

I leave Lev to stew. The more I examine Samantha's behavior, the more I see I'm not who she wants. I'm what she needs to get what she wants. The unfortunate part for her is that I don't want her, and the Bradfords are the true power. Ariah's return stalled her plans. She still had the Selection to work things in her favor. However, we all fell in love with Ariah, and that fucked her in the ass with no lube. It's why she resorted to trying to get rid of Ariah, and when that didn't work, she helped orchestrate Owen's kidnapping for the second time.

"I never thought of it that way. Sam's been so in your face about wanting you. I thought you were her endgame, and the power would be a bonus," Lev explains.

It's what everyone thought, including myself. "You weren't alone. We all did. I didn't start examining Sam's true motives until we found out how much she was doing."

Walking over to my window, I peer out at the setting sun—frustrated that yet another day has ended and Ariah's still out of reach. I know we're on the cusp of turning things around, but that doesn't help me now, especially after hearing she's not well. Each slight against her feels like our doing, and I hate it—I hate myself for my part in it. I'll do everything in my power to ensure she doesn't go through her entire pregnancy thinking we abandoned her for a lecherous leech.

My door opens for a second time, and Owen and Wyatt enter. "Are you sure we can't replace her saline implants with cement and throw her in the pool?" Owen inquires, crossing his arms and leaning against the wall near my bathroom.

"No," Sebastian replies, stepping inside and closing the door. "At least not yet."

I rub the bridge of my nose, attempting to hold back my snicker at the imagery. Wyatt makes no such attempt. His raucous cackle fills the room.

"That's how she has to die. Promise me that's how she dies. Someone, please tell me we can make that happen," Wyatt begs, and I lose my fight—we all do.

The whole room bursts into peels of laughter.

"Can you see it? Her tits would become an anchor," Owen coughs, catching his breath.

"She'd be tits up because her tits weighed her down," Sebastian jests.

This is almost as funny as what happened at the party over the weekend, but I'm not sure anything will ever pass that. Wiping the tears from the corner of my eyes, I refocus the conversation. "How is she?"

The room quickly quiets. "She's resting. Her dad let me in to see for myself, but he wouldn't let me stay," Wyatt answers.

I clench my fists. My nostrils flare as I grind my teeth. I'm so over this whole thing. "Where is Teagan on the chip?" I growl.

Reaching into his pocket, Lev pulls out his phone. "Seventy percent there."

My shoulders slump. We're closer, but we're still not there yet.

"We still have to play this like Senator Baker and Samantha are in control, but their time's almost up," Sebastian declares. "The night at Le Toucher is step one in their ultimate downfall."

I shake off my sullenness at his words and hope they ring true. Our girl inches closer to her due date each day, and we need to be there to support her through it.

32
OWEN

"You can suit up, Jefferson, but you need another week before you can take the field," Charlie states as he directs me to follow his hand. Then he tips his head, signaling he's finished.

Huffing, I hop down from the exam table. "You said that last week."

"Well, considering it was only a couple of months ago that you had swelling in your brain, cracked ribs, and a concussion, I'd say erring on the side of caution makes the best sense," he replies.

I want to argue, but I know he's right. I was really hoping to get time on the field today. Football isn't life to me like it is to Lev, but I enjoy being on the field with my brothers. It's been too long since I've been able to do that.

"Still benched?" Wes asks once I enter the locker room.

"Yup," I grumble, reaching into my locker and grabbing my jersey.

Wyatt claps my shoulder and squeezes. "Now you can keep an eye on our girl. A little birdie told me she's coming tonight since she's off bed rest."

I perk up at that news. My angel will be here. The wheels in my head are already churning.

"Just don't get caught," Wyatt leans in to whisper, and I smirk.

He can always read me like a book. One look, and he knows I'm plotting a way to get Ariah alone. It's not a want—it's a must-have.

"I won't," I promise, then pull my jersey over my head and leave the padding behind, opting to wear my jeans. If I can't play, it doesn't make sense to suit up completely, especially not for what I have planned.

I'm putting my pads back into my locker when the coach calls for everyone's attention. I'm only half listening to the pep talk. Something about winning the game to continue Lincoln-Wood Univeristy's undefeated streak against one of our division rivals and making the alums proud.

He shouts for us to bring it in, and at this point, I'm just going through the motions—one step closer to who I want—*my angel*.

I run with the team through the tunnel, nearly gagging at the sight of the witch cheering with her squad. Samantha would be okay if she weren't such a selfish, evil hag. She could be easy on the eyes or a ten for someone. Not us, but someone out there. Her brother, for instance.

"What has you grinning from ear to ear?" Lev inquires as he searches the stands.

Ignoring his question, I join him. It doesn't take long for me to spot her. "Found her."

Lev follows my gaze. "There she is," he sighs, as lost as I am in her beauty.

She's glowing. The color has returned to her face—Ariah's in the box seats with her father, Shay, and Shay's parents. Tobias Bradford is absent for obvious reasons. Only a select few know he's back in Edgewood.

"Do you think she's warm enough," I mumble, elbowing Lev to look away. Samantha and her trolls are watching, and the last thing we need is for her to throw a temper tantrum on the field. It's already suspicious that she hasn't pitched a fit over her mother's death.

Wes and Wyatt approach as Lev responds, "Yeah. I'd say she's warm enough between her sweater and the wool blanket Shay just pulled out."

"I wonder if she's wearing her new charm bracelet," Wes ponders out loud.

If I plan this right, I'll get to see for myself and report back.

"Time for the team huddle," Coach Briar barks, and the guys run it in. When I don't move, he shouts, "Jefferson, get your boney half-broken ass over here."

Grumbling, I jog over in time to hear our initial strategies depending on which way the coin toss goes. The defensive coach is still speaking when the ref blows his whistle. Our captain, who also is our quarterback, runs onto the field. The ref announces the rules for the coin toss before flipping the coin, and since Eastland University is the away team, they get to call it.

"Tails," their captain yells as the ref catches the coin.

"Heads, Lincoln-Wood gets it," the ref booms, and our quarterback decides to defer the kickoff, setting us up to receive the ball during the second half. Then, the game begins.

I watch the game but keep a steady eye on Ariah, hoping for a moment to strike. We're halfway through quarter one, and neither team has any points on the board. EU has the ball and is third and one at the sixty-yard line.

The ball is snapped, and before their quarterback can get in position to see who's open, our defensive tackle is on him, and as Eastland University's quarterback falls to the ground, the ball pops out. Both teams scramble for it. EU—hoping to recover it, and LWU—hoping to capitalize off the fumble.

Wes scoops up the ball and shoots up the field, dodging offensive players. He's nearly clipped at EU's ten-yard line, but Wes spins, hopping over the player who is diving for his legs before running it in.

Cheers erupt across the stadium, but I barely hear them. My focus is lasered in on my angel. She's out of her seat, whooping and shouting, and I make a mental note to tell Wes. The dick needs some cheering up—we all do. But Wes is taking the brunt of it. He agreed to be the one who was cold while we got to act indifferent. And while we all will owe her recompense, Wes will have to prove none of what he's said was true.

Ariah leans over, whispering something in one of the marked-for-death bodyguard's ears. I think that's Fernando or Nando, whatever the fuck he's called. He nods and follows her out of their box.

Peering over to the cheer squad, I notice Samantha's eyes glued on Wes's ass. She's practically foaming at the mouth. My guess is she's picturing the "sex" they had at the party. I'm almost giddy, picturing the horror that will mar her face when she discovers the truth. Her shock might even elicit an actual reaction from her usually frozen features. I use her distraction to sneak out of the stadium.

I'm halfway up the third flight of stairs when Thomas comes into view. "What are you doing up here?" he asks, arching a jet-black brow in my direction. "Aren't you supposed to be on the field?"

"Still on the injury list," I reply.

His chin dips in understanding. "So, you're not playing. That doesn't explain why you're on this floor."

I swallow my retort. If I have any hope of getting past Thomas to Ariah, I'll have to play nice. "I just need to see her, T. I've been trying for weeks to get her alone, just once," I plead.

"You know you're treading on dangerous grounds, right? You have a device in your arm that could be set off at any given time," he explains.

My nostrils flare at the reminder, but my determination is renewed when I remember it's homecoming. "If Samantha did anything here, her existence would be wiped from history. Today is the perfect day to push the envelope."

Thomas glares down at me for another second before turning to speak into his earpiece. "You've got ten minutes. By halftime, you need to be back on the field like you never left, and if she refuses to speak to you, you're out."

"Got it," I readily agree, darting past him up the final set of stairs.

The best part of how this stadium is constructed is that each family suite has complete privacy—no shared hallways or bathrooms. So the only person I see is Fernando, and he shoulder-checks me. "What's your problem?" I snap.

"Rich, asshole pricks like you," he retorts.

"Says the rich prick to the other rich prick. I think you're projecting, but none of that currently matters. Move out of my way, or I'll slice you a new airway."

Chuckling, he says, "You think you scare me, Pretty Boy?"

"You've underestimated me if I don't, and that's an error on your part. One I'll happily rectify after I see my girl. Now move the fuck out of my way." I spit through clenched teeth. My hand is already wrapped around Lizzie.

"Escucha, cabrón, no me asustas," he shoots off in rapid Spanish, thinking I won't understand. "I'm letting you through because it's an order, but if you hurt her, your little knives won't save you from me, comprende?"

My lip curls. "Yeah, I got you, *Asshole*."

Fernando steps out of my way, but he mumbles, "Pinche malditos idiotas niños ricos y sus estuoidos pendejos cuchillos." Then, I pull open the door to the bathroom.

I slide Lizzie back into her holster and run my thumb along Lola's handle.

"Nando, I'll be out in a minute."

Closing my eyes, I bask in the melodic sound of her voice, and for the first time in months, I truly breathe.

The stall door opens, but she remains frozen in place until I hear her gasp. "Owen."

Ariah's mouth hangs open, but the words are stuck in my throat. I can't believe she's here, and I'm in touching distance with nothing and no one keeping us apart.

I let my feet move since my mouth won't work. I don't stop walking until I'm standing toe-to-toe with her. Watery silver eyes peer up at me, and I lift my hand to cup her cheek, finally finding my voice.

"Angel."

33
ARIAH

I lean into his touch, one I thought I'd never feel again. I refuse to make any sudden movements in case this is all in my head. I want to live here forever.

A tear escapes at the sound of him saying my name, the one only he calls me... *Angel*. It plays on repeat, a skipping soundtrack I never intend to fix.

"Don't cry, Angel," he murmurs, wiping the rivulets of tears now flowing freely down my face. "Don't cry," Owen repeats.

I suck in a lungful of air at the brush of his lips against my skin. Owen clasps my neck, bringing his forehead to mine. "You're... you're really here," I stutter, lifting my head.

"Home," he growls, pressing his mouth against mine, and I'm lost. All thought and reason vanish as our tongues dance.

I allow myself to bask in the feel of him a moment longer before I push him away. "What are you doing here?" I demand, praying my voice doesn't betray me. "Shouldn't you be down on the field watching your friends play and your *fiancée* cheer?"

Owen winces, hurt and anger burning in his hazel eyes. "She's not my anything," he snaps, running his fingers through his unkempt hair.

"What the hell do you mean?"

He sighs, rubbing the back of his neck. "I can't explain—"

I snort, interrupting him. "Oh, let me guess. You can't tell me, and I have to trust you?" I cross my arms and continue. "Well, that 'I can't tell you, but you have to trust me' bullshit line is getting old. It should be the town slogan. 'Welcome to Edgewood, where lies run rampant and promises are never followed through.'"

"Ariah, please, " Owen pleads, but I will not be deterred.

"No."

"Angel," he mutters. This time more in warning.

I know I'm pushing him. I know from seeing him over the last couple of months he's struggling, and I shouldn't goad him, but I still don't take heed.

"You need to get the fuck out of here and go return to the bitch you all chose to marry. Me and my babies will be just fine without you—"

Owen crosses the room, startling me with his swiftness before I finish my sentence. His fingers sink into my hair, tugging gently until I peer into his eyes. "*Our* babies."

My breath hitches at the feel of cool metal on my heated skin. Chills shoot down my spine straight between my legs as he slowly rests the blade against my thrumming pulse.

I want to be angry at myself for being turned on, but the sensation triggers memories of when Owen's knife touched my skin. I have to fight back the moan, trapping it in my throat.

"I can feel you, Angel—see the lust and excitement in your eyes. Lola and I have missed you."

Lola.

I weep at the mention of the knife that will only ever be mine, then blink away all its sentiments. He's probably given Samantha a blade of her own or, worse, used Lola on *her.*

"Bet you say the same thing to her," I snap.

"The only thing I'd ever want to feel is her blood pumping from her body after I've gutted her for what—" His lips thin, and I watch as Owen seems to fight with himself in real-time.

I scrunch my nose in confusion. *Why the hell would he want to gut his fiancée?*

He flexes his jaw, showcasing the sharp set of his cheekbones before he speaks again. "It will all make sense soon. I promise, Angel. But I didn't come in here to discuss *Samantha!*" He says her name like a curse, further perplexing me. "I came to see you," he growls before the sharp tip glides down into the crook of my neck, nicking my skin and drawing blood.

My hiss morphs into a moan when Owen's mouth replaces his knife. The thudding in my chest multiplies as he sucks the flesh between his teeth, making my nipples pucker and my knees go weak.

Owen releases his grip on my hair and wraps his hand around my waist, preventing my fall.

I should be pushing him away. He's no longer mine. But some part of me knows they'll always be mine.

Except they're not. They didn't choose you!

"No, this isn't right," I mumble, sobered by my intrusive thoughts.

My protests are met with a nip of teeth and a hand slipping between us into my leggings. Owen expertly works his fingers into my panties and begins rubbing slow circles against my clit.

I groan, making one last attempt to find the willpower to push him away, but when two fingers sink into my pussy, I grip his muscular forearm and tug him closer.

Unlatching from my neck, Owen's mouth crashes down on mine, and I moan at the taste of him. The sound urges him on. One hand fists my hair while the other spears in and out of me.

"M-more," I gasp, riding his finger already on the precipice of release.

No further words are exchanged. Owen walks me backward toward the couch in the lounge area, only pausing long enough to pull my leggings and boyshorts off.

I squeal when he hoists me in the air, forcing me to wrap my thighs around his waist. Then he kneels, lowering me until my ass rests on the top of the couch.

Owen lifts my legs over his shoulders, positioning his mouth at my entrance. I claw at the material of the sofa when his heated breath puffs against the spread lips of my pussy.

"So fucking wet and perfect," Owen groans before his tongue swipes the length of me. My head lolls back when his lips latch around my clit.

"Shit. . ." I try to find words. It's been so long.

Rolling my hips, I grind against his stubbled jaw, matching his pace. He volleys between sucking my clit and thrusting his tongue in and out of me until my juices run down my thighs, and I'm begging him never to stop.

He grumbles something, but it's incoherent, and I don't care to figure it out, too lost in the way he devours me like he'll never get enough.

My back braces against the wall as Owen's hand moves between my legs, sliding his middle and index fingers inside me. I clench around the two digits as he hums his approval. I hear something about wishing I was squeezing his cock as my hips buck from the vibration.

Owen pushes his ring finger into my puckered hole, then pistons in and out of both holes at a relentless pace. Each thrust tugs me closer to the edge.

His tongue swirls around my clit, sucking until my back bows. Then he nips the bundle of nerves, and a scream rips from my mouth. The oxygen drains from my brain, spots dance in my vision, and my body jerks as I catapult over the cliff into one of the most intense orgasms I've ever experienced.

I'm not sure when his fingers slip from inside me or when he places me on the couch. My body still twitches with aftershocks when his lips press against my rounded belly. "I can't wait to meet you both. I'm the crazy dad," he murmurs. His warm breath tickles my skin, and I'm frozen for the second time since he appeared in the bathroom.

Tears run down my face at the love in his tone. I choke back a sob, but he knows. I prepare to sit up and shove him away for daring to make me feel this way, knowing they broke my heart.

A loud bang sounds at the door. "Time's up, fucker. Get out, or I'm coming in." I recognize Fernando's voice.

Owen curses, then helps me up. Once I'm standing, he grabs my leggings from their spot, and I blush, aware of my disheveled state.

He's assisting me when there's another knock. "Let's go," Fernando shouts.

"I'm going to chop his hands off if he pounds on that door again," Owen mumbles.

My nails dig into my palms as I try not to worry about what just happened and what it all means.

"Don't," Owen pleads, and before I can ask, he lowers his mouth to mine.

Then he's gone, and I'm uncertain of everything.

●

"You were gone for a very long time. I didn't know pregnancy meant having fifteen-plus-minute bathroom breaks," Shay teases. I know my cheeks are red with embarrassment when she giggles. "Your secret is safe with me."

"I don't know what you're talking about."

She smirks. "Tell that to your backward leggings."

My gaze drops, and sure enough, the small logo in the top left corner of my pants is no longer present. "For fuck's sake," I groan, pulling my sweater down to cover the evidence.

"Which one was it?" she starts. "Wait, don't tell me. Let me guess." She pauses, pretending to think when she already knows the answer.

I roll my eyes. "Cut your shit. You already know who."

"But it's so much fun watching you squirm," she teases.

We're walking toward the SUV. The game is over. LWU kicked ass, and I'm ready for a well-deserved nap.

"I know he fucked me so good. They both did." The all-too-familiar nasally whine carries across the lot.

"You had sex with both of them?" one of the cheerleaders squeals.

Samantha's icy glare meets mine. "Yes, Wyatt and Wes at the party they threw last week. I have the pictures to prove it."

My gut roils. Wes, I could believe. His vile words still play on repeat. Wyatt. . . My heart hurts.

"She's probably lying," Shay states, rubbing my back.

Shaking my head, I reply, "She's theirs. It makes sense they would."

Another part of me dies, and with it goes all the hope I felt after my encounter with Owen earlier.

Samantha grins, knowing she struck a blow. She can claim today's battle, but I intend to win the war.

I climb into the back of the Suburban. Thomas is at the wheel. Reigns sits in the passenger seat while Fernando and Elias are in the back with Shay and me. My dad left, promising to stop by the house tomorrow.

Peering out the window, I state, "Take me home. I suddenly need a shower."

34
WES

"You guys coming to the party?" Jonas, our cornerback, questions, wrapping a towel around his waist before he grabs his shit to shower with.

I mull over his question as I dry off. We're still riding the high of our win. If we keep this up, we'll clinch the top seed in the playoffs.

Running my hands through my damp hair, I reply, "Nah. Not tonight, man."

"Aww, come on, Wes," Jonas groans, and my jaw ticks in annoyance. "It's been a while since we've seen the Edgewood Heirs live up to the reputation that precedes you guys."

My hand stills. *Why is he pushing this?* "We just threw a party."

Jonas shrugs, leaning against the locker. "You were three men down and barely laughed, much less partied. Then you and Wyatt disappeared with your sexy-as-fuck fiancée." My eyes narrow to slits at the mention of the soul sucker. "Sorry, man. I didn't mean any offense. I'd be territorial, too," he exclaims, misreading my change in mood as his eyes widen in fear.

The question is, do I let him think his assumptions are correct? It would serve our bottom line. We need everything to go as planned, and I'm sure Jonas will run his mouth to someone who will spread the word until it eventually gets back to Samantha.

"It's in your best interest to move the fuck on," I growl as I put on my LWU t-shirt and matching gray sweats, choosing a vague enough response to elicit my desired reaction.

Straightening, Jonas's gaze flits from side to side before he clears his throat. "But you'll all be at that Groveton after-party for sure, right?" he asks, shifting the conversation back to what he assumes is a safer topic.

It works because I completely forgot about it. The annual GC versus LWU game is two weeks away. Which only gives us three weeks to deactivate Owen's chip. Not to mention, Ariah's more than halfway through her pregnancy, and we've already missed too much time. I refuse to let her go longer than necessary without us by her side. She won't be in the delivery room alone. So, the big rager Groveton is hosting this year is nowhere on my list of priorities.

What if it's too late and she doesn't forgive us?

I scoff at that thought. Like I'd ever give her that choice. An endless reel of every slight we've caused her plays in front of my eyes. Every time we've hurt her since I made the unilateral decision to save Owen and choose Samantha. The anguish in her stormy gray eyes haunts me. But it's the fire that replaced the hurt that terrifies me the most. It was the same look she had the first day of school—the one that eviscerates anything in her path. The same one that slammed her head into my nose when I dragged her into the janitor's closet and then made me work to earn her forgiveness once I realized my colossal fuck up.

"Wes," Jonas shouts, pulling me from my spiral. "You good? I was calling you for at least a minute."

"Yeah, man. I'll catch you at practice on Monday," I state, pulling my hoodie over my head and grabbing my duffle bag. I need to get the fuck out of here. The locker room walls feel like they're closing in on me.

I pass Lev, Wyatt, and Owen on my way out. "I'll be by Rubi," I mutter, then quickly exit, not waiting for their responses.

A cool fall breeze hits my face as soon as I step outside. I sneer.

Another fucking reminder of how much time has passed and what little we have left.

"Wesley." My eyes close at the sound of Samantha's voice. "Wait," she commands. I ignore her, doubling my pace, hoping to get to the car before she can corner me. Her claws dig into my skin. "I said wait," she hisses.

Turning, I glare down at where she grips my arm before I hear giggles. *Of course, she's not alone.* Exhaling, I fight my instincts to recoil at the feel of her touch, then school my features. "What can I do for you, Samantha?"

She whips her head around. "Leave," she barks, and her new fan club scrambles out of sight. Once they clear, Samantha swivels her neck to face me. "Why the fuck did Owen leave the game?" she seethes, and it takes everything in me not to snap at her like I usually would.

Sticking to the plan, I force my shoulders to relax and smother my mounting frustration before I say, "What are you talking about?"

Samantha studies me. The slight twitch of her nose is the only indication that she's confused by my reaction. "Owen left the stadium. Where did he go?"

My head begins to throb. I know exactly what she's referring to. Owen dipped for a long-ass time, and when he returned, he looked like someone who finally got their fix. He went to see Ariah, and he accomplished whatever he set out to do. I try not to let my anger at him for putting her at risk show. "Maybe he went for a walk." My answer sounds unbelievable, even to my ears.

Crossing her arms, Samantha sneers. Her face blooms red as her inflated lips thin. I'm impressed they don't burst. "I'm not a fucking idiot, Wesley. I know he went to see the gutter trash." I remain still, displaying none of my rage at her name-calling. Her inky eyebrow arches. She can't figure out the game I'm playing. "Just tell your asshole friend who seemingly has a death wish, that the next time he tempts fate, I'll call his bluff," she huffs, storming away.

"Fuck," I exclaim, rubbing my hand against my stubbled chin as I stride toward the car. It's not long before I hear them approach.

Lev says something I can't hear from where I'm standing, but Wyatt cackles, and his laugh is identifiable from space.

Owen unlocks the Jeep as they make their final approach. "What's got your face scrunched in disgust like Samantha's landfill snatch is before you, and you have no choice but to eat it?" he jokes, and I shudder at the thought of ever having to see her pussy again.

"Where the hell did you disappear to?" I ask Owen, tossing my bag in the back of Rubi. He's all teeth as he passes me, then opens his door without answering. "Are you just going to pretend you don't hear me?" I growl, hopping in the backseat.

Wyatt snickers next to me as Owen starts the jeep. "I feel like you're being purposefully daft, Wes. You can't smell our girl on him?"

"We all fucking agreed," I snap. "You're putting her in harm's way for your own selfish reasons." Grinding my teeth, I try to get my anger under control. "I know this has been—*is* hard. Staying away from Ariah is like flaying your skin with a butter knife. And even when you think you snuck one by Samantha, you haven't. I just had to deal with a very pissed-off banshee threatening to end you."

Owen's whips around. His jaw muscles flex. "I needed to see her," he argues.

"No. You wanted to see her," I retort, not breaking my stare. We haven't been this careful for him to go rogue and fuck our carefully laid plans to waste. Hurt replaces the rage in his eyes before they close, and the rebuke I was prepared to deliver dies.

"Wes's right, O. You can't take that chance. Not with Ariah's life. None of us can," Wyatt sighs from the front seat. He looks bone tired, and not just from the grueling game we just finished playing. The overall weight of the situation is wearing on him. "Samantha has made it well known she's tracking our every move."

"This is all my fault," Owen chokes. "I should never have gone out alone that night. She begged me not to, and I didn't listen." He leans back against the headrest, staring at the car's roof. "I told her I'd be safe. Instead, I got myself taken, forcing you to break her heart."

His confession catches me by surprise. "We've all fucked up.

Each one of us has a hand in this," Wyatt states, and I hum my agreement. "I could list our transgressions, but what will that accomplish?"

"We need to stay on track. The pendulum is swinging back in our favor. We need to get through Le Toucher, then we'll have more leverage. Teagan is in the last stages of writing the code to deactivate the chip in your arm. Once that happens, there's no holding back. We can destroy Samantha Davenport and her brother," Lev explains.

Owen turns, staring out his window into the darkness. Another moment passes before he nods his agreement, then sits up and starts the car.

I rub my brow, feeling like a dick because I know he'd never intentionally endanger Ariah, but Samantha is looking for any excuse to mete out any punishments. Especially those that will hurt Ariah. So, until we're ahead of this, we all need to steer clear.

35
ARIAH

I watch as Owen sails another throwing knife through the air, and it lands dead center. "Bullseye," I shout, throwing my arms in the air like a cheerleader.

Owen turns, pulling me into his chiseled chest. "Mmm, the sound of you cheering, your delectable ass bouncing." He hums while lowering his hand to grip said ass, "is making my dick hard, Angel." Chills run down the length of my spine, causing me to squirm.

The evidence of his arousal pushes into my stomach, and like a wanton she-wolf in heat, I roll my hips. The action presses his shaft against my pussy, creating friction and stimulating my clit.

"Will you two cut it out? Unless you're letting me join in," Wyatt teases.

"Do we have to?" I groan, rolling my hips again. The feeling is too fucking great to stop now. I don't think I could if I wanted to.

Wyatt smirks, leaning over and pinching my erect nipple. "Unless you want your dad to come out here and see you. I'm not sure seeing his baby girl riding her boyfriend's dick is on his bingo card this year, or any year for that matter," he chuckles, and like a bucket of ice water was dumped over my heated skin, my lust cools.

"You should've led with that," I mutter, punching his shoulder.

Wyatt feigns hurt, clutching his arm. "You wound me. Now kiss me, and make it better."

"Isn't it kiss it and make it better?" Owen grumbles, adjusting his very hard cock in his jeans. I bite my lips, watching his movements. Noticing my attention on him, Owen squeezes his shaft, displaying his want for me. I'm tempted to drag him and Wyatt upstairs until I hear my brothers' giggles as they round the corner of the house.

"I swear those two have a LoJack on when one of us is about to make you come." I hear Wyatt snort under his breath. The memory of the time in the hallway at his father's house comes to mind, and I giggle.

My lips curl into a smile. "Come on, let's go see what everyone's up to," I say, pulling them both along. It isn't long before we're inside, where Dad and Jamie are waiting in the kitchen.

I fight to open my eyes, knowing I'm locked in a dream. Part of me wants to stay in this dreamscape where they were mine, while the other part is angry at the reminder of their trickery. My eyes flutter, fighting to wake, but I ultimately lose my battle as the Sandman tugs me back to his world.

"There you are," I exclaim, approaching Owen. His brows are furrowed, and his lips are thinned. He always looks so pensive until his gaze lands on me.

Owen's features smooth out, his shoulders loosening as his eyes light. He closes the distance between us, cupping my face in his hands. He presses his forehead to mine, then whispers, "I'm never too far behind you, Angel. Remember that if you ever try to run from me."

I snort, resting my hand over the "A" carved into his chest. "What if I like it when you chase me?" I taunt before pushing away from him and darting into the woods. "Catch me if you can," I exclaim without looking back.

Darting into the woods behind my house, I run, hoping to gain enough of a head start. Owen is fast, so outrunning him isn't an option, but outmaneuvering him is. I duck behind a bush when I hear him shout, "I'm coming for you."

Steadying my breaths, I wait for him to run past. He stops directly in front of my hiding place as if he can sense me. A rustling sound somewhere close by draws his attention. "Angel?" he shouts, and I have to fight not to giggle and give away my position. Dad would shake his head if I did. "No sudden movements, Ry. Be stiller than the air around you," he'd say. 'Be slyer than a fox and more observant than an owl.'

I wait until Owen's footsteps sound faint, indicating he's far enough away to take off safely. Strands of my midnight blue hair blow in my face, and I wish like hell for a hat or my hoodie to hide it under. In this lighting, my hair stands out like a beacon.

The giant red oak appears off in the distance. I'm almost to the clearing. In about another sixty or so yards, I'll be out of the copse of trees.

I'm nearly at the field when an idea hits me, and I duck behind a tree. Peeking around the trunk, I watch Owen continue in the wrong direction, then begin stalking my prey. Licking my lips, I relish how quickly the roles reverse. We're almost at the tree when I make my move, stepping on a few branches, ensuring he hears me, and then running.

"There you are," Owen's voice booms, and I squeal in excitement. This is more exhilarating than being chased. I hop over the outstretched roots of the oak tree into the clearing toward the hill and hear his feet hit the ground. He's close.

"Come and get me," I tease, knowing he won't be able to resist. I take three steps before he wraps his arms around me, turning so he takes the brunt of the fall. We roll over a few times before we finally come to a stop. I'm on top, my hands pinning his shoulders to the ground as I hover over him. Both our chests are heaving. "I like this game," I jest. "The hunter ends up being the hunted."

"I was always the one hunting you, Angel," he states confidently, attempting to grip my waist, but I force his hands over his head.

Ghosting my lips along his throat until I reach his ear. "Were you chasing me, or was I luring you?" I ask before licking the shell of his ear.

"Is that right," he murmurs, his hazel eyes heating as I lower my lips to his. The taste of him is magnified by the adrenaline pumping through my veins. Owen groans, freeing his arms from my feeble hold before trailing his fingers up my side.

He thinks this game is over, but it's only just begun. Nipping his bottom lip, I spring up and take off to the forest on the other side of the clearing.

"Oh, you better run, Angel, because the next time I catch you, you're mine," Owen exclaims.

I hear him drawing closer, the thud of his feet against the grass growing louder. But I don't dare turn back. That's how you sprain an ankle and get caught. I dart into the woods, hopping over rocks and ducking under low-hanging branches.

"Gotcha," Owen says, and I shriek as he lowers us to the ground. I didn't

even hear him approach. His face dons a lascivious smile as he now traps my arms over my head, pinning my wrists with his left hand. "Did you think you could ever escape me, Angel?" His other hand snakes under my shirt until he grasps my breast and squeezes, sending a jolt between my legs. My eyes close, and I squirm while he teases my nipple. I could come off this alone. Owen growls, and my eyes snap open to meet his gaze. Darkness flashes in Owen's eyes. Something I would've missed if my eyes weren't glued to his. "There isn't a stone I'd leave unturned, an ocean I wouldn't run dry, or an afterlife I wouldn't traverse to get you."

I peer into his lust-filled, tormented eyes, feeling the magnitude of his words as Owen strips himself bare. His vulnerability is raw, striking me in my heart. "O—," I begin, but he silences me with a brutal kiss, conveying the truth to his declaration with his lips.

Lost to the fire burning inside me, I don't come up for air until he slams inside me. "Fuck. You're always so ready for me, Angel. Squeezing my cock as only you can," he confesses, powering into me. "I'm going to take you fast and hard. No interruptions this time." My hips roll up, meeting each one of his thrusts. My pussy stretches around him as each snap of his hips pushes him deeper.

Owen grabs my throat, using it to control my pace. I throw my head back. "I'm so close," I whimper.

"Not fucking yet," he commands, releasing my neck and pulling out of me long enough to flip me onto my knees. Then he grips my hair, yanking me into a bowed position and latching onto the pulse point at the base of my throat.

Owen's pace doubles as he bites down on my neck, pinching my nipples. I scream, clenching around him, but his pace is relentless. It's not long before I'm careening over the edge. Moments later, Owen's thrusts become jerky, and he pulls out of me, turning me around to face him. I watch as he rips the condom off and fists his dick. "Stick out your tongue," he orders, and I quickly oblige. Our gazes lock just as warm jets of cum land on my tongue and across my face. "Don't swallow."

Leaning forward, he wipes his cum from one side of my face before covering his mouth with mine. As our tongues dance around his cum, Owen lowers his hand between my legs and swirls circles on my still-swollen clit. Closing my eyes, I throw my head back with a moan, and some of his nut trails down my chin.

"Please," I breathe, my chest heaving. "More," I beg, and he rolls my clit between his fingers.

Gripping my hair, Owen pulls my head back, licking the trail of cum up my throat and kissing me while he pinches my clit. Heat pools in my stomach as he rubs me through release. I begin to shake, tremors racking my body when he brings his mouth to my ear. "One day in the distant future, I'm going to fuck our baby into you. I'll fill you with so much cum that you have no choice but to have multiples. I won't stop until there are little versions of the both of us on this Earth."

The idea of him or any of my guys trying to impregnate feels so primal. I hope they all know that's off in the very, far from now, distant future.

My chest heaves as I come down from my orgasm, seeing Owen's attention locked on me. "Owen, I l—"

I startle awake, groaning as my fingers plunge in and out of me while my thumb works my clit. "What the fuck, Ry," I mumble, yanking my fingers away. This is the third time I've woken up with my hands between my legs since my lapse in judgment in the football stadium bathroom. "You really need to stop this shit," I chastise myself. I know I'm extra horny because of the pregnancy, but I need my body to understand there are no dicks available to help us with that problem.

Picking my phone up, I check the time. "Holy shit, it's three o'clock." I sigh, then check my messages. There's one from Shay.

> ROD BESTIE
>
> Wake your ass up. We need to get ready to take your brothers out trick-or-treating tonight, ho. Guh wash yuh ass. See you at 4 PM.

Groaning, I roll from my body pillow, placing my feet on the floor, then push myself off the bed to stand. "Shower, brush my teeth, and get dressed," I mutter, heading for the bathroom.

"I still don't know how I feel about that one," Shay confesses.

Turning, I follow her gaze. "Oh yeah, Conner. He's not the most jovial, but he does his job well. So he stays for now," I state.

Shay studies him a moment longer before shifting her attention back to the boys. "The twins look so freaking adorable," she whispers low enough so only I can hear. The first time she mentioned them looking cute, they scowled and said they were scary monsters. I had to hide my smile behind my hand and fake cough to cover up my laugh.

They're both dressed in black denim jeans and a black hoodie and are wearing glowing purge masks. I should be alarmed that they wanted to go as masked murderers that pillage parts of the U.S., hunting for their next victims, but they look too damn cute.

Security follows as they run to the door of the next house while Shay and I stand on the sidewalk at the end of the driveway. "Those two are a trip," Elias states.

"That's putting it lightly," Fernando adds. "Remember the first two weeks with them in Colorado?"

I snort, "Just a little initiation."

"Initiation? Those two tricksters hid hard-boiled eggs in the back of my closet. The stench took weeks to disappear," Reign grumbles.

Shay doubles over in laughter. Her lioness tail pops up as she's bent over. "Chuh, I wish I was there. I can only imagine what they put unnuh through." As she stands back up, you see the full extent of her bomb-ass costume. Her dreads double as her mane, and the tan jumpsuit is backless, showing off the lioness tattoo that covers her entire back.

I'm dressed as a skeleton. My face is painted along my jawline up to my nose, and I'm in a black jumpsuit with two skeleton babies on my growing stomach. "It was amazing. I can't tell you how many times these three were pushed into the pool," I snicker, not bothering to try and cover up my amusement.

The twins charge down the sidewalk like chaos in human form.

"Ry, look," Kellan and Kylan shout, shifting my attention to them. "They gave us Halloween Lego sets," Kylan exclaims as they both hold up their boxes.

"That's amazing! Put them in your bags so you don't lose them," I instruct, turning to Shay and mouthing, 'Seriously?'

She giggles. "Welcome to Edgewood."

Rolling my eyes, we continue around the neighborhood. We're on our last two houses on this street when five imposing forms stand, blocking the sidewalk. It doesn't take a rocket scientist to know who they are.

I groan, looking over at Shay. "Are they really here?"

"Unfortunately," she mumbles.

Wyatt is dressed as Heath Ledger's Joker. Very fitting. All their costumes are. Sebastian is some Disney prince. Wes is the Hulk. *Oh, his might be the most accurate.* Lev's Sherlock Holmes, and Owen is dressed as Tate Langdon from *American Horror Story*. Of course, he's also in a skeleton costume as well.

As they walk nearer, Reign, Elias, and Fernando stand in front of Shay and me. Conner and the rest of the twins' guards do the same.

"Fancy meeting you—" Owen's words are cut off as Kellan and Kylan run around their guards, and I quickly follow behind them. I'm just not fast enough to stop either of them.

Kellan punches Wes in the nuts. "You guys were mean to our sister," Kel shouts over Wes's grunt of pain.

"She was so sad because of you, assholes," Ky adds, elbowing Sebastian in the stomach.

"I almost forgot how protective you two are of your sister," Sebastian gasps.

Kylan heads for Lev, preparing to kick him. "Ky, stop," I command, and he turns.

"But they—" Kylan begins, but I hold my hand to my lips. Their guards corral them away from the Heirs.

"They aren't worth the trouble," I state, meeting each of their eyes before turning and walking away.

As I'm nearly back to where Shay stands smirking, I swear I

hear one of them murmur, "Just a little while longer, and you'll be ours again."

Whirling back around to call bullshit, they're already almost out of sight. *It was your brain tricking you. They don't want you. It would be best if you stopped having hope.* I massage the space between my brows. "Let's finish up and go home," I say, annoyed that they ruined what was such an amazing night.

"Don't," Reign commands, making me look in his direction.

"What?" I ask.

Gripping my shoulder, Reign replies, "Don't let them steal your joy. Tonight was fun. They don't get to change that."

"He's right," Shay chimes in. "Those idiots do not deserve a second thought. Not to mention, your brothers are some kickass protectors."

"Yeah, we are," Kellan and Kylan shout in unison, making me laugh.

Smiling, I agree, "You two most definitely are. I'd be lost without you." Then I grab their hands. "Let's go to the next house."

36
SEBASTIAN

"You understand the plan for tonight?" I ask as we pull into the parking garage at Le Toucher. Since the club is closed for Senator Baker and his guests, the only cars here belong to the staff working tonight.

Owen puts the car into park, grabs his mask, and slides it on so it sits on his head before he peers over his shoulder. He, Wes, and Wyatt have a more hands-on role in tonight's festivities. "Yeah, Bash. We get to wreak havoc and cause mayhem once the President's daughter is taken. Why is Matthieu interested in Isabella anyway?" Owen inquires, shutting off the ignition.

It's a loaded question. One I don't have all the answers to. But I know enough that Bella will learn time doesn't make the heart grow fonder. Instead, it hardens stronger than graphene. "Childhood acquaintance," I mutter, opening the passenger door.

"Right, that's why you have King here," Wyatt snorts, and he isn't wrong. King's presence is a neon sign that it's far from business as usual.

"Just remember what you're supposed to do and be in your correct spots. Even a second late, and this all goes to shit," I retort. Wyatt snickers at my obvious direction change.

I scan the black aluminum keycard, gaining entry to the private elevator. We're entering Le Toucher through the tunnel entrance. So, instead of heading upstairs, we're going down. We stop on the first level, and the control panel lights up. I move to stand in front of it, leaning forward for the retinal scan. We descend two more floors before the panel opens, and I'm directed to place the tip of my index finger on it, palm side up. "Fuck," I grit at the prick of my finger. It's not that it hurt so much as it surprised me.

"Good Evening, Sebastian Blake Grant. Mr. Devereux is waiting to greet you. Please proceed to the entryway and have your second access card prepared," the computerized voice instructs.

"Well, aren't we fancy," Wes mumbles, turning to Lev. "I'm sure you'll have something like this installed in the next month."

Lev arches a brow but doesn't lift his head from his phone. "Ordered and scheduled for delivery in two weeks," he says, finally looking up from the screen once the elevator door slides open.

Exiting the elevator, I pull the second card from my breast pocket as we approach the club's lower-level door. I quickly scan and enter the code Matthieu provided me the last time I was in his office. Seconds later, the lock disengages, granting us entry.

"Good. You made it," Matthieu states.

My nose scrunches. "Did you think we'd back out?"

He's shaking his head before he replies, "No. We've all got far too much to lose for that to be the case."

I'm tempted to ask why he asked the question when another door opens, and King walks through with ten men.

Matthieu lifts his arm, turning his wrist to check the time. "Perfect. We're ahead of schedule."

"Devereux, my team's ready. Just point us in the direction you need us, and they'll get set up," King says. His thick Russian accent is still prevalent even all these years later. He's Lev's contact, but I've had my fair share of encounters with the rightful Pahkan of the Volkov Bratva.

The two trade brief salutations before Matthieu relays his instructions. "Senator Baker will arrive in thirty minutes. They will spend twenty minutes being provided with the rules for the night before heading to their cocktail hour. Then the game they've requested to play commences thirty minutes after that." Matthieu adjusts his cuff links and continues, "You received the picture of Isabella?"

"Dah, only an idiot wouldn't know who the first daughter is, but yes, my men know who to grab," King responds.

Matthieu nods. "It's imperative she's taken before the red lights flash, signaling the start of the second round of the game. She can't be part of what happens next."

"Understood," King replies, then fires off instructions to his men in rapid Russian. I only understand every third or fourth word, but it's enough to know that if they fuck up, their heads will no longer be attached to their necks. Once they have their marching orders, they disappear down the hall with Michel, Matthieu's head of security.

Wyatt tilts his head to whisper in my ear. "Still think he eats the souls of his enemies," he jokes.

I smirk. "And bathes in their blood."

King's gaze focuses in our direction. "Good to see you again, Levi," he declares.

"Likewise, Wolf," Lev says, gripping his forearm. The two of them exchange pleasantries in Russian. "Any progress with your uncle?"

The muscles in his jaw flex at the mention of the man who slaughtered his entire family. "Plans are progressing. My contact has discovered that my uncle has a girlfriend—*Reina*," he spits her name like a curse as he steps back. I'm curious to know what she's done to earn his ire.

Grinning, Lev quips, "Fun times ahead, then?"

A cruel smile curls onto King's face as they drop their hands. "What better way to announce the end of my uncle's reign than to take what he covets the most? Then send her back as puzzle pieces."

There should be a rebuke—a suggestion to spare her life. But there are no saints here—just monsters who'll do whatever it takes to get what they want.

King scratches his beard. His cold eyes survey the rest of us.

"Ah, the infamous Heirs. It's good to have you all in one place finally," he pauses, walking over to where we stand. "Though I hoped it'd be under better circumstances when we met."

"What could be better than a night of blood and terror?" Owen quips.

A genuine look of admiration lines King's face. "Ah, Owen. Always a pleasure to be in the company of someone whose thirst for blood nearly rivals mine."

Dipping his chin, Owen replies, "Hopefully, one day, in the near future, we can make a game out of it—perhaps the person who collects the most blood."

"Oh, count me in," Wyatt interjects, and we all follow suit. There's not a snowball's chance in hell any of us would miss out on an opportunity to slaughter our enemies and win bragging rights.

A throat clears, drawing our attention to Matthieu. "It's time for everyone to get into position. Senator Baker has arrived, and he's brought along five more people."

"How was he able to get them in without us knowing?" I inquire.

"The Senator called an hour before you arrived requesting to have guests added to his list. I was ready to refuse when I found out they're currently members," Matthieu explains.

Lev already has his phone out, his fingers flying across the screen, adjusting for unknown new players. "How many new guests are there?" he mutters, obviously annoyed with the last-minute additions.

"Five," is all Matthieu states. He's being purposely obtuse, only answering questions he's being asked instead of providing us with everything he knows.

Sighing, I check my watch. We have twenty minutes before tonight's festivities to begin. "Well, don't keep us in the dark. Who are they?"

The slight twitch of his right eye is the only indicator he doesn't appreciate my pushing the issue. However, he knows we can't afford to go in blind. We all stand in silence, waiting for answers. He huffs, then finally says, "The Council."

37
LEV

"What the fuck is the Council doing here?" Wes seethes, pacing the length of the room. "Have they been in on this all along?"

I don't bother to stop him from processing the bomb Matthieu dropped before insisting we follow him to the area we'll have as our headquarters for the night. Time is ticking away as we follow behind him, but the stench of betrayal coats the large surveillance room—barely allowing us enough air to breathe.

As Wes continues to wear a hole in the floor, Wyatt, Owen, and Sebastian stand behind me, watching the Council mingle amongst known enemies. "I might believe our fathers are behind this, but there's absolutely no fucking way Aaron Bradford would do this to Ariah," Owen mutters.

"How well do we know him to assume that?" Sebastian retorts, lifting his hand to list his thoughts. "The man was forced into hiding for decades, his spot as the rightful leader of the Fraternitas was given away, and his family was torn apart." Looking at Owen, he arches his blond brow. "Should I continue because I can do this for days?"

He isn't lying. Aaron has lost a lot, and, in many aspects, he's still being forced to sacrifice more of himself and his family. That alone is reason enough to jump ship."

"You can count your fingers as much as you want to, Bash. It won't change the fact that Aaron Bradford would sooner gut himself like a fish before he sold out any of his kids," Owen snaps back, clenching his jaw as his ears redden.

Wes stills. "Owen has a point. At no point in time has Aaron given any cause for suspicion."

"That could make him the perfect Judas," I offer, and Wyatt snorts. "What, you don't think it's possible?"

"You all need to be more rational. I'm usually the one with wild accusations," Wes states, finally giving up his pacing and sitting down.

I grimace. There's nothing rational about anything that's happened in the last year. Maybe not even in the last few centuries. If someone were to examine how and why the Fraternitas was established, they'd think it was out of some conspiracy-theory-suspense novel.

"It's perfectly reasonable to believe the Council could conspire with the enemy. They could easily think it's the best way to continue to keep power," Sebastian suggests.

Before anyone can respond, Matthieu appears on screen, entering the room and greeting Senator Baker and his guests. "Senator. It's good to have you back." He pauses, swiveling his head. "And with guests this time."

Stepping forward, Wes's father extends his hand. "Matthieu. It's been a long time."

"Donald." Matthieu nods, doing the same. "Always a pleasure."

They shake hands before someone lets out an exaggerated sigh. "Can we get on with this shit? I came here to fuck and kill, not sit around," Brian shouts, drawing the attention of everyone in the room.

"What the hell do you mean kill?" *Isabella.* The president's daughter wasn't entirely in the loop. Her crystal-blue eyes, ringed with gray, stand out against her porcelain skin and wavy raven hair that falls past her shoulders. Matthieu's gaze is fixed on her, but she looks everywhere but at him. His jaw momentarily clenches before his features smooth out. The calm exterior that he's known for carefully sliding back into place

Senator Baker's nostrils flare at his outburst. "Please forgive Mr. Porter. He seems to have left his manners at home this evening." Brian's face reddens at the apparent slight.

"Trouble in paradise," Wyatt snorts, and I hum in agreement. This night just got a little more interesting.

"It appears so. We might be able to use that to our advantage," I murmur.

Matthieu strides toward the bar before he speaks. "Tonight, you will all experience the highest heights one can attain through pleasure and pain." He turns, extending his arm toward the doorway as Henri and Amélie enter.

"Fuck. He's gorgeous," Samantha groans. Her eyes trail over Henri's tall, broad frame with lust, and he smirks. Samantha squirms in her seat, pressing her legs together.

"Isn't that the woman from the Chosen ceremony?" Wes questions, shifting my attention to Amélie. She looks about the same height, but that's where all the similarities end.

I shake my head. "Didn't she have black hair and blue eyes? Plus, her facial structure is different."

Leaning, Wes studies Amélie. "There's something about the smile, but I guess you're right."

Once they both reach the front, Matthieu continues, "The rules are simple—there are none. You have full reign of the facilities. The game will begin in fifteen minutes, and your targets for the night will be released." He takes a final look at Isabella before he says, "Happy hunting," and exits the room.

"What did the fuckwit mean by kill?" Isabella demands, storming over to stand in front of Senator Baker.

An oily, slimy grin, eerily similar to his half-sister's, appears on the Senator's face. "He means, dear, sweet Bella," he lifts a knuckle to her face, but she steps back, only making the Senator chuckle. "He means tonight we'll be hunting and fucking whomever we catch, and after we're satisfied, we can do whatever our heart's desire to them."

"I didn't sign up to kill anyone, Matthew. Let me the fuck out of here," Isabella sneers.

Throwing her head back, Samantha laughs. "Of course, you'd be too freaking soft for this shit. I told you not to invite her, Matthew. You should've listened." Her gaze lands on Aaron. "Much like your daughter—too fucking soft."

Aaron's eye twitches, barely enough to be noticeable, but he remains silent. It's Wes's father who speaks, "Is this why you invited us here?"

"I was hoping we could come to some sort of agreement, seeing as how we have you by the proverbial, and after tonight, maybe literal, balls," Senator Baker singsongs.

My face scrunches in disgust. "Stupid, arrogant fucker."

Donald's eyes glint with amusement. "Is that so?" Senator Baker's smile falters. His earlier confidence slips. It's apparent he's not used to dealing with Donald Edgewood—a lesson he'll soon wish he'd learned before slinging threats. Wes's father peers up at the camera and says, "Devereux, we're leaving." The door slides open, and then each member of the Council exits, ignoring the demands of the Senator to stay.

"I told you there was no way they could be involved," Owen gloats.

"I'm leaving," Isabella hisses, stalking toward the entrance, but nothing happens. "I said. Let. Me. The fuck. Out of here," she demands, whirling around.

At her words, the Senator's earlier smugness returns. "No one else leaves before the sun rises. Survive the night if you want out," he spits, yanking her head back as he settles behind her. His hand glides up her torso, then squeezes her breast until she screams in pain. "Your Daddy should've taken my offer to run as Vice President. Let's see how serious he takes me when I send him a video of you being fucked stupid."

The door to the surveillance room opens, and Matthieu walks

back in and freezes at the sight of Isabella in the Senator's clutches. "Are you sure we can't kill them now?" he growls.

"Brian and the other two senators, sure. Samantha and Baker—not until we get the chip deactivated," I explain, swiveling in my chair to face them.

Inhaling, Matthieu collects himself before pressing the intercom. "The game hasn't begun. I suggest you let her go unless you want this night to end very differently, Senator Baker," he commands—his French lilt more prominent as he tries to control his anger.

The Senator snarls at the reprimand, tugging harder on Isabella's roots before he shoves her away and stomps to the bar to demand a drink. I glance down at my watch. *Ten minutes.* "O, Wes, and Wy, you all should get going to be in position," I instruct, turning away from the monitors.

A smile forms on Owen's face. His hazel eyes blaze with the promise of retribution. "Porter is mine."

●

Sebastian sits to my right as we watch the carnage before us. There might be some sympathy for the slain and those still left if they weren't traitors.

"Do you think they realize they're killing their own people?" Sebastian laughs, entertained by one of the Senators slitting the throat of one of his men, unknowingly. He stands proudly over the masked man he killed, too focused to realize a true hunter stealthily moves behind him. Much like a doe in a field, he isn't aware until it's too late. Amélie's knife slams into the back of his neck with such force that it pierces his cervical vertebrae, poking through his Adam's apple until the sharp tip, coated in the man's blood, is visible from his throat.

Never taking my eyes from the lethal assassin, I ask, "Is she always like this?"

"From all the stories I've heard, yes. This is my first time actually seeing her or Henri in person. I've only ever seen footage of their work."

Amélie pulls the blade from his throat and watches as he drops lifelessly to the ground. She says something in French before spitting in the dead Senator's face. "What did she say?" I inquire, wishing I'd learned French alongside the five other languages I speak fluently.

"Pigs deserve to be gutted," Sebastian replies, and I quirk a brow.

"Indeed they do," I mumble, switching screens.

Henri has Samantha tied and kneeling as he fucks her face. Not ready to lose my dinner, I bring up another screen. Senator Baker and Brian are screwing a girl in a bunny mask. The gag in her mouth muffles her screams. "On three," Matthew orders. Seconds later, they pull from her and spray their load on her face.

"Where are the guys? Bring them up," Sebastian requests.

I bring up three feeds. Owen is waiting in the room next to Brian and Senator Baker. Wyatt is chasing Isabella toward King and his men. When Wes appears on screen, he's holding a bat. His arm rears back before he swings forward into the head of the other Senator, knocking him off the man he's thrusting into. Teeth fly, and blood sprays as Senator Wheelan shrieks in pain. That's when I get a better look at the other guy.

"Holy shit, was Troy fucking a corpse?"

"Doubt it matters now since he's one himself," I joke.

Massaging his forehead, Sebastian tries but fails to remain serious. "Bring up Wyatt again."

When he reappears on the monitor, Wyatt is still methodically forcing Isabella to head exactly where we need her to be to accomplish this part of the plan. "Leave me the hell alone. Do you know who the fuck my dad is?" she spits, yelling over her shoulder. Isabella tossed her stilettos before she left the lounge area. Now, she is running barefoot in one of those shiny jumpsuits that make her look like Catwoman or a Domme.

"Where's the fun in that, Isabella?" Wyatt taunts her in his Ghostface mask. "I'd run faster unless you want your night to end here." Wyatt watches her double her speed and take off down the corridor. He pauses, giving her more time to get away. Once she disappears, Wyatt turns, lifts his mask, and winks at the camera.

"Remind me to smack him in the back of the head later," I mumble, rolling my eyes as I delete all traces of his identity from the servers. "Idiot never remembers the rules when he's in character like this."

Switching angles, the feed changes—the cameras follow each forced turn Isabella makes. "Isabella. Come on, I only want to tell you a secret," Wyatt teases—his distorted voice echoes off the walls. Mascara-filled tears stream in rivulets down her flustered face. I snap a picture and then text it to Matthieu. I'm sure he'll use this later. As much as he claims this is for revenge, I've seen the way he drank her in. He'll use this to jerk off to, I'm sure.

"We're ready. Is Operation Fledgling still a go?" King verifies.

Matthieu's voice comes over the comms. "Get her out of there. Baker is looking for her, and he's closing in quickly."

"Wy. Hang back. Isabella is about to find the door leading to King. We need you to hold off Senator Baker," I command.

"My fucking pleasure," he growls.

Baker turns down the hallway where Wyatt is goading Isabella. He lifts his hand and stares down at his watch. "Where the hell is she going?" he mutters before making a left.

"He's got a tracking chip in her somewhere," Sebastian announces.

"Not a problem," King replies.

Isabella stops short of slamming into the wall. She spins until her gaze lands on the door. Licking her lips, she bends over, trying to catch her breath. "Where the hell are you, you stupid cunt?" Senator Baker barks. He's a turn away from Wyatt, but he is so loud that Isabella shoots up. Her back is ramrod straight as she surveys the area around her.

"You can do this, Izzy." She hesitates before slowly inching forward.

"I hope you've enjoyed yourself so far, Isabella, because it will be the last time you'll ever experience it," the Senator croons, grabbing his dick through his pants.

My eyes volley between screens, watching in rapt attention as Senator Baker finally reaches Wyatt, and Isabella urges herself to find the courage to move.

"You've stopped moving, Bella. I'm going to enjoy fucking your sweet pussy as I slice you open," Baker shouts as he passes Wyatt. He takes two steps before Wyatt springs forward, wrapping his arm around the Senator's throat.

Wyatt locks in his hold, gripping his forearm to apply more pressure. Then he steps back, using the Senator's flailing as leverage. Baker scratches at the padding on Wyatt's shirt.

"Let me fucking go." Isabella's screams pull my attention to the monitor where King is placing a black bag over her head. Isabella fights, her arms swinging wildly, but it's too late. King bites the cap off a syringe and effortlessly pushes it into her neck. Seconds later, she falls limp in his hold.

My attention reverts to the monitor Wyatt's on in time to witness the last of the Senator's struggle. "Night night, bitch," Wyatt snaps, releasing him to drop with a thud to the floor. Wyatt wastes no time lifting his leg and stomping on Baker's still very erect dick. Then he leans over and grips the unconscious fucker by his hair. "Your reign is about to end," Wyatt seethes, rearing back and punching Senator Baker in the face.

"That's enough," I order. "We can't kill him, Wy."

Snarling, Wyatt stands and kicks Baker in the face, and blood erupts from his nose. The Senator grunts but doesn't move. Wyatt lifts his gaze to the camera. "There, I didn't kill him," he snaps before storming off.

I scan all the feeds to determine what we should watch next. Sebastian taps my arm, then points to the monitor to our right. My pupils double in size at what I see. "Holy fucking shit."

38
OWEN

"Do you know who the fuck I am?" Brian barks for the millionth time as I secure the last lock, chaining him to the wall. I want to cut out his larynx so he'll finally shut the fuck up. "Your boss was paid handsomely to let us kill and fuck whoever we caught," he continues to yammer on. Ignoring him, I secure the last lock, tugging the metal link, ensuring there's no chance of escape unless I let him out. "You're a dead man when I get free from this. I'm going to chop your balls off and make you eat them."

Stepping back, I tilt my head, studying Brian. I wonder if he's realized he has no power in the situation. He chose the wrong side.

"This club will be ash, and you'll be my bitch once Senator Baker hears of this," he mutters, and I cross my arms, listening as Brian rambles on about the horrible fate that awaits me once he's free.

Brian's empty threats feed my need for revenge. He has no idea it's me, and I relish that fact. Hidden behind the powder-white goaltender mask—a tribute to one of the all-time great horror movie characters—I watch Brian squirm against his bindings. His gaze darts around the room until it connects with the wall to my left.

"This isn't how this is supposed to work," he stutters. His irises double in size as he fights harder to break free from the metal cuffs holding him in place.

Leaning my head back, I inhale the scent of his fear. "You're finally paying attention," I snort, lowering my gaze to meet his eyes—confident the voice modulator hides my identity. The veins in his neck bulge, straining against his pale skin to the point I swear I can see the thudding of his pulse triple from my spot in front of him.

I'm not sure if it's the wall of terror, as I call it, filled with an almost endless supply of toys and tools meant to elicit the screams of their victims or my voice that terrifies him.

"Who the fuck are you?" he bellows, throwing some bass into his tone, but it does nothing to mask the tremble of his limbs or the hitch in his breath.

Ignoring his question, I turn and stride toward the wall.

"Don't you hear me talking to you, asshole?"

My brow arches beneath the mask, almost impressed by Brian's bravado. Though I'm quite sure it'll be replaced with trepidation soon enough.

I spot my weapon of choice before I come to a complete stop. Reaching up, I grab the Pear of Anguish from its glass enclosure on the fifth row of cherry-wood shelves. My eyes light as I peer down at the deceptively innocent device that will produce the desired effect—*immense pain*. The pewter contraption feels cold in my palm. Its pear shape is undoubtedly the reason for its name. Personally, I would've gone with Petals of Pain instead because it resembles a flower in bloom once cranked open. There's something poetic about something of perceived beauty being used to garner screams. *Pain is beautiful.*

As I turn to head back, something glints in the lights in the room, capturing my attention. A slow smile crests my face. An onyx-handled titanium machete sits across two hooks. The nearly two-foot blade is one Jason himself would be in awe of. It's almost as if fate wants me to have it.

Who am I to deny fate?

Lifting the machete from its spot, I study the blade, appreciating the bladesmithing before heading toward a terrified Brian. "Wh-wh-what are you going to do with those?" he croaks, widening his eyes in terror.

Placing the machete on the table, I retort, "Don't worry. You'll find out soon enough."

Brian glares—his nostrils flare, eating away at some of his fear. "Enough of this bullshit. I want out. Red," he shouts, and I cackle.

"There are no safe words here. This isn't a BDSM experience. I'm not your Dom—you don't get to tap out. Ever," I seethe, closing the distance between us. Brian freezes, his eyes doubling in size with each step I take.

Yes, you stupid shit, feed me all your fear.

Standing at his right side, I pull Lizzie from the brown leather holster secured around the waist of my dark blue jumpsuit. "You're fucking done when I say you are," I snap, slicing along his ribcage. "And before this is over, you won't know if living is worth it."

A scream rips from Brian's mouth as I dig into his side, burrowing a hole big enough for the device. "P-please," he begs. "I don't know who you are or who paid you to double-cross the Senator, but I know he'll triple it for my safe return."

My hand stills. "Are you really this stupid? Let me guess, you also thought you were brought here for all your good deeds?"

Gritting his teeth, he snarls, "You're dead."

"Do you seriously have *no* idea who could've orchestrated this? I thought you were the brains behind it all—big man on top," I spit.

Another shriek of agony fills the room, and I almost wish this was the aphrodisiac it used to be. "Those fucking Heirs and they're dumb sl—," Brian gasps, unable to finish his sentence as I slam the pear-shaped device into his side.

"Didn't your daddy ever teach you to know when you're outgunned so you don't say stupid shit," I tsk. I'm eager to remove the mask so he can see who holds his existence in their hand, but I still need answers—ones I know Brian would sooner go to an early grave than confess.

"Matthew will quadruple whatever they're paying you," he groans once the air returns to his lungs.

"Will he? Let's test your theory, shall we," I taunt, twisting the device so it expands. Then I bop my head to the beat of his screams as I pull out my phone and dial.

"What do you want? I'm busy hunting. Unless you're calling to confirm you've dealt with that shit-stain weasel, Porter, I don't want to—." The line goes dead.

Brian gawps, his mouth opening and closing like a fish out of the water before he furrows his brows, narrowing his gaze on me. Determination sets back in. "That wasn't him. You're lying! He wouldn't abandon me after everything I've done for them. What game are you playing?" he confidently states, and he's right to be. While that was the Senator's voice, it wasn't him speaking, but he didn't need to know any of that.

Rolling my eyes, I sneer. "Enough wasting time with your frivolous pleas. Senator Baker can't save you." I crank the handle, twisting until I feel resistance. "Why did the Senator really want to come tonight?"

Brian yells, his eyes scrunching close, and his teeth snap together as he tries to ease the pain, but there is no easing it. His betrayal has earned him endless pain. Sneering, I twist the handle again, and he bellows, "To kill the President's daughter and the two other Senators for their scheming against him!"

"Now we're getting somewhere," I state, happy for the answer but pissed I have to start with the questions the Fraternitas are eager for. All I want to do is kill the slimy Judas and know how to rid ourselves of the desperate, brother-fucking wankstain, Samantha Davenport. "Why does Baker want Isabella dead?" I ask, cranking the handle two more times.

Brian sucks in a lungful of air before his breaths steady. "I'm not telling you shit."

"Wrong answer," I snarl, turning the device once more. Drool runs down the sides of his face, but I can tell he's not ready to budge. I'm not sure if I'm annoyed or elated by his refusal to cooperate. I need to get answers so I can be done with him, but I also want to make him suffer more than I did at his hands this summer.

"Fuck you," Brain says, then spits. I don't move, allowing spittle to fly through the air and land on my mask. My top lip curls as some of his saliva hits my face through the holes.

Reaching around, I grab the machete and wildly swing, giving no thought to where it will actually land. "You really can't seem to get it through your thick skull, can you, Brian?" I growl as the blade connects with his thigh, easily cutting through flesh, muscles, and tendons. His shrill cries echo off the walls. "You're a dead man. How slow your death is—that's up to you."

"He wants the President to have to leave the campaign trail to mourn the loss of his daughter while also dealing with the media fallout from where she was found dead," Brain explains between staccato breaths.

"And the two Senators?" I question, yanking the blade from his leg. Brian's teeth clench before he throws his head back and yelps. I'm almost tempted to use his ugly face like a piñata and the machete as the stick.

I'm preparing to swing the blade again when his gaze meets mine. "They were going to release information." He huffs, then continues, "They'd switched sides. . . decided they didn't like where they would fall. Didn't have enough power. They planned to inform the President in hopes of currying favor."

I made a mental note to tell Lev to look into the Senators, but I'm sure he'll study the footage from this room in minute detail. "Who else has control over the chip in Owen's arm?" I demand, feeling like a pompous ass for speaking in the third person.

Brian's pupils double in size. "H-how did you know about that?"

My brows scrunch in confusion. "What do you mean?"

"Only those in the innermost circle of Senator Baker and the Fraternitas know about that. Which means," he trails off, lowering his head momentarily before snapping it back up. "Which one of the fuckhead Heirs are you?"

"And here I thought you were a complete dunce." Seeing no reason to hide my identity, I lift the mask so it sits on the top of my head and turn off the voice modulator. As he takes me in, the color leeches from Brain's face when he realizes who is questioning him.

His jaw drops open. "No. . . no. . . no. You're not allowed to do this."

"Surprise, motherfucker," I smirk, then sail the blade through the air and connect with his other side. "Now, answer my fucking questions, or the next shot will be your head."

"Please stop. I'm sorry, man. I was doing what I was told. I'll tell you anything. Whatever you want—their plans. The names of the traitors that are still in the Fraternitas ranks. Anything. Please. I'm begging you."

"Who else controls the chip in my arm?"

Hanging his head in defeat, Brian sighs. "Senator Baker and Samantha. If anything happens to either of them, an alert goes to the device, then you and whoever is in a one-mile radius go boom."

"Can we just take them?"

"No, they're biometrical. So only they can disarm the chip. And as you already know, if you kill them, you die. If you remove the devices, you die. If you piss either of them off enough—"

Clenching my fist, I cut Brian off. "I die. I got it."

"Wrap this up. He doesn't know anything else important," Lev instructs in my ear. I knew the fucker would be watching.

Huffing, I yank the blade from his thigh and unscrew the device from his side. Brian sags in relief until he looks up. I watch as it sinks in. The moment he finally understands. He's not getting out of here. This is where his actions will be meted out. Death is the only thing coming for him, and I'm the reaper that will deliver his soul straight to hell.

"You're a coward, and your thirst for power led you here," I growl, rearing my arm back. I slam the Pear of Anguish in his eye and crank the handle five times before he can blink. Brian wails, his body convulsing from shock, and I watch as the spot that used to house his right eye caves in. Not satisfied because he's still bleeding, I two-fist the machete and swing, connecting with his throat until its progress is stopped by bone. But it's enough to end his cries.

I don't bother to admire my work. Sliding my mask back in place, I turn on the modulator and exit the room. There's still more hunting to do.

39
WYATT

We all remain quiet as the elevator descends to the SCIF on the sublevel of the Fraternitas. We had barely finished our debrief with Matthieu when our phones went off in unison. The Council was summoning us.

"You know they're going to want an explanation," Wes mutters, breaking the uncomfortable silence.

If this were any other time, I would make a witty retort. Who am I kidding? Gasping in faux shock, I say, "Where would we be without your deductive reasoning skills?"

Everyone laughs. "Shut up, asshole. I'm just saying maybe we should've talked more on the drive over," Wes states.

"I think we're set for what needs to be discussed," Sebastian announces, then peers around the elevator, saying more with his eyes than his words. *Don't reveal more than what's necessary.*

The door slides open, and we file out only to be greeted by every member of the Council. My gaze immediately zeros on Ariah's father. Aaron Bradford's composure appears calm and collected, but his eyes burn with fury. An older man who looks like Aaron in twenty more years and another Bradford family member stands beside him.

"Glad to see you boys have decided to grace us with your presence," Donald Edgewood mocks. The set of his jaw is so much like his son's when they're annoyed.

Sebastian elbows Owen as Lev elbows me. Owen and I look at each other and smirk while rolling our eyes.

"You know the routine. Lock your shit away, go through the scanner, and enter the SCIF. We're limited for time, and there's a lot that must be discussed," Mr. Edgewood instructs.

It takes about thirty minutes for each of us to go through the security protocol to enter the room. A screen is already being lowered as we take our seats. "I thought this was Council business?" Wes questions, staring at who I assume is Ariah's grandfather and possibly her uncle, which are shocking developments in and of themselves.

I only interacted with the guards and Aaron when I visited Ariah in Bronston. If I'm right, the Bradford line went from being extinct to having three generations of family members.

"We're asking the questions here," Wes's father barked.

"Yeah, that's no longer going to work for us," Wes snaps, meeting his father's glare in a challenge. "We're either equals at this table, or we walk."

Aww, our little Wes is growing a pair. I had to grip the arms of my chair to refrain from clapping. This showdown has been a long time coming. Mr. Edgewood spent years after Owen's kidnapping verbally abusing his son, and Wes always took it. The reasoning behind it didn't matter. It would take years for them to work things out if they ever did. But Wes needed to find his voice before any of that could happen.

"Excuse me?" Mr. Edgewood spit.

"We don't have time for this, Donald. My granddaughter's life was already at risk before the stunt these fuck-ups pulled tonight," Ariah's grandfather levels us with a glare before turning his vehemence on the Council. "If your fathers were alive, they'd be kicking your asses. What have you idiots been doing while I was in hiding, picking each other's noses? You're behaving like children instead of leaders."

I cough to cover up my snort. Tobias Bradford was not dead. Tonight's meeting just got more interesting.

"What do you mean?" Owen says, jumping from his seat. "How has what happened tonight put her in more danger?"

"Sit down," Sebastian commands. "We need to recognize that to keep Ariah safe, we need to work together. It's the only way we'll ever be able to get our girl back."

A smile curves on my face. *He's finally getting it.* I know Wes seems like he'd be the most difficult one to be on board, but it's actually Sebastian. Wes is a broody asshat, but he's like a giant teddy bear. He's been writing to her in his journal for months. Sebastian is jaded—his heart was ripped out and put through a shredder by Vivian. She fucked Sebastian's father and married his former best friend, and she still had the gall to try and win him back. I flex my jaw at the thought of the dead wench's name. Sebastian will have to open the vault that stores his heart before he gives Ariah the key to unlock the chains binding his love.

"Why don't we all calm down," Aaron says, gazing at everyone around the table. He pauses until Owen, Mr. Edgewood, and Ariah's grandfather sit down. "Now, what were you doing at Le Toucher tonight?"

Leaning forward, Sebastian rests his hands on the table. "We've been planning for tonight since summer."

Donald's face draws tight—his face flushes red. "Why are we only hearing about this now?" he mutters through clenched teeth.

"Because Ariah's life is at stake—*hers and our babies'*. The plan you've been employing is moving slower than a snail," I quip. "We refuse to be separated from Ariah or miss her pregnancy longer than we have to."

Aaron nods. "While I respect that, I won't have any of you playing chicken with my daughter's and future grandchildren's well-being. So, tell us what you've all been up to."

Wes meets each of our eyes, waiting for the confirmation we're on board. Once he has it, he replies, "First, tell us who this guy is."

Before anyone can answer, the man in question announces, "Liam Bradford. Ariah's uncle." The younger Bradford brother meets each of our stares with derision, obviously unimpressed with what he sees. "Now that we've gotten the pleasantries out of the way. Let's cut the bullshit and move on to topics that really matter—*Ariah*."

Satisfied with the answer, Wes says, "Okay." Then, for the next two hours, we divulge everything, from the meeting with Samantha's mother, which they were already aware of, to how close Teagan is to breaking the code to deactivate the chip in Owen's arm.

"When do you expect Teagan to have what she needs?" Mr. Jefferson inquires. I know he also is concerned with keeping Ariah safe, but I'm sure his son is his main priority.

Taking the lead, Lev explains, "We're hoping for any day now. We want to be free of Matthew Baker and his soul-sucking, vindictive half-sister, Samantha Davenport, before the engagement party."

I hum my agreement. "We don't want Ariah to believe we'd actually marry that delusional bitch."

"We've answered all of your questions. Now, explain how you knew about tonight and why you were there," Owen requests.

Sighing, Aaron answers, "We discovered Baker was going to Le Toucher with Samantha almost weekly to fuck freely," he begins, scrunching his nose in disgust, then continues. "While what they are doing is repulsive, it's inconsequential. We already have enough footage and evidence of those two to wipe their existence from the Earth once we free Owen."

"Okay, but what does that have to do with your appearance at Le Toucher, and how did you even know about tonight?" I challenge, growing annoyed with them skirting our questions.

My questions make Tobias smirk. "Did you forget Matthieu is part of the Fraternitas? Who do you think fronted the money for him to open the clubs?" Tobias's grin grows at the obvious shock on my face. "Le Toucher is more than a sex club—it's a full fantasy experience. It's also the easiest way to store information for future use."

The collective gasps from our side of the table as Ariah's grandfather demonstrates how the Fraternitas continues to wield its power.

"Okay, the Fraternitas is the great and powerful Oz," Owen jests. "Now, why were you there, and what does that have to do with Isabella?"

Wes's father's nostrils flare before he replies, "They wanted us dead. Tonight was a test run. If they could get away with murdering the President's daughter, they would employ the same tactic to kill us."

"That's a dumbass idea. If anything happens to you, we take over, and Ariah will have a seat at the table," Sebastian states.

Donald nods. "That's true. However, the expectation is that you'd be bound to Samantha, and they can use the power of the Fraternitas to guarantee Baker the presidency."

"Power-hungry dumb fucks," I mumble. I was long past tired of their shit.

"Yeah, I'd kill myself before I let that happen," Owen declares, standing and pacing the length of the room. He's trying to keep himself calm.

I rub the tension building between my auburn brows. They picked the wrong Heir to kidnap and chip. Out of all of us, Owen will self-destruct before he ever allows for any of what the Senator and the sewage cunt to ever come to fruition.

Lev's hand whips out, grabbing Owen before he can pass again. "Stop with the martyr shit, man. It won't ever come to that. Now sit the fuck down," Lev snaps.

Everyone's evolving. I preen like a proud peacock with all the backbones growing in here.

"Now, if everyone's done with their outbursts, let's see if the plans we've devised will work," Wes exclaims.

Lev reaches out to Teagan for an update on the timeline for decoding while we strategize. Four hours later, it's almost ten in the morning.

"If we stick with this plan and keep each other in the loop on the next steps, I'm confident we'll be free to eviscerate Matthew Baker and Samantha Davenport," Wes's father declares.

Rising from my seat, I follow the others out. They better be right. Otherwise, I'll activate my plan—one that gets Ariah safely away from here forever.

40
ARIAH

"Okay, the babies are developing on target. However, you, Mom, need to lower your stress levels," Dr. Jaffri instructs as I sit up.

Wiping the gel off my stomach, I reply, "I'm keeping a low profile these days. Only going to school then home unless there's an event or meeting I need to attend." Sliding off the exam table, I massage my back. "I swear these two have it out for my back."

"I wish I could tell you it will get better, but as they grow, they'll situate themselves in positions that may be uncomfortable or even painful," she explains as we walk to her office. "I would look into doing yoga, pilates, or swimming. These are all great options."

Groaning, I sink into the chair across from her desk before I ask, "Does that mean I have to stop training?"

"Yes, especially after your fainting episode. No hand-to-hand combat until you're cleared." My shoulders slump. "I know this part will be hard for you, but I never said you couldn't still throw knives or use a punching bag."

My posture straightens. "So what you're saying is no kicking the asses of the three stooges in the hallway. Got it."

Dr. Jaffri shakes her head before her face turns serious. "It is vital that you heed my warning about stress. Women pregnant with twins are two to three times more likely to develop preeclampsia than women carrying one baby. Do I need to remind you of all the risks and possible complications that may happen?"

"No, I heard you loud and clear."

"Perfect, in that case, I'll see you at our next appointment."

Nodding, I exit her office. "How did it go?" Elias asks as I approach them.

Briefly, I gaze at where Conner stands. The six-foot-five former soldier was back on my security detail. He's helped to guard me on a few other occasions, but we never built a rapport. He's always so stiff. I never know if it's safe to joke with the guys when Conner's around. He's always annoyingly serious. I don't think the man has smiled once in his life, not even as a child.

Refusing to let the stick up his ass stop me, I quip, "Great. She said you all get a reprieve from me handing you your asses until after the babies are born."

"I'd say you were mistaken, but I've seen you train in Colorado," Reign laughs as Conner's jaw clenches. I roll my eyes, ignoring Mr. Stuffy.

I reach for my hair sticks before I check for the throwing knives safely holstered in my armband at the mention of my training in Bronston. "I'm glad you recognize my greatness," I tease as we walk down the hall.

"Shoot, even your training here," Elias adds. "I can't imagine how lethal you'll be once you no longer have to be cautious of the b—"

We're halfway to the elevator when Elias is cut off as the building begins to shake. Small tremors rattle the windows like a seismic wave has hit us. "Is this an earthquake?" I ask, searching for a nearby room and hoping it has a table. Seconds later, the building shakes again, harder this time, and I swear I hear a boom. Then, suddenly, they surround me. "What's going on?"

They guide me down a hall to what looks like an emergency exit. "Our team outside has been compromised," Fernando explains while punching in the code.

"They're on this floor," a man shouts from somewhere down the hall. "Spread out and find her. It's kill on sight, boys. But, instead, let's capture her alive and have a little fun first."

"He's mine," I whisper. I was going to bleed him out slowly.

There is a soft chime as the doors to an elevator slide open. "Nope, that's the exact opposite of your doctor's orders," Elias mutters. "Thomas is already ten minutes out. For this reason, we always have three teams on standby close by."

I wanted to pout. It's been so long since I could draw someone's blood that I could cry. "Only you would get teary-eyed about being unable to stay and fight," Reign taunts, and I roll my eyes.

"It's not funny," I retort, punching him in the shoulder.

Conner clears his throat. "What's the plan once we get her into the room?"

"Stay on guard until we get the signal," Fernando answers as the elevator opens to what appears to be the basement. They quickly usher me out, moving us down a corridor before banking a left.

"Is this building structurally sound enough for us to be down here?" I ask as Reign opens another door with his thumbprint. "So you've had a contingency plan in place for this?"

We're through another door that leads to a set of stairs that only goes down. "Come on, Ry. I'm almost hurt that you'd think we didn't cover all our bases."

No one says anything until we're down the three flights of stairs, through another secured door, and enter a room. "Thomas and his team are four minutes out. We need to hang tight for now," Reign states.

Sighing, I walk around, taking in the space. Gray, plastered walls line a windowless room that is filled with all the necessary amenities. There's a fully stocked kitchen and some form of a living room. I leave the main area to see what else is in this bunker under my doctor's office. Conner follows behind me. "You know you don't have to keep an eye on me. We're in a secured space," I inform him.

"If it's all the same to you, Miss Bradford, I'd rather be safe than caught flatfooted," Conner replies in a clipped tone.

I continue my perusal, not wanting to come off like a spoiled princess who doesn't let people do their job. There are about six doors in this hallway, four of them bedrooms. Each consists of a full-size bed, a bathroom, a desk with a chair, and some books.

Having seen enough, I say, "I'm ready to go back." Conner nods, then steps out of the way for me to go ahead of him. Shrugging, I move past him. We're almost back into the main space when the hairs on the back of my neck prickle.

I hear the distinct sound of a bullet being chambered. "Samantha sends her re—" Before he can finish his statement, I whirl around, drawing one of my blades from my arm holster, sailing it through the air down and to my right. "Fuckkk," Conner shouts, reaching for his groin. I use his momentary shock to disarm him. I opt for a hand chop when what I really want to do is sidekick him into the afterlife. Conner drops the gun, and I kick it away from him.

Footsteps sound. "What the hell is going on?" Reign asks. Fernando and Elias must follow quickly behind him, but I'm too focused on my target.

Conner moves to yank the knife from where I hope the blade lodged his dick to one or both of his balls. Before he can fully wrap his hand around the knife, I kick him in the nutsack, and he drops to one knee.

Taking advantage of his position, I pull the metal hair sticks from my messy bun and jam them both in the sides of his throat. I relish the feel of the fuckhead's blood coating my hands and the shock in Conner's eyes as his brain tries to catch up with the fact that he's about to die.

Conner reaches for the metal protruding from his neck, but it's too late. I step back, raising two fingers to the middle of his forehead. "You should've been paying attention in the elevator. Don't worry, *Samantha Davenport* will join you in hell," I spit, then shove his head, causing him to fall back.

"Seriously, Ry?" Elias groans as I stand over Conner and peer down into his vacant, pale blue eyes.

"He started it," I retort.

Fernando snorts before he comes to stand beside me, checking for any injuries. "I guess you got your blood, Hellcat."

Inhaling, I smile at the realization, then bite the inside of my cheek. "Fuck, can one of you get my knife and my hair sticks for me?" I beg, realizing if I squat down to get them, it's going to be a bit of a struggle to get back up.

When I'm met with silence, I turn and gaze at each of them. The assholes are working hard to hold back their laughter. I flip them off and walk into the main room as Thomas opens the door covered in blood. "Tough day at the office?" I jest.

Thomas scans me from head to toe, taking note of my bloody hands. Satisfied I'm not hurt, he quips, "Seems as though you've lightened my workload."

Elias, Reign, and Fernando enter the living room. "A team's been dispatched for clean up. Do we have any idea how Conner made it through the background checks?" Fernando asks, cursing under his breath in Spanish. Something about fucking turncoat weasels and how they deserve to be hung and left for vultures.

I smirk, but then I remember the men upstairs and why I was there. "Dr. Jaffri?"

Thomas's face softens. "Safe."

I sigh in relief. My shoulders slump as the adrenaline dissipates from my system. Elias scoops me into his arms and whispers, "Let's get you home."

Humming, I rest my head on his shoulder and close my eyes. "I'm going to gut that bitch," I mumble before sleep finally takes me.

●

"Miss Bradford, we've heard your grievances," Tamara states from across the table.

"I don't think you have. Things aren't getting better. They're getting worse, and if you want me to fulfill my end of things, you'll provide the information and support I'm seeking. I refuse to have my family looking over their shoulders for the rest of our lives," I pause, needing to rein in my rage. "Generations of Bradfords have already done that. We won't anymore," I reply.

Silence hums through the room, and I begin to wonder if we are at an impasse. I won't budge on my demands.

She smiles. "You'll be an excellent addition to the Novus Ordo Seclorum. The Princeps chose wisely." She stands, and I spend time admiring her. High, sharp cheekbones are highlighted in a bronzer that accentuates the reddish-gold undertones in her umber skin. Tamara's burnt orange suit is paired with a cream silk blouse. *This woman emanates power.* "You'll have your information and support when the time has come, Miss Bradford. Complete your task before the Tribunal, and we'll handle the rest." And without a backward glance, she exits the room.

Huffing, I sit back in my chair and rest my hand on my stomach. "Mommy is going to open the gates of hell to protect you." I feel flutters against my palm, and tears build in my eyes. The guys will either get on board or get run over. Their fiancée, however, is a bitch on borrowed time.

41
LEV

Music blares through the speakers. The bass vibrates off the walls. "Are you sure this was the only place she could meet us?" Sebastian asks as he has to stave off the attention of another sorority girl.

"They're like an invasive species," Owen grumbles as we move through the room.

I wait until we reach an alcove, awarding us some amount of privacy, before I answer Sebastian. "We are running out of time with the engagement party being next week. This is our best shot."

I stop speaking as another group of giggling sorority girls approaches. They preen, pulling their shoulders back and widening their smiles. They must recognize our disinterest quickly because they frown as they scurry past, making no attempts to engage us in conversation.

"This is the only place remotely safe enough. Samantha wouldn't step foot into a Groveton party, much less one the Jacobis are throwing," I explain, and shiver at the memory of her after tonight's game. We were, once again, subjected to the unfortunate circumstance of pretending to be happily betrothed.

Senator Baker, along with several other high-ranking businessmen, attended tonight's game, forcing us to pretend to be happy partners. Samantha took advantage of our predicament by trying to rub herself against Owen, of all people. Wes had to grab her hand and hold it before Owen lost it and cut off her entire arm. Her sly smirk was all the evidence necessary to show she knew precisely what she was doing.

"Why exactly is she afraid of the Jacobis?" Wes inquires, pulling me from my thoughts.

I turn to meet his gaze. "Let's just say they didn't take Samantha's bullying of Eva kindly."

We walk deeper into the packed Sigma Alpha Psi fraternity house. It's one of the many parties being thrown tonight on Groveton's Greek Row. The premise is simple. Each house—fraternity and sorority—throws a themed party, and students from everywhere attend. This house is masquerade-themed—the perfect place to meet with Teagan. The annual event is hosted by the winner of the prior year's football game. Next year, it'll be at Lincoln-Wood.

I smile, remembering our win. It was third down, and we just received a penalty pushing us back fifteen yards, landing us at the thirty-five-yard line and out of the red zone. We just left the huddle with our play, quickly getting into position before there could be a delay of game. After the snap, Groveton expected us to go long, and they were correct, but I pretended to hand off the ball to one of our running backs. Groveton's defense responded by running in, leaving our receivers more room to move. That's when I sailed the ball down the field to a tight end for a touchdown.

"How long before Teag gets here?" Sebastian leans over to ask. He's not thrilled that this is where Teagan decided to meet. The original plan was to meet at Le Toucher on Halloween night, but she needed more time.

Peering into the sea of bodies, I spot who I'm looking for. "As soon as the room is completely distracted," I reply and tip my head, silently instructing them to follow.

We barely make it three feet before a girl stands in our path. She isn't that much taller than Ariah, but her curly hair hangs loosely past her shoulders. The majority of her face is hidden behind an

"Great. Now that this is settled, operation 'distracts the masses' will commence," Coop says. A Cheshire grin creeps up his face.

"What do you have in—" I rest my hand on Wes's forearm, ending his question.

I wait until Colter and Cooper exit their room. "It's better we don't know what they've orchestrated to serve as a distraction."

Nodding, Wes asks, "How long do you think we'll have to sit up here before we get the go-ahead?"

Throwing my hair up into a bun, I respond, "Thirty minutes tops."

Then, for the next fifteen minutes, we discuss how we'll outfit the warehouse to become the ultimate place of torture. "We'll spend time adding more after we kill Samantha and Matthew Baker. I see no reason this building should be a one-time use," Owen suggests before we change subjects to discuss our plan for capturing them.

"Once the device is deactivated, I say we just knock her out and lure Baker outside, then do the same to him. Between the five of us, we will be more than able to get them into the back of Rubi," Sebastian suggests.

"I call dibs on Baker," Owen and Wyatt say in unison. They both look at each other and then burst into laughter.

Rubbing the furrow between my brows, I retort, "Let's wait until Teagan explains what will be required to remove the chip from Owen's arm." We'd been up here for almost an hour when my phone finally buzzed. I retrieve it from my front pocket and notice several notifications filling my screen.

> COLT
>
> Coop & Liam definitely have the place distracted.
>
> TEAG
>
> I'm about to enter with a group of students I've been walking across campus with.
>
> LEECH
>
> How much longer do you assholes plan on being at that fucking party?

> **COLT**
> I suggest you all start coming down now before this party gets even wilder.
>
> **LEECH**
> One of you fuckers better answer me. I've seen the pictures. If I find out that any of you even remotely participate. . . Kiss Ariah goodbye.

I growl at Samantha's message. "I'm releasing the footage of Samantha and Brittany," I snap, and they all smile.

"It's about time we started this part of the plan. When will it be posted?" Wyatt probes, mirth gleaming in his eyes.

> **ME**
> Be down shortly. I need to use your computer.

A second barely passes, and I already have his response.

> **COLT**
> You know you never need to ask.
>
> Don't forget the encryption.

Standing, I walk over to Colter's desk. I want to roll my eyes at his reminder. Like I would ever do that. Minutes later, I answer Wyatt's question, "I have it set to go live tomorrow morning. Then, the video from the night of our party will be posted during the engagement party, and the news that she's been sleeping with her brother will be posted after the party."

> **TEAG**
> I'm here. Where the hell are you? If one more person asks me if I want to ride some part of them, I'm stabbing them.

"Let's head down," I snort before responding.

> ME
>
> On our way.

We swap out our simple black and white masks that only cover our eyes—replacing them with a white shell mask. Half of our mouths are skeletal, the other half appears to have its lips sewn shut with black thread, and a black upside-down cross sits between our charcoal-lined eyes.

"Holy fuck," Wes exclaims when he reaches the bottom of the stairs.

"What is it?" Owen asks.

Not to be left out, Wyatt demands, "I want to see. Move out of the way."

Sighing, I peer over to see Sebastian with the same look of apprehension once we hit the main floor. He gasps, and I jerk my gaze to a full-on orgy. "Well, this is one way to distract people," Sebastian mutters.

My shoulders shake as I try to hide my amusement, but my laugh dies once I step into full view of the scene unfolding. Couples, throuples, and more engaging in various stages of fucking. In the center of the room, some girl is riding the face of a girl being fucked senseless by a guy who's also being fucked by Coop. Each slam of Cooper's hips sets off a domino effect.

"Is that Eva?" Wyatt shouts, but none of us reply.

I'm so stunned by the scene before us that I don't realize Teagan's presence. "When you said they'd be distracted, this isn't what I envisioned," she quips, pinching Owen's arm.

"Ouch, Teag. You didn't have to do that to get our attention," Owen mock whines before scooping her in a hug.

Teagan flicks his Adam's apple. "Put me down. I don't want to draw any unnecessary attention our way," she commands, and he begrudgingly places her on the floor. Then she moves to stand next to me, holding out her fisted hand. "Take this. It's what O will have to wear."

Opening my palm, I catch the black leather bracelet and place it in my pocket. "Is there anything else we need to know?" I ask.

Teagan shakes her head. "Not yet. I have a few more kinks to smooth out on my end, which I'll finish in the next couple of days. Once that's done, I'll have final instructions." Then, as quickly and quietly as she came, she disappears into the crowd.

I take one more look to see it's definitely Eva. Her face is now visible. She's on all fours with her face buried between the girl's legs as she rides Colt, and the mystery man takes her ass while Coop fucks him. Seeing more than enough, I say, "Let's go. We got what we came for."

42

ARIAH

"Don't think I forgot that we need to discuss the crazy guard who tried to kill you," Shay admonishes.

"Can't we just pretend it never happened?" I query, not wanting to rehash Conner's attempt on my life for Samantha. "One day soon, I'm going to deflate her lips before I gut her."

Shay pauses, registering my statement, then cackles. "Who said pregnancy would diminish your thirst for blood?"

"Most specifically, Samantha's. She's been vying for me to kill her since the first day of school. Who am I to deny her?"

"Okay, La Femme Nikita. Temper your urges until my niece and nephew are born. Then we can award the bitch a death worse than Vivian's," Shay states.

Huffing, I reply, "Fine. Let's talk about something else then. Reminders of the fuckwit security guard raise my blood pressure."

Shay moves the conversation to a more interesting turn of events. "I still can't believe Sam and Brittany have been screwing each other," Shay snorts. "After all that shit she said about us last year, I guess I shouldn't be surprised, but the projection levels were high." I could only gawk when the video of Samantha behind the girls' dorm was sent out via mass text and across all social media platforms. I might have felt sorry for her if she hadn't done the same thing to me only weeks ago.

"Did you hear how she reacted?" I ask. "There have been so many different stories spreading."

Shay's amusement is written all over the glee on her face. "The best one was when she ran from the math building and tripped in her eighteen-foot stilettos, scratching the right side of her face."

Giggling, I stride toward the en-suite bathroom and wash my face. My stylist team will be here any minute now to help me get ready for this joke of an engagement party. My laughter ceases at the realization that the Fraternitas is forcing me to go. I groan. Each attempt to get a pass from going was swiftly denied. "I can't believe they're forcing me to attend," I spit, stepping back into my bedroom.

Shay clasps my hand. "I'm surprised you were allowed to miss the bridal brunch and shower."

I smirk. "Thank fuck for bed rest."

We stare at each other, then burst into laughter. "The twins are already Team Mommy," she chuckles.

"An instant get out of jail free card." A knock on my door interrupts our goofing around. "Come in," I shout, and the door opens, and in comes a rack full of dresses, three hairstylists, a makeup artist, and a nail technician.

"Hello, Miss Bradford, it's always a pleasure to dress you," Bree exclaims. She and her team were brought on in Bronston.

Sitting on my bed, I reply, "The pleasure is mine. Even when I'm dreading the event." Then Shay and I wait for Bree to begin showing me my dress options for the evening. The first five dresses were far too loud. While they all would flatter me, I want a dress that doesn't scream, 'Look at me.'

"This is the one." Bree's thick Italian accent is more prevalent with her excitement. My gaze freezes when I look up. A stunning floor-length, blush pink spaghetti-strap dress with a plunging V-neckline is before me. "It's a velvet dress covered in mesh with two slits up to the thigh. The floral pattern, along with the empire waist, is perfect for your growing belly." She smiles at me before continuing, "This, paired with the rose gold, pink diamond-encrusted jewelry set, will be the perfect statement piece."

Her assistant brings out the necklace, earrings, and bracelet, and it's Shay's turn to gasp. "Those are from a limited collection made by a French jeweler who only ever creates one-of-a-kind pieces." Shay whips her attention to Bree. "Only the most exclusive families have access to this woman. How did you do it?" she inquires with no accusations in her tone.

"A private benefactor purchased them under the condition that they go to you, Miss Bradford," Bree explains.

Scrunching my face in confusion, I verify that I heard her correctly. "Did you say someone bought these for me?"

Bree nods. "Yes. Every dress selected for tonight was chosen to match this one-of-a-kind set. You'll be wearing well over half a billion dollars in jewelry."

My heart stops beating. Why the fuck would anyone buy me a billion-dollar anything? "Who's the benefactor?"

"I'm not permitted to reveal that. Everyone on my team has signed an NDA, and any perceived violation will be met with a career-ending blow," Bree explains. She remains professional, not reacting to her words except for the fear gripping her mahogany eyes.

Not wanting her to lose her livelihood, I drop it. "Let's get my bestie and me ready." Then, we're waxed, plucked, and pampered into stunning perfection for the next three hours.

"Beautiful as always, Miss Bradford and Miss Warren," Bree says, clapping her hands in ratification. She knows her team has once again gone above and beyond her expectations.

Shay and I express our gratitude before walking downstairs, where everyone waits for us. "Fuck! She can't go out looking like that," Elias mumbles. "Ouch," he exclaims, glaring at Reign. "Why the hell did you hit me?"

"Because, idiot, she doesn't need your permission to wear what she wants," Fernando adds.

Sighing, Elias snaps, "I know that. I didn't mean she had to change. I just—"

"You three cut it out, or you'll be taken off tonight's detail," Thomas commands. "Now, head to the car."

I clear my throat, hiding my laughter. Those three were ridiculous sometimes. "Will Dad meet us there?"

Thomas nods. "Yes, he'll be waiting for your arrival. Then he'll take his place with the Council."

Stupid fucking Council. They were all in for a rude awakening if they think I'll forget this anytime soon. Everything they've known will no longer exist in a few more weeks. I smile at that thought. "Time to get this train wreck of a night over with."

●

"This match has been a long time coming," says the MC. "Samantha Davenport, Wesley Edgewood, Wyatt and Sebastian Grant, Lev Washington, and Owen Jefferson have known each other since childhood."

Rolling my eyes, I mutter, "Is it possible to want to crush someone's larynx?"

Shay turns, arching her perfectly sculpted brow at me. "When do you want to begin?"

And this is why she'll always be my ride-or-die. She's always ready and willing to encourage my fuckery. "This is why you can never leave me, bitch."

She smirks. "And where exactly would I go?"

"I don't know, but I have rope, tape, and a place to keep you just in case you decide to try it," I quip. We both laugh at our ridiculousness.

"I knew I loved them before I could even count." Samantha's nasally-ass voice announces, making me want to lose the little bit of food I ate before coming to this damn party. "While there was a small hiccup during the Selection, I knew I was their chosen. It was kismet."

Overhearing Samantha drone on and on about their destiny to be together, I grab Shay's hand, pulling her over to the bar. "You know she's delusional, right?" Shay encourages. "I've known those idiot men as long as Samantha has." She pauses. "And after Owen was kidnapped, they've always despised her."

"Tell that to my broken heart and the gaudy rock on her left ring finger," I retort, then order a club soda with fresh berries and a lemon slice.

Gritting my teeth, I work to stave off my tears. I'm just not sure if they're from sadness or anger. *Probably both.* Shay envelops me. "If they're too stupid to see who they passed over for the entitled train wreck they chose, then they all deserve endless years of misery with each other until one of the guys snaps and kills her." She releases me as the bartender places my drink on the bar top. "Now, let's address the real problem. Why are you drinking unflavored beverages? What in the bingo night at the VFW are you subjecting my niece and nephew to?"

I throw my head back and laugh before picking up my drink. Shay looks on in horror as I close my lips around the straw and do a happy dance as the flavors hit my tongue. "Hey, no picking on the pregnant woman. She's allowed to have what she craves. Now, let me be great!"

Shay shakes her head as she grabs her mojito. Then we find our table and get lost in conversation, drowning out the endless speeches, praising the happily engaged group.

Two hours pass, and my love for my ensemble vanishes. I should've gone with my gut and pretended not to be well enough to attend this bullshit. My face hurts from all the smiling and conversations I've endured. At some point, Samantha and the guys left their own shindig. Now I'm here listening to women babble.

"Didn't she look lovely?" A blonde woman shouts over the music to the brunette woman she's standing with. They both appear to be in their late thirties or early forties.

The brunette frowns, and worry fills her face as she responds, "It's a tragedy her mother couldn't be here."

Where are her parents? I haven't seen Samantha's father or mother.

"Oh, and that poor girl that's pregnant. Rumor has it that she's claiming it to be one of the boys, but they've all denied it," the annoying blonde states, and I curse the Fraternitas and the stupid contract for forcing me to be here. They titter on about who the father could be and how foolish I am forever believing I had a chance. "Can you believe she had the audacity to show up?"

"I didn't want to come to this stupid fucking engagement party in the first place," I grumble, spinning away from the two women I'm adding to my ever-growing list.

Huffing, I fight with my damn dress. It feels so restricting, and my feet fucking hurt. Socializing at twenty-six weeks pregnant should be illegal. I barely like people to begin with. Everything feels off, and I want to be anywhere but here. I curse when tears begin to pool in the corner of my eyes.

"We can sneak out the back. No one will ever know," Shay whispers, sensing my growing frustration.

"I wish. If I leave, all the plans I've been working on will fall through. I need the Fraternitas to believe I'm a docile, willing participant."

Shay snorts. "Docile? Do they know who you are? If they think, for a minute, you're anything but—" She's cut off.

"Hush it. Let's go grab another drink," I suggest.

We stand and then begin walking toward the bar. Reign and Elias are quick to follow.

"Oh look, it's the reject," Brittany slurs, stepping into our path.

Someone's hammered.

"Did you say that in the mirror to yourself?" I challenge. Brittany's nose scrunches as she curls her lip in anger.

She takes a step forward, but Reign blocks her. "I wouldn't do that if I were you."

Brittany looks momentarily stunned, but she quickly recovers. "Whatever. I'm over this whole thing. Owen sent me to find you."

Rolling my eyes, I retort, "Right, because Owen sending you to deliver a message to me is ever going to be believable."

"Whatever, suit yourself. Don't say I never tried to do you any favors," Brittany spins, almost taking out a passing waiter and the tray of hors d'oeuvres. "Stupid bitch Sam better be happy," I swear she mutters before skulking away.

43
OWEN

"You understand what needs to happen?" Lev asks me.

Nodding, I reply, "Yes, but how do you suppose I get Samantha to follow me anywhere? That soul-sucking bitch knows I hate her."

"We're playing to Samantha's vanity. Wes will tell her you both want time alone, and she's to meet you in one of the rooms," Lev explains.

Arching a brow, I say, "I still don't think this will work, but I'll do just about anything to be rid of her."

Lev hands me the leather bracelet. I turn it over, inspecting every inch of it. "Where the hell is the device that will zap the control the Senator and Samantha have over us?" I probe.

"It's nearly unnoticeable to the human eye," Lev explains, turning the bracelet so the bottom side with the "A" carved into the center of a heart is showing. He pulls out his phone, brings up his camera, and zooms in. That's when I see it. "It's embedded into the A. Teagan's work is impeccable, isn't it?"

While he admires Teagan's craftsmanship, I'm more impressed by the blatant *fuck you* this provides. "Teag made Ariah the person that ultimately will save me," I chuckle, but I have to wonder if this is foreshadowing. I don't want Samantha breathing the same air as my angel. Even if Ariah could take her out, I don't want it to ever come to that.

"Here, put this in your ear," Lev instructs. "This is how Teagan and I will relay any information to you guys."

Speaking of the guys. "Where are those assholes?"

"Currently, they're keeping an eye on things. Once you're in position, the plan will commence, and instructions will be relayed."

I tip my head in agreement and then put the earpiece in. It's small enough to remain hidden unless I turn and show someone my left ear. Lev gives me another once over, ensuring we're ready before he exits the room.

"Did you guys see how fucking breathtaking our spitfire is?" Sebastian groans.

"In about an hour, we'll be able to start earning our spots back into her life," Wes adds.

Sighing, I look around the space, trying not to let my need for Ariah cause me to make a mistake—one wrong move, and this all could turn to shit. I'm in one of the offices at the country club. A large, cherry-wood L-shaped desk sits feet from a floor-to-ceiling window, offering a beautiful view of one of the many man-made ponds. Shifting my focus, I take in the built-in bookshelves that cover the expanse of every wall but the one behind the desk. I shake my head of distraction, then look for where I want things to go down.

"Okay, Wes is moving in," Lev announces. "Be ready, O. Samantha should be to you in three minutes tops."

Inhaling, I finish surveying the room. My gaze lands on a table. It's also made from cherry wood, but that's not what grabs my attention. The six office chairs surrounding the table are perfect. I wheel one into the center of the room.

"Samantha stopped to whisper something in Brittany's ear," Sebastian states. "I'm not sure what she said, but Brittany looked angry as she stomped away."

"How long before we can kill her?" Wyatt grumbles, making me laugh. I can't wait to have them all at our mercy. It's long overdue.

Sitting, I try to compose myself. *Remember, this is for freedom. None of it is real.* The only thing providing me with a semblance of peace is knowing Ariah will never know what I'm doing to get back to her. "She's less than twenty seconds away," Lev informs me.

The door opens, and I dig my fingernails into my palm to prevent me from scowling as the bane of our existence fills the doorway. "Where's Wes?" Samantha questions, taking a cautionary step into the room.

"He'll be here shortly," I reply in a tone that shocks me. It's not clipped or angry—it's almost welcoming. "Come in. I see no reason to wait for him to arrive."

Her lips curl up into a salacious grin, almost like a cat who caught a canary. "You'll have to pardon me if I find this change of heart insincere," Samantha retorts, but she still steps into the room, closing the door behind her. "You and Wyatt are two of the last people I ever expected to see the light, if you will. But after Wyatt and Wes fucked me at that party, maybe all things are possible."

"Keep her talking," Teagan commands. "I've already begun the process. We need to get her close enough so your bracelet can pair with her watch."

I internally groan at the idea of her getting any closer than she is. *This is for my angel.* Biting my lip, I smirk. "I won't bullshit you and pretend I've had a complete change of heart."

"What the fuck are you doing?" Lev hisses.

I want to yell for him to trust me. There's only one way to make this believable. "But this is more about need. I have needs, and you're available."

She scowls, then quickly covers it with a smile. "Well then, why deny yourself?" Samantha begins to walk toward me before she stops—her fake smile morphing into mischievous glee. "The only way I'll take you seriously is if you let me cross out the A on your chest with the same knife you let her carve it with and let me replace it with my initials."

I'd sooner cut out her heart and blow myself up before I let her sully Lola. "I don't have that knife with me," I reply, my voice still leaning more toward neutral than pissed off.

Huffing, she retorts, "Fine, any knife will do. I want all traces of the gutter troll off you and replaced by me."

"Fucking bitch," Teagan snaps. "Let the skank think she's won. This is the perfect opportunity we needed."

I want to tell Teagan it's easy for her to say because she won't have stale pussy wafting into her nose.

"Brittany just stopped Ariah and Shay. I can't hear what she said, but our girl whipped something back, and Brittany took off seething," Wes shares.

I ignore him and pull a blade from my ankle holster under my black sock. I'm not sure which one this is. I haven't named any of my new ladies yet, but I'm saving this one to run through the spot in Samantha's chest where her heart should be. "Let's get this over with," I state, flipping the knife for her to grab its handle.

"Never let someone say you're not romantic," Samantha laments before stopping in front of me. She takes the blade and then straddles my hips, pushing her heaving chest into my face. I have to fight the urge to shove her off me when she starts grinding on me.

Samantha cuts the buttons off my crisp white tuxedo shirt as she grinds down on my flaccid dick, trying to make it hard while exposing my chest to her hungry eyes. Then she angles the knife, hovering above the initial of a person I'll sacrifice myself for. Teagan's plan better work because I have no intentions of letting Samantha cut through shit.

"Closer, O. I need you to move the wrist with the bracelet closer for this to work."

Groaning, I clasp her hand as the knob on the door turns.

"Shit, Ariah's outside the door," Lev shouts, and I close my eyes, pleading with every deity for Ariah to skip this door.

Samantha must have stolen a look because she smiles as she picks up her pace, exaggerating her moan, making me want to reach into her throat and rip her trachea out.

I can feel my angel's eyes boring into the side of my face.

"Don't move. I need just another minute," Teagan instructs, but I want to rage. I will completely obliterate the love of my life's heart in another minute.

Samantha's hand descends, and I hear Ariah gasp, forcing my attention to her.

"You need to get her out of here in case this doesn't work," Lev demands.

Gritting my teeth, my nostrils flare, and I channel the anger for the person on top of me. "Can't you see we're fucking busy? Get the fuck out of here!"

My eyes close at the sight of Ariah's tears.

"No, stay and watch as I carve the last of you from them, and then maybe you'll finally recognize your place, you gutter troll," Sam sneers. A combination of pleasure, victory, and menace fills her usually stiff face.

I'm going to fricassee Samantha's entrails and feed them to her sister-fucking brother.

I will my angel to move. *Leave baby, please, I'm begging you.*

"She needs to go now," Teagan snaps. "This will be done any minute now, and if it goes wrong, I don't think I need to explain the rest to you."

"Get the fuck out," I spit.

My heart shatters at the bereft look on Ariah's face as she stumbles from the room, slamming shut the door to her heart forever.

I'll fix this, Angel. I promise. I silently pledge.

Samantha's hand roams, and her touch feels like acid against my skin. "I'm glad you finally chose right," Samantha squawks as she lightly drags the sharp point of the blade up my chest. I have to force myself not to ram my knife through her neck to shut her up.

"You know how annoying you've all been. *Ariah this* and *Ariah that*. So fucking annoying," Samantha prattles on. I only hear every third word of her whining—just enough to ensure she's not about to stab me.

Time ticks by, each second putting even greater literal and figurative distance between Ariah and us. It feels like another eternity passes when Teagan finally shouts, "We got it!"

My shoulders sag in relief as I repeat her statement, "We got it?"

"Yes, you're fucking free!" Teagan squeals, and I hear the guys cheering.

"We got what?" Samantha questions, her earlier smile sliding off her face as she scrunches her nose and pauses her movements.

Wasting no more time, I push her off me and stand, ignoring her disgruntled shriek. "Rid of you," I seethe, striding past her. My hand is on the doorknob before she replies.

"You're fucking dead!" Peering over my shoulder, I laugh as I watch her push the detonator over and over to no avail. Samantha's accusatory icy blue glare up at me. "What the fuck did you do?"

"Whatever was necessary to rid ourselves of you," I snap.

Her face blooms four shades of red before she laughs, "Do you think she'll take you back after what she just saw? I'm not a complete idiot. I knew you fucking dicks were up to something," Samantha singsongs as she stands. "Why do you think I had Brittany tell her you called her?"

My blood turns cold. *No, Ariah will forgive me. I just need to—we need to explain everything.* "Shut the fuck up, Samantha. Your time is about to expire. I'd run if I were you," I bark, then open the door. I look up and down the hallway, but my angel's gone. That's when I see it—a trail of red. "Fuckkk! This can't be happening," I mutter as I run in the direction of the path of blood while Samantha's mocking cackles chase behind me.

44
LEV

"Fuck, fuck, fuuucccckk!" I shout, losing the battle on my composure. Everything was perfect. Not a minute out of place. How did we screw this up so badly?

"You'll make her understand," Teagan encourages.

I loosen my bowtie, then unbutton my collar, hoping the foot compressing my throat eases. "How can you know that for sure?"

"Because of the love in that girl's eyes. You'll all have to fight hard for it, but she'll see reason once you explain."

Trying to take solace in Teagan's words, I work harder to finish the last stage to deactivate the chip. Even though neither Samantha nor anyone else with a detonator can blow Owen up, we still need to ensure it's safe to remove. "I can only hope you're right, Teag. Ariah has changed each of us for the better. Her love made me confront my demons because she could never truly have a place in my heart if I wasn't up to doing the work to heal. None of us are even halfway, but we're closer than we've ever been before," I confess.

"And that's exactly why I have zero doubts that you'll earn her forgiveness. You're all willing to do the work—it's not just lip service. Each of you wants to be worthy of her," I hear her sigh. "Now get the fuck out here and go see your girl. I'll finish this, and then I have an idea I want to test."

I don't wait for her to change her mind or ask if she's sure. I pull my earpiece out and jump from Owen's Jeep, racing inside to meet the guys. Ariah's already en route to the hospital, and I have no intention of arriving far behind them.

45
OWEN

I'm nearly to the end of the hall when I have to stop short. Reign, Elias, and Fernando are blocking my path.

"Move, I need to get to her," I growl, then step back to avoid Reign's fist.

"You think you deserve to see her after what you caused?" Elias barks.

I don't have time for any of this. I can still see the crimson trail on the carpet. "We'll explain everything later. Now, move the fuck out of my way before I make you."

"You assholes have done more than enough. We did warn you, and while Ariah is like a sister to us, that doesn't mean we can't still remove you from her life until someone she deserves comes along," Reign snarls. "None of you are good enough to drink her piss."

I grit my teeth and shout, "You don't think we know that? You don't think each slice to her heart is like fifteen to ours for having to be the ones wielding the knife? *She's our everything!*"

"Cut the shit. Whatever you did tonight could cost her the twins. Nothing you say will convince any of us your intentions are pure," Elias glares at me in disgust. "What the hell were you thinking? We distinctly told you at her doctor's appointment if you all fucked this up, we would never let you close enough to hurt her again."

I don't have time for this shit. I need to get to her.

"Ariah was just checked into Labor and Delivery," Wyatt states. I almost forgot I have the earpiece in.

"Keep me posted. I have the three musketeers in my way at the moment," I inform whoever else is on our line. Curling my lip in frustration, I stare down the wall blocking my path. The idea of pulling out my throwing knives and making them bleed is very tempting, but I know that won't endear Ariah to me. "Look, you can hold each other's balls for all I care—just do it out of my way. This is your final warning," I spit.

Fernando stalks closer from the right as Reign and Elias come from the left, leaving me enough room to dart between them. Wasting no time, I run past the three of them to meet up with the guys.

46
WES

Samantha rushes down the hallway, and I stick my foot out, tripping her, secretly hoping she breaks her nose or her lips deflate on impact.

"What the fuck, Wesley," she shrieks as she rolls to sit on her ass. Her shrill voice almost bursts my eardrums.

She tries to get up, but I put my foot on her forehead, pushing her back down. "Did you enjoy your little power trip while it lasted? You thirsty bitch," I seethe. "Did you and your brother feel justified in your quest for power?" I press the heel of my onyx Crockett and Jones Highbury dress shoes down so hard that I know it's cutting into the flesh of her forehead and will also leave a beautiful bruise.

"Let me go," she screeches her demand.

I tilt my head so she can see the five-alarm blaze in my mahogany eyes. "Did you let us go?" She closes her eyes, attempting to turn her face, only for her to hiss in pain. Smirking, I watch as scarlet droplets roll down her face. "That's what I thought."

"You better take advantage of your momentary freedom because once we reactivate the chip, I'm raining hell on your world, starting with that cheap whore you all can't seem to give up," she yells.

Narrowing my gaze, I retort, "I guess you really are as dumb as you look." Then I lift my heel off her, replacing it with my hand around her throat and squeezing. "You've been out-maneuvered. You showed your hand too early. Don't you know the house always wins," I snap as I hoist her by her throat off the ground.

"What is the meaning of this? Let that poor girl go," a woman with blonde hair orders, and I throw my head back and laugh at the looks of disgust she and her brunette friend exchange. "How dare you treat your fiancée this way."

Samantha whimpers, playing the victim, and I roll my eyes —*victim, my ass*. She's as much of a damsel in distress as I am kind. They can believe her bullshit all they want. It won't stop the death awaiting her. "Mind your fucking business unless you want the weight of the Fraternitas on both your poorly dyed heads," I command.

They gasp in shock, ready to leave, when a familiar voice booms, "Now, is that any way to treat a woman?" Senator Matthew Baker coos. "I would've thought my brother taught you better than that."

This asshole still believes he's related to me. I open my mouth to rebuff him when Sebastian's curt tone fills my ear. "Don't tell him shit. We need him to find out at the right time."

My lip curls in annoyance. "Why?"

"Lev believes we can work it in our favor. He needs to see it at the end of the engagement party. Let Samantha go and meet us outside. We need to get to the hospital. Ariah's more important."

Huffing, I release my hold, and she crashes to the ground. Then I step over Samantha and past Senator Baker, sneering down at him before I run to meet the guys.

47
SEBASTIAN

"What the fuck?" I snarl, running my hands through my hair. The once perfectly styled look is in tatters, but none of that matters. I look at the row of our cars. Each one has its tires slashed, and various expletives are keyed all over them. And by the fumes attacking my nose, I'm confident each car is sitting on empty.

"Shit. This isn't good," Owen groans. "We don't have time for this."

The sound of more dress shoes running across the pavement indicates the rest of the guys are here.

"Tell me we have a spare car around here," Wyatt sighs, and I don't have to look at him or anyone else to know their brows furrow in worry.

Wes pulls a set of keys from his pocket, then starts his father's midnight black Maybach SUV. "Won't he be pissed you took this?" I ask.

"Not under these circumstances. One of us should text the Council we're leaving and that O is now free—shit, we all are," Wes suggests as we pile into the car.

I nervously chew at my lip. It's not a habit I've shown since I was young. It's a clear indicator of my worry. Ariah can't lose the babies, and we can't lose her. I'll fight fate itself if it tries me. We've been through enough. *Fuck!* She's endured more than any one person should ever have to. Especially while pregnant.

"What if she loses the babies," Wyatt chokes out.

"That's not an option on the table," Owen snaps. "She and our babies will be fine. You'll all see. They'll be more than fine even." It sounds like he's trying to reassure himself as he tries to convince us, but I'm with him.

Lev's fingers are flying over the keys on his laptop. "She's been given a room, and her vitals are high, but she's outside the danger zone."

"Did you hack the hospital computer?" Wes chimes from the front.

"He absolutely has," Owen grins. "I'd kiss you if I knew you wouldn't punch me for touching you."

Wyatt snorts as his shoulders relax slightly. "I second the kiss. I might even throw in a handy," he jokes, and we all burst into laughter.

Minutes later, we're pulling into the hospital, leaving the keys with the valet. "Scratch this car, and I'll eat your firstborn," Wes threatens, and the poor guy looks like he just about shit himself before scurrying away.

No one speaks the entire elevator ride to the fourth floor. Once the doors open, I crack my neck. It's time to get our girl.

48
WYATT

We walk down the hall like five of the seven deadly sins. My usual unsettlingly calm heart beats triple its normal speed. I can feel her pumping through my veins, renewing my will to live.

My cool confidence isn't manufactured—ninety-nine percent of the time, every fiber of my being oozes surety. Tonight. . . tonight's events rocked me to my core. Hearing Owen's fear over the comms froze me still. Carrying the weight of everyone's doubts so we don't lose hope drains me, but I wouldn't change a thing.

When the Fraternitas issued their order, I followed the girl with the autumn hair. By the time Ariah arrived in Edgewood, my only goal was to make sure the guys fell. She's it for us. Ariah is our missing puzzle piece—the five-sided oddly shaped one at the center.

I'm so deep in thought that I don't realize we're standing outside the Labor and Delivery door. Inhaling, I watch Owen pick up the phone and wait to connect with someone from the nurses' station. "We're here to see Ariah Bradford," he says into the receiver. There's no speakerphone, so only Owen can hear what's said.

"What do you think the hold-up is?" Wes grumbles when we aren't given immediate entry.

"We're her fiancés, and she's carrying our babies," Owen explains, trying to remain calm, but with each clench of his jaw, I know his fuse is close to going off. "No! That's not acceptable." He pauses. "What the fuck do you mean we're not allowed in?"

I snort. Of course, they won't allow us in—we're responsible for this. "We should've seen this coming," I mutter.

"How do you figure," Sebastian asks as Owen continues to argue our case.

"If the roles were reversed, and it was Ariah's father who hurt her to the point of being hospitalized, would we let him within one hundred feet of her?" Peering at him, I continue," I'm surprised they let us in the hospital—shit, that we were even allowed in the parking lot."

Seconds later, the door opens. Owen slams down the receiver. "Stupid fuckers. I knew they only needed the right motivation to let us in."

We don't make it one step before a wall of guards blocking our path inside. Thomas is at the center—Reign is to his left, along with three more guards, while Elias and Fernando are to his right with two other guards. "You boys need to go home," Thomas begins.

Reign cuts in. "No one wants or needs any of you heartless assholes here."

"You've each done more than enough," Elias adds.

"Move the fuck out of the way," Lev snaps.

Fernando tilts his head, and his eyes light with excitement. "Or else what? You'll sic Mommy and Daddy on me," he mocks.

Lev's nostrils flare. "No, I'll wipe you from the board. Your continued existence in Ariah's life is because I allow it. So, don't tempt me to call your bluff. It only takes one alert, and your father will know where you are."

"Enough," Aaron hisses, stepping between Thomas and Reign. "Tonight, my daughter was hospitalized, and I won't let the reasons for that anywhere near her until she's one hundred percent recovered." Aaron rubs the bridge of his nose before familiar gray eyes snap open. "I know why everything that transpired tonight had to happen, but give her the time she needs before you smother her with your pleas for forgiveness. She deserves it and so much more."

I meet Aaron's gaze, "At least let us know she's okay. I'll make sure we leave—just tell me Ariah's okay."

"What?"

"Fuck that, I'm not leaving!"

"Wy, have you lost it?"

"No!"

Wes, Owen, Lev, and Sebastian argue.

Raising my hand, I reply, "It's more important for her to rest than for us to see her." Then I face Aaron, waiting for him to answer my question.

"She's sleeping and being closely monitored because her blood pressure keeps spiking," Ariah's father explains.

The guys let out collective sighs. They understand tonight isn't the best time to push. "Tell her we'll give her all the time she needs," Wes states. Aaron nods, and the door to the floor slams shut in our faces.

A slight smirk grows on my face as we head down to our car. *Wes promised you time, Love. I only promised you tonight.*

49
ARIAH

"We need to get you to the hospital, Ry. You're bleeding," I faintly hear Reign's pleas, but I'm still drowning in the scenes looping through my mind. Samantha on top of Owen, riding him. His shirt open as she lowers the blade to stamp out my existence. . . Owen's hurtful commands to leave like I'm some pathetic stalker who doesn't get it.

"Can't you see we're fucking busy? Get the fuck out of here!"

No, no, no, I don't want to go back there. I can feel my heart turn to ash all over again. How could he be so cruel? Until that moment, I held out hope.

"No, stay and watch as I carve the last of you from them, and then maybe you'll finally recognize your place, you gutter troll," she sneers. Victory etches across her usually stiff face.

Samantha has been right all along. They used me until they were ready to discard me. My love for them has only been a game. A sharp jolt across my stomach throws me back into the darkness.

The blood in my veins boils to a fever pitch. Eviscerating my existence as I've known it, replacing it with one that rivals Wanda Maximoff's rage for all her sacrifices and Catalaya Restrepo's thirst for revenge.

Clutching my stomach, streams of tears fall down my face, but someone's calloused fingers keep wiping them. "Cuidado mariposita, tus alas apenas Han comenzaron a volar," *Fernando whispers, pressing a kiss to my forehead.* "Thomas, we need Aaron. Ariah needs to go to the hospital." *Hospital? What for?*

"When will we have more answers?" *I can make out the worry in my father's voice.* Why can't I wake up? *I want to shout, but I'm once again losing the battle with consciousness.*

"Let's get you out of here, Ry," *Dad whispers, carrying me in his arms. He must've used the rear exit because the brisk November air brushes across my skin, doing very little to cool my rage. I hear the doors slam shut and feel the seatbelt as someone fastens me in before the car drives off.*

"How far away are we? Shouldn't we call an ambulance?" *Reign questions.*

I don't need a hospital, I'm fine. "No," *I protest, ready to tell them I want to go home.* "I don't need—" *I begin, but Shay's crying cuts off my words. Why is she crying? Is Brendan here? Did he do something to her?*

The distinct smell of hospital fills my nose as questions swirl between clips.

"Ry, we need to get you to the hospital before something happens to you or the babies," *Shay pleads through hiccups and tears.*

My best friend needs me, and I'm unable to help her. Why she doesn't tell me she can't take this anymore is beyond me.

"Nineteen-year-old white female, in and out of consciousness, experiencing bleeding and high blood pressure."

"The twins are fine. Their heartbeats are strong and aren't showing any signs of distress." *I think I hear Dr. Jaffri explain.* "We're keeping her sedated for the time being. While bleeding and Braxton Hicks can happen during pregnancy, Ariah's blood pressure continues to be high."

Whatever they've given me works through my bloodstream, pulling me back into sleep.

My eyes fly open at the sound of monitors. Awareness of my surroundings quickly settles in. Something slowly squeezes my arm—a blood pressure cuff. I peer up at the fluids running through the IV on my wrist.

"Good, you're awake," *Dr. Jaffri says, stepping fully into the room. That's when I notice that I'm in some sort of suite. My full-*

size hospital bed can easily fit two people. There's also a tawny-brown leather couch with two matching recliners and a large flatscreen television. I can't see where the closet is or how the bathroom looks. I just know this isn't like any hospital I've been to. "Ariah? Did you hear me?"

The look on Dr. Jaffri's face tells me she's been calling me for a while. "I'm sorry. What did you say? I was a bit distracted," I tell her.

"You've been having these episodes more often lately, and while some women do experience pregnancy brain. I'd like you to note how often they occur. Your anxiety may also be the cause or help contribute to your lack of focus," she explains.

I nod in agreement, then ask, "How are my babies?"

"Both are doing very well." Dr. Jaffri pauses, grabbing a stool and sitting beside me. "I can only imagine what you were feeling last night. The good news is the bleeding wasn't excessive. Some women experience spotting or even get their period while pregnant."

"And the cramping?" The pain I felt at the engagement party was on a different level.

Dr. Jaffri offers me a warm smile. "Braxton Hicks. It's fairly common during pregnancy. However, stress can make them occur more frequently. So, it will be essential that you bring your stress levels down for the next few months."

Relief floods my body, causing the tension in my shoulders and throbbing in my head to ease. I need my babies to be safe and healthy, and the only way to ensure that is to stay the fuck away from the Fraternitas, the Heirs, and cunt-face Samantha Davenport.

"Whatever you're thinking about right now, stop it," she orders. *That's easier said than done.*

Taking a deep breath, I try to focus on my babies' heartbeats and the peace I'll find now that the Heirs are behind me.

As my heartbeat begins to slow, the door to my hospital room swings open again. This time, it's Dad, Jamie, Kellan, and Kylan. "Ry," the twins shout, running for the bed.

"Boys," Dad warns, rooting Kylan and Kellan to their spots. "Remember what we spoke about before we came?"

They sigh, then lift their puppy dog gaze at me. "We just want to make sure you're alright."

Jamie steps between them, grabbing their hands, "You can still do that. We just need to be careful. Not too much excitement."

"Ariah, dear." My eyes flick toward the door at the sounds of my grandmother's voice. She's carrying a vase of beautiful flowers. White lilies, red magnolias, and purple lewisias are arranged amongst baby's breath and greenery.

"We're so happy to see you awake," my uncle says as he walks in with my grandfather and a giant stuffed bear hugging two cubs.

I can feel the tears threatening to spill over. "Come sit with me," I pat my bed, urging my siblings over as I quickly wipe my eyes.

"Not too long," Dr. Jaffri orders. "Our girl needs her rest." Then she faces me, "If you can keep your blood pressure down for the next twenty-four hours, I will release you on the condition that you remain on bedrest for two weeks. But we'll discuss it in more detail after your family visits."

My grandmother places the bouquet on the table close to the window. "I like her. She has an excellent bedside manner."

"Dr. Jaffri is the best," I confirm. "She's kind but firm and has no problem telling it like it is."

"You had us so worried," Grandad states, kissing the top of my head.

Uncle Liam stands on the other side of my bed. "I think it's time we find better ways to spend time with each other, niece."

Giggling, I reply, "Yeah, let's forgo any more exciting moments and keep our time together as most families do. Holidays, birthdays, and family trips."

He snorts his agreement, and for the next few hours, I enjoy my time with my family without any thoughts of the men who shattered my heart.

Maybe there's hope for me yet.

50
SEBASTIAN

Massaging my temple, I try to find the patience to deal with the nurse who's just trying to do her job, but it's taking everything in me not to wield the force of the Fraternitas in this hospital. "It's been two days, and we refuse to wait any longer," I state, clenching my teeth.

"Sir, this is outside of our con—"

"Don't you dare finish that sentence, or it'll be the last words you'll speak as a nurse," I spit. She has no idea of the tenuous hold I have on my temper. I never want her to find out, but Nurse Gloria is on thin ice. I'm her last hope. This may not be her doing, but she'll be collateral damage, and I won't bat an eyelash when she is.

"Mr. Grant, might I remind you that you were given specific instructions to stay away? Haven't the five of you put Miss Bradford through quite enough?" *Nurse Gloria* chastises.

Growling, I retort, "Since you know all our information, you should be aware that Samantha Davenport is no longer our anything."

I can feel her judgment through the phone. "Mmhmm. So, now you've gone and broke multiple girls' hearts."

"Ariah's heart is the only heart we care about not being broken," I snap. *Gloria is five seconds from being past tense.*

"That sounds great, but that doesn't change the fact that none of you are permitted to see her. That order is above my pay grade." She sighs. "Just stay away. I'm sure you can all harass her once she's home, though I don't recommend any of you going near that girl again. You all have caused her nothing but heartache."

My phone buzzes. I pull it out of the front pocket of my gray sweatpants while pretending to still be listening to Nurse Gloria's eight-year lecture.

> **WES**
> Any luck?

He already knows the answer—we all do. There is no scenario where we would be able to see her.

> **ME**
> Negative. We're not getting in here, and she goes home today. I think we'll have a better shot then.

> **WYATT**
> We have one more ace up our sleeves.

> **ME**
> What did you do?

Wyatt's text bubble appears, disappears, then reappears. While I await his response, I listen back in, and sure enough, Gloria is still babbling. "Enough," I command. "This is your last chance to do this in a way that ensures your livelihood. Either you let me, or I'll—"

I hear the click and then the dial tone, indicating that the line's been disconnected, and I see red. Gritting my teeth, I gaze down at the offending receiver to confirm that my ears aren't deceiving me. *Gloria fucking hung up on me.*

Pulling out my cell phone, I ignore the incoming text messages and call my uncle. We've been playing nice for too long. Two nights ago, we broke ourselves free, and Ariah needs to know why we stayed away. She needs to know we never once stopped fighting our way back to her—that she's our endgame.

"Bash. How are—"

"They still won't let us in to see her," I shout, cutting my uncle's greeting short.

"Of course, they're not. They've been given specific orders to not let any of you in."

What the actual fuck? If he weren't my uncle and one of the only good father figures outside of Ariah's, I'd tell him to where he could fuck off.

The Council is more of a hindrance than a support system. "Why the hell would the Council sanction something so damn asinine?" I question.

Clearing his throat, he declares, "Because she needs and has earned this time. Ariah's been made to suffer at the hands of Matthew Baker, Samantha Davenport, and all of their cronies." Sighing, my uncle continues, "I thought you all agreed to give her time—that you all understood why it is necessary?" His response sounds more like a question than a statement.

Logically, I understand his reasoning, but logic and reason aren't in the driver's seat. Instead, I'm close to kicking in the door and saying fuck the alarm system and the privacy of other patients when I see a person dressed in what appears to be surgical gear—blue scrubs with the matching head covering and mask. The only things visible are their hands and eyes.

"Bash! Are you listen—" I hang up when they scan their badge. *Perfect timing.*

Shadowing their steps, I keep my head down, following close enough behind to sneak in but not enough to alert the person to my existence. I'm about to pass through the door when a hard shoulder slams into me. "Where the fuck do you think you're going?"

Fucking Reign! This asshole has been, quite literally, raining on our parade since he was put on Ariah's security detail—a move we are happy with a majority of the time. Reign protects her like a brother, giving us shit whenever we fuck up. Now, I'm reevaluating our initial support. He's made the last few months harder than necessary. Especially since I know he has some knowledge of the situation. My fists clench at my side, preventing me from swinging. *He's only doing his job.* I try to remind myself before responding. "I need to speak with her. She needs to know so many things—mainly that we never truly abandoned her."

He pushes at my chest, "I honestly don't give a fuck, Prince Charming. You and your merry band of idiots need to back the hell off. She doesn't need any of your shit right now."

Glaring at him, I try to breathe away my fury. "You don't think having Ariah think Owen was fucking Samantha while she carved the "A" off his chest is adding to her stress?" I argue.

"I know it is," he snaps, pushing me again, and I know the last tether of my control is about to break. "Add that to the laundry list of things you've all done, plus the endless number of responsibilities she's shouldering. If something doesn't give, she'll go into early labor. Is that what you selfish pricks want?" When he steps forward to push me this time, I let him—he's right. "Everything that's transpired has been at your pace. All the smoke and mirrors—all of the secrets—they've been on your terms."

Running my hands through my hair, I sigh, "It's not like—"

"Just shut the fuck up," Reign raises his hand to silence me. "Do I know foul things were in play and that Samantha, the chick you'd all run through a wood chipper alive, was part of it? Of course, I do—we all do. Shit, if Ariah weren't so hurt, she'd see through all the bullshit. I honestly believe she knows, but Ariah's holding her cards close to her chest just in case."

We promised more time, and we barely gave her two days. Ariah's not Samantha—a leech without conscience or regard for anyone but herself, and she's no Vivian—a delusional inconsiderate bitch.

"You're getting it now. For a doctoral student, you're not too bright. I guess it's true—book smarts don't equate to street smarts."

Narrowing my eyes, I retort, "It's interesting you're preaching so hard. I won't bring up memories that hurt. You and your *friends* have your own crosses to bear. Just know it's a bit hypocritical to tell us to stay away when you all did the exact opposite. I know what brought you all to Lincoln-Wood. Maybe you're talking to the man in the mirror."

Reign opens his mouth, but it's my turn to hold up my hand. "Save it. I understand what it means to feel helpless in a love you've only just discovered. Maybe the three of you should extend that grace to us." Done with him, I take the stairs, needing to feel the breeze on my face. Inhaling the fall air, I open my car door and check my phone—three missed calls from my uncle and a text message in our group chat. Deciding to call my uncle later, I start my car and bring up my messages.

"For fuck's sake," I shout to no one before I break out into laughter.

> LEV
> Owen's in.
>
> WYATT
> Operation get our Queen back has commenced.

Operation, get our Queen back indeed.

51
ARIAH

"A nurse will be in shortly to help you get dressed while we wait for Dr. Jaffri. Then, we should be out of here in the next hour," Elias says as he holds the door handle.

Nodding, I wait for the door to snick closed before I rest my head on the pillow. The sound of whatever show is playing on the television seems lightyears away. There is too much to process, but I can't calm my mind enough here. I need my discharge instructions so I can go home and think.

The engagement party was a fucking disaster from start to finish, and no one would tell me everything that transpired. Not even Shay.

Sighing, I rest my hand on my belly before turning to see my babies' strong heartbeats. I put them in jeopardy, all for some archaic ass rules. I should've fought harder to be excused or ignored the summons altogether. "I won't put you in danger again," I whisper, smiling when I feel a fluttering of movement against my palm.

I peer at the time, wondering when this nurse will arrive. I'm ready to return to my house on campus, but because I'm on bedrest until we return from fall break, everyone disagreed and suggested I return to the Bradford Estate in Edgewood. Rolling my eyes, I remember the serious look on everyone's faces when I made the request.

"You're on fall break, Ry. No one will even be on campus for the next two weeks," my father explains, hoping I understand.

We have been at this for the last fifteen minutes. "If no one will be on campus, then I have nothing to worry about. We can increase security measures," I try to reason.

"After Conner, your detail is made up of ten cleared men. There isn't enough time to vet anyone, and ten men are not enough," Thomas points out.

A throat clears, pulling my attention to my uncle. "Where's the niece who knew she needed a protective detail and that she isn't Natasha Romanoff?"

Oh, they're laying it on thick.

"She's tired of hiding and is ready to collect the blood of my enemies and make Samantha Davenport drown in it," I retort, and they snicker.

My dad offers other reasons, but I'm making my last stand.

"But, Dad—" I begin to say, imploring his understanding before he cuts me off.

"Absolutely not, Ry. It's too dangerous. The Senator is in the wind, and none of his known associates have heard from anyone," Dad states.

I make one last pleading look toward my family, only to be met with silence. My grandparents, my uncle, Shay, and Thomas shake their heads.

Shay uncrosses her legs and stands. "Ry! Girl, I know you want to throw a middle finger up to everyone who's hurt you, and rightfully so."

"You're damn right I do. And I will. I have plans for everyone that has screwed my family and me over, but that's not my point. I'm tired of having to bend to their will. Hiding behind the walls of the Bradford estate feels like we're still playing their game, and I'm fucking done with that shit. It's time to initiate the first part of my plan."

Shay crosses the room and holds my hand before she continues. "Slow down there, G.I. Jane," she jests.

I snort, quickly covering it up with a cough as I school my features while she continues. Lifting her hand, she ticks off each reason. "You've been kidnapped, almost sex trafficked, sent the body parts of other students, and we won't bother to count the number of times someone has tried to either blow you up or stab you. Until you're back on your feet, you need to take your ass home."

"Fine," I groan, giving my bestie the 'Et tu Brute' side-eye. Freaking traitor.

Rolling her eyes, Shay smiles. "Cut yuh bullshit, my girl, yuh dun know I'm right."

I didn't want to go home, but I understood why I had to in the end. My stubbornness is rooted in my need for some control in my life. I feel like I'm being controlled at every turn, but they're all right. I can't let my thirst for autonomy cause me to make stupid decisions.

Reign already left to get the car ready, and Elias and Fernando are standing guard outside my room while Thomas is with Dad, preparing the house for my return. Now, I just have to wait.

Another five minutes pass before there's a knock on the door. "Come in," I shout, and a person in blue scrubs and a mask enters.

"Miss Bradford?" the person asks, and I nod. "I'm Daniel. I'm here to review your discharge information and assist you with getting dressed."

"Okay," I reply, eager to leave.

Daniel gently closes the door. "Can you please just verify your full name?"

We go through all the verifications as he approaches. It's not until he's closer that I see a familiar tattoo peeking out from his scrubs. My eyes widen. "What the fuck are you doing here," I seethe.

Pulling his mask down, Owen raises his index finger to his mouth. "Shhh. I don't want them barging in here."

"I should scream so you can be removed. The nerve of you being here after everything," I hiss, feeling the tears threatening to fall.

"Please, Angel," he begs. "Let me explain."

My nostrils flare, and my lip curls in disgust. "Take your explanations and shove them up your ass."

"Only if you're holding the dildo," Owen smirks, momentarily shocking me into silence. He takes advantage of my stupor. "Things have not been as they seem. I can't tell you everything now because our time is limited, and we don't want to risk your health."

Regaining my ability to speak, I retort, "So, I imagined Samantha fucking you as she carved through the 'A' on your chest?"

I shouldn't care, not after everything they've done and all the pain they caused.

Owen reaches behind his back, pulls out a brown leather-bound journal, and offers it to me. "This will explain better than any words we can offer."

I stare at his proffered hand before leveling him with a glare. "Nothing any of you say will fix this."

Owen frowns. A forlorn look paints his face as he works his jaw. His hazel eyes lock with mine, and I watch as despondency morphs into determination. "Angel," he whispers my name like a prayer, "I know we've fucked up at every turn, but we promise to make this right. Which starts with explaining it all."

The earnest look in his eyes gives me pause. *Should I hear them out?* Reading it doesn't mean I forgive them. Holding out my hand, I accept the journal.

Owen sighs in relief as there's another knock on the door before it's pushed open. "Jefferson, you need to be out of here in the next five seconds," Reign snaps.

I watch as Owen's hand drops to the front of his scrubs, reaching for what I'm sure is one of his knives. A smile crests his face as he rolls his shoulders back, ready for a fight. "I'd love to see you try, asshole. I owe you a facial," he sneers.

"*I'd like to see you try*," Reign retorts, tossing Owen's words right back at him.

My hand shoots out before they can come to blows, grabbing Owen's wrist. "You two can measure dicks another time," I command. "Owen was just leaving. Weren't you, O?"

Owen's gaze meets mine, releasing his grip on his blade before he reaches up, caressing my bottom lip with his thumb. "Anything for you, Angel," he murmurs so only I can hear. Then Owen turns, walks toward the door, and pauses long enough to exchange death glares with Reign, Fernando, and Elias. "I'll see you fuckers soon," he mutters before disappearing from sight.

Yawning, I stretch, sitting up in my bed. It's my third day home, and after doing nothing but sleeping, I'm finally feeling more like myself. Turning, I glance at the journal I've left untouched. Part of me is nervous that I'll feel a greater sense of betrayal, but I also understand I won't know until I do.

I sigh, picking it up and running my fingers over my name engraved into the leather cover before I open to the first entry.

June 12, 2023

Ariah,

Today, I had to betray the trust of my brothers and crush your heart in the process. I did it to save Owen, and I can't lie and tell you I wouldn't make that same decision every time the scenario replayed. By the time we reached your house, you were gone, and so went the hopes of explaining what had to be done. Where did you go, and why did you run so quickly? Why didn't you fight?

Save Owen? Fuck, was leaving without confronting them a rash decision? Inhaling, I prepare myself for whatever comes next.

We still don't have all the details, but Owen was taken, and I was given explicit instruction to choose Samantha, or he'd be killed.

My breath hitches, robbing me of the necessary air to process what I've read.

I made the decision—not any of the other guys, and I'm not sorry for it. I hope you understand that. I'll never be sorry for doing what's necessary to protect the people I care about. But I need you to understand one thing, Ry, we're coming for you soon, and I'll drag you back here kicking and screaming until you hear us out because you're my forever girl.

Until then, I'll write the words I've struggled to say.

Wes

Song: Back to December- Taylor Swift

My pulse doubles, and my skin prickles with awareness as my mounting panic forces my eyes to close. I can't even focus on Wes's usual highhandedness. *They were forced, and Owen was missing.* But they never said a word. No one made any attempts to reach me once Owen came home. Snapping the journal, I center my thoughts before they spiral out of control. As eager as I am to discover their truths and the cause for their continuous betrayal, I can't read anymore for now.

Huffing, I grab my cell phone off my pillow and send the text.

ME

I'll meet with Wyatt tomorrow afternoon.

Not ready for their reply, I put my phone back on Do Not Disturb. I need more time to process before any of them can visit. A big part of my heart hangs on to the hope this won't break us.

52
WYATT

The last place I want to be is at some dumbass election campaign rally in some town I never knew existed in the United States. Yet, here we stand in Applebrook, Maine, hidden in plain sight.

I thought Edgewood was exclusive. Some of these towns have unofficial requirements to be able to move in. Otherwise, land is passed down through generations.

Cheers erupt around the packed campaign rally for the Presidential hopeful, better known as a dead Senator walking, Matthew Baker. I watch as another pompous prick walks up to the podium. "Did you know MC stands for master of ceremonies?"

"And why did we need to know that useless fact right now, Wy?" Sebastian asks.

Shrugging my shoulders, I adjust the collar of my army-green bomber jacket, blocking Maine's brisk fall air. "Aren't rallies for learning?" I quip, earning me an elbow in my side from Owen.

"Oh, this crowd is about to get a crash course in family relations," Owen replies, barely keeping a straight face.

Smirking, Sebastian adds, "You think he'll get a campaign boost from this rally?"

"Is everything in place, Lev?" Wes asks, getting us back on track.

"Baker is about to be announced," Lev states, then busies himself with some portable device. "I'm in their network, and the video is loaded. I only need to hit play once he's on stage."

The MC sings the Senator's praises—how he stands for good family values before spouting more lies the Senator promises to accomplish.

Holding out his arm in Baker's direction, the MC exclaims, "Without further ado, coming all the way from the great state of New York, Senator Matthew Baker."

I roll my eyes at all the 'Baker Will Make This Country Greater' signs.

Owen pulls one of his blades from its holster. I think it's Mary, but I can't be sure. "I could end this now if you just say the word."

Wes starts to speak but is cut off by the Senator. "Thank you, Applebrook. It's a pleasure to be with you all today. Before I get started, I wanted to make a special announcement."

Looking at Lev, I mutter, "What the fuck is he talking about? I thought today was just another campaign rally?"

"I'm not sure, but we're about to find out," Lev states.

"Applebrook, please give a warm welcome to my wife."

My eyes nearly pop out of my skull. "Are you seeing who I'm seeing?" I mumble, blinking to ensure my vision is clear.

"What. The. Absolute. Fuck?" Wes whispers.

Senator Baker grabs his wife's hand, pulling her in for a kiss before he continues. "Samantha Baker."

"This is better than a telenovela," Owen cackles.

"Please tell me we're going to hit play now?" I exclaim.

Lev is lowering his thumb toward the tablet. "I don't see why not. I couldn't have scripted—" Sebastian's hand shoots out, halting Lev's movements.

"Wait," he commands, making us all turn to him.

"Why the fuck would we do that? We can end his political aspirations right now," Wes states.

Sebastian leans in before responding. "This is perfect. There's a debate coming up in a few weeks. The way I see it, Samantha is leashed for now. So, we can spend this time with Ariah."

"I vote we do it now. Our plan isn't hinged on outing their relationship," Wes suggests.

"Or," Sebastian starts. "We can wait until he's on primetime television with millions tuning in."

We peer at each other, seeing if there are any objections. "Perfect. It's settled. Samantha's given us plenty of material to work with. Let's return the favor and make her life a living hell."

Smiling, I hum, "Operation end the bitch is a go."

⬤

Wiping my sweaty palms on my jeans, I step forward and ring the doorbell. Sneaking in to see Riri—zero nerves. Walking through the front door like a proper fool does—more nerves than I know what to do with.

The front door opens, and Aaron stands in the doorway. "So good of you to finally use the correct entryway," he teases.

"Aren't you a regular comedian?" I jest, and he laughs.

His hand clamps down on my shoulder. "Don't fuck this up. She's been through enough, and once she finds out everything, I'm sure we'll each have our turn on the chopping block," he confesses as Tweedle Dick, Tweedle Dumb, and Tweedle Dead Man step into the room.

"You assholes don't know the meaning of healing, do you?" Elias quips.

Narrowing my gaze, I smirk. "Unlike the others, I know your role is strictly platonic. As long as you keep her safe, you'll all continue to breathe." Refusing to take the bait, I climb the stairs two at a time until I stand outside Ariah's bedroom door.

The scene at their home in Colorado flashes through my mind as I mimic my actions from that night. My forehead rests against the door—my hand holds the knob as I inhale her scent, hoping this isn't the last time I'll see her. "I'm here, Love," I whisper, resting my palm on the door. She's inside, but my feet feel frozen in place.

"I know you're out there, Wy," Ariah announces, and I hear the amusement in her tone.

Turning the knob, I open her door, then step into her room. Ariah's sitting up in bed, drinking a smoothie. She's wearing one of the band tees I had included in the weekly care packages we sent. The avocado sits next to her body pillow. "Riri," I choke out, attempting to swallow the overwhelming emotions whirling in my chest. It's been too long, and the last time I was with Ariah, her cries nearly broke me.

A small smile appears on her face as she places her drink on the nightstand. That's all I need to cross the room. I capture her face in my hands, tilting her head up while lowering my lips to hers until I'm devouring her. She opens her mouth, allowing me access. Hints of apple, mango, and ginger burst across my tastebuds, but none of them compare to the flavor that is her. My hands move to grip her hair when I'm suddenly on the floor.

"Did you think you'd come in here, kiss me, and all would be forgiven? You have lots of explaining to do, asshole," she heaves. My gaze heats when her skin flushes red. Ariah licks her puffy, freshly kissed lips, and my cock comes to life. *Down boy.*

Pushing off the ground, I reply, "I expect nothing less. I'm here to answer all the questions I can."

Her strawberry-blond brow arches. "I'm going to say this one time only, so please pass the message on. Anyone who comes in here with that 'we can't tell you' or 'this is for your protection' shit will catch an elbow to the throat and a fist to the groin," she snaps.

"Fuck, I've missed you, Love," I profess.

Ariah crosses her arms. "You have one minute to start talking, or I'll kick you out."

I bite the inside of my cheek, drawing blood, trying to get my erection under control. "You have to cut that out, Riri, or I'll say screw your one minute and fuck you until you remember my dick is tattooed on your walls."

"Wyatt, please," she pleads, but I see the yearning burning in her gray eyes. Ariah blinks, regaining her composure. "We need to talk. I've been reading Wes's journal and have spoken to Shay, but there are still so many missing pieces."

Shaking off my lustful thoughts, I point to the spot on her bed, and she inclines her head for me to take a seat. "I'm not sure how far into his journal you are because Wes never let anyone read it. Hell, he tried to hide it for the longest time, but we all knew he had it," I begin, running my fingers through my hair.

Ariah shifts in the bed, adjusting her pillows before refocusing her attention on me. "Continue."

"That day was never supposed to happen," I growl, clenching my jaw. My anger rises at the memory of the turn of events. "None of us knew Wes's intentions until he announced *her* name. And trust me, Love, he paid for it."

Ariah asks more questions, and I continue to answer, from letting her know Wes was on everyone's shit list until we found out about Owen to the way we raced to her house to explain it all to her.

She nods. "Wes recounted that day's events and further detailed all your asinine reasons for why you couldn't at least tell me Owen was missing."

"First, explicit instructions were given that Owen would die. Secondly, you left," I mutter. "You packed up all of your shit without asking any questions and left us—left *me*!"

Surprise glints in her pewter eyes, and I fist my hands at my side. I didn't realize how hurt I still was about her leaving. "Wyatt, I—"

Her words seem to die in her throat, and I wonder if it's due to the anguish on my face. "I could see how you might doubt Wes, Lev, and even Sebastian's feelings, but O's and mine—ours should never have been in question."

"Everything happened so fast, and Wes's words," Ariah shakes her head. "His words left very little room for questioning. So, pardon me for not sticking around after being told I wasn't good enough. A message Wes and Lev looped for months."

The hurt in her gaze matches the cracked heart in my chest that stopped beating since she left. *Rein it in, asshole.*

I spring up from her bed and kneel beside her before clasping her hands in mine. "When the world is in chaos, and you're unsure which way to turn, know I'll always be your North Star, Love. Did it gut me that you weren't confident in my feelings for you? *Yes*, because my love for you knows no bounds. But I also know in the end, leaving kept you safe."

After standing, I sit on the edge of her bed, then lean forward, licking the tears trailing down her cheek, and groan before I pull back. My eyes glaze over. The hunger that simmers under my skin bursts to life.

"Focus," she snaps, breaking the spell.

I chuckle and sit back. "Can you blame me? I've been picturing you being back in my arms for months."

Ariah's neck flushes scarlet. "Wyatt, if you don't take this seriously, I'm going to ask you to leave," she exclaims.

She's right. The only way we make this right with her is to tell the truth. While our intentions are good, keeping information from Ariah has only made the situation worse and given Senator Baker and Samantha more power. Hopefully, after she knows everything, she'll forgive us.

Titling my head, I drink her in one last time before responding, "Okay, Love. Ask away."

53
ARIAH

June 20, 2023

Ariah,

I was hoping you and Owen would be back and this journal would no longer be necessary. Instead, I'm sitting at my desk writing to you while the search for Owen hasn't turned up shit. Every lead led to nowhere. Our ranks are filled with traitors, those loyal to Filiae Bellonae and Senator Baker. It's why none of us have reached out. It's not safe. We know two things:

1. Someone wants to take over the Fraternitas, and they're using the Selection to gain what they believe is a major in, and

2. Your life is in danger.

So, even though it's been too long since you were in my arms—my forever girl. For now, it's better for you to believe we don't want you.

Our hope is that we only have to cause you temporary

pain. Something we'll gladly spend the rest of our lives making it up to you.

Wes

Song: If I Would've Known- Kyle Hume

I want to rage at the words on the page. Owen was missing, and no one wanted me to know for my safety. Why does everyone try to treat me like antique porcelain? I won't crumble into dust at a soft breeze.

Throwing the covers off my legs, I head to the bathroom, shower, dress, and pull out my floor mat. I need to release the anxious energy coursing through my body.

Owen was fucking missing. The empty look in his eyes on the first day of classes catapults to the front of my mind.

Secrets abound. *Everyone is hiding something from me under the guise of protection.*

Inhaling, I suck in a lungful of air through my nose and expel it out through my mouth. Then, I begin my stretches. With each roll of my head, I can feel the tightness between my shoulders loosen.

"My girl, what are you doing out of bed? Go find your zen under the covers, " Shay chides, breaking my focus.

"I'm doing Tai Chi Chuan, bitch. You're in a completely wrong country."

She cuts her eyes at me. "Well, you can Namaste and stay inna yuh bed."

"Once again, correct continent but wrong country," I snort, shaking my head as she sits on my couch. "What are you doing here so early?" I ask, peering at the clock on my wall.

"I know Owen gave you their journal, and I wanted to make sure you were okay," she states, wringing her wrists. Something she does when she's nervous about something.

Pausing mid-stretch, I study her. There's a furrow between her brows, and she's gnawing her bottom lip. "What is it?"

Never one to mince words, Shay's soft brown eyes lock with mine. "I knew the guys weren't really with Samantha. Sebastian came to visit me while I was recovering." She stands. "Don't worry, I chewed him and all the guys a new asshole, but once I knew they had to choose that dutty hole gal in order to save Owen, I agreed not to tell you. We both know you would've never stayed away if you knew."

The more she speaks, the wider my eyes open. *She's known.* Why didn't she tell me? Shay's been at my side since the beginning. I open my mouth to get answers, but she holds up her index finger, signaling me to wait.

"I need to get this out. I know you have questions and probably feel betrayed, but Ry, I promise it's not that. Just let me finish."

Nodding, I plop down on my mattress and listen. She shares everything from the beginning. How much she's known but couldn't tell me. Shay's father's side of the family has been in Edgewood for a long time, but her mother is a transplant. Which means stricter rules govern them.

"I was on thin ice from everything I'd helped you with since moving here," she confesses.

Massaging the knot in my left shoulder, I try to process everything she's telling me. I don't want to believe that the girl who's become a sister to me only got close to me because she was ordered to. *So much for lowering my stress.* "Was any of it real?" I challenge, and her nose scrunches in confusion. "Our friendship," I shout. "Was any of it real?"

Shay looks like I struck her in the heart, and I wait for her to snap back. Instead, she breathes, composing herself. "I know you're hurting, and it feels like another betrayal from someone close to you—"

"It doesn't feel like it. It is like it," I hiss, cutting her off. "Let me make sure I have this right. You sent me false leads when I was trying to discover the history of the Selection and withheld vital information not once, not twice. Fuck, not even three times. It's happened so many times I've lost count."

I shoot up from my bed and pace the length of my bedroom floor. *You need to calm down. You can't overstress, or they'll put you back in the hospital. Remember the twins.* A tear escapes, sliding down my cheek to my lips. The salty taste angers me even more. I'm so fucking emotional now. All this bullshit crying.

"Please try and understand. The friendship we have has nothing to do with the Fraternitas. *It is real.* You're the batty tuh mi bench. The ackee to my saltfish and fried dumplin," Shay jokes, then wipes away the tears streaming in rivulets down her face with the back of her hand. "I had no choice. My mom's position in town was on the line. I'd given you one too many clues and answered far too many questions. If I so much as breathed wrong, we'd have been exiled."

I grit my teeth, halting my steps. She's right. Everyone in this town is regulated by rules, both spoken and unspoken. Closing my eyes, I reign in my hurt and anger. If I were in her place and my family was hanging in the balance, there would be no hesitation. Calmer, I sigh, then open my eyes to face her. "I'm still pissed, not so much at you. The Fraternitas and every organization like it will suck your soul and sell your future generations to the highest bidder." Walking toward her, I wrap her in a hug. At least, I try to. The beachball in front of me makes it hard to fully embrace her.

We both laugh, wiping the remnants of our tears away. "Just so you know, I had rope, duct tape, and a blindfold ready if you would've said you were no longer my friend," Shay jests.

"Fucking stalker," I quip.

Smirking, she retorts, "Hey, you never know when you might need to subdue someone. I believe in being prepared for all situations."

"Now you just sound like Wyatt," I tease. We both look at each other and burst into laughter.

As we sit on the couch, Shay continues to tell me everything she knows, cementing my decision. When she gets up to use the bathroom, I pull out the phone and send a text.

ME

Move forward.

UNKNOWN

... ...

I hear the sink faucet turn on and know I'm about to run out of time. Biting the inside of my cheek, I run through the plan again. So many lives will be impacted. I can only hope that when it all comes to fruition, everyone I love will be standing with me. The pipe turns off, and I start to put the phone away when another text alert sounds.

> UNKNOWN
>
> Everything's in place. Dispose of this phone, and we'll be in touch when it's time.

A Cheshire grin grows on my face. Step three has begun.

●

After the tense conversation I had with Shay earlier and reading four more passages from Wes's journal, I desperately need a break from all the intense emotions. The pain and grief poured from Wes's words struck me at my center. I can still taste his regret in every penned word.

"You scared us, Ry," Jamie mutters as we get ready to watch a movie with Kellan and Kylan. Her jewel-green eyes well with tears.

"Don't cry, Jams. I'm here, and everything is going to be okay," I say, trying to reassure her.

She shakes her head. "Nothing's been okay since Dad was taken three years ago. We've been on an endless loop of heartache. Our family has been destroyed. Moving here was supposed to fix it, but it only got worse."

Leaning over, I press a kiss on the top of my sister's head. "It has been a very long three years. Before we lost Dad, we lost Mom."

"No, we never had her. Mom never existed."

I rub the crease on my forehead, happy the boys are still downstairs picking out their movie snacks. "Oh, Jams, she existed. Hold on to the moments that brought you joy, but never get lost in them. Let go of the moments that hurt you, but remember the lessons that came from that pain."

She begins to sit up, so I follow suit. "What do you mean?"

Smiling, I reply, "Even though we discovered our mother was never who she pretended to be, we shouldn't let her rob us of the happy memories. We've gained so much. More family and new friends to create new moments with."

I brush the last of her tears from her face. She looks so much like our mom. "We did," she exclaims. "It just sucks that we had to lose her in the process. I miss her."

She hangs her head, and I tip her chin so she'll meet my gaze. "And there's nothing wrong with that. You're allowed to mourn her. To feel a hole in the place she used to be."

Jamie's lips quirk seconds before she wraps her arms around my neck. "Thanks, Ry. I love you."

"I love you, and any time you want to talk, I'm here. And if you ever want or need professional support to help you process what you're feeling, let one of us know."

Her grin grows as the twin terrors come piling onto the bed with what looks like the whole kitchen. "Time to watch *Venom*," Ky screams.

"No, I want to watch *Guardians of the Galaxy*," Kell shouts.

I snatch the remote off the bed. "Snooze, you lose. First up is *Iron Man*. We're watching these in order."

"Aww, come on, Ry."

"Booo, I want Sonic."

"I've got you, boo," Jamie declares before tackling them and tickling their sides until they give in. Their peals of laughter bounce off the walls. I rest my head on my hand, watching my siblings goof off.

This is what I'm fighting for.

54
ARIAH

"Your blood pressure is still higher than I'd like, but it has come down. Have you been keeping your stress levels down?" Dr. Jaffri asks, notating my record as I sit on the exam table.

As she continues to input information, I peer around the room, taking in the medical equipment. Over my first few days home, they've converted an area of the estate into a home doctor's office.

I can feel Dr. Jaffri waiting for me to answer. I thought I'd have more time before my next visit. I've only been home for four days, and between my argument with Shay, the visits from the guys, and Wes's journal, I'd say it's a miracle I'm not back in the hospital.

"Isn't my appointment next week at your office?" I counter, hoping she doesn't realize I'm avoiding her question.

Placing her tablet on the counter, Dr. Jaffri levels me with a pointed glare. The type you get when you know you've been caught with your hand in the cookie jar before dinner. "Open," she orders, holding the thermometer probe to my mouth.

My lips part, and I mentally prepare for the lecture I know is coming. "Ariah, you're an intelligent young woman. So, I know I don't need to tell you the seriousness of your condition," she begins, pulling the thermometer from my mouth before disposing of the probe cover.

"You're carrying twins. Two developing fetuses. That means double the work on your body to ensure you give birth to two healthy babies," Dr. Jaffri continues, her teal stethoscope in her hand, lifting the headpiece, placing the earpieces in her ears, and holding the chest piece to my back. "Deep breath," she orders, and I immediately follow instructions again. "Which also means you need to. . ." She moves to another spot on my back, and I inhale. "Take care of yourself."

Suitably chastised, I say, "I'll do better. There are a lot of high-stress situations I'm juggling currently."

"You can't pour from an empty cup," Dr. Jaffri cuts in, and I nod my agreement. Her message is received. Loud and clear.

We talk as she continues the exam, explaining what to expect as I prepare to enter my final trimester. We briefly discuss birthing plans.

"I would like to have my babies at the hospital and not the medical facility at the Edgewood Estate," I declare emphatically. Even though we're working on our relationship, I refuse to be left in the lurch if they decide they're done with me again. "I'll discuss heightening security measures with my father and security team. They'll coordinate with you and the hospital."

Dr. Jaffri smiles. "I'll get in touch with your head of security and get things moving."

Fifteen minutes later, she makes her final notations before packing her doctor's bag. As she readies herself to leave, I remember she never actually answered my question earlier.

Rising from the exam table, I straighten my shirt and say, "You never did tell me why you saw me today at home instead of next week in your office."

With her bag in hand, Dr. Jaffri is at the door when she turns and replies, "Mr. Washington ordered an in-home visit immediately."

My face scrunches in confusion. "Why would Lev's father concern himself with my prenatal care?"

"Oh, no, dear, you misunderstood. *Levi Washington* demanded I see you today," she clarifies before exiting the room and leaving me with my mouth hanging open.

●

I stand in shock, staring at the video gaming equipment that was installed in my room while I was at my prenatal appointment, immediately knowing this is also Lev's doing.

Walking further into the room, I approach the sleek, brand-new jet-black desk, then sit in the midnight blue, purple, and black ergonomic chair with extra lumbar support and some sort of footstool beneath the desk. A lit-up wireless keyboard and mouse, matching the color of the chair, are set in front of the two monitors mounted to the wall. But none of that is why I shoot up from my seat as my eyes well with tears that threaten to spill over. Bookshelves filled with special editions of some of my favorite books stand on both sides of the desk.

I run my hand along the spines, pulling one book after another out to examine the signed copy of each beautifully sprayed-edged hardcover book with foil accents.

It's at this moment that I'm grateful I'm alone and Lev isn't here because I certainly would've forgotten myself and fucked him senseless, ignoring the fact I'm still upset with him.

Sighing at the reminder of their betrayal, I turn away from the bookshelf, striding toward my bed. It's only then I see a brand new tablet with a pen. Sitting on my bed, I push a button, lighting the screen. Lev must have put some high-tech shit on it because it unlocks as soon as my face comes into view. Some pre-installed apps appear on the home screen, but I ignore them all once I notice the one for graphic design.

I reach into my pocket, pulling out my phone. It barely rings before his face appears on the screen. "Making appointments and infiltrating my room to have a gaming system installed. Is ordering doctor's visits and sneaking into a woman's room to install things a kink, Lev?" I ask, quirking my brow.

Not looking the least bit apologetic, Lev's heated stare meets mine before replying, "You know exactly what my kinks are, Dove. Should I bring my ropes over to remind you?"

I feel the blush rise up my neck into my cheeks and my traitorous pussy clenching at the thought of his rope against my skin again. The last few times weren't nearly enough.

Lev's eyes follow the sweep of my tongue as it glides over my lips. His nostrils flare before the lust in his gaze melts, quickly replaced by his usual stoic mask. "You've been under an enormous amount of stress. The kind that, according to my research, can bring on preterm labor. We can't have that," he states, and a big part of me wants to push his buttons, riling him up until his composure cracks. I love it when Lev's carefree. He's always carrying the weight of the world on his shoulders. They all are.

"As Dr. Jaffri so aptly reiterated," I grumble, and he smirks.

"You know she only means well. We all want to make sure you're supported and taken care of. For so long, we had to do it from the sidelines," he frowns.

Shifting on the bed, I lean back against my pillowed headboard. "From the sidelines?" I echo as confusion knits my brows.

Lev's lips curl into a sly grin. "You haven't made it to that part of the journal yet, I see." He pauses, and I hear his fingers flying over a keyboard. "I think we should all be on the phone for this part," Lev explains before four more faces join the call.

"Angel," Owen groans. "You always look more fucking beautiful than the last moment I saw you."

Rolling his eyes, Lev blurts, "Chill out, Romeo. You can Rico Suave her on your own time. I added you bums to the call for a reason."

"Hater," Owen retorts, and I laugh.

"Definitely a hater," Wyatt adds without looking away. His hazel eyes drink me in. "Isn't he, Love?"

I've missed this.

The reminder of why I've had to miss anything glares like a beacon, lighting the path to my frustrations. Do I understand why they made the decision? *Absolutely.* That doesn't negate that no one felt I was strong enough or smart enough to navigate our current situation. I'm still sitting in the dark without all of the details, for fuck's sake. I snort. "Don't you dare put me in the middle of this."

"What if in the middle of us is exactly where we want you to be?" Sebastian quips, shocking me.

Five sets of hungry eyes convey just how on board they are with that plan. "Oh, that sounds like a fantastic idea," Owen gleams.

Clearing my throat, I refocus the conversation. If I stay on much longer, I'm sure I'll end up where they want me, and they haven't earned back that right. "You'll have to entertain each other. A nice circle jerk." My nipples harden at that image.

Wyatt zeros in on my mouth just as I bite my lip. "You'd love that, wouldn't you, Love? All of us getting each other off to thoughts of getting you off?"

My entire body's on fire. My already swollen breasts feel even heavier while the urge to slip my hand between my legs and make them watch rides me. The bitch-ass devil on my shoulder whispers, 'Do it,' and I have to turn my head to break the spell.

"Turn it down a few notches, Wy. That's not why we're here," Lev mutters. "Ariah wants to know what I meant when I said we've been supporting her from the sidelines."

"So you haven't gotten to that part of the journal," Wes states, and I nod, confirming. "It means that once you returned and we knew you were carrying our baby, we've been sending you gifts and ensuring any craving or want you've had is met."

I freeze, my heart stalling in my chest as I remember all the stuffed animals, the fruit baskets, pillows, and baby gifts. "That's been you guys?" I choke out, not sure I can manage to say anything more.

"We only wish we could've done more. Fuck, we should've been with you from the very start," Owen growls.

"Another reason the Senator and Samantha are dead," Wes spits.

My eyes narrow to slits at the mention of her name. "What exactly does a college student freshly out of high school have to do with any of this?"

"Finish reading," Lev instructs, and I'm thankful a screen separates us because, of fucking course, I don't get a straight answer.

Rage suffuses my skin, crawling up my limbs until I'm suffocating in it. "There are always hoops to jump through only to get half-ass answers with everyone in this fucking town. I'm so sick of it," I seethe, clenching my teeth so hard that the muscle in my jaw causes my left eye to twitch.

I spring from my bed, my chest heaving as I try and fail to regain my composure, but I can feel my blood pressure boiling past its tipping point. "Why can't anyone give me a goddamn straight answer that's not riddled with vagueness?" I snap, waiting for someone to answer me, but they all remain silent. Varying looks of sympathy are etched on each of their faces. Hitting my threshold for bullshit for the day, I glare at them and then end the call.

55
WES

The spot where I keep my journal remains vacant, reminding me that it's with Ariah, and she's getting an unfiltered glimpse of my soul. Rubbing my forehead, I try to remain positive. After hanging up on us during the video call, she hasn't spoken to anyone. It's been radio silence for three days. I need her to understand why remorse isn't an emotion I feel in this situation.

"Wesley." I spin my computer chair at the sound of my mother's voice. A bright, warm smile is on her face as she enters my room.

Guliana Edgewood is dressed impeccably—cranberry pants that taper at her ankles with a cream-colored off-the-shoulder cable knit sweater and matching heels. Thin gold bracelets adorn her wrist, pairing well with her wedding ring and diamond stud earrings.

"Mom, what are you doing here?" I inquire, standing to hug her.

She steps back, pulling from my embrace. "Do I need a reason to come and see my son?" she counters, turning to survey my room before her eyes find mine. "You haven't been home this entire fall break."

"I just needed a few days to be alone," I explain, rubbing the back of my neck. "There's still over a week left of break. I promise to come home this weekend."

My mother's knowing gaze tells me there's no need to explain further. She's the only other woman I let my guard down for. "This will be over soon enough, Wesley. You rid yourself of the lecherous viper. Now, the real work begins—earning Ariah's forgiveness."

"I know." I sigh. "But it's easier said than done."

Amusement fills my mother's features. "If love were meant to be easy, so many people wouldn't get it wrong," she insists before sitting and crossing her legs. "More people are in relationships disguised as love. So the first chance their love is tested, it doesn't weather the storm."

"I didn't mean it like that," I say, trying to get her to understand. "I spent months trying to run Ariah from town, and I spent even longer denying there was any attraction." A fact I'll take to the grave. I gave Wyatt and Owen shit for their obsession with Ariah, but in truth, I was enthralled—am enthralled. The day I received her file, I studied it until I memorized every detail. I did it under the guise of knowing my enemy. "But the minute I allowed myself, it was so effortless to love her."

My mother's lip quirks. "I'm going to impart a little wisdom on you. Falling in love is easy. Staying in love takes more effort, but growing in love takes work. If you're unwilling to do the work, Wesley, you'll need to let her go because Ariah is not a girl who'll accept half-assed effort."

I ruminate on her words before I profess, "Ariah is my forever. I'll do more than whatever it takes to love her like she deserves." Then I peer down at my mother, waiting for her to meet my eye before I declare, "But there isn't a scenario where I'll let her leave me."

She stands, smoothing out her clothes before grabbing her rust-colored Dior purse. "Good. I'm glad I didn't give birth to a quitter. Now come and have lunch with me."

●

"Why do you think we're here?" Owen asks as we exit the elevator outside the Council's chambers.

An hour after I had lunch with my mother, my father called, requesting we all come to the Fraternitas.

"I'm sure it has something to do with Senator Baker," Sebastian replies.

"Has something new happened?" Wyatt inquires as we proceed down the hallway.

Turning, I wait for Sebastian's response. Things have been eerily quiet. Outside campaign events, we haven't heard anything from the Senator or his wife. It would be suspicious if Lev didn't inform us that Senator Baker has Samantha under close watch. Which means we won't have to deal with her delusional ass.

We're standing outside the chamber doors before Sebastian answers. "Not that I know of, but given that he planned to force us to marry Samantha to secure his position for the presidency, one can deduce that Baker is planning something."

I hum my agreement, opening the door. The Council sits five original families strong. It's still strange to see a Bradford occupying a seat that has been vacant for decades. Ariah's father sits to the right of mine, and I can't help but wonder why he doesn't demand his rightful spot.

"Boys, have a seat," my father instructs, waiting for us to sit before he continues. "First, we'd like to congratulate you on a job well done. You five have made the Fraternitas proud. Now that the bomb has been removed from Owen, we can weed out the other traitors in our ranks." My father points to the tablets on the table. "On these, you'll find the information of at least three dozen people who need to be questioned and then eliminated."

Picking up the device, I bring my eye up to the scanner. It beeps, prompting me to place my palm on the screen, initiating the biometric thermal scanner to open the tablet.

"As you see, we've tiered them based on rank within the Senator's organization, level of suspected knowledge, and position within the Fraternitas," Owen's father explains.

A fist slams against the table, forcing my attention to where Owen sits. "This fucker is mine," he snaps, holding up an image of a man with a slender build. He's barely six feet tall with oily chestnut hair and murky-brown beady, dead eyes.

I read his name, but it's Sebastian who voices the question. "Who the fuck is Grady Templeton?"

"A dead man," Wyatt answers. "If the look on Owen's face says anything."

Owen's usually light hazel eyes darken, narrowing to slits. "He's the asshole I separated from the head of his dick over the summer. The one I plan on making a eunuch for whatever's left of his miserable life."

Memories of conversations play in my mind. Unlike when he was younger, Owen has shared some of what happened to him. He didn't share everything, but it's far more than he's ever done before.

"So, he's first, then," Lev says, speaking for the first time. His fingers are already fast at work, digging up every detail of Grady's life. By the time he finishes, we'll know the last time Grady flossed his teeth.

I grunt my agreement and study the rest of the names on the list. I don't know if there's a family in town who didn't play a part in trying to destroy the Fraternitas. And not for the first time, I wonder if the organization we pledge allegiance to will survive.

Wyatt springs from his chair first. Sebastian, Owen, and I are quick to follow suit. "Have a seat. We're not finished here," Ariah's father demands.

My gaze flits to Lev, wondering if they have an idea of what we'll discuss next, but he shrugs.

"As you know. My daughter is pregnant and hell-bent on returning to school." Mr. Bradford begins, and I know whatever he says next will be a fight once Ariah discovers his plan. "This means she'll need around-the-clock protection."

The door opens, but I don't bother to look away from Aaron. I already know it'll be one of the Council's assistants bringing our new assignments.

"It also means accommodations will need to be made for Ariah and Shay to move into your house on campus." I groan, instinctively knowing I won't like whatever Mr. Bradford is about to share.

"Not these jerk-offs," a voice that grates on every last nerve I have mutters.

Whirling around, I meet Reign's, Fernando's, and Elias's glares with one of my own before I spin back. "Absolutely the fuck not," I growl.

"This isn't up for debate," Aaron declares, looking over my head. "With any of you. My daughter comes first. The rest of you can get fucked if you think I care about your personal feelings above her safety."

I clench my fists at my side, knowing he's right. That doesn't change the fact that I want to clothesline all three of these idiots for the shit they've been pulling. Ariah's ours—she's my forever. Fuck them for implying otherwise. "Fine," I finally grumble.

Ariah's father stands, placing both palms on the table and leaning forward. Arching his brow in a way that reminds me far too much of his daughter, he snaps, "I wasn't asking for your approval, Wesley. Now, all of you get the hell out."

56
ARIAH

July 10, 2023

My Forever,

Owen's been missing for weeks, and every lead to finding him is a dead end. Almost as soon as we discovered Jameson was in on the kidnapping, our hands were tied. We don't know exactly what the Senator plans to do, but he intends to use Samantha to do it.

But it doesn't matter what tactics they use. We'd all sooner die than marry her. The Senator may have us under his thumb, but we're working overtime to chop off his hand and shove it up his ass (I can almost hear your laughter as I wrote this).

Time feels like it's moving in slow motion and at warp speed all at once. Every day that passes is another reminder that my best friend is missing and our girl is gone. I'm not even sure how we'll tell him you're no longer here when he returns. Owen's going to flip his shit.

You've been a light in all of our darkness, but you've been the Angel that saw the Devil but loved him anyway. That's what you mean to O. Out of everyone I hurt with my decision, you and Owen are the two that weigh the heaviest on my heart. Wyatt, Lev, and Sebastian are pissed but understand why. Owen will shout we fucked up and chose wrong—your love is worth his life because, without you, he's already dead.

I need you to know, Ry, while I'll let you be pissed and raise hell, I won't let you leave us because we'll never let you go.

Wes

Song: Control - Zoe Wees

I clutch my heart as I reread Wes's journal entry for the fifth time. I haven't been able to move past this page in days. I'm too terrified to read the horrors Owen faced and the devastation he must've felt when I wasn't there when he woke up.

How do I face that?

How can I face them?

With each entry, my anger toward them wanes, but my frustration explodes. Annoyance with them, with myself, and with the whole fucking situation.

Sighing, I close the journal. I know I need to keep reading, not just to find answers but because I see Wes letting his guard down with each passage he pens. His willingness to be vulnerable helps me understand the parts of him he keeps hidden.

I know Wes isn't one-dimensional. He's a rich, broody asshole walking around with a chip on his shoulder because he has something to prove.

"Ry." Jamie's voice pulls me from the endless swirl of thoughts swimming around my head.

Looking up, I see her standing in my doorway. "Hey, Jams, what's up?"

She shrugs. "I wanted to come hang with you."

I smile, patting the empty side of my bed. "Hop in."

Her face lights before she runs, diving head first onto my mattress. "Cannonball," Jamie giggles as she bounces. It's a sound I'll never tire of hearing. Any chance my twelve-year-old sister gets to be a tweenager, I bask in it.

"How's school?" I ask as she sits up and leans her back against my headboard.

I watch the joy melt from her face, a scowl now in its place, before she turns away from me. My hackles rise, and I'm already planning ways to make whoever is causing her face to twist in anger pay. "Jams?"

She still isn't looking at me when she confesses, "Not as great as it used to be." I wait, not wanting to push her. "There's this boy at school who's been trying to bully me."

Yup, I'm going to go to jail for knocking out some snot-nosed sixth grader.

"Who is it?" I press, trying to remain calm.

Turning, Jamie's lips thin. "Killian Porter," she hisses.

Porter. Why does that last name sound so familiar?

Clenching and unclenching her fists, she huffs, "He says his brother went to high school with you."

"Brian Porter?" I question. He's the only Porter I know, but I can't understand why his shit stain of a younger brother is harassing my sister. "Okay," I prompt, hoping for more details. I remember Brian from high school, but as far as I can remember, we've never had any significant interactions.

"Killian said his older brother's missing, and it's because of you. That ever since we moved here, you've caused nothing but trouble, and now his brother is probably dead because he crossed the founding families, so their family is ruined," Jamie explains, answering my unspoken question.

What the fuck?

I'm way past tired of people blaming me for their problems. It's getting old fast. I don't think I've ever spoken five words to Brian. Shit, outside Jameson's class, I never saw him, and now his douchey younger brother is trying to intimidate Jamie. "Why does he believe I'm responsible for that?" I wait to hear whatever poor excuse he gave her.

She rolls her eyes and responds, "It has something to do with the Selection. Supposedly, you ruined everything. Our whole family did when we moved here."

"Me?" I ask, scrunching my face in confusion. "How the hell did he arrive at that conclusion?"

She shrugs. "Killian just keeps saying that his mom was always crying, and his father was always stomping around the house livid, blaming Brian for being a traitor."

None of this makes any sense. What the fuck does Brian's behavior and sudden disappearance have to do with me? Massaging my temples, I try to tamp down my annoyance. A task that grows harder each day I'm back in this town. "How'd this lead to him bothering you?"

"Well, he calls himself teaching my *whore of a sister*," Jamie mutters.

The tops of my ears burn red in loathing. If Brian isn't truly missing, he will be once I get my hands on him. "The jerk thought I was easy prey, cornering me in a hallway after gym on Friday. So, I kicked him in the dick."

Spluttering, I cough to clear the spit that flies down my throat and cackle. "Jams," I scold, but it falls flat. It's hard to take your older sister seriously while she's holding her side, laughing as she puts her hand up for a high-five.

I know this isn't the reaction I should have, but I have time to work on that. Plus, I'd argue that she was in her right to defend herself. None of my siblings will take anyone's shit.

Jamie's palm and mine connect, and I hug her. We spend the remainder of the night talking and watching television. I make a mental note to ask the guys if Brian's missing and why I would be responsible for any of it.

57
ARIAH

Rubbing my bleary eyes, I internally curse myself for staying up so late to read Wes's journal.

After Jamie left my room and went to bed last night, I immediately snatched it off my nightstand, hoping to find more answers within its pages.

Standing, I stretch, then rush to use the bathroom. I'm unsure which twin is doing the cha-cha slide on my bladder this morning, but their message has been heard loud and clear.

I flush the toilet, wash my hands, and brush my teeth. Owen's coming over this morning to talk.

Shutting my eyes, I breathe, remembering the text I sent him after I read he was found. It's one of the shortest entries so far, immediately setting off alarm bells. I read entry after entry until my eyes refused to remain open. There was no mention of the condition Owen arrived home in. Until then, Wes made it a point to share so much detail. The absence of it made it nearly impossible to sleep. Hence the dark circles staring back at me as I stand in front of the mirror in my closet.

"Angel," I hear Owen call from inside my bedroom, pulling me from my trance. I throw my hair in a messy bun and head out to meet him.

"Owen," I whisper, scanning him for any obvious scarring. I find none, but remember that he didn't play in the homecoming game.

My cheeks heat. The memory of his face between my legs, in the bathroom of the football stadium, vividly plays in my mind.

He smiles, a knowing grin painting his face. "I know, Angel," Owen groans, closing the distance between us. "I know," he repeats, cupping my face.

I find myself leaning into his hand, basking in the warmth of his touch as I peer up into his hazel eyes. "They took you," I whimper as his thumb brushes my jaw, wiping away tears I didn't realize were falling.

"But they couldn't keep me. I'm okay, Angel. The important part is that you're safe, and now we have you back."

I choke back a sob, hating his answer. "It matters," I shout, pulling from his embrace and pushing him. But the asshole doesn't even budge. Instead, he tilts his head and smirks, pissing me off even more. I want to shake the shit out of him. Why is he always so dismissive of his safety? I scream in frustration, pounding my fists against his chest. "They fucking took you, and no one thought I needed to know. And here you stand, grinning like a cat who caught a canary."

The smile melts from his face. "They were only trying to—"

"Keep me safe," I seethe, finishing the regurgitated statement I was long past tired of hearing. "Fuck all of you and your goddamn need to keep me safe. It's bullshit, and you know it."

Dropping my arms, I step back, knowing I need space to calm down. Owen reaches for me, but I back away. Because fuck him and fuck them. Actually, fuck every person who thinks I'm incapable of making decisions for myself.

"Why doesn't anyone comprehend that I should be included in any conversation pertaining to *my* safety? Do you honestly believe I would put myself at risk?" I rasp, my face twisting in anguish. I'm no longer angry or annoyed. Hurt and disappointment unfurl in my chest like a poisonous gas, suffocating me slowly, making me question everything. "Do none of you trust me? Is that it?"

Owen's eyes widen. "Of course, Angel—with our lives," he declares, clasping my hand before I can step out of his reach and pressing it against the spot where my initial is carved. "If anyone feels your rage at having their choice taken from them, it's all of us. Wes being forced to make the split decision to let you go or save me set off a domino effect of forced decisions we're still trying to fix."

I freeze, my eyes close, picturing the journal entry before blinking back open. Wes's words were coated in fury, resignation, and hope. "He chose right," I exclaim, making Owen frown.

"Seeing you—getting back to *you* fueled my fight. So, when I came back and found that you were gone because they picked me instead of you, I was beyond pissed. They fucking chose wrong!"

He must see the horror on my face because he rushes on, "I was the one who fucked up. You told me to stay. I promised you I'd be safe and would come right back to you. I allowed my ego to put us all in a precarious position, and you paid for it. Anything that happened to me once I was taken was my cross to bear—not yours."

Inhaling, I dig my nails into the palms of my hand to prevent me from slapping the idiot upside his head. "If you ever sacrifice yourself for me, I'll bring you back to life to kill you myself."

Owen's features darken, and his nostrils flare like he's trying to compose himself. "It's a death I'd welcome before I see any harm come to you or our babies—a sentiment I know all of us share. We'd sooner welcome the Apocalypse, ending humankind as we know it."

My lips thin, and the tightness in his jaw slackens, morphing into another freaking smirk. "Luckily for you, none of us plan to let even death separate us. "

I glare, trying to pull from his hold, but his grip only tightens. It's not enough to hurt. It's just enough to give me pause. "Yet here you stand, ready to die and leave me," I mutter.

Owen tugs me into his chest and cups my face in his palms, angling my head until I meet his eyes. "Never," he growls, lowering his lips to mine.

Moaning, I relax, allowing myself to get lost in the feel of his mouth on mine. His tongue slips between my lips, and I meet his advances with my own. My hands travel up the expanse of his broad, muscular chest before I wrap them around his neck. I can't press completely into him because two bundles of joy have decided to be cock blockers.

The reminder of pregnancy splashes cold water over my face. I want to get lost in his arms forever, but we have a lot to discuss.

Sighing, I step back, and Owen grumbles, making me snort. "We need to finish talking. I have questions. Ones that need to be answered before I can let any of you back in."

He studies me more for a moment, then groans, "I know. I don't have to like it, though."

My snort morphs into a full laugh as I shake my head, tugging him to sit on my couch. None of my questions will be answered if we sit on the bed.

"You would laugh at my pain," Owen grumbles, gripping himself through his pants.

Biting my lip, I reason with myself, arguing that just a few touches before we discuss things can't hurt. *Down, you horny bitch.* I hear him snicker and pinch his side. "Now, who's laughing at who?"

His hand glides up my thigh and squeezes as a mischievous smile crests his face. Owen leans over, wrapping his lips around my peaked nipple and sucking through my shirt while cupping my other breast. I throw my head back, welcoming the sensations coursing through my body. My pussy clenches, and I desperately want to table our conversation until we both come.

Owen nips the raised peak before renewing his assault. His hand drops from my chest, dipping beneath the fabric of my lounge pants. My legs fall open, giving him greater access, and he rewards me by swirling the tips of his fingers over my clit.

Desperately needing more, I lift my hips and grind in sync with his pace. I'm about to say fuck it when his mouth and hands disappear. "Time to talk," he teases, and now I want to murder him for a completely different reason.

"Stupid touching me and getting me turned on when you know

we need to have a serious discussion fucker," I mumble. Only serving to make him laugh harder.

My eyes narrow to slits as I reach down and grab his shaft, pumping him through his sweats. "Fuck, Angel," Owen grunts as his gaze heats. I increase my pace, and he reaches for me. I pat his hand away and release my grip on his dick.

Owen protests, and I smile in victory. He shakes his head, then clears his throat, adjusting himself before raising his hands. "Okay. Okay. I surrender. Ask away. Just know once we're finished, I'm going to make you choke on my cock after you ride my face."

Licking my lips, I catch my breath and give him a few moments to collect himself before I ask, "Why couldn't any of you tell me?"

"We couldn't risk you getting hurt. There were and still are too many unknown variables, and none of us are willing to put you in harm's way. Especially once we found out you are pregnant." He pauses, staring deep into my eyes before he continues. "A snowball has a greater chance in hell than any scenario where we allow you to get hurt. We stayed away as much as it pained us. I was a literal walking time bomb."

I clench my fists. All my earlier lust is doused at the reminder of the explosive implanted in his body. I'm going to peel Samantha's skin off before feeding what's left of her to that fucking prink of a senator.

Part of me warms to their steadfast need to keep me safe. The other part still wants to stomp on their dicks for not at least telling me.

"But the football game?" I inquire.

"It was a very slim window of opportunity I selfishly took advantage of. I was drowning without you. Seeing you but not being able to love you the way you deserve cracked me open. It was a stupid move. One of the guys made sure I understood."

A scene I've desperately tried to scrub from my memory flits across my mind. "The engagement party. When she. . . when she. . ." I can't make myself say the words.

Understanding my struggle, Owen replies, "It was the only way to get her close enough to deactivate the chip. I'll be sorry for how I treated you that night and what it caused for the rest of my life." His eyes well with tears, a lone one cascades down his face, but before they can finish its descent, I lean forward and lick it away. Then I lift his hand to the "O" near my heart.

"That musty cunt rag and the slimy senator don't get any more of any of our heartache." I rise and straddle his lap before continuing. "They only get to lay at the feet of our rage before we end them."

58
LEV

"Did you get the folder I sent?" I ask Teagan as she walks back into the frame with a plate of cake.

"Sure did. I'll look at it once I finish this red velvet cake," she replies, plunking down in her chair.

Snorting, I work on inputting the string code. Even though Baker and Samantha are on the campaign trail, we need to be ready. They won't take their plans being thwarted well, so it's only a matter of time before they strike back. "I think we can—" I pause, squinting to make sure I'm seeing things clearly. "Are you eating your cake with a knife and spoon?"

I watch Teagan do a happy dance while she cuts a piece of her cake and then pushes it onto the spoon. "Judge your mother, bitch, and let me be great," she quips, kicking her feet up on her desk.

Stifling a laugh, I shake my head and refocus on the task before me. We've been working on a way to permanently take control of any chips and the devices made to activate them.

Moments later, my phone buzzes. Picking it up off my desk, I notice it's Ariah calling. "Dove," I breathe, grateful she's on the line.

"Hey, Lev," she replies as I hold up a finger, signaling I'll be back to Teagan.

I clear my throat, stepping into my bathroom for more privacy. "Are you okay?" I inquire, worrying something's wrong.

"Yeah, I uh. . . I was reading Wes's journal and had a few questions about the explosive they implanted into Owen."

My shoulders relax, and the tension I don't realize I'm feeling eases. "Of course. Ask me anything."

"Do you mind coming over? I'd really prefer to do this in person. It would be the most secure way to discuss what happened."

I fist pump the air, ecstatic she wants to see me, even if it's only to answer questions. Then I remember she's waiting for an answer. "Absolutely," I state, trying to sound composed. "What time did you have in mind? I'm finishing up a few things, but I should be done in the next two hours."

"Perfect," Ariah exclaims. "I want to read more of the journal and take a nap. I'll see you in a few hours."

"I'm looking forward to it." We exchange goodbyes, and I wait until she hangs up. Even more motivated, I burst through the door.

Teagan looks up, her plate now gone. "What has that ridiculously happy smile on your face, Washington?"

"My woman wants to see me," I blurt out.

Smirking, Teagan states, "I take it things are going well then?"

"It's moving in the right direction," I confess because Ariah wanting to see and speak to me is everything I've been wishing for since June.

"Well then, I guess we should get a move on," Teagan infers, and I nod, sitting before she pulls the code up on our shared screen. "This part right here," she circles with the computerized pen. "We need to switch a few commands, but I'm positive this is what we need."

I study our work, reading to see what we need to change to make this work. Pointing to three other areas, I suggest moving around two more lines before we rerun it.

•

O

Get out of the car, you chicken shit.

WY

What he said. You're not going to make things up to her from inside your car. Pussy up already.

Of course, they would hit me with the rip the bandaid off and take my ass inside approach. "Dicks," I mumble to myself.

BASH

Stop your muttering and get going already.

My head snaps up, looking for the camera that obviously must be hidden in my car. How the fuck else would Sebastian know I'm still sitting here.

ME

Are you assholes watching me?

WES

Nope, but now I know what I'm doing the next time you piss me off.

ME

I'm sliding my phone in my pocket when it goes off again. Ready to curse whichever ass is taunting me, I yank my cell back out. But it's not them.

UNKNOWN

Enjoy your fun while it lasts, bitch. I'm going to gut Ariah and hang your babies from lamp posts.

My vision blinks out at Samantha's threats. She thinks she's smarter than me, but the dumb skank is useless without a programmer. I hacked her the first time she sent a message.

Gritting my teeth, I snap a screenshot and drop it in our group chat. Seconds later, I'm staring into four sets of matching furious eyes.

"Remind me why we haven't killed her or, at the very least, sent King to toss her into a bodybag we can hang like a piñata, then hit with spiked bats?" Wyatt seethes.

"I still vote we replace her implants with cement and drop her in a tank of piranhas," Owen snaps.

I'd be a liar if I didn't say both ideas sound like perfect plans. Unfortunately, we still have to play this just right. "I'm not saying these aren't options, but we agreed to a different plan."

"Isn't there anything we can do? She can't continue to make threats with no consequences," Wes hisses, clenching his teeth until his jawbone flexes in his cheeks.

While they continue to share creative ways for Samantha to die, I open my laptop and hit publish on the video I've been holding for an occasion just like this. One by one, their phones go off.

"Fuck yes," Owen shouts.

Grinning, Sebastian announces, "I'll have Matthieu put this out through all of his channels as well.

"Please tell me I'm not the only one hearing horses run right now?" Wes snickers.

I watch Samantha's mentions triple in seconds. She's trending now. "It's only fitting Samantha has her own soundtrack when this hits every porn and social media site available."

"She's lucky that's all we're doing for now," Sebastian mutters. "She should get the Vivian treatment and more."

Humming his agreement, Wyatt says, "That would be too good for the cunt, and no pig deserves to eat something so poisonous."

Owen twirls one of his throwing knives between his fingers. "Maybe I should dip my blades in snake venom and then play frisbee tag."

Four million views and counting.

"You dicks can continue to brainstorm. I'm going to see our woman," I quip before ending the call and exiting my car.

I'm standing outside Ariah's front door when my phone goes off again. Slipping it from my back pocket, I answer without checking the Caller ID. "Don't you asses have a death to plan?"

"Yes—yours. You trash whore," I snarl once I register Samantha's voice. I'm kicking myself for not checking to see who called before answering.

"I hope you enjoy your little stunt, Levi. It'll be the reason I take someone you all love."

Growing tired of her threats, I volley back one of my own. "If you're smart, you and the Senator will tuck your tails between your legs and run because we're coming for you. There isn't a place in this life or the next that either of you'll be safe—I'll snatch you from death, then send you back in pieces," I sneer, then disconnect the call.

The door opens, and Ariah stands before me, her eyebrows furrowing in concern. "Everything good out here?" she asks, stepping back so I can enter.

Wasting no time, I pull her side flush against my chest, resting my palm on her stomach and breathing her in. Notes of watermelon, mint, and ginger fill my nose, melting my anger away. "Everything is alright, Dove," I murmur, kissing the top of her head.

"You've been sitting outside for the last fifteen minutes. I was about to send out a search party," she jokes, making me smile.

"Crisis averted. Call off the dogs." I tease, and Ariah giggles—the sound is like music to my ears. There was a point over the summer when I thought I'd never hear her laugh again. I want to stay in this moment, lost in the feel and taste of her. The need to destroy anyone or anything that threatens her surges through my veins, revitalizing all my broken parts and making them whole.

Ariah leans back, slightly turning in my hold, craning her neck to meet my eyes. "Is this. . . this okay? I don't want you to be uncomfortable, even if I could spend forever in your arms."

"What do you mean?" I question, scrunching my face in confusion.

She points between us before replying, "Our bodies. . . touching."

Peering down to where our bodies are joined, I take in Ariah's hands on my chest, waiting for the sensation of thousands of fire ants crawling over my skin—it never comes. "It's the best feeling I've ever had," I confess before reluctantly releasing her. Even though this is a giant step, I don't want to tempt fate and push myself too far.

She grabs my hand, leading the way upstairs to her room. We don't speak until we're sitting on her sofa.

"Tell me why you really were sitting outside, Lev," she coaxes. The freckles on her face have grown darker as she progresses through pregnancy.

While ensuring Ariah is no longer in the dark and part of making decisions, there's no reason to repeat any of Samantha's vile words. So, I choose to tell her the what and only some of the why. "I was releasing the video we have of Samantha from the night we threw the party. She's been stirring up trouble," I explain.

Ariah grimaces, processing my words before dipping her chin. "The party where Wes and Wyatt—"

"They didn't," I cut her off, not wanting her to go down that road. "She just thinks they did."

Crossing her arms, Ariah arches her strawberry-blond brow, and I have to fight not to drop my gaze to her glorious tits.

Have they gotten bigger?

"Ouch! Shit," I yelp, rubbing the spot where she pinched me before she lifts my chin.

"My eyes are up here. Focus and answer my questions," Ariah chastises, rolling her eyes.

Licking my lips, I sneak one more peek and then nod. "What did you ask me?"

"What video?"

"The one where she tried to roofie the guys, but Wes and Wyatt poured their drink into hers and covered her in horse nut."

Her gray irises light in amusement. "Are you telling me you released footage of Samantha Davenport covered in horse cum?"

"It was so much more than just being covered in it." I turn green at that memory. "She even rubbed one out. It's not an image I ever want to think of again."

Ariah's head falls back as she cackles—full-belly Santa chuckle until she's red and tears run down her face. "So when she was going around campus bragging about fucking Wes and Wy, it wasn't them at all."

I shake my head, "Nope. It was some monster dildo O and Wy bought."

Ariah lets out another peel of laughter before her mouth snaps closed. Then she unsuccessfully tries to get out of the couch. "What's wrong?"

"Pee. . . I need to pee and fast," she blurts out.

Jumping up, I lift her and carry her to the bathroom.

"Out," she shouts. I'm about to argue that she has no reason to hide but think better of it.

"I'll be just outside the door if you need me." I'm met with silence before I hear the toilet flush and the faucet turn on.

Ariah steps back into her bedroom and looks up at me, beaming. "Thank you. We almost had a tsunami on our hands."

I snort as we walk back to the couch. "If you did, we would've sorted it out. Sent out search and rescue."

"You're a regular comedian today, aren't you?" she retorts before clearing her throat. "While we're on the topic of people who play stupid games and then are surprised when they win stupid prizes. Tell me how that dumb cunt was able to catch you all so flat-footed?"

59
ARIAH

November 6, 2023

    My Forever Girl,
    Tonight, we get you back, regaining the power we temporarily lost.
    Tonight, we send the Senator and the sewage cunt troll back under the bridge they climbed from.
    Tonight, I'll get to hold you and explain the decisions I made, leading us to this moment.
    Tonight, we right wrongs, choking what little life our enemies have left. We'll skewer those who tried to break us and hurt you in the process.
    Everything is in place, and we've rehashed the details down to the second. This is the night we've been working towards since I had to choose to save O.
    Teagan's been working tirelessly with Lev to deactivate the chip in Owen's arm, and as long as nothing gets fucked up, you'll be back in our arms. Well, at least after you nut-

punch each of us. But I'd let you do it a thousand times if it guarantees we get you back.

Owen will be forced to do and say things to gain Samantha's trust. It's the only way to get him close enough for Teagan to work her magic.

We need you to know that we'll confess all our fuck ups. Choosing to keep you and Owen safe won't be one of them. There are things to atone for—protecting you will never be one of them.

We're sorry for whatever you're made to endure at this farce of a party. We tried to get the Council to excuse you, but they said it would be more suspicious if they allowed you to break the rules of the contract. We just need you to hold on just a little bit longer.

We're coming for you, Ariah—you and our babies.

Wes

Song: Coming Home -Skylar Grey

I reread the last line through watery eyes, then snap Wes's journal closed.

They were always coming for me. I know they said it, but it is so hard to trust with all that's happening.

Clearing my throat, I grab a tissue from the box on my desk and wipe my face. I know without looking that I'm a blotchy mess. Seeing what they planned compared to what actually happened that night will forever be burned into my memory.

Even after my conversations with Owen and Lev, part of me is still raw. I want to argue that there had to be another way. One where Owen didn't need to pretend or be that close to Samantha, but that's selfish. I'd be the first to tell him he was foolish if he didn't do what was needed.

I open my laptop and type Senator Matthew Baker's name into the search bar. I need to know the man who's been trying to destroy my family. The smug bastard's face pops up on the screen. Site after site sings his praises.

"Youngest Senator in the country."

"Baker's on the fast track to the White House."

Matthew Baker's rags-to-riches story would be impressive if he hadn't done so on the backs of people around him. I stare at the latest picture of him. He's standing alongside his new *wife*, Samantha "Cunt Face" Davenport, or I guess it's actually Baker now. Her smile is just as fake as it's always been, but there's something in her eyes I've never seen. *Fear*. Samantha's glacial blue eyes appear haunted.

"Good. I hope you're a miserable bitch that makes his life just as unbearable," I mutter. They deserve each other. I scroll further down, pausing to read the articles detailing Senator Baker's countless accusations. Many that should disqualify him from holding public office, and even more that prove he needs to be behind bars.

Standing, I massage my lower back as I walk, which is more of a waddle these days, and lock my door before returning to my desk. Then I open the bottom drawer, removing the false bottom to retrieve my safe. It's not long before I pick up and power on the burner phone, inserting the SIM card and calling the only number preprogrammed on the cell. There's barely a ring when the call connects. "Ariah, is everything okay? We aren't scheduled to speak until you return to school next week."

"Yes, I just need information on Senator Matthew Baker," I reply, smiling.

As the months have passed, the relationship I've built with the person on the other side of the line has strengthened me. Especially their belief that the tides are turning in my favor.

"Matthew Baker isn't someone you go after alone. He's very well connected." Though it's not needed, the warning is heard loud and clear. But one look at the little information available on the Senator confirms how powerful his reach is.

Sighing, I state, "I understand. This is just a preliminary search. I have no plans to go after him until I know who I'm dealing with."

"I'll have Tamara send you the file. Does this mean you're ready to begin the final phase?"

Biting the inside of my cheek, I ponder the question. It's one I've been asked at the end of each call. There have been many instances over the last few months when I nearly said, "fuck it," giving the green light to destroy it all.

The last phase will light the fuse to a bomb, eviscerating everyone and everything in its path, unwilling to yield. I'm not ready for the nuclear option. There are still opportunities to gain the desired outcome without trampling over the men I love. "Almost. I need to determine if they're worthy of being saved or if their end is inescapable."

"I knew I chose wisely. Take the time needed, but if the Senator forces our hand, then I'll make the decision, and I cannot promise it will be in their favor." I'm being given the same warning. One that leads me to believe I'm still being tested.

A moment passes, before I realize I'm nodding like we're in the same room. "Understood." The call ends, and I wait for the text to come in.

Fifteen minutes later, the burner phone buzzes, alerting me to log into the encrypted site.

Pulling out my computer, I enter the login information before removing the SIM card and putting the phone away.

"Holy fucking shit," I exclaim as I stare at the laptop in shock. My stomach churns as I click and read through the stories of Senator Matthew Baker's exploits with underage girls and the depraved things he's done to them.

"How the fuck have you been able to get away with all this shit?" I mumble, rubbing at the crease on my forehead.

I squeal, my heart feeling as if it's going to bolt from my chest when a fist pounds on my door. "Ariah, bitch are you in there? You have ten seconds before I break down this door." Shay's voice registers as I work to steady my breath.

"Coming," I shout, logging out and closing my computer before I stand, then head for the door.

"My girl, you didn't hear me knock or call your name the first three hundred?" she questions, arching her sculpted brow.

Stepping out of her way, I invite her in. "I didn't hear you until you almost scared me into an early labor."

Shay cuts her eyes at me. "No sah. Don't call down dem deh crosses down pon mi."

I smirk, proud I understood what she said. "I didn't hear you. I'm sorry."

"It's cool," Shay retorts, studying me. "By the looks of your shorts and tank, you forgot we're supposed to go shopping today."

"Shit, I thought that wasn't until this afternoon."

"Ry, it's two o'clock," she states, peering around me and looking at my desk. "What were you doing in here?"

Not wanting to lie, I opt for a version of truth. "I was just surfing the web and lost track of time."

She surveys me as if she can smell that there's more to the story. "You sure that's all? You look Casper-pale, like you were caught with your hand in the proverbial cookie jar."

If only she knew. "Promise. Why don't we shop online instead? I don't feel like walking around anyone's mall with these two Irish Step Dancing on my bladder."

She snorts. "Remind me of all this when I tell you I want kids in the future."

"You dork. Go sit down. I'll grab my laptop, and then we can start," I laugh, glad when she strides for my bed, successfully distracted.

Pinching the bridge of my nose, I sigh before heading for my desk. Once I have my computer, I glance over my shoulder, watching Shay as she busies herself on her phone.

I hate being unable to confide in her, but with her confession last week, I refuse to jeopardize her or her family. Steadfast in my resolve, I shake off any doubts. This is how I protect the people I love.

●

"What the hell do you mean Shay and I have to move in with the guys?" I splutter, gripping the table's edge as I stare at my father, grandfather, and uncle.

After Shay left, Dad called me down to his office. That was twenty-five minutes ago. The conversation started with security protocols for next week when I return to school. I thought the meeting was coming to an end until the guys strolled in with Reign, Elias, and Fernando close behind. That's about the time he dropped this nugget in my lap.

"You know this is for the best. We need you protected at all times," Granddad explains, and it takes everything in me not to roll my eyes. To say I'm over all the men in my life unilaterally making decisions for me is the understatement of five millennia.

Standing, I slap my palms against the table and glare. "Moving in with them for my protection isn't the problem here. It's everyone's inability to speak to me," I shout, jabbing my index finger against my chest before continuing. "About decisions pertaining to my damn life."

"Told you so." I hear Wyatt murmur.

"Shut up, asshole," Wes stage whispers.

My gaze travels over the guys as they sit on both sides of me in time to see Sebastian elbow Wyatt.

"Ow. Your elbow is sharp, fucker. We told them this wouldn't go well if they did it this way. It's not my fault they didn't listen," Wyatt grumbles, rubbing the spot.

I shake my head, hiding my smile before returning my attention across the table. My father's gray eyes soften. "We only want to keep you safe, but you're right, Ry. We should've come to you to discuss things first. So, for that, I'm sorry."

Feeling somewhat vindicated, I sit back down. "Look, I know everyone in this room is looking out for my safety, and I appreciate you all for it, but you *all* need to remember to include me," I command, leveling every person in this room with a look that better put the fear of my wrath in them. "Now, what are these plans?" I inquire. Then, for the next hour, we discuss the move.

"Does everyone understand their roles?" Uncle Liam asks.

"As long as they know we're in charge, we'll have no issues," Reign declares, and I smack my forehead. This will go downhill in three. . . two. . .

"Listen, dickhead. I've had about enough of all of your bullshit," Wes growls. "She's ours to protect, which is the only reason you're allowed within one centimeter of her."

My count might have been off, but I'm not wrong about the dick-measuring contest taking place in this room. *Fucking men!*

"If you're too dense to see that we've only ever seen Ariah as a sister, then it's good we're the ones making the calls regarding her security," Fernando adds.

Closing my eyes, I pray to whatever divine entity is listening that they'll spare me all of this bullshit.

"Enough," Uncle Liam barks. "None of you are fucking in charge of anything. Thomas makes the security calls. Now all of you zip your damn mouths closed. The adults are talking."

I knew someone up there loved me. Unable to hide my amusement, I burst into laughter, cackling until my sides begin to hurt, and I swear I pee a little.

"Good. I'm glad everyone's finally on the same page—moving day is tomorrow, gentlemen. We'll see you in the morning and not a moment sooner," my grandfather states, dismissing everyone but Dad, Uncle Liam, and me.

I stand to exit the room behind them. "Not you, Ry. We need to discuss a few items with you," my father says.

Nodding, I wait until they file out, and the door snicks closed before I speak, "Is everything okay?"

"Yes. We need to update you on a few things," Uncle Liam answers.

"Okay," I offer, hoping they'll spit it out. Dad comes around the table, and my heart rate kicks up. "You're scaring me. Are you sure there's nothing wrong?"

Sitting, my father clasps my hand. "Once we've gotten rid of Senator Baker and whoever else he's working with, I'm going to take my seat as the head of the Council so that I can change the rules barring women from the Fraternitas."

My eyes widen in shock. "Really?"

"Yes," he replies. "It's been long overdue. There's no good reason the Fraternitas should only be open to men."

I beam with excitement. *Maybe I won't have to go with the nuclear option after all.*

60
SEBASTIAN

"Make sure you don't scratch that," I order, pointing at the men climbing the stairs carrying Ariah's dresser before turning to watch the parade of movers coming through the door.

I can't begin to express the calm that has fallen over me knowing that Ariah's here. The collective sigh of relief we all had was palpable.

"Shit." I hear one of the men mutter at the same time another shouts, "Watch where you're going, Bobby."

Spinning, I watch as *Bobby* nearly drops the very item I told him not to. "What the fuck does it look like I'm doing, Frankie, twiddling my thumbs by the water cooler?"

The two idiots continue to argue, holding up the line.

"Hey," I bark, garnering their attention. "Quit bickering and get fucking moving."

They grunt their understanding and proceed upstairs, where Wyatt and Owen are overseeing things. They'll do their jobs if they know what's good for them.

I make a mental note to check with Lev about which company

Ariah's father hired. He's in the security room with Thomas and the other three shits going over the tech he's installed.

My teeth clench at the reminder of the three stooges that are always one word away from being minced meat. While Reign, Fernando, and Elias aren't our favorites, they keep her safe. A task that should be easier now that we're under one roof. So, for now, they stay.

I moved in last week. Wherever Ariah is, I will always be. The time apart from her was worse than I could ever imagine. They say absence makes the heart grow fonder. And while it did, it's not a lesson I endeavor to revisit.

A few more movers enter the house with boxes as I follow the sound of Shay's voice.

"All your men under one roof. The amount of dick you're about to be riding!"

Oh, this is a conversation I'm happy to be overhearing.

Creeping closer, I peer down at my sock-clad feet, glad I opted out of putting on shoes.

"Shay," Ariah gasps in faux shock before she bursts into giggles.

"What? Don't act like you aren't eager to have one of them shift your womb," Shay retorts.

Inching even closer, I stop at the edge of the entrance to the living room, waiting for her response.

"I've been so fucking horny. It's like my libido is supercharged, knowing the guys are around," Ariah replies, and I smirk.

The image of her spread before me as I make her come for the third time pops into my head. She won't have that issue for much longer. I won't be surprised if Wyatt sneaks into her room tonight.

"Just let me know when yuh plan fi ride the cocky so I can pop in my earplugs."

Ariah bursts into laughter as they continue their conversation. I wait for them to move on to another topic before finally announcing my presence.

"Ladies," I greet.

Ariah's stormy gray irises glance up as she smiles. "Bash," she breathes, and I fight to keep a tent from rising in my sweatpants. She must see the hunger for her burning in my eyes.

"Okay, you two. Cut it out. Save the seduction for when I'm not sitting right here." Shay snickers, waving her hand and severing our connection.

Turning, I quirk my brow, and Shay mirrors my action.

"Don't give me that look, Sebastian Grant. You can have Ariah time later."

Snorting, I shake my head. "Fine," I grumble, holding my hands up in mock surrender. "I need to talk to Wes anyway." I glance at Ariah once more before crossing the room and heading to the basement.

When I find him, Wes is cleaning his ink in one of the back rooms.

"How's everything going upstairs?" he asks, applying the ointment to the half-sleeve tattoo.

I study the amazing design Owen created. The primarily grayscale piece masterfully displays an intricate pattern, creating the illusion of smoke before it morphs into the profile of the woman we love. Haunting silver eyes stare a hole through your soul as embers fall, illuminating a hand partially covered with half a lioness—the jaw drops, exposing razor-sharp teeth as she roars. The symbolism is not lost on me.

"Has she seen it yet?" I probe, earning me his pointed glare.

"Has she seen yours?" Wes fires back.

Absentmindedly, I reach for my left rib. It's not time to reveal mine.

"Point taken."

We each got personalized tattoos last week when Allinah and her team from Hel's Ink came. Lev had to be sedated. He's getting better, but it's still the only way he can endure being touched.

"I'm sure we'll all reveal them to her soon enough." He pauses, pumping hand soap into his palm. "I don't want her to think it's a ploy for her to forgive me. I won't tell her until we've talked."

I nod. I've never seen Wes like this with anyone. Not even his mother, who is the only other person he's not a complete dick to.

"You know she'll forgive you, right?" I have to ask him.

"I'm not as sure about that as you all seem to be."

Sighing, I rub the back of my neck. Wes has been the hardest on himself for not seeing Samantha for the threat she is. She was supposed to be a gnat that would disappear once we made our final pick. He underestimated her—*we all did*. A mistake we'll never repeat.

"Wes. She's read the journal. I'm sure she understands why."

"Do you know the fucked up part of this?" Wes growls, whipping around to face me—his chest heaving as his nostrils flare. "I'm not letting her go. Even if she never forgives me. Even when I told her I would—I wouldn't—*I couldn't*. There isn't a fiber of my being or an alternative universe where Ariah Bradford isn't mine. *She's my forever girl.*"

He pulls up the cameras. An image of Ariah still talking with Shay appears on the screen mounted to the jet-black wall. I stand, watching the woman who restarted my heart, pushing me to deal with my demons, from across the room, laughing with Shay.

My gaze flits toward his before returning to Ariah. "She's our missing link," I profess as he stands beside me.

"No," Wes exclaims, causing my attention to snap in his direction. He sighs, turning to walk away.

I'm preparing to argue when he stops in the doorway, peering over his shoulder, and declares, "She's the gold filling our broken pieces, reminding us that there is beauty in our damaged parts." Then, he exits the room, leaving me with the weight of his words.

61
ARIAH

"Please tell me you have a copy of the video of Samantha flicking the bean with Mr. Ed's nut?" Shay pleads.

My lip curls at the mention of Samantha's name. "Absolutely not. I have no interest in seeing that cunt. Literally."

Shay groans. "All traces of that video have been scrubbed. There isn't a site you can find it on. Even the articles about it have disappeared."

I'm not one for revenge porn, but I can't say I was upset about Lev leaking it. Samantha gloated that night, taunting me with the news she fucked both of my guys. My jaw tenses at the reminder. It's what made seeing her on top of Owen harder.

"That's unfortunate but not surprising. Her slimeball husband is running for president. I can't imagine having your wife's face plastered all over the media while they accuse her of bestiality makes for a great campaign ad," I grumble.

We've been sitting in the living room while the guys handle the movers. Wes caught me trying to carry a box of my books upstairs. After taking it away from me, he told me in no uncertain terms that I'd be punished if they found out I was lifting anything heavy. Then he personally escorted me in here, kissed my forehead, and headed for the basement. That was almost two hours ago.

Shay's been here with me for the last forty-five minutes, and outside of Sebastian's visit, I haven't seen any of the guys. I think back to our earlier conversation, and she's right. I am excited to stay here. I've missed them. Seeing them around campus and being on the receiving end of their icy behavior cracked a part of me. I know it will take time to heal.

"Presidential race or not, I wouldn't want anyone to believe I had a fetish for having sex with animals," Shay quips, pulling me from my thoughts. Then she stands, absentmindedly brushing the invisible dust from her plum-colored pants before focusing on me. "I'm going to head upstairs and check on how the movers are doing before I head out to visit my family. Are you coming?"

Shaking my head, I lay back. "Nope," I state, popping the 'p.' "This couch is nirvana, and I don't plan on ever leaving."

"I wouldn't dream of it," Shay chuckles. We chat for another few minutes, then she turns and exits the room.

Exhaling, I try to expel all the bullshit, allowing the stillness to settle me. So much is changing in such a short amount of time. I remember moving here and thinking this was the fresh start my family needed. That notion lasted for the five-minute drive to Edgewood Academy.

I snort, picturing Wes, *my broody asshole*, attempting to intimidate me when he carried me out of the lunch room. My mood quickly shifts. Fall break ends in three days, which means having to see the sewer rat and not punching her.

"What has your face frowning so hard?"

My eyes snap open to see Owen leaning on the bluish-gray wall.

"I'm trying to remind myself I can't stab your *ex-fiancée*," I mutter, knowing I'm being a brat. The entire engagement was a farce. None of them wanted her. However, that doesn't change the hurt that reverberated through me each time they chose her over me.

Quirking a brow, Owen moves away from the wall and lifts his shirt, displaying two different chestnut-brown leather knife holsters. "Which one do you want? We can live out my Mickey and Mallory Knox fantasies," he gleams. Any other time, the beautifully crafted blades would mesmerize me. This time, it's the sliver of his ink-covered skin enthralling me. More specifically, my name scrawled across his throat.

"When did you. . ." I point to his neck. "Get this?" I murmur, awe-struck by its beauty. Intricately designed angel wings bracket my name written in some form of calligraphy.

"I need you with me always," he replies. "Plus, it's a great annoying chick repellent."

Snorting, I retort, "I don't know. Some may see it as a challenge."

Then he raises his shirt further, exposing even more of his chiseled abs as he reveals another knife. "Not if they want to live."

He says something else, but I'm too busy lost in the vividly-playing images of me licking and nipping my way down Owen's well-defined chest until he loses control and fills my mouth with his cock. He'd groan, yanking my head back, forcing my mouth to open wider as he slams his cock into the back of my throat until tears trail down my face. Lust pools in my belly, shooting straight to my pussy, and soaking my teal boyshorts.

Now, I want. . . no scratch that, *I need* to live out that scene more than I need air. It's been too long since I felt any of them so deep inside, fucking me senseless until even the flicker of an eyelash would require too much work.

"See something you like, Angel?" The smooth tenor of his voice snaps me from my fantasy.

"I don't know what you're implying. I was just admiring your knives," I mutter, but the heat rising in my cheeks screams like a fluorescent beacon, signaling my blatant lie.

Smirking, Owen lowers his shirt, hiding his lickable Adonis belt, and strides into the living room before squatting in front of me. "Oh, but I think you do," he coaxes, peering into my eyes.

My breath hitches at his nearness, and I wet my suddenly dry lips. Owen tracks the movement before tracing the same path with his thumb. "I think you want nothing more than for me to lay you out on this couch and fuck you while I use Lola to play with your clit."

"I. . . you. . ." I stutter, trying like hell to seem unaffected, but that's what I want him to do. The cool metal kissing my skin as he slams inside of me is exactly what I need.

Leaning forward, Owen licks the seam of my lips before capturing the bottom one between his teeth and nipping it.

"Ouch," I hiss, pulling back. "You bit me." The distinct metallic taste of blood assaults my tastebuds. My fingers brush the spot, confirming what I already know. "And you broke the skin."

Owen's lustful gaze zeroes in on the crimson blood now coating my fingertips. "Fuck," he groans as he clasps my wrist. Then, without breaking eye contact, he lowers his head, bringing my hand to his mouth.

My nose flares, and my body hums as anticipation skitters up my spine, leaving a trail of goosebumps in its wake. I watch in rapt attention as Owen wraps his lips around my fingers and sucks. Rolling his tongue, he pulls me deeper into his mouth. "Owen," I cry, panting from the sensation building low in my belly. *Need.*

"Angel," he pleads like a prayer, and with one word, he lights a fuse, setting my skin ablaze. Releasing my fingers, Owen cups my cheeks, then rises to his knees and presses his mouth to mine.

Giving up all pretense of indifference, I groan, reaching up and fisting his hair as I deepen the kiss. The taste of my blood still lingers on his tongue, only serving to soak my panties further.

I hear the distant sound of a throat clearing, but we're both so lost in each other that neither of us stops to see who's here. It isn't until whoever is in the room clears their throat again, louder this time, that I try to pull away, earning me another nip.

"You better behave, or he'll strip you and fuck you while I watch," Lev warns, announcing his presence. "Won't you, O?"

Owen reluctantly pulls back, dropping his hand from my face. He confirms, "That and so much more." Then, he leans forward to whisper in my ear, "But you'd like that—Lev watching while I bounce our pussy on my cock."

I clench, growing wetter. At this point, I'm certain my arousal is soaking through my lounge pants. Biting my cheek, I swallow back my whine. Mischief dances in their stares, and I know they're up to something.

"The question is, will it be for pleasure or punishment?"

Then Owen smirks. "As a matter of fact, I think a lesson is in order. She fought to stay here, potentially putting herself in danger. That can't go unpunished. Can it, Lev?" Owen quips, as Lev strolls into the room.

I track his movements until he positions himself behind me. Then Lev bends, his breath tickling the column of my throat, and murmurs, "It most certainly cannot," before biting my neck.

My nipples grow to hardened peaks that desperately ache to be sucked. "Oh? Is that right?" I gulp, trying to regain my composure. The fuckers are teasing me. "And let me guess, you two will be the ones doling out my punishment."

Gliding the tips of his fingers up and down my arms as he rises, Lev traps both of my wrists in his hold. "I'm glad you understand. This way, we don't have to waste time explaining," he states before reaching into his back pocket. Moments later, he produces a bundle of black rope.

"So, you just happen to carry around rope?" I question, tilting my chin to peer up at him.

"You never know when the occasion might call for it," Lev retorts, running the rope along my collarbone before gliding it over my breasts.

My pulse thrums at the feel of the coarse fibers brushing my hardened peaks, making my walls contract, feeling empty and angry that neither Owen's nor Lev's dicks are pistoning inside. "Fuck," I exclaim, already close to coming.

Owen tugs at the loose knot of my pants, refocusing my attention on him. "Be a good girl, Angel, and let Lev tie you up."

"Here? In the middle of the living room, where anyone can

walk in? Aren't the movers still here?" I rapidly fire off my questions but lift my hips so Owen can tug down my boyshorts and pants.

Cool air hits my drenched naked sex as Owen bends forward, inhaling me. "If I knew I wouldn't peel off the skin of any man that smelled you with a cheese grater, I'd wear your scent like cologne," he declares.

"Owen," I shout as he curls two fingers deep inside me. All of my earlier resistance and protests are long forgotten. I lean against the couch, closing my eyes and surrendering to their whims.

Lev weaves the rope around my wrists and up my arm, creating a pattern I can't see as he binds them together. "Do you honestly believe we'd let anyone outside of the five of us ever see you naked and still have eyes?" Lev probes as he continues to bind my forearms together. "The movers are gone. Shay went to visit her family, and I turned off the camera to the living room with the explicit threat of death if they stepped a foot outside of the security room."

Before I can process Lev's words, Owen pulls me toward him until I'm sitting on the edge of the couch. "You better answer him," he warns, then he spreads my thighs and buries his face between my legs.

"Shit. . . oh my. . . fuck," I mumble, unable to make a coherent response. Owen's tongue flicks against my clit as he thrusts two fingers in and out of my pussy before sliding one into my ass.

I barely have time to adjust when Lev fists my hair, yanking my head back and crashing his mouth down on mine. I gasp as one of Lev's hands slips under the collar of my Slipknot t-shirt. He tweaks my nipple at the same time Owen works a second finger past the ring of muscles, scissoring his digits as he pumps in and out of my body.

Owen hums against my pussy, and I clench, basking in their unyielding assault on my body. Bucking my hips, I grind down on Owen's fingers and enjoy the way his stubble rubs my clit.

"That's it, Angel, ride my face like you'd ride our cocks," Owen grunts, momentarily lifting his mouth. "Because one day soon, every fillable hole will be owned by us." His teeth graze my clit before he wraps his lips around the bundle of nerves, sending sparks up my spine.

My body coils like a spring, and I know I'm fucking close to coming. Lev pinches my nipple as he releases my mouth, and I huff in frustration. "Come back," I demand, and he chuckles, loosening his hold on my hair.

"Don't worry, Dove, we're just getting started," Lev declares. Then he releases my hair before he walks around the couch and climbs up, so his bulging erection stares me in the face as he stands over me, straddling my legs.

Mewling, I crane my neck, peering up at his looming figure and wishing I could touch him. My bound hands are itching to be free to roam the plane of his muscled chest. I know he's restraining me so he can control when and how he's touched, but I hunger to have his body pressing against mine.

Lev's heated bluish-gray eyes connect with mine. "Fuck my face," I command, yearning for the salty taste of him before he comes all over my face. I watch as Lev lowers his sweats, and his cock springs free. I lean forward to lick the pre-cum off, but a tug of my strawberry blond locks holds me in place just as Owen renews his conquest to own my body.

"Owen," I gasp as he inserts another digit, further stretching the tight ring of my ass. My arousal drips down between my spread legs, coating his fingers. "I'm so close." Then he swirls his tongue and sucks as he flicks my clit. I shatter, my walls spasming around his digits.

I barely recover from my first orgasm when Owen starts edging me toward another one, pumping and thrusting deeper. "Look how fucking sexy you look with my fingers pounding into your ass," Owen rasps.

"Pl. . . please," I beg, rising to meet each stroke. "Don't fucking st—"

Fisting my hair, Lev slams his length down my throat, halting any further words when he thrusts in and out of my mouth. "That's it, Dove, take this cock down your throat like a good girl," he hisses, snapping his hips forward.

Lev's face twists in pleasure, his mouth falling open as he feeds me his cock. "You like it when Owen fills your tight holes while I fuck your mouth, don't you?" I hum my agreement, and he growls, "You're going to keep coming until I bathe you in my cum."

The pressure in my core mounts, and I know I'm about to explode again. Lev doubles his pace when I let out another muffled scream. Owen's relentless as his fingers pound into my pussy and curl up, hitting the same spot over and over again.

I moan, breathing through my nose, creating a vibration as I swallow Lev's shaft. His movements become jerky, and I know he's close. We're both climbing higher, and I'm determined to make him come when I do.

Relaxing the muscles in my throat, I close my mouth around Lev's cock, swirling my tongue over its crown. "This goddamn fucking mouth," he shouts, thickening while he tries to allow me to control the tempo.

Owen bites my clit just as he hits the same spot inside, making my pussy clamp down. A moment later, his fingers curl in my ass, discovering a place I didn't even know could feel so good, and I cry out my release just as Lev roars his own. Hot spurts shoot down my throat, and I suck even harder, determined to drink what he has and more.

"That's our fucking good girl. Swallow everything I give you, and not a drop less," Lev praises, releasing my hair and pulling out of my mouth.

Sighing, I fall back against the cushion, spent and eager for bed. Lev tucks his dick back into his pants before climbing down off the couch.

After they both help me get dressed, they peer at me with a reverence one can only give someone they truly see. No words need to be spoken. Everything is simply understood.

A smile grows on my face as they both press a kiss on my forehead.

Owen is the one to lift me, and I must have dozed off because when my eyes flicker open, I'm in a bed. Based on the spiced, smoked brandy smell, I know it's not my own. But I don't care. This is the most peaceful I've felt in months.

Inhaling, I snuggle into Wes's broad chest and fight to stay awake. I need to talk to him, but he's so warm. "Shhh, sleep. Whatever we need to discuss can wait." I mumble something incoherent before my eyelids grow too heavy to keep open.

Wes rubs my belly, and just before I drift back to sleep, I swear I hear him whisper, "I love you."

62

ARIAH

It's been two nights since I moved in, and things don't feel as settled as I'd want them to. There are still some unresolved issues that need to be addressed. I stare down at the table set for six.

"Are you sure you're cool with going home tonight?" I ask Shay. I didn't want her to have to deal with the storm brewing.

Shay looks at me like I failed a shapes and colors test. "Why would I mind going home to get stew peas and rice?"

I laugh and shake my head. "How could I forget? You probably would've left me tonight anyway once you found out what your mom was cooking."

"You know me so well. No one gets between me and my food," she says, batting her eyelashes.

Rolling my eyes, I reply, "I wouldn't dream of it."

"Miss Bradford," the chef calls from the kitchen. "Dinner will be served in twenty minutes."

Butterflies flutter in my stomach. I'm nervous. *What if we can't actually fix this?*

"Stop it," Shay admonishes. "Tonight is going to work out. It's clear you all love each other. Even the densest person can see that."

I scratch the back of my neck, contemplating her words. *Love.* "Love is not enough to sustain a relationship. Trust and love go hand in hand. I have to be able to know they won't abuse my feelings for them so they can take advantage of me. After every—"

My eyes shut, hoping to ward off the pain. Inhaling, I center myself so I don't fall apart where I stand. "After everything, I need to know it's not another ploy. I'd murder them. Mercilessly," I hiss, glaring as I ball my hands into fists. I'd be on the next episode of *Snapped* or *Cold Case Files*. My training this summer will go a long way in ensuring I'm never caught.

"Okay, Harley, stow your stabby hair sticks," she teases. "And remember, you're too pretty for prison, but if you absolutely need to kill one of them, I'll stage a prison break before they even read the charges. Then we can hide at my family's estate in Jamaica."

Her joke eases the tension, and the tightness in my shoulders dissipates, making my mood far less volatile. Smiling, I retort, "As long as you promise hot guys, I'm there."

"No the fuck you're not—not if you want the island of Jamaica to still exist," Lev growls.

I snap my head toward his voice and almost melt where I stand. Lev's hair is in a messy bun, showing off the shaved sides of his head. He's wearing gray, black, and white flannel and distressed dark-wash denim jeans. His jaw flexes, accentuating the sharpness of his stubbled jaw.

"Wipe yuh chin, bitch," Shay giggles, snapping me from my trance. Then, she turns to Lev. "And I'm going to pretend you didn't threaten my country."

Shay leans over and hugs me from the side before reminding me to make them work for it. I smile, squeezing her back before we part, and she exits the room, leaving Lev and me alone in the room.

"Hot men?" he quips, arching his brow as he strides over to me.

"What about hot men?" Owen questions, entering the dining room. Wes, Wyatt, and Sebastian quickly follow behind.

Lev answers, brushing his thumb along my cheek. "Ariah, here, thinks she can run off to Jamaica with Shay, be with hot men, and leave us behind."

Sebastian bends to kiss me. "Oh? Is that right, Spitfire?" he murmurs, breathing along my neck. "Ten," is all he has to say, and shivers travel the length of my spine, making my pussy involuntarily clench.

"I didn't actually do it. So, how does that count?" I whine.

Smirking, Sebastian's fingers trail up and down my arm. "As if you *actually* need to do anything. Eleven," he hums, and I yelp when I'm pulled away from him.

"What men?" Wes demands, pulling out my chair. I sit, and he takes the seat next to mine.

I stare into his chocolate-brown eyes in shock. Wes has barely spoken two words to me since I've moved in. Outside of threatening to punish me for trying to lift boxes during the move, it's been radio silence.

He's part of the reason I'm terrified to settle in. Wes's journal professed so many mixed emotions. He was angry, unremorseful, conflicted, and hurt. I can still feel each stroke of his pen as if it were a blow.

"Now you're speaking to me?" I quip. I guess now is as good a time as any to do this.

In for a penny or whatever.

Wyatt sits to the left of me, with Lev sitting next to him while Owen and Sebastian sit on the other side of the dining room table.

Clenching his jaw, Wes pauses and then speaks, "I wanted you to get settled before we had this conversation." He picks up the cloth napkin before me, unfolding it and laying it across my lap. My eyebrows nearly hit my hairline. "Don't look so surprised," Wes jokes. "I do have some manners. Just not in the bedroom."

Snickering, Wyatt states, "Smooth. Don't speak to Riri for days, weeks even, and you're showing up to dinner with your dick in hand instead of an apology."

Wes glares. "I'm not sorry," he grits out. "I'd do everything I did a million times over if it meant we ended up here with Ariah, the babies, and Owen safe."

"Let's at least feed Ariah before you two set off the next world war," Lev commands as the servers bring in the dishes.

Steak, mashed potatoes, corn on the cob, and asparagus are placed in front of me, but I'm stuck on Wes's words. *I'm not sorry... I'd do it again.* "Choosing to save Owen isn't the problem. It's that you, all of you," I point my steak knife in each of their directions. "Didn't ever fucking consult me," I snap, slamming my hand on the table.

"Why don't you put the knife down, Angel? Then you can yell at us like we deserve," Owen suggests.

I want to snap back, 'fuck you,' but he's right. "I should stab you for all the fucking liberties you've all taken," I seethe and place the knife down.

"When exactly did you want us to ask you? Huh?" Wes challenges. "Was it when you ran out of the room, or maybe it was when you packed your bags and ran off without so much as a word?" Wes's voice rises with each question. "Wait, let me guess. It was when you cut off all communication with us?"

"Fuck you," I scream, standing. My chest heaves, and I ignore the thunk the chair makes when it hits the ground. "Fuck you for thinking you have a right to be angry at me for leaving after you ripped my heart out!"

My skin feels tight with rage, and I want nothing more than to punch Wes in the face before I step on his balls.

"Dove," Lev tries, but fuck him too.

"You all think it was easy? Like I was living my best life in Colorado?" I snarl. "I was broken and could barely get out of bed for weeks."

Wyatt's palm lands on my arm, but I shake him off. "You need to sit down before you hurt yourself or the babies," he orders, picking up my chair. I turn, my nostrils flaring, and I'm rearing for a fight, but the Wyatt that greets me is one I've never seen. "Sit." His tone brokers no argument, and I absentmindedly obey.

"Now we're going to discuss this like adults with two kids on the way," Wyatt continues.

I'm still blinking at him when Sebastian says, "There's a lot of hurt and anger to go around. No one at this table is absolved from any wrongdoing. We all made mistakes along the way. The key is learning from them."

Sebastian's words quell my fury enough to see reason. "You're right. I'm at fault as much as any of you. I'll be the first to admit that my emotions fueled me," I sigh, grabbing my glass of water and sipping.

"And we should've consulted you——"

"So she and Owen could've died?" Wes states, interrupting Sebastian. "There's no scenario where we could tell her shit and you all know it. Stop fucking placating her, and be honest."

Wes spins to face me. "I wasn't going to let Owen die or put you in harm's way. So, if that means your feelings get a little hurt, then so be it. It's better to be alive to feel them than to be dead and be in the know."

I peer down at my plate, my appetite long gone, before meeting Wes's turbulent gaze. "I would never ask you to do anything that could hurt any of you. If you think that, then you don't know me, and maybe we aren't what I thought we were becoming."

"That's bullshit, and you know it, Ariah," Lev replies. "Do we have shit to work out? Hell yes. But that doesn't mean this——" He waves between us. "—isn't real or right."

"You're hurt, Angel. Rightfully so. But don't you ever try to say some fuck shit like that again, or I'll have Lev tie your ass up in a room until we each convince you otherwise," Owen declares.

Wyatt snorts. "And daddy count 'em ups, over there, can tally how bad you've been."

"Is everything a joke to you guys?" Wes snaps. "She needs to understand we won't compromise on her safety."

"Says the dick who was talking about not having manners in the bedroom," I retort.

Wes balls his hands into fists on the table as his shoulders tense. "Is anything I say to you going to be thrown back in my face as an argument? If you're looking for an apology for my choices—you won't get one."

Reaching my quota for bullshit in one sitting, I push back from the table and rise out of my chair. "You, Wes Edgewood, are the biggest, dumbest tool." Then, I storm from the room, not caring how terrible my clapback is.

63
WES

"You better go fix this shit, you twatwaffle, or I'm going rearrange your face like Picasso," Owen threatens.

"Why? So you can dip your d—"

The serrated edge of the steak knife presses against my Adam's apple. "Finish that sentence, Wes. I dare you," Wyatt spits, and I know I've gone too far.

Even if she can't hear me, Ariah doesn't deserve my vitriol for a situation she was thrust into. "I won't," I state.

Wyatt waits, his hazel eyes doing nothing to mask his fury.

"I don't know what your deal is, man, but fix it. I won't tell you again—any of you. We've fucked up enough for ten lifetimes. We brought our bullshit to her front door. Now we're going to make it right," Wyatt commands.

My nostrils flare at his reprimand. Everyone is like *fix it—make it right*. "What do you think I've been doing, Wyatt? Sitting on my ass?"

"Wes," Lev tries, but I wave him off and stand.

"None of you assholes had to be the one to reject her. You got to just avoid her. I—" I beat my chest. "I had to be the one, for months, to make snide comments or publicly show that dumpster fire cunt, Samantha, affection."

They all stare at me—none of them making a move to speak. "Fuck this shit. I don't need this bullshit right now," I exclaim, striding from the room.

"I always have to be the damn bad guy," I mutter, climbing the stairs two at a time until I'm standing outside Ariah's room door. We're doing this shit tonight.

Gripping the handle, I turn it, barging in, and she shrieks. "What the hell, Wes?" Ariah's half-naked—her towel the only fabric covering her. "Get out," she shouts, standing by her bed, but I ignore her.

I slam the door behind me and lock it before I face her. "No. I'm done with your bullshit too."

"My bullshit?" she retorts as I step closer.

"Yes. Your *bullshit*. You and everyone else in the goddamn house. I did what I had to in order to ensure we got you both back." I'm standing in front of her when I speak again. "*We* didn't keep anything from you—you left."

Ariah's face scrunches, and tears well in her steel eyes, but I'm not deterred. "How exactly were we supposed to inform you of our plan without tipping off the one person who would've decimated our world if she found out?"

Springing forward, she bats at my chest with one hand while the other holds the towel securely to her chest. I'm going to pretend my cock isn't hard with her fight.

"You, obviously, were able to tell some people since my best friend had to keep it a secret. So, you tell me, *Wesley*," she exclaims. "How was it safe enough for Shay to know, but I had to walk around with a cracked heart."

I groan. "Let's stop belaboring this point. Better you have a cracked heart that beats than a whole one that's still."

That must be the wrong thing to say because she releases the towel. Her hands ball into fists, and she rears back and clocks me in the jaw. "I've had more than enough of your shit. You big, entitled, rich snob. Are you so used to always getting your way and thinking you never have to apologize?" she questions as I run my fingers along my jaw.

"I forgot how much of a brat you are," I grunt, grabbing her wrist before she can strike another blow.

Ariah grits her teeth, and I want nothing more than to wrap my hand around her throat and slam her into the wall before impaling her. "You're so lucky I can't kick you in the balls from this angle."

"What's that, Ariah? Fill your pussy with my cock?" I walk her back until the backs of her knees bump into the bed, forcing her to plop down on the mattress. "Always happy to oblige," I smirk, climbing onto the bed and holding her hands above her head.

"Do you seriously believe that all I've said meant for you to accost me?"

I run the fingers of my free hand over her already-hardened peaks. "Is that so?" I challenge, bending to suck her nipple into my mouth.

Ariah doesn't say anything, but her breath momentarily hitches before she begins to squirm. "Wes," she grumbles, half a moan—half a rebuke, but I don't stop. She isn't saying no. My minx is only putting up a fight because she missed playing with me.

Sucking harder, I pull her nipple between my teeth, grazing the raised peaks as my hands move further south, briefly stopping at the swell of her belly. Then I'm spreading her folds and rubbing slow circles against her clit.

"Why do you have to—ahh. . . fuck," she screams when I thrust my middle and ring fingers into her tight pussy.

I begin to pump in and out of her, my thumb brushing her clit with each stroke. Ariah whimpers, and I increase my assault, wanting to bring her close to the edge without tipping her over. She's been a brat, and brats get punished.

Lifting my head, I reluctantly release her nipple from my mouth. "I am fucking your tits, first chance I get," I confess.

"Never let anyone tell you you're not romantic," Ariah quips, her sarcasm evident.

"But you don't want roses and chocolates," I retort, releasing her wrists. As expected, she rises to her elbows, but I'm up, lifting her legs around my waist before pushing down my sweatpants and boxer briefs.

I don't wait for her slick comeback. Instead, I snap forward, sinking in so deep my pubic bone touches her stomach.

"Fuckk," I growl at the feel of her bare pussy taking my cock. She couldn't escape me before, but now I'll lock her ass in the tower and surround that bitch with a moat full of some mythical killing machine.

I lean forward, bringing her right leg over my shoulder as I grip her neck. "You want hand necklaces and dirty fucks," I exclaim, rolling my hips.

She attempts to reply, but my pace is relentless. I'm not giving that smart mouth a chance to do anything but scream my goddamn name.

Our gazes lock, and her lips part as her walls constrict around me. All thoughts of punishing her are tossed right out the window. Filling her until my cum is dripping out of her is the new goal.

"Wes," is all she says before spasming so hard she triggers my release.

"Ariah," I bark. My vision whites out, and my ass clenches as I come harder than I ever have since I learned what sex was.

My chest rises and falls as the blood returns to my head. Slowly, I pull out my dick and stare at her pussy, leaking my cum. Biting my lip, I slide two fingers back inside her, pushing my seed back into her pussy.

Ariah flutters around me, and I slip my two digits out, scooping the evidence of our combined pleasure up. Then I lay on my side next to her, resting on my forearm. I coat one of her nipples in our cum before taking it into my mouth. I suck until she's a quivering wreck, then lift my head and press my lips on hers.

She allows herself to get lost, and I'm preparing to fuck her again when she bites me. "Shit," I hiss. "You bit me."

"Oh, I'm sorry. Did you think our conversation was over because you made me come?" Ariah begins. "You barged in here to talk. So let's talk."

I clench my jaw but nod. "Okay, fine. Let me clean you up first." I stand. "Climb up on the bed. I'll be right back."

By the time I grab a washcloth, wet it with warm water, and stride back into the room, Ariah's leaning back on her pillows. I position myself between her spread thighs and start to wipe when she speaks.

"You don't realize how much what you all did hurt me," she states. "Like, I don't let people in, and I let all of you in. Then, you proceeded to shatter me."

I drop the rag on the nightstand and lie next to her before enveloping her in my arms. "But now you know why and understand that it had to happen. I don't understand why you're having such difficulty seeing why I had to choose Sam and why we had to stay away. Both yours and Owen's lives were at stake."

Ariah attempts to pull from my hold, but I hold her tighter.

Huffing, she looks away from me. "I just don't want to feel railroaded," she mumbles, slumping her shoulders.

Slipping my knuckle under her chin, I lift her face to peer into my eyes. "That's not at all what I want to do. None of us want that. Ariah, you're a force—not some pretty princess locked up in a tower waiting for some fairytale princes to save her. But you also have to understand the spot we were in."

Her lips part, ready to speak, but I place my index finger on them and continue, "Owen, the brother none of us could save all those years ago, was taken again. He was taken, and the demand to get him back alive was giving you up. It was never going to be permanent. You're my forever. I needed to move accordingly. None of them knew. My jaw remembers that fact vividly."

"Wes," she starts, leaning into my touch. "I was never mad about your choice to save Owen and keep him safe after he returned. It's just like I said before. I don't want the men in my life treating me like some damsel in constant need of saving. Who knows, I'll probably be the one saving you."

I arch a brow. "Is that so, Miss Bradford?"

"What? Don't think I can save you, Wes?" She smirks, and I brush her hair out of her face.

I love seeing her like this, properly fucked and carefree. Her smile grows when she sees me watching her, and I want everything to stay like this. No outside bullshit while we celebrate her and our babies.

Babies. I still can't believe we're going to be parents. There have been moments when I've wondered who the father is. I have a feeling, but I can't be sure.

Samantha tampering with the condoms in my nightstand drawer still pisses me off. We're so young, and Samantha stole the choice from us, but she can't steal our love for the twins and their mother.

Ariah stills, and I watch as her focus shifts to my arm. Her gaze volleys between my tattoo and my face a few times before she finally speaks. "That's. . . you got a. . . that's a—" I smirk at her loss for words.

"It's beautiful," she whispers as I admire her. She is the lioness—fiercely loyal, majestic, and protective of her pride.

Cupping her jaw, I run my thumb over her lips before bending and gently kissing them. "I wanted to capture the beauty in your strength. Something that symbolizes how I see you," I explain when I break our connection.

Ariah tilts her chin up, studying me. "You have such a way with words, Wes. I truly love it," she confesses, and I get lost in her captivating silvery eyes—eyes that have witnessed so much but remain steadfast.

"Are you still with me there, big guy?" Ariah teases, snapping me from my thoughts. I chuckle as I lift her, positioning her to straddle my lap.

I can't say I ever thought I'd like the idea of fucking a baby into my woman and watching her belly grow our children, but fuck if my dick isn't hard again at the thought.

"There's no place I'd rather be," I murmur, bending and capturing her nipple in my mouth.

She groans, grinding her bare pussy against my erection as she tugs my hair, pressing my face into her breast.

Ariah's hips roll, moving faster up and down my shaft, and I can feel her arousal coating my cock.

"Fuck," she whimpers, her breath hitching when I bite her nipple.

Needing more, I grab my length, pulling my mouth from her breasts as I thrust up into her, impaling her on my cock.

Ariah gasps, throwing her head back as I piston in and out of her as I growl, "That's exactly what I plan to do."

64
OWEN

"Do we remember the rules," Reign asks, narrowing his glare on us.

"We're not five, asshat. There's no need to go over security protocol for the tenth time," Sebastian snaps.

It's the first day back to class, and I'm already feeling stabby. I'm convinced Elias, Fernando, and Reign have a death wish.

"Apparently, you are because one of the first things we covered was not giving us a hard time. Ariah's safety is number one. Everything and everyone else is inconsequential," Reign retorts.

We're all standing in the middle of the entryway, arguing over the semantics for when we're on campus. "And what, you think we want something different?" Wes sneers.

"No, but we know you're all prone to rash decisions, and we can't afford that," Elias explains, checking his watch before he continues. "We need to be out of here in the next fifteen minutes. Just do what you're told, and we won't have any issues today."

Tilting my head, I study the pricks ordering us around. Elias, Reign, and Fernando continue to rattle off their rules. *Don't go anywhere unguarded. Don't try to slip the security detail. Wait for us to clear all buildings, rooms, and vehicles.* And on and on they go. My hand twitches at my side, itching to pull Mary's ornate handle from its holster. It's been too long since she's tasted blood, and I think it's time to rectify that—starting with these fucks.

"Can we hurry this along?" Wyatt demands, smirking at all of us like he's in on some secret none of us are aware of. "It's a waste of all our breaths to continue to debate this. Thomas has outlined what needs to be done. We'll follow those protocols. Save the bickering for something that hasn't already been agreed upon."

"Exactly," Ariah states, and I turn in time to see her and Shay walk down the stairs. "We'll follow the rules, and you'll all stop the alpha pissing contest so we can get to school."

Sharp gray eyes survey the room as she descends the final step. *She's fucking breathtaking.* She's wearing black leggings, a cream-colored sweater with a collar that droops enough to see her delicious freckled skin, and knee-high burnt orange leather boots. Her body is changing, and I'm pissed I missed the first signs—time we'll never get back—my jaw clenches at the reminder of time lost.

"Won't you?" Ariah persists when none of us respond to her reprimand.

"As long as it keeps you safe. Otherwise, all bets are off," Wes declares as Ariah and Shay stand by the table. Wes hardens his gaze when Ariah meets his stare head-on. A silent exchange passes between them, making me smile.

Since the night Wes and Ariah had their *fight*, he's been different—they both have. The electricity passing between them is infectious, and I have to remember to control my dick.

Wes flexes his jaw, refusing to back down while Ariah meets his eyes in challenge. I feel like a voyeur watching their exchange as the silence between them stretches, making my cock lengthen uncomfortably.

"We need to go," Sebastian announces, breaking the spell.

Ariah blinks, and her cheeks flush scarlet as awareness of the people around the room observing them sets in.

"I'll meet you assholes in the car," Ariah mutters, tugging Shay's hand and stomping off. Fernando and Elias quickly move to precede them.

"Don't take long. We need enough time to check her classroom," Reign instructs, then turns, leaving us inside.

Sebastian scowls at Reign's retreating form. "Dibs on Reign," he huffs, and I snort. Though the idea is extremely tempting, and their deaths play on a loop in my head, they keep my angel safe. So, for now, they remain alive.

"You're all still letting them get to you. They aren't, nor have they ever been, a threat to us," Wyatt begins, sliding his arm through the straps of his backpack. "Everything they've done has been to make all of us pay for the hurt we, intentionally or unintentionally, caused her."

Wyatt's halfway to the front door when Lev clears his throat. "You've always known who they were to her but never said a word," Lev states. His statement isn't accusatory. It's more of a confirmation. Wyatt always holds information about Ariah close to his chest until he believes we're worthy enough to share.

Pausing, Wyatt peers over his shoulder. "Most of you are only just getting your heads out of your asses." His hand wraps around the door handle. "Now, don't fuck it up, and then I won't have to keep shit from you." Then, he steps through the door, leaving us to stew.

"We seriously need to tie his ass up," Wes mutters as he whirls around and exits the house.

I'd agree if I didn't know Wyatt has only the best intentions for Ariah. We all do, and we all have and will continue to take care of her. I am going to nick the smug fucker, though.

"That's it. I'm sending a virus that shouts, 'I like butt sex' to Wyatt's cellphone," Lev exclaims as we funnel out behind Wes to the convoy of waiting SUVs.

●

The day is passing by with no issues. In fact, it's been how the entire first semester should've gone—Ariah by our sides as we laugh and walk across campus for the dining hall, showing everyone just how much she's the center of our universe, and Samantha making herself scarce, hopefully to the point of no return.

"Wait here. Let us scan the cafe before you all go in," Fernando orders. He's holding his arm up to prevent us from walking inside, and I have to suppress an eye roll.

"Behave," Ariah whispers, grinning up at me. I return her gorgeous smile with my own. This moment, right here, makes every scar I suffered at the hands of Senator Baker's lackeys worth it. I'd bear four times as many as long as it means I'm here now.

Clasping her chin, I lean down and press my lips against her supple blush-pink ones. I sigh when she eagerly returns my affection, her body molding against mine, and groan when I have to pull back. "Never letting you go," I murmur, nipping her lip before I resignedly lift my head.

"I swear I'm going to need to buy better noise-cancellation earphones," Shay giggles, making Ariah flush scarlet.

"Oh, hush. You're all the way at the end of the hallway," Ariah retorts.

Shay arches her brow. "Exactly, not nearly far enough away to drown out the many." She pauses, eyeing each of us. "Many orgasms you'll be having."

Ariah's mouth drops open as the blush spreads from her cheeks to the remainder of her face and down her throat. "Shay," she admonishes, and I have to bite my cheek to prevent myself from laughing.

"Okay. All clear," Fernando announces, saving Shay's and my life.

Wyatt steps beside her as we enter the dining hall and head for our table. "I mean, where's the lie, Riri? We have every intention of making the neighbors know our names," he states, winking before he spins out of her reach.

"Don't be surprised when I make you sleep outside, Grant," Ariah declares, and Wyatt covers his heart.

"You wound me, lass. Would you treat your love with such an extreme punishment?"

We all burst into laughter as we set our bags in the chairs. Wes claps Wyatt on the shoulder, "You did this to yourself. Have fun in the hall tonight."

Ariah works hard to hide her amusement when Wyatt kneels before her, thou'ing and doth'ing until she bursts into giggles. She and Shay are both clutching their sides as they sit, coughing and trying to breathe.

Clearing her throat, Ariah begins to stand, "I'm going to grab some lunch."

"You sit. I've got you, Angel. Southwestern salad with feta and Oreo brownie milkshake," I confirm, kissing the top of her head as she sits back down.

She beams. "No. I've been craving birria tacos. Nando bought them the other day, and I had some."

"Some? Girl, you ate his whole order," Shay teases, and Ariah shrugs, pointing to her stomach.

"These two are very demanding. Nando was happy to part with his food, weren't you?"

Ariah's gaze falls on her guard. "Of course. I didn't want the only tacos from the only place in town where I can get birria done correctly on the one day of the month they make them."

"Idiot," Reign mumbles, then quickly covers up his ridicule with a cough.

Usually, I'd enjoy seeing the shithead squirm under Ariah's scrutiny, but feeding her is more important. "We can work on the tacos after we get home. For now, tell me what you'd like instead."

Ariah cuts her eye at Fernando once more before peering at me. Her shoulders slump. "I guess I'll have the salad, but I want a cookies 'n cream milkshake with bananas and strawberries."

Nodding, I stride across the dining hall and over to the salad station. I order Ariah's chopped southwest salad with chicken, extra feta, and olives. While the chef prepares her food, I head to the dessert bar and have them start her milkshake.

Fifteen minutes later, I have Ariah's food. I'm nearly back at the table when a familiar nasally squawk makes my skin crawl. "Oh look, it's the trash whore and her merry band of rejects."

I've never met a girl who was so purposefully dense in my life. Samantha Davenport has more audacity than sense.

Outside of Reign, Elias, and Fernando, who all have their hands in varying states of readiness, everyone at the table ignores Samantha.

"I'd state the obvious, but I don't think you have enough brain cells to rub together and figure it out," Elias spits. "So, why don't you do yourself a favor before we ignore the order not to kill you."

Does she heed his warning? Of course not. *Have you met the cunt?*

Samantha babbles on as I creep closer. I meet Fernando's eye, and he imperceptibly dips his chin.

"There's nothing you bitch made assholes can do to me. I'm a Senator's wife, and your soon-to-be first l—"

I don't allow her to finish babbling. Instead, I remove the lid, then dump the milkshake over her head, cackling when the banshee shrieks. I step back before any of the drink can get on me as she attempts to spin around.

Standing back, I watch my handy work in action. Heels and spilled liquid may make for a terrible time for Samantha, but they make for an extremely entertaining and satisfying time for everyone else—me, most specifically.

"That's always been your problem, Davenport. You never know when to shut the fuck up," I growl.

Samantha tries desperately to remain standing, but like Humpy Dumpy, she has a glorious fall. "You little sh—" Her ass hits the ground so hard I think one cheek actually bursts.

"I give this a zero out of ten. Way to stick the landing," I taunt. Not totally satisfied, I pour Ariah's salad on Samantha's cherry-red face, which is contorted in rage. Then, one by one, Lev, Wyatt, and Sebastian follow suit, emptying their drinks.

Wes is the last to walk up to her prone form. He holds out his hand, and Samantha turns a cold, shit-eating grin on Ariah before reaching for his hand. "I told you he was always m—" Samantha's so busy talking she misses when he swerves her hand and pushes her forehead so hard that her head smacks the floor with a thud.

Grabbing the garbage can closest to us, Wes towers over her, pressing his booted foot on her chest, and I look on in glee. Samantha opens her mouth to speak just as Wes removes his foot and pours the trash all over her face. "The only trash here is you. Now stay the fuck away from us, or next time I'll have Lev dump acid on you instead of his soda."

The dining hall breaks into raucous laughter. I survey the room and smile at all the cameras, recording Samantha as she fails to stand. Finally fed up, she pulls off the designer heels she had bought the night we followed her and grabs the leg of the table closest to her. Which also happens to be near me.

Never one to look a gift horse in the mouth, I kick the table, causing her to fall flat on her face. Pressing her onto the floor, I snarl, "Now you're exactly where you've always belonged, on the ground beneath our feet."

65

SEBASTIAN

The week has flown by. Samantha hasn't been seen or heard from since the incident in the dining hall.

I smirk, remembering how her eyes widened when she realized Wes wasn't there to help her. I've watched the video at least a dozen times. Lev also may or may not have hacked into and posted it on every digital billboard along the I-95 and I-84 corridor.

"Everyone, please take your seats. We have a lot to cover before finals," Lilliana instructs from the lectern.

Exams are in two weeks, then we have a month to spend away from all the bullshit. I can't say I'm not looking forward to spending the holidays with our girl.

A phone rings above the chatter in the room. I turn toward the noise and see Professor Monroe's eyes widen in surprise. She hastily pulls the device from her cranberry wool sweater pocket, whirling around to answer. The class continues to bustle about, taking their seats and pulling out their laptops.

"I have to go," Liliana blurts, scrambling to grab her things. "It's time... Charli—"

Waving my hand, I say, "Go. I was teaching today's lecture anyway." I know it's the call she's been waiting for. We briefly touched base prior to class. I didn't ask for details, and Liliana didn't offer them. But I know Charli is one of her partners, and by the look of joy on the professor's face, I assume this is good news.

Liliana smiles. "Thank you. I need to be there for her. I'll be in touch." Then, she dashes out of the room.

"Today, we're going to be discussing the Heather McGhee book you all should've read during fall break," I explain, stepping behind the podium. I wait until the room quiets before I begin. "How does McGhee's overall premise tie into our conversation about the impact of policies on society?"

A hand shoots up, and I tip my chin, signaling the student to speak. "One of the big takeaways was how discriminatory policies against marginalized groups have economic impacts."

"And that's a crock of shit," someone snaps. My gaze moves toward the sound of the voice. *Beau McCarthy.* This should be good.

I move from behind the stand, stride over to the desk, then sit on the edge of it. "Why do you say that, Mr. McCarthy?"

The smug youngest son of an oil tycoon smirks. "Because everyone has an equal opportunity to make it here, and all this bullshit about laws making it so only certain people win is nonsense."

"Says the guy whose family has never had to worry about food being on the table for generations," Ariah mutters, rolling her eyes.

Beau's hands fist on top of his desk. "That's not because of some law. Let's be honest here. All this talk about how the government makes policies to benefit some over others is just another way to try and pit people against each other."

"No. You can't have an honest discussion about economics without acknowledging oppressive systems in place that continue to foster inequities," Ariah retorts.

Beau grits his teeth. "What do you have to complain about? You fucked your way out of being white trash."

You can almost see the silence with the way the room quiets. I gleam, watching Wes's, Wyatt's, Owen's, and Lev's hackles rise. Owen slips a butterfly knife from his boot, flipping it open as he prepares to stand. Ariah's imperceptible shake of her head freezes them in place. Following her lead, I refrain from any reprimands.

Aloof to his colossal mistake, Beau continues. "Bitches like you always complain. *'This country is so horrible. The rich are so corrupt,'*" he mocks, not noticing the predator lying in wait.

My jaw locks. That's a step too far. "Mr. McCarthy, I suggest you learn to read the room," I growl, but Beau never knows when to shut the fuck up—a problem that plagues his older siblings as well.

I roll my shoulders back, glaring at the prick, oblivious to the pain awaiting him. *Beau's fucked.* Owen's knife flips between his fingers—Wes cracks his knuckles while Wyatt's expression declares Beau's imminent death, and Lev's fingers are flying across his keyboard. Destroying the McCarthy family by releasing the insider trader information his father's been using to try and recoup the family fortune that wife number five is snorting up her nose, I'm sure.

Ariah holds up her hand, halting all our movements. "I always find it hilarious how fragile the male ego can be when challenged. Are you so insecure that resorting to unimaginative name-calling is the best you can do?" she quips.

Fuck, she's amazing.

"It's not name-calling if it's true, you dumb slut," he spits, slightly angling his head to peer at her. "You're always strutting around here like you own the place—proud to be pregnant before you're twenty with no idea who those bastards' father—"

Springing from her seat, Ariah presses the blade that is no longer in Owen's hand into his carotid. "Finish that sentence, Beau. Please do it so that I can decorate this room with your overprivileged blood," she snarls, and he hisses as a trickle of crimson liquid runs down the column of his throat.

My cock stiffens in my jeans, and I stand, striding over to the podium to hide my very obviously growing hard-on. I'm safely behind the lectern when I decide I'm going to fuck her after I punish her. My dick is so hard it hurts.

Beau remains silent, and Ariah quirks a brow. "It's always assholes with no spine that talk the most shit when they can hide behind their mommy's Dior skirts. Well bitch boy, mommy can't save you. So finish your goddamn sentence!"

Ariah's demand filters through the air as she pushes the metal tip harder into his flesh. The scent of urine fills the room.

"Did you just piss yourself?" Wes laughs, briefly pulling my attention away from where she's holding the knife against his neck to the undeniable wet spot on Beau's pant leg.

My gaze travels up in time to see molten rage painting Ariah's complexion. Her nose scrunches as her gray eyes narrow to slits. "I could set up a gang bang on the professor's desk after hours to sell it to some porn site, and it would be my fucking prerogative. I could give less than a fuck what you have to say about it."

"Over my dead body," Lev mumbles, but Ariah's so focused that I know she can't hear him. Otherwise, a few choice words would be thrown in his direction.

Beau barely breathes. His snot mixes with blood as fear emanates from his body in palpable waves.

Ariah lowers her mouth to Beau's ear and declares, "But what you, or any other stupid fuck, won't ever be allowed to do is disrespect my kids. I'll slice off your lips and shove them up your ass since you like to talk so much shit."

"Fuck, I think I just came in my pants," Owen groans, and I can't help but silently agree.

It's time for everyone to leave. "Class dismissed," I announce, adjusting my cock. "We'll pick this up next week. Until then, I strongly suggest reading so you don't embarrass yourself like Mr. McCarthy."

No one moves. "That means get the fuck out," Wyatt barks, springing everyone into action. People don't bother to pack up, snatching their belongings and rushing out of the room instead of incurring our wrath.

"Okay, Dove. Let us take the trash out. I think he understands he fucked up. Don't you, Beau?" Lev mutters before kissing the top of her head.

"Y-y-y-yes," he stammers, barely opening his mouth for fear of being cut any further.

Wyatt slaps his shoulder. "You're not a complete dumbass, after all. Which is unfortunate because I'd love nothing more than to have her covered in your blood."

Ariah's nostrils flare and her chest heaves like the idea excites her. *Oh, my Spitfire has a thirst for blood.* That image makes my dick grow even tighter in my jeans.

"Let me take this, Angel," Owen says, coaxing his knife from her hand. His mouth curls into a smile at the sight of McCarthy's blood on his blade before he lifts it and wipes off the blade across Beau's cheek. "Can't have you tainting the purity of the metal with your subpar DNA."

Resting his palm on Ariah's stomach, Wes bends and kisses her temple. "Wait here with Bash while we take out the trash," he instructs while meeting my eye. Then he lifts Beau from his seat by his throat and storms out of the room. Lev and Owen immediately follow behind him.

Wyatt steps in front of Ariah and then dips his head until his mouth ghosts along her neck. "We're going to need to reenact this scene later tonight, Love," he murmurs, lowering his lips to hers. Then he's pulling back and running to catch up to the guys.

Turning, I walk toward the classroom door and flick the lock. "Desk. Now," I order, already unzipping my pants.

"Bash," she begins but stops. Her gray eyes heat as a flush blooms across her chest.

Ariah moves, and I meet her in time to assist her. "That's it, Spitfire. Lean back and spread your legs for me," I groan, grateful for the knit sweater dress she's wearing once she's seated.

Resting on her elbows, Ariah's thighs open, and I bite my knuckle. I was right. She's turned on. My eyes remain glued to the evidence of her arousal, and all semblance of my patience evaporates.

I stalk forward, bending over to push her dress up until it bunches around her hips. "Bastian," she whimpers, pulling my focus from the outline of her pussy.

The sight that greets me makes my dick twitch, reminding me of its confinement. The rise and fall of Ariah's fuller breasts stretch the fabric of the dress, making her nipples poke through the material, and I ache to pluck one while I suck the other.

"Fuck me," she pleads, licking her lips.

Needing no further encouragement, I pull out my cock. "This is going to be fast and hard," I exclaim, aiming the swollen tip at her entrance. We groan together as I sink inside her. "God, I never want to be anywhere but inside you ever again."

Ariah's moans mix with the sound of skin slapping skin as I thrust inside of her. I watch as her mouth falls open. Her incoherent demands for more urge me on.

Lifting her leg so it wraps around my hip, I increase my pace and deepen my strokes. Wanting her to feel more, I slip my fingers between her spread lips and begin to work her clit. Slow light circles build up to fast and intense pinches.

"Fuck," she gasps, clamping her walls around me. I don't think I'll ever get used to the feel of her bare pussy welcoming my every thrust.

My shaft grows harder when I peer into her lust-pooled eyes. Blush colors her cheeks, and her head falls back with each snap of my hips. Ariah lets out a cry of pleasure, urging me to fill her more. I lose all sense of self, fucking her with wild abandon when her pussy grips me.

As if sensing my hesitation, Ariah braces on her forearms and rises to meet me thrust for thrust. "You better not take it easy on me, Bastian. I'll push you off me and finish myself if you do."

Her threat made clear, I slow my strokes, removing my fingers from her clit. "I think you forgot how this works, Spitfire." Reaching forward, I grip her throat, feeling each rapid beat of her pulse. "How are you supposed to address me?" I demand, arching a brow.

"B—" I tighten my hold around her neck, pulling out so only the crown of my cock is seated inside her drenched pussy.

She whines, and I smirk. "You know what you have to say if you want me to fill your needy cunt," I tease, rolling my hips forward just enough for shallow thrust.

"Sir," she mewls, and I slam inside of her. "Ho. . . fu. . ."

Releasing her throat, I piston my hips, grinding into her tight walls on each down stroke. "Such a good pussy, taking my cock so well."

Ariah's eyes roll back, and I feel her flutter around me, but I won't let her come unless we're falling over the cliff together.

Scooping my arms around her thighs, I increase my thrusts, and I know when I've hit the right spot because her walls try to clamp my dick in place.

I lift my eyes, drinking in the beauty of her body and all its changes as it grows to accommodate our babies. *She's fucking beautiful.*

Groaning, I thrust. . . one. . . two. . . three times in a successive staccato rhythm as I lower one leg. Then I pinch her clit, and she screams, spasming around me. My balls draw tight, and my cock stiffens.

"Ariah," I shout. Stars blink in my vision before whiting out as jets of my cum shoot inside her.

I don't know how long it takes for my awareness to return, but when my eyes finally reopen, my Spitfire looks blissfully sated. Droopy eyes fight to stay on me.

Not ready to leave the warmth of her pussy, I rest her legs around me and lean forward and kiss her belly. Ariah murmurs something I can't make out as I lift my head. I'll kill for her—*for them.*

I whisper a promise, "Even after the last beat of my heart, my love will always belong to you."

66
WES

"I see Beau's withdrawn from LWU. This is your doing?" I inquire, gauging Lev's reaction to my question.

After I yanked the stupid fuck from class by his neck last week, Wyatt, Owen, Lev, and I ensured Beau understood his presence at Lincoln-Wood is no longer allowed. The sentiment was made extremely clear with Owen's knife work. It'll be difficult for him to flap his gums, at least until his face heals.

"Yes. Inquiring minds want to know," Owen adds as Wyatt looks up from his computer. Ariah is attending a meeting with her father, grandfather, and uncle. So, she won't be in class, making this the most opportune time to have this conversation.

Lev clears his throat, training his gaze on the three of us. "I think you already know the answer to that," he states, a smug grin appearing on his face before he turns back to the front of the room where Sebastian discusses the role the media has in generating public opinions.

It's our last class before our final next week. "Mr. Edgewood, would you care to explain how social media has been able to change the landscape of societal norms?" Sebastian asks as he hands a stack of packets to the first person in each row.

Sighing, I proceed to detail the ways social media platforms are being utilized to report news the mainstream media won't. Then, I expound on the movements raising awareness surrounding issues like mass genocides, extreme fascism, and corporate greed.

"We're living in an era where news outlets can no longer dictate what we have access to. Which, if unchecked, can be as harmful as it is helpful," I explain, grabbing the study guide from the person in front of me.

Sebastian nods and then continues with the lecture. The discussion goes on for another twenty minutes before I stand.

Wyatt quirks a brow, silently questioning where I'm going. I mouth 'the bathroom' before heading for the door and exiting the lecture hall.

Smirking, I walk down the hallway. In the last few weeks, we've eliminated Senator Baker's hold, freeing ourselves from Samantha's reign of terror, and we're rounding up all of their co-conspirators. But most importantly, Ariah's back safe where we can protect her, supporting her through the last stage of her pregnancy before our family grows.

"Wesley," Samantha's nasally voice screeches and the hairs on the back of my neck stand.

Stupid idiot. You jinxed yourself.

Ignoring her, I quicken my steps. I'm not in the mood to deal with her—not today—*not ever.*

"I know you heard me. And unless you want that bitch of yours to be shot, you'll stop."

She's bluffing, but I can't chance it. We don't know where Ariah went. When we asked, the only response provided was that she'd be safe.

Refusing to risk it, I shoot off a quick text to Thomas before sliding my cell into my jeans pocket. Then I whirl around and snarl, "You always seem to push the limits of my patience. Threatening Ariah is a surefire way to make us all go nuclear."

"And underestimating my reach is a *surefire way* to have two dead babies left at your doorstep next to the whore I cut them out of," she snaps.

I survey the hallway, looking up and down the corridor. Not that an audience will stop me from choking this bitch out before I toss her out the ninth-floor window. "I suggest you tread lightly and use the time we allow you to still breathe more wisely."

Samantha crosses her arms, stopping far enough out of my reach. "You assholes are always so fucking cocky. It's why I was able to get so close. You're all the same—led around by your dicks and distracted by your egos."

"Says the cunt we were able to fool." Her jaw ticks at my retort. "Why don't you and your *husband*, the Senator, go infest your toxicity somewhere else? There's nothing left here for either of you," I seethe, forcing my hands to stay at my sides.

"This is your last chance," she snarls. "Be with me, and you'll have more power than you know what to do with."

My phone buzzes in my pocket, and I check my watch, confirming what I knew all along—*she's safe*.

Recognizing I no longer have to engage, I roll my eyes. "You nor Baker intimidate us, so save your villainous monologue. You've lost all your leverage, and I'm not going back and forth with you," I state before I turn, giving her my back.

I'm seven steps from the restroom when she shrieks, "Remember this moment, Wesley Edgewood. It's the moment you cost yourself everything and everyone you love."

I pivot just enough for her to see the fury in my cold brown eyes. Her glacial gaze meets my glare, but I'm past caring. Ariah's safe. So fuck her.

"Funny, you think you have any ability to threaten me into anything," I bark. My nostrils flare, indignation settling in my chest. "Here's my advice, *Samantha*. Run—run fast and far because the next time we meet, I'll crush your windpipe, applying pressure until your eyes bleed. And once your fucked mind registers your life is slipping away, and you begin clawing at my forearms, I'll snap your neck."

Then, I leave her frozen in place, gawping with her mouth hanging open.

67
ARIAH

I look at my razor, then down to my protruding stomach. I can barely see my feet, much less my pussy.

Huffing, I sit on the bench in the glass-enclosed shower, thankful it's not cold. I've been in here for thirty minutes and still can't figure out a way to shave. I've tried to put my leg up on the marble bench, which is more like a twin-size bed it's so big. Then, I was sitting with my legs up and spread. Also not successful.

"Practice safe sex, they said. . . there's no way you'll get pregnant with the implant and condoms, they said. Well, I did, and now I have two ninjas duking it out on my bladder while hiding my damn puss—"

"Riri," Wyatt shouts, and I shriek.

I hold my hand over my now racing heart. "You scared the shit out of me."

There's a short pause, then seconds later, the glass shower door opens, letting in a gust of cold air as Wyatt steps into my shower naked, his cock jutting out.

"Uh uh. You keep that away from me. It's why I'm in this predicament now. Wait, is that my name on your dick?"

He chuckles, amusement gleaming in his eyes. "I come in peace.

And yes." He stands proudly. "*Property of Ariah* is absolutely tattooed on my cock."

My mouth hangs open as I gawk, looking between his shaft and his smug, grinning face. "Did all of you tattoo yourselves?" I question, momentarily forgetting my dilemma.

"*Maybe*. You'll have to go on a scavenger hunt to find out for yourself," he jests. Then he surveys me. "We were worried. You've been in here for quite some time."

His question reminds me that I still need to shave. "There's been some slight complications," I grumble.

Wyatt's gaze volleyed between my face and my razor before his lips curl into a mischievous smile. "Need some help?"

My nose scrunches. *Am I that desperate?* I mean, I have a wax appointment in a week. Then I remember how freaking uncomfortable I feel when my panties brush against the hair growing back.

Yup, I'm that desperate.

"I need some help trimming the hedges," I blurt, and the dick's hazel eyes fill with mirth.

"Trimming the hedges?" he repeats, quirking a brow.

Death. . . I'm going to kill him, then bring him back to life so I can end him again.

"Yes. Prune my rose bush. Groom my cat. Bald my vajayjay," I mutter, and he laughs. He fuck-ing laughs. "I should punch you in the balls."

Smirking, Wyatt retorts, "Now, Love, don't tempt me with a good time."

Yup! Definitely punching him in the balls!

I can feel the water building in my eyes, threatening to fall, and I want to scream. Noticing my change in mood, he stops joking.

Wyatt crosses the porcelain-tiled shower and kneels in front of me before he clasps my face into his palms. "I'm sorry, Love. I was only trying to make you laugh. You looked so upset," he explains, leaning over to kiss the trail of escaped tears.

"It's not funny, and I'm not laughing," I huff, ready to kick him out, which only makes me want to cry even more. "Everything feels so overwhelming today," I confess.

Wyatt stands, grabs my shaving cream, then holds his hand out for the razor. I blink through bleary eyes and stare at him. "Are you really going to shave me?"

Hormones, one hundred and fifty-seven. Ariah, two.

He tips my chin so I'm peering up at him. "I love you, Ariah. There isn't a thing I wouldn't do for you."

The earnestness in his words hit me square in the chest. I didn't realize how much of my heart was missing while they were gone. That realization hits me like a ton of bricks. *When did they become so important to me?*

Wyatt knew before we all did. None of us believed him. I'd been skeptical at first, rightfully so. On day one, Wes made it abundantly clear I was nothing and no one. Lev wasn't very receptive, either. But Owen and Wyatt challenged every resistance and blew up every barrier I had in place.

My tears spill over again, this time blurring my vision. "Wyatt," I choke between my sobs. He puts the shaving cream down and lifts me onto his lap so I'm facing him.

"I love you," I whisper, looking into his eyes. Our connection, like the one I have with each of my guys, is powerful in its uniqueness. Each burns with an intensity I've never felt before.

He beams, capturing my face and pressing my lips against his. I hum, wishing I could stay in this spot and in this moment.

Deepening our connection, I whimper as our tongues move in sync. Neither of us tries to exert control over the other. He presses three more gentle kisses against my mouth before pulling back, and I whine.

Wyatt laughs, running his thumb along my jaw. "Let's get you shaved before I forget why we're in here." Then, he lifts me from his lap and grabs my razor and shaving cream.

He kneels between my legs. "Lean against the wall," he instructs, and I scoot back.

Bending, he kisses my pussy lips, and I'm suddenly no longer annoyed with him, nor am I concerned with shaving. Heat licks my skin as he slowly lathers my mound before gliding the razor over my skin.

I lick my suddenly parched lips as my head falls back against the shower wall. Each pass of the blade makes me clench, sending a jolt straight to my clit.

"Keep still," he scolds, lifting the razor. "I don't want you to get cut." Then, he begins his slow, torturous strokes again, and when I think I'm going to combust if he doesn't make me come, he stops.

"Wyatt," I plead, forcing myself not to move.

He stands, grabs the detachable shower head, and turns it to the high pulse setting. "Now, let's get you clean," he growls, rinsing away the soap. I feel him spreading the lips of my sex. "Open up for me, Riri. I need to inspect my work."

Widening my legs, I lift my head, feasting on the carnal need displayed in his heated gaze before he aims the spray between my legs.

"Fuck! Please. . . please." I cry, not knowing if my pleas are for him to stop or give me more. But nothing more needs to be said. Two thick fingers barely fill my entrance before they stop. He's teasing me, swirling circles on my clit before pulling the spray away. Then he aims the nozzle directly at my bundle of nerves and my hips roll, lifting to match the pace.

I whimper at the loss of pressure when I hear the thunk of something dropping. "I need you on my cock," Wyatt grunts, springing to his feet and sitting on the bench. "Straddle me."

Wyatt holds my waist, ensuring I don't fall as I climb on top of him. Positioning myself, I sink slowly, one barbell at a time, giving myself time to adjust.

"Holy fucking shit. I knew this would be even better," he rasps, thrusting up as he slams my hips down.

"Yes," I scream, feeling every inch of him bare for the first time. His piercings rub my walls, creating a sensation that makes my pussy clench.

Wyatt hisses once he's buried to the hilt, and I feel so fucking full. "I don't know if I'm going to make it. It's been too long, and your sweet pussy is gripping my cock, demanding to be filled."

Bucking his hips, Wyatt sets a grueling pace, and I feel so much all at once. "Don't stop," I beg, grinding down before I lift back up and slam down his length.

"Never," he grunts, bouncing me up and down to meet each slam of his dick. His movements become jerky, and I know he's about to come.

"Fucckkkk," Wyatt shouts as warm jets of cum paint my walls, but he doesn't stop. Instead, he stands, and I wrap my legs around his waist and my hands around his neck as he carries me into my room.

I'm being lowered to the bed when he pulls out. "No," I protest.

"Oh, I'm nowhere near being finished with you, Love. Turn over and get on your knees," he commands, helping me.

Wyatt positions himself at my entrance, rolling his hips until I'm completely full of him. His fingers glide up my spine as he leans forward. Then he holds onto my shoulders, using the leverage to pump his length deeper inside.

One hand drops from my shoulder, but Wyatt's strokes never stop. I feel a cool burst of air before his palm connects with my ass, and I clamp around him.

"Jesus. . . Fuck. I'm going to fuck you to sleep, then fuck you awake," he promises, and my walls clench. The prospect of being asleep and being woken up on his dick is appealing.

Wyatt's hand moves from my shoulder to around my throat as he sits back slowly, pulling me into an angled sitting position. Then both his hands grip my ass before he doubles his pace.

"Oh. . . hhh. . . shit. . . ttt," I stammer. My voice vibrates with each bounce on his cock. I can feel myself growing wetter. The sounds of my arousal around him have me panting, edging me that much closer to my release.

"I need to see your face when you come, Love," Wyatt states before he slowly pulls out of me.

Bending forward, I begin to crawl toward my headboard. "Ouch," I squeak when smacks my ass.

"Don't move," he demands, halting me. Moments later, I feel his body heat. "Open those thighs for me, Riri. I want to see my cum dripping from my pretty pussy."

Gasping, I part my legs. Wyatt growls, and my nipples grow taut. His cool tongue licks the length of my slit, sucking our mixed arousal. "W-Wyatt," I breathe, fighting the urge to fall. "I need to turn."

He hums, making me shiver. Then his lips are gone, and he's helping me get situated. I'm lying back on my pillows when he fills me in one stroke, stealing the air from my lungs. Next, my legs are being spread before Wyatt is holding them open by my ankles.

Staring down at me, he rolls his hips, the muscles of his stomach flexing, showcasing every one of his abs. "You're dripping for me. Your pussy is so fucking wet it's dripping down my balls."

I throw my head back when his hips snap forward, grinding down before pulling back and snapping forward again. Each time, his pace increases. I'm so damn close.

"Fuck. I could watch your pussy swallow my dick for hours, but I feel your walls clamping down on me. Do you want me to make you come, Love?"

My only response is gripping my pillows and rising to meet his strokes as my walls begin to flutter. "Oh shit, Ry. You're so fucking —." He never finishes his sentence. On his next thrust, I scream. My orgasm rips through me with such force I explode.

Wyatt's back bows, and I feel his cum shoot inside me. But he quickly pulls out, releasing my legs and grabbing his shaft. He stands, straddling my waist. He grabs my hair, and I open my mouth, sucking him down my throat.

"Fuck. Fuck. Fuckkkk," he roars as he begins to fill my mouth. "I need to see you covered in my cum." Then he pulls from my mouth, and jets of cum hit my face and down my chest. Wyatt releases one last groan before a smile grows on his face.

Wyatt kneels in front of me and grips the back of my neck. "I knew you'd look beautiful drenched in my cum," he groans, leaning over and licking a path up my chest. His lips wrap around my nipple, and I reach down and grab his head.

My body comes alive again as his tongue swirls around the raised peak. "It's too much," I squeak but hold him in place when he attempts to move. "Don't you dare."

Wyatt laughs, nipping me. The action makes me squirm. Then his fingers disappear between my legs, parting my folds and playing in my juices before lightly rolling my clit between two digits.

My legs begin to shake as my body hurdles toward another orgasm when he bites down on my nipple, rubbing small, fast circles until I bellow his name.

Spent, I collapse on the bed and hum a contented sigh, succumbing to sleep.

I'm not sure how long I've been out before my mattress dips. Something warm and damp wipes across my cheek, rousing me.

"Shhh, Love. Go back to bed. I'm only cleaning you up so we can go to bed," Wyatt murmurs. I feel his lips as they brush against my forehead just as I give in to sleep.

68
OWEN

"So I finally get to meet the infamous Heirs," Ariah's doctor says as she squirts a warming gel on the probe.

We're at Ariah's thirty-two-week prenatal visit, and I want to tell her doctor to hurry the fuck up so we can see our babies.

This is the first time we get to be in the room, and Dr. Jaffri is babbling away about everything but our twins. I try to remind myself she's Ariah's doctor and I shouldn't threaten her—though it's tempting.

"A few unforeseen circumstances kept us away, but we sorted everything out. We'll be at every appointment moving forward," Lev states.

"Ah, Mr. Washington. It's finally great to meet you in person," Dr. Jaffri replies.

Ariah looks up, puzzled by their familiarity. We probably should've disclosed this part during dinner the other night, but things are going so well. I don't think any of us want to fuck shit up this close to the end of her pregnancy.

"Just how close are you with the obstetrician?" Ariah's gray eyes narrow, and I know we will be discussing this on our ride home. She knows we've had some communication with Dr. Jaffri, but she isn't aware of just how much contact we've actually had. Luckily, the whooshing of heartbeats pulls her keen stare away as she refocuses her attention on the monitor.

Two sets of hands, eyes, and ears appear on the screen, and my heart stops. One of our babies is sucking their thumb while looking like they're sleeping. The other looks like they're trying to punch their way out of her uterus.

"Ah, she's a busy one today," Dr. Jaffri chuckles, moving the probe over to our daughter.

"She's definitely something," Ariah mutters into the quiet room.

I'd look around to see if the guys are as in awe as I am, but I refuse to look away.

"Well, I can see who the ringleader's going to be," Wyatt jokes.

"If either of them is half as tenacious as their mother, we're in trouble," Sebastian quips.

Laughing, Lev adds, "We're in trouble. Have you met us? Two mini-versions of any of us are going to wreak havoc. They already have us wrapped around their tiny fingers."

"Not me," Wes declares. "You idiots, sure. Me? I'll be the level-headed one."

"Oh please," Ariah interrupts. "I'll be the only rational one in the bunch. You'll all be big softies, saying yes when they ask you to sneak them ice cream or let them stay up past bedtime."

Without looking away from the monitor where our daughter is moving so much her brother begins to stir, I reply, "She's got us there. We should take bets to see who'll be the first to break."

"Everything looks great. Both babies are hitting all the benchmarks. As long as you continue to limit your stress, you should be in the clear," Dr. Jaffri explains, lifting the probe from Ariah's stomach.

Then, she wipes off the gel before removing her gloves. "The nurse will be in to print your ultrasound pictures for you. Otherwise, you're all set, and I'll see you in one week."

"Before you go, can we discuss these knockout-strength jabs I feel in my vagina," Ariah requests.

Dr. Jaffri grins. "That's quite the analogy, Miss Bradford. That would be lightning crotch."

My gaze whips up before I blurt, "Lightning what?" Then I turn to Ariah. "Why didn't you tell us you were having such severe pain?" I question before shifting my attention to the doctor. "Is she okay? Are the babies okay?" I know I'm rambling, but anything with the name *lightning crotch* can't be good news.

"It's perfectly normal, Mr. Jefferson. Some women experience sudden sharp pains throughout their pelvic region or the vagina, especially in their third trimester, that are not signs of labor."

I expel the breath I didn't know I was holding at Ariah's obstetrician's answer. "As long as she's safe."

"She is," Dr. Jaffri affirms.

I help Ariah lower her shirt and sit up as the doctor departs. By the time she's up and ready, the nurse prints the images and hands them to Wyatt.

Reign, Fernando, and Elias are waiting when we step into the hall. "Good visit?" Reign asks, taking the point position once we enter the elevator.

Ariah nods. "Yup. Outside of the heavyweight boxing match our daughter is having, everything is great."

Once the doors slide open, Reign and Fernando step into the lobby, where more guards signal it's safe. That doesn't stop us from creating a protective circle around our girl.

Noticing our movements, Ariah rolls her eyes, pretending to be offended by our actions. "Oh no, save me from that dust particle," she wisecracks, and I snort.

"Fifteen," Sebastian retorts, and she turns beet red, clamping her mouth shut. I need to be in one of his counting sessions if they make her blush this much.

Thomas is outside, holding the door open to the SUV. As Thomas walks to the driver's side, Wes helps her get into the backseat. "Ready to go, Ry?" he asks once he climbs in and buckles his belt.

"Yes. I need to take a nap," she murmurs, resting her head on Sebastian's shoulder while Lev clasps her hand.

Wyatt and I exchange a look, knowing how monumental this is. Lev has his own demons to tackle, and he's working to do that. The fact that he grabs and holds her hand shows how far he's come.

We ride in silence once we hear Ariah's soft snores. "She's been so tired lately," Sebastian states, brushing her strawberry-blond hair from her face. I watch as she subconsciously burrows further into his side.

"According to my research, as she gets closer to her due date, she can grow more tired," Lev says, rubbing circles against the back of her hand with his thumb as he continues. "We should also ensure she has the right lotions at the house. Her skin will tend to be dryer. Oh, and we need to keep an eye on any swelling."

Pregnancy Encyclopedia Lev's lips part to rattle off more information when I notice movement out of the corner of my eye.

"What's that?" Reign asks, grabbing my attention. Looking up from Ariah's sleeping form, I watch as Reign points at a car that seems to be darting in and out of lanes on the busy road.

Thomas is already barking orders, and the convoy closes in, switching around to hide which car we're in. "Hold on," he orders, and Sebastian pulls Ariah tighter to him as Lev grips her hand just as one of the SUVs in front of us is rammed from the side.

I lean over and pull my Nimravus Tanto aluminum-handled blade from my ankle holster. My fingers itch to sink it into the heart of Senator Baker, who I know ordered this.

"Baker's days on this earth are over," Wes growls, voicing my suspicion.

Wyatt lifts his shirt, revealing his gun, but I shake my head. "Last resort," I mumble. Ariah's still sleeping, and I desperately want to be home before she knows what's happening here.

My head whirls at the screeching of breaks. A silver Lincoln Towncar drives up next to the vehicle Fernando is driving and fires a shot, but Fernando slows and whips right, nearly running the car off the road into a guardrail, but the driver maneuvers the wheel enough to stay on the road.

The back window of Fernando's SUV rolls down, and the familiar barrel of an AR-15 appears, letting off four successive shots. The driver from the other car loses control, driving head-on into the guardrail before flipping the silver sedan upside down.

"Thomas, get us the fuck out of here," Wes snaps.

"What the hell is going on," Ariah's sleepy voice becomes alert instantly.

Whipping around, I see the knife I gave her in her hand, and my chest swells with pride.

"It's under control," Reign assures her.

Ariah's nostrils flare. "That's not what I asked," she retorts, looking around. Ariah's body tenses, but we're already turning off the main road.

"Let's talk once we're inside. Right now, I need you safely in the house," Thomas demands.

Ariah huffs, but she doesn't argue.

The tight set of my shoulders slightly loosens when it looks like the cars following us are being held off as we race away.

We drove for another few minutes before turning into our driveway. We're out of the car and inside before I truly relax.

The relief lasts long enough to get Ariah upstairs. I press a kiss on her forehead and promise to be back shortly. She doesn't put up an argument, which under any other circumstance I'd question, but rage lights my nerve endings, and I need to release it into the flesh of someone.

I race down the stairs and barge into the security room.

"How the fuck did that happen?" I shout, slamming the door.

Thomas roars, "We don't know yet, but once we find out, there won't be a place for the people responsible to hide."

Good.

I've only seen Thomas this visibly pissed a handful of times, all of which never boded well for the person on the receiving end. Between his barking orders, while Elias, Fernando, and Reign look seconds away from imploding, we're all eager to get our hands on whoever this is.

Lev's running through the footage, tracking the route the attackers came from. He brings up a still image, and I clench my molars so hard I think they'll crack.

"Grady," I hiss and begin pacing.

"Stuck the chip in your arm, Grady?" Wes inquires.

Nodding, I ask, "Did the fucker survive?"

"His body isn't with any of the remains, and the footage shows one car fleeing the scene before the shooting began."

"Fucking coward," I shout, clenching my fists. He needs to be dealt with. "I want his head on a spike," I seethe, heading for the door. I need out of this room.

Holding the doorknob, I turn and command, "Find him.

69
ARIAH

"Can you please refrain from giving me a heart attack for at least one week, woman?" Shay exclaims, bursting into my room.

"Are you still certain your future is in forensic science? My money is still on you finally seeing you belong in Hollywood," I retort, trying to lighten the mood. The look on her face screams, *'Don't try me, Satan, not today.'*

Shay crosses her arms, narrowing her brown eyes at me as she walks further into my room. "Don't start that again. You know damn well I have every right to be worried."

"I'm okay, Shay."

"Are you sure?" she probes. "Because what I've gathered from all the security running around the house, the situation today was far from okay."

Sitting up, I meet my best friend's gaze. "I was asleep for about ninety-five percent of it. Like only woke up when we were a few minutes from home."

Her head falls back as she roars in laughter. "Only you, Ariah Bradford, would sleep through a car chase that ends in gunfire."

Shay's shoulders shake as she tries to catch her breath. She's near wheezing when she stops laughing.

"I'm glad I could amuse you," I mutter, hiding my laughter.

Clearing her throat, Shay schools her features. "Seriously though, Riri, I'm going to need you to chill, or I'm putting you under house arrest."

"No threats necessary. I have no plans to seek out another shoot-out."

"Good," she says, bending to hug me. "I need you to be okay."

I squeeze her tight before letting go and replying, "I am. Now, where are you off to?"

"My mom is making a pre-Christmas dinner since my uncle will be in Jamaica for the holidays."

My mouth waters. "I'll need a plate. I don't even know what's on the menu. I just know I need a plate."

She snickers. "Don't worry, you'll get your plate. I don't want a stye on my eye."

I scrunch my nose. "How does not bringing me food cause you to get a stye?"

"Old Jamaican wives' tale. Deny a pregnant woman her cravings and boom—stye."

"Whatever gets me a plate," I snort.

She sighs. "I don't know what I'm going to do with you."

"Love me forever," I quip, and she rolls her eyes.

Bending, she gives me another hug. "I'll be back later."

"Tell your mom I said hello," I shout at her retreating form.

My door opens almost instantly after Shay leaves. Lev's standing in the doorframe. "Do you need anything?"

I smile when he strides across the room, then lifts my chin, ghosting a kiss on my lips. "I'm okay."

Lev peers into my eyes a moment longer before standing. "We're going to head out for a bit. Thomas, Fernando, Reign, and Elias are here if you need anything."

"Be safe," I demand.

"We will. Just following up on a lead," he explains, running his knuckle along my jaw. Then he gives me another once over before he leaves.

I wait at least thirty minutes before I move from my bed and enter my closet.

Stepping inside, I lock the door behind me, then head for the safe. When I moved in, the safe was a hidden place to keep the cell phone hidden.

I place my palm over the panel, disengaging the lock before reaching for the burner inside and powering it on. Then, I listen out for any signs someone is coming as I put in a new SIM card. Once the phone is set, I waste no more time and shoot off a text.

> ME
> I need to meet.

It doesn't take long before the chat bubble indicates they're typing.

> UNKNOWN
> Are you sure? I'm sure the Heirs will want to keep a closer eye on you.

She's right.

Reaching into my pocket, I pull out my cell and dial.

"Ry! Is everything okay? I heard about the car chase. Are you hurt?" My dad bombards me with a rapid-fire of questions.

"I'm fine. Not a hair on my head out of place," I tell him. "But listen, Dad, I need you to pick me up."

I hold my breath, waiting for his response. He's the only one that can get me out of this house.

"Absolutely not! Did you forget someone tried to kill you today?" he questions, and chills run up my spine.

Like I could forget.

My shoulders drop. I need to have this conversation, but I can't tell him why I need to leave.

"I just need to—"

"The answer is no, Ariah," he exclaims, cutting me off. "It's too dangerous for you to leave. As a matter of fact, I'm going to contact Dr. Jaffri and have the rest of your visits take place at your house."

"Didn't we have this conversation?" I shout, my aggravation at being spoken about like I'm not in the room boiling over. "I need to be part of these decisions."

"Ariah, there will be times when you won't be—can't be consulted," he replies tersely. "

Sighing, I retort, "Dad, I understand all of that, but in instances like this, I *can* and *should* be consulted."

There's a long stretch of silence. I let the pregnant pause linger because I refuse to back down. They're smothering me, and I need them all to see me as an equal in this.

My dad huffs before he finally speaks. "You're right, Ry. You should be consulted, especially as it pertains to your prenatal care. What would you like to do?"

Fist pumping the air, I respond, "Thank you, and yes, let's move the remainder of my appointments to the house."

"Okay, I'll make the arrangements." There's another lull in the conversation before he clears his throat. "I just want you safe, Ry. I can't lose you," he insists.

Guilt hits me square in the chest. "I'm sorry, Dad. I'm not trying to worry you. I'll stay put. I promise."

He's quiet for some time before finally saying, "I love you, Ry, and I'm so proud to be your father."

Tears prick my eyes. *Now, why would he go and make me all emotional?* "I love you too, Dad," I reply past the lump in my throat, then hang up.

When I pick back up the burner, five messages await me.

> UNKNOWN
>
> I don't want you leaving that house, Ariah.
>
> Nothing you have to speak to me about is worth risking the twins or your safety.
> Promise me you won't leave.
>
> I'm sure we can discuss this over text message. If need be, a call.

> You better not have left the house.
>
> Ariah???

Geez. Everyone's laying it on thick tonight.
Massaging between my brows, I begin responding.

> **ME**
>
> Sorry. I was speaking with my dad.
>
> I already promised him I'd stay put. But I really need to talk to you, and I'm not sure texting or a phone call are the best ways to go about it.

Three dots appear before I continue. I stop texting, waiting to see her reply.

> **UNKNOWN**
>
> If you have your laptop nearby, I'll send you a VPN number. We can connect that way.

I exit my closet, grabbing my laptop before returning and sitting on the sofa. The number comes through moments later, and I quickly sign on.

My eyes nearly pop out of my head. The woman, the one I've been talking and planning with. The one Tamara introduced me to as one of the Princeps. It's. . . it can't be. I blink, double-checking my eyes aren't playing tricks on me.

No longer able to hold back, I blurt, "Holy fucking shit. It's you."

70
SEBASTIAN

Senator Matthew Baker is a dead man. Obviously, our warnings haven't been enough to relay our message—fuck with her, and it's game over. Our hands were tied before, but now, nothing will hold us back.

"We've got Grady. Can we have him delivered to Le Toucher?" Lev asks, looking over his left shoulder at me from the front seat.

My lips curl in smug satisfaction at how quickly the vermin was rounded up. "For what we have in store—yes."

There's no way we'd interrogate the dumb fuck at the house. If I had it my way, Ariah would never see or know danger ever again, but I know her, and that will never happen. That doesn't mean we need to bring the threat directly to her doorstep, especially with some of the complications she's been experiencing.

"King found him pretty quickly," Wyatt states.

Lev shakes his head. "It wasn't King this time. Thomas sent out a team. Grady was far too easy to find to involve King."

"Where was the prick hiding?" Owen inquires from the driver's seat.

"His office," Lev replies. "The idiot thought he could sneak in through the basement and not get caught."

Fucking moron.

"Of course he did," Wes snorts, untwisting the cap of his bottled water. He brings it to his mouth and takes a swig before he continues. "It's comical how the Senator convinced people he'd protect them."

Humming my agreement, I add, "Their arrogance makes them like shooting fish in a barrel."

Wyatt snickers. "Which is an insult to fish everywhere."

We strategize the remainder of the ride to the club and can't wait to give Grady the day he deserves.

Once security waves us through the gated entrance, we drive a couple of minutes to the underground parking garage, where Owen pulls into the assigned parking spot.

"Which room do you think we should use tonight?" Wyatt asks as we walk toward the elevators.

Mulling over his question, I grab my badge from my jeans pocket and scan it before replying, "Any one on the basement floor will more than suffice. Every room down there is designed for its victims to enter but never leave, at least not alive anyway."

"Fuck yes! Time to carve the Christmas ham," Owen gleefully announces.

The elevator comes to a stop, opening to the entryway of Le Toucher. "Welcome back, gentlemen," R'chelle greets with her megawatt smile.

"Chelly," I reply. "A pleasure as always. Is Matthieu waiting for us in his office.?"

She nods. "Yes, he's been expecting you. I called him once security let you in." Then, she walks us down to Matthieu's office and knocks.

"Come in," the brute grunts before she opens the door.

Matthieu stands in front of his desk, brutally slamming his dick down some naked girl's throat. He fists her black hair, ripping himself from her mouth and coming all over her face. He releases his hold, and she drops to the floor at his feet. That's when I notice who it is.

"Go clean yourself up, Isabella, and get the fuck out of my sight," Matthieu growls.

Wasting no time, the President's daughter scurries from the room. "Have a great meeting," R'chelle says as she closes the door.

By the time I look back around, Matthieu's tucking his dick away as he rounds his desk. "Grady will be in the Purgatory den," Matthieu informs us once we take our seats.

"Are we all just going to pretend you didn't just nut all over the President's daughter's face?" Wyatt chuckles.

My lips part to say much of the same when something glints in the light. "Is that a wedding ring?" I ask, staring at the onyx band covered in black diamonds sitting on Matthieu's left ring finger.

Smirking, he turns the ring. "It is. Isabella and I were married this morning."

"How exactly did you convince Isabella to marry you?" I ask, rubbing the bridge of my nose.

Matthieu isn't an impulsive man. Which means this was his plan from the start. "As if she had a choice," he exclaims. "If she didn't want me to tank her father's re-election campaign by releasing the videos of her at one of my many different sex clubs, her only option was to say *'I do.'*"

"Ariah would serve us our freshly severed balls if we ever attempted that," Lev states.

"I don't doubt that for a minute," Matthieu responds.

Scratching my chin, I watch my friend intently. The smug asshole is preening. "And how did you manage to get the President to call off the search?" I probe. "Because I can't imagine a world where Jonas Atwater lets you marry his daughter."

The smile momentarily slips from Matthieu's face as his jaw ticks. Then, the muscles in his face relax into a sly grin. "Bella's family were all in attendance. Our virtual witnesses, if you will," he replies.

Sighing, I shake my head, hoping Matthieu doesn't believe he's won. With everything I know about Isabella, she's no wallflower. I'll be shocked if she isn't biding her time before she strikes. It's exactly what Ariah would do.

"You better sleep with one eye open," Owen offers, "Unless, of course, you're looking forward to the fights that will undoubtedly come."

Matthieu's grin grows. "You leave Isabella to me. She'll quickly learn just how much she belongs to me."

Skeptically, I nod and let him hang on to the illusion that he has complete power over his new wife. "If you're so confident, put your money where your mouth is," I challenge.

"What did you have in mind?" Matthieu shoots back.

I steeple my fingers and smile. I'll let him enjoy his temporary victory because I know he'll lose. "We can figure that out later." I stand, "For now, my brothers and I have a fish to scale."

●

"Wake up," I shout, slapping the unconscious fucker across the face.

Grady's head whips to the right so hard and so fast that I wonder how his neck didn't snap. Blood sprays as a tooth flies from his mouth.

"Fucking pathetic," Wes seethes, wrapping his fingers around the hook-tipped tow chain. "I strongly suggest you realize how screwed you are and stop protecting the Senator. He doesn't give a shit about you."

When he remains silent, Wes launches his chain-wrapped fist into Grady's ribs.

"Go. . . to. . . hell," Grady wheezes, and I have to give him credit begrudgingly. We've been at this for about two hours, and he continues to be obstinate, revealing nothing.

I watch as Lev disappears into the back room. "If I were you, I'd speak up. You see him," I point in the direction Lev went. "Out of all of us, he's the most sadistic. Obsessed with watching people die in the most gruesome ways."

Grady's one good eye widens in fear. "You're finally understanding you're in the belly of not one but five beasts," Owen says, yanking his head back before dragging the fish scaler down his face.

"Ahhh! Pl—" Grady wails, ready to beg, but no one in this room will grant him a moment's peace, even in death. That's why this room is so fitting for where he'll meet his end.

I peer around at the rich crimson and obsidian colors in this space—like a place Dracula or Lucifer would readily call home. My gaze trails over to the bar, where scarlet-tinted decanters line ink-black shelves before moving to the four-poster bed with the headboard made of skulls painted black. What people don't know is that each skull was a victim, and I think I've found Grady's spot.

My attention returns to where Grady is chained to the wall by his wrists and ankles as Lev returns with a bottle. "Acid?" I ask when he stops beside me.

"Something better," Lev gleams. I quirk my brow in question, but he only replies, "Soon."

Coughing up blood, Grady spits, hitting the front of Wyatt's shirt. "You idiots. . . are over. . . your. . . heads."

"We need answers, Wy," I warn, knowing what's probably coming next could kill him.

Wyatt briefly meets my eyes before darting forward, grabbing Grady's Adam's apple, and slamming his head against the cement wall. "I think you've miscalculated," Wyatt begins as Grady attempts to turn from Wyatt's hold, but he's being rendered immobile.

"Your importance in this situation. We don't need you," Wyatt growls. "Senator Matthew Baker and his mildew cunty wife will die regardless of your unwillingness to answer our questions."

I'm so distracted watching Wyatt that I don't see Wes and Owen move until they're standing on either side of Grady to hold each of his eyes open with gloved hands.

Lev strides forward, and I say, "This is your last chance to do this the easy way, Grady. Whatever happens after this refusal will be on you."

"Fuck. You," Grady garbles just as Wyatt moves slightly to the side, never releasing his hold, making room for Lev.

"Hold him still. You don't want any of this on your skin," Lev commands before dropping something in each of Grady's eyes.

The shrill cry that Grady bellows echoes throughout the room.

They all release him and move back as Grady whips his head around, uselessly trying to free his arms to rub his eyes.

"If I were you, I'd stop all your shaking and tell us who's backing Senator Baker, or you might miss the window for the anti-venom," Lev states.

Grady freezes before he screams, "What did you do to me?"

"We gave you some incentive to stop wasting our fucking time," I retort. "Now, who ordered you to orchestrate an attack on us?"

Grady's head falls. "The Senator's wife."

"I'm going to let that bitch choke on her overinflated lips," Wes barks, then whirls to look in Lev's direction. "She dies. That cunt is done. Release everything. I want her end to be long and tortuous."

We all nod our agreement. It was always meant to end this way. Samantha Davenport is the definition of delusional and dangerous, and we've underestimated her one too many times. But no more—her world implodes now.

"Does Baker have anything else planned?" Wyatt snarls.

There are a few beats of silence before Grady finally slurs, "The babies. He plans to take the babies."

The blood running through my veins turns to ice at his confession. "How?" I snap. "How exactly is he planning to do this?"

"He's planted at least five nurses on the maternity ward for when you deliver the babies," Grady coughs. "Once the twins are taken to the nursery, they'll be smuggled out, and then the same chip we put in lover boy over there—" Grady mutters, flicking his head toward Owen. "—will be injected into them. Then if you refuse to cooperate, *'boom,'* they'll be baby confetti."

Grady tries to lift his head as he laughs, and I move on autopilot, snatching the knife from Owen's belt holster and charging him. I only remember the first thrust of the blade into his spleen.

"Bash... Sebastian. He's dead... he's dead," I hear in the distance. "Come on, Bastian. There's nothing left."

The red haze clouding my vision slowly lifts just as Grady's head rolls to the ground with a thud.

71
LEV

After the information we forced out of Grady, we met with the Council and determined it was safest to move into our wing in the Edgewood Estate. There's a medical unit where Ariah can safely deliver the twins. Security has been tripled, and no visitors are allowed outside of when Shay or Ariah's family comes to visit.

Christmas and New Year's came and went. We kept everything very low-key. There were no grand parties or any other holiday activities, and I have to say, I like it that way.

For far too long, there's been endless pomp and circumstance. It's not that we should never host any events, but we will certainly do less of them once we take our seats on the Council in three years.

"Have I told you sperm-wielding dickheads how much I want to stomp on your balls?" Ariah huffs from the couch in our den, eating the bowl of goat soup Shay brought her.

We're all relaxing and watching a movie. Owen and Wyatt are both massaging Ariah's feet while she's tucked into Wes's side.

She's thirty-six weeks and is quick to remind us that our dicks are the devil, even though she'll kill us whenever we say we'll keep our cocks away.

"Your love language is definitely physical touch and words of affirmation," I tease and then have to duck when a cream throw pillow sails through the air.

"Jerk," she mutters. "How's that for touch and affirmations?"

Springing from my seat, I stride across the room, signaling for Owen and Wyatt to move. "Someone needs to be reminded to keep their hands to themselves," I quip, smirking.

"Is that so?" she challenges, taking my proffered hand as I help her up. Once she stands, I clasp her hand, and we begin to exit the room.

"So, you're just gonna take her away from all of us?" Sebastian jokes, and I nod.

Wes laughs. "That's cold-blooded, man."

I peer over my shoulder and smirk just as we reach the doorway, then retort, "Unapologetically so." Then, I pull a giggling Ariah up the stairs to my room and lock the door.

"Are you going to teach me a lesson now?" Ariah asks, batting her eyelashes and pretending to be coy. But there's no time for meek and mild—not tonight.

"Strip," I order, striding for my closet. I grab four bundles of black jute rope and walk back into my bedroom.

Ariah stands naked—skin flushing rosè as her full, heavy breasts rise and fall with each breath. My eyes travel down the expanse of her body, admiring the beauty that is her pregnancy. I know she'd tell me to fuck off and that pregnancy is far from beautiful. I know she's right, but that doesn't stop me from basking in her glow.

My dick lengthens in my black sleep pants at the thought of having her trussed and fucked. Without a pause, I step forward, dropping the rope on my bed before kneeling in front of her.

"What are you—" she begins to rasp as my lips kiss the brownish vertical line along her stomach.

Raising my hands, I gently place them on her belly as I follow the line, tracing it with my tongue.

Ariah's legs part granting me access to her pussy. I slide two digits between her spread thighs. She moans as I groan, "Fuck, you're already wet for me, Dove."

I withdraw my fingers from inside her and stand, pushing the digits into her mouth as I lower my head and capture her lips, sharing the taste of her arousal.

"Mmm," she hums as our tongues tangle, but I need so much more. I need her to fall apart on my cock.

Pulling away, I pick up one bundle of the rope and face her. My chest gets tight at the thought that crosses my mind.

Can I really do this?

She peers at me. "What's going on in that head of yours? I can see the gears in your head spinning a mile a minute."

For her.

Inhaling, I sit on my bed and tug her in between my legs.

I'd do anything.

"I want you to tie me up," I rush out.

Ariah's eyes widen, her gray irises triple in size as my heart slams violently in my ears. "Are you sure?"

She's every reason to see past what haunts me. The push I need to heal. Not just for me—for the little boy gearing up to be a dad. He and I are owed peace in spades.

"Y-yes," my chest rattles as I choke out my words. "I've thought about this and am ready to try."

Worry creases her beautiful face as tears glisten before falling down her cheeks. I quickly move to swipe them away. I don't want her to be sad.

"No, Ry, please don't—don't cry."

A small smile peeks through. "I don't know why I'm crying." She wipes away a budding tear. "Stupid hormones."

That makes me laugh. "Would you like me to tell you what the research says about hormones during pregnancy?"

"Don't you dare," she mock scolds before freeing my hair from its bun. "I. . . I didn't expect this. It's. . . it's just so—I'm sorry I'm fucking this up."

I shake my head. "Never. I can't promise I'll make it through, but I need to do this." I hand her the rope, then yank my shirt over my head.

My throat constricts, and my palms grow balmy. "We'll go at

your pace. Whatever you need, Lev," she states, and I want to ask her if I can get that in writing because I'd need a video to believe she's following anyone's lead.

"Wrap the rope around my—" I close my eyes, trying to free the words stuck in my throat.

"Breathe," Ariah whispers. "Whether you do this or not tonight, be proud of yourself for reaching this point."

The heat of her skin encourages me to open my eyes, and when I do, Ariah's compassionate gaze is trained on me.

I nod, and she unravels the rope. "Just a simple one to start," I rasp. The jute fibers brush lightly over the flesh on my wrist, and I freeze—memories of the past assault me. Beads of sweat dot my forehead, and my skin feels like a million fire ants are crawling all over me.

"Stop," I bark. Ariah immediately lifts the rope, and I feel a sliver of ease. "I... I don't think I can do this—I want to, but—"

"You don't have to explain, Lev."

Clenching my fists, I angle my head to look at her. "But," I heave. "It's been far too long. I need to—"

"The only thing you *need* to do is take your time and go at the pace your body permits."

I turn away, wiping my sweaty hands on my pants. "This shouldn't be so damn hard. It was over ten years ago. I should be better," I hiss, whipping to face her. I'm angry at myself—the disappointment is like a thick, suffocating film against my skin. I'm desperate for an outlet to regain some semblance of control.

"How can I—"

"Go to the wall where the hooks are and spread your arms," I growl, gritting my teeth.

Rein it in, asshole.

Standing, I grab the rope and wait a few minutes to compose myself, burying my nightmares safely back in their 'don't fucking open' box in the deepest depths of my mind.

It was stupid of me to try this. I thought I was ready.

"Are you going to just stand there with your dick between your legs?" Ariah goads, knowing it's just the motivation I need.

"That mouth, Dove. I'm going to stuff it full the next time I have you on your knees," I state. Then, I'm before her and work methodically to secure her wrists to the industrial strength hooks and lock them in place so there's no chance of her falling. I won't be gentle. I can't.

I move, looping and tying until onyx rope crisscrosses her breasts, leaving only her nipples free of any bindings.

"Fuck, you look amazing," I murmur, wrapping the cord above the swell of her stomach, then through her legs and around her right thigh before doing the same to her other side.

Ariah's breathing picks up each time I brush her clit. "Lev," she whines. "Stop teasing me."

Smirking, I drop my pants, fisting my cock. "Is this what you want, Ry?" I groan, running the crown up and down her slit.

"Yesss," she whimpers, trying to lift herself so I'm positioned at her entrance.

I tsk, grabbing the last two bundles of rope around her thighs before securing the strands to the outer two hooks. Now, she dangles perfectly.

Stepping forward, I grab my shaft, line it up with her pussy, and thrust inside. I don't wait for her to adjust. Gentle can be for round two. This one is to sate the demon riding me—the ghost enveloping every cell in my body.

Ariah's scream when I pull out and slam back in spurs me on. She's begging for more, for me to go harder—to go deeper.

Pulling out of her, I squat and bury my face into her dripping cunt. "This fucking pussy," I mumble over her squeals as my fingers massage her juices into her puckered hole. Then I stand, reach into the drawer, and grab the vibrating anal beads and fingertip vibrator. I've been eager to use them on her since I bought them last month.

I slip the vibrator over my index finger before commanding her to open her mouth. Ariah leans forward, wrapping her swollen lips around the beads, and I work them, bead by bead, into her mouth before kneeling and sliding it slowly into her waiting ass.

She bucks with each inch it goes in. "Shit. . . fuck. . . holy shit fuck. . ." she moans as I find the perfect setting. Once her hips begin to undulate, I know it's time.

Holding my dick, I rest the head just inside her entrance, and her pussy is already fluttering. She rolls forward, but I slip out, leaving only the tip inside. "You get dick when I give you dick. Do you understand?" I question, but she doesn't respond. So, I slap her clit five times.

"Ohhhkayyy," she exclaims as I rub circles against her bundle of nerves. Then I snap my hips forward and fill her in one deep stroke. "Lev," she cries, tumbling over the edge, but I'm just getting started.

Without stopping, I grab the vibrator and turn it to max pulse. "I'm going to fuck this pussy until it's weeping, and then I'll fuck it some more," I grunt, pistoning in and out of her walls as I lower the vibrator to her clit.

Ariah curses, and I swear she must be speaking in tongues because most of what she says is unintelligible, but each clamp of her walls on my cock is the only language I need her to be speaking.

"That's it, Dove. Come for me. I want your pussy to milk my cock empty."

My words heighten her arousal, and I can feel her contracting as my balls begin to draw up with each buzz of the anal beads. I angle her hips up so she can meet my sharp, deep thrust.

I'm fucking close, and I need her to come with me. Ariah bounces with each stroke, her pussy growing tighter and tighter. "That's my fucking girl," I shout. "God, I love the way you take me so well. This tight needy pussy, begging to be owned. But it should know," I pause, turning up the setting on the vibrator as I lean forward and pinch her nipple. "Five men already do. You." I thrust. "Are." I pull back. "Ours," I roar, snapping my hips forward.

"Shi. . . shh. . . iittt," she screams, and her pussy convulses around my cock, triggering my release.

My whole body shakes as jets of cum shoot inside her with each spasm of her pussy.

Slipping my softening cock from her entrance, I lower myself to the floor while holding the vibrator in place.

"Give me what I want," I demand, pushing my leaking cum

back inside her as I watch her walls contract. Then her body momentarily stiffens before a sound I've never heard bellows through the bedroom.

I withdraw my fingers and replace them with my mouth just as she squirts. My cock is half-mast as I growl into her pussy, savoring the taste of us. It's only then the beast riding my back hums before going silent.

72
LEV

"The debate's starting," I inform them before changing the channel. Then, I pull out my laptop and begin keying in the string of code.

It's been a week since I officially let Ariah in. Something changed for me that night. I'm nowhere near better, but for the first time, I was able to try.

I'm lost in my head as my fingers fly across my keyboard when a video call pops up, and I answer. "Hey Teag. Are we set on your end?"

"Yup. The footage is already scheduled. Once Samantha joins Baker on stage, I'll hit play. I already took over the network servers, barring anyone from the TV station to cut to commercial," Teagan explains.

"Good to see you again, Teagan. I'll ignore the fact that you also withheld information from me," Ariah states, leaning over to peer at my screen.

Teagan shrugs, not remotely affected by Ariah's icy demeanor. "You better than most understand. There's no way I could ignore a direct order."

The two of them stare at each other for another moment before nodding. Some silent agreement is made between them.

"So, what exactly is this plan?" Ariah asks before Wyatt scoops her up, making her squeal as he sits her in his lap.

Chuckling, I reply, "We're going to broadcast a compilation of video evidence of everything we have on the Senator and *his wife* to the world."

"Every news network and social media platform will get a copy of the footage as well as a detailed outline of the sequence of events," Wes adds.

"In other words," Owen says, bending to kiss Ariah's forehead before he takes a seat on her other side. "Tonight's the night we burn their worlds to the ground, leaving them nowhere to hide."

Ariah smirks. "When is everything supposed to happen?"

I type in another line of code, granting me access to the Baker's bank account. I enter a few more commands, then turn to face Ariah. "At the end of the debate. We want to make sure they don't see this coming," I answer, and she beams.

"You mean this will be over tonight?" Ariah probes.

I want to tell her, '*Yes*,' but I won't jinx it. The last time we allowed ourselves to be optimistic, she—. Closing my eyes, I try to block the memory of Ariah's blood in the hallway.

"Hey," Teagan interrupts. "We have five minutes until the debate begins. Where are you with the Senator's bank account?"

"Teag, you wound me. Do you doubt my capabilities?" I retort, lifting my hand to my chest in faux outrage.

She snorts. "Answer my question, dickhead. We have minutes left."

"All funds, even offshore accounts, have been wiped. Senator Matthew and Samantha Baker are officially broke," I grin.

I see movement on the television out of the corner of my eye as the two moderators come into focus. "Good Evening. Thank you for joining us here in the nation's capital for the 2024 Presidential Primary Debate. I'm Jillian Moore." One states before the other moderator introduces themself.

"And I'm Bryant Montgomery. Seven presidential hopefuls must pass a critical test tonight to become their party's Presidential nominee."

Tuning out the remainder of the introductions, I focus on my next task. "Is the file ready for the Secret Service?" I ask Sebastian. His role was to have Matthieu use his new *ally* to gain access to the head of the Secret Service.

"The documents should be landing on Chad's desk in twenty minutes," Sebastian replies.

I'm preparing to lower my head when Ariah speaks. "Why not before?"

"We need them to run," I explain. When I see a confused look on her face, I continue. "Once the Secret Service gets the information, they'll station agents at every exit except the one we want unguarded.

Ariah's nose scrunches in confusion. "If you think that answer clears anything up, I ask you to please try again."

"There's a shoot-to-kill order in place, Angel. If either of them attempts to flee, agents have been instructed to take the shot," Owen answers.

"And we want very much for them to run," Wyatt adds, rubbing her lower back.

While they continue filling Ariah in on the plan, I have Teagan double-check that all the footage is on the drive. "We can't leave any room for doubt. The country needs to see who their precious Senator truly is."

"I see this is payback for my earlier snub, Levi," Teagan grumbles, rolling her eyes. "You know the answer to that. So, I won't dignify that with a response."

Snickering, I continue to set our plan into motion as I sip my drink.

"Senator Baker," Jillian calls, pulling my attention from my computer. "One in nine girls and one in twenty boys will have experienced some form of sexual abuse before the age of eighteen in this country. Unlike TV shows, we know that a family member or an acquaintance commits the majority of these heinous acts."

I nearly choke on my juice. "I forgot we added questions," I rasp, clearing my throat.

"Excuse me, what?" Senator Baker inquires as his face turns beet red.

Wyatt cackles. "Wait until he gets the next few."

Jillian repeats the question, "What will you do to combat the alarming rates of children being subjected to these life-altering experiences?"

Senator Matthew Bakers stumbles and stutters over his words, obviously flustered by how spot-on the question is.

Each candidate gives some variety of the same answer, promising to end all forms of child abuse. I grit my teeth at their hypocrisy, knowing at least three of them also like to molest underage children.

"Secret Service is on the move," Sebastian announces, and I check the time. Perfect, another thirty minutes, and it's show time.

Round after round of questions and arguments occur as each candidate grandstands, postulating their fitness for office.

"Senator Muller, thank you," Bryant says as the camera pans over to him. *It's time!* "This concludes our first primary debate of the election year. We hope these questions helped spark thought and an eagerness to make an informed decision come November."

The camera shifts to Bryant's left, landing on Jillian. "We want to extend our thanks to Bradford Hall Theater for hosting us."

"Wait, did he just say Bradford? As in my family?" Ariah squeaks, rubbing her stomach.

"You okay, Ry?" Wes probes, standing. "How long have you been having contractions?"

Ariah peers up at him. "I'm fine, I promise. This is the first one, and we all know I've had at least two false alarms."

We all narrow our gazes on her, not wholly convinced. She's thirty-seven weeks. . . with twins. That means she can go into labor at any time.

"I'm fine. Stop fussing before you miss the finale you all planned without me," she mutters, frowning.

My gaze flits to the TV just as Teagan says, "It's live!"

"Samantha, you had one job, none of which told you to kill your friends," Blair hisses.

"Fuck off, you lying bitch. You promised me the Heirs and reneged. So I didn't know what was necessary to get what I'm owed," Samantha snarls.

A shrill cry causes the microphone to screech. "Turn it off," Samantha demands. "Matthew, make them shut it off."

The video skips to Samantha in bed with Brian and Brittany. She's talking shit as Brian fucks her ass, and Brittany sucks her pussy.

"Matthew's too stupid to realize I'm using him. He hasn't even figured out he's not Wes's uncle—he's not Wes's anything."

The look on the Senator's face as he shouts at the production crew to shut it down—*priceless*.

Two more clips roll—one is of Samantha closing the lid of the tanning bed on a still very much alive Meagan flailing her arms. The other is of Samantha delivering Bethany's lips in a box outside the diner.

"You mean to tell me that deranged bitch is responsible for all of those deaths? How's that even possible?" Ariah growls, but before we can respond, the grand finale plays.

"You should've made sure that bitch aborted that bastard. Now look," Blair Davenport shrieks.

Samantha darts across the stage, heading for the control room. Security grabs her before she can even make it down the first step. "Turn it the fuck off," she stomps before the burly man hoists her in the air. Her arms windmill until she's securely in the Senator's arms. Samantha keeps fighting, but it's too late.

The money shot is already playing.

"You're overreacting, Blair," Samantha's father sighs. "You and our daughter have always had such a flare for the dramatics."

Blair's face goes four shades of red in under two seconds.

"It's not an overreaction when you find out your goddamn daughter is fucking your illegitimate son so she can take the Bradford girl's spot."

The entire theater hall stills. Gasps ring out, but I'm unsure if it's here or at the debate. "She's married to her brother?" Ariah shouts. "She's fucking her brother?"

"No, Matthew. Let me go. I can explain," Samantha cries.

Gripping Samantha by her hair, the Senator begins to drag her from the stage. "Shut the fuck up. You evil, conniving bitch." Baker's arm raises, swinging down with such force I swear I can hear the whoosh in his mic.

Samantha goes limp, and he catches her, then storms out of sight.

"Holy shit," Sebastian blurts. "You think the hit killed her?"

If only we could be so lucky.

"Doubt it," Wyatt mumbles.

There's a crash before gunshots ring out. "Don't shoot, you idiots. The President wants them alive," some asshole orders.

I watch as Owen crosses the room and leisurely leans against the wall. "I'm guessing Franky isn't happy that those two are primarily responsible for Isabella being taken," he smirks.

Laughing, I add, "Or the fact that the Senator was trying to kill her." Even though part of me wants to melt the plastic tramp in acid after playing kickball with her face, a larger part of me is glad we won't have to worry about either of them ever again.

"Fuck! We lost them. Tell the gamma team to cut from the right. Then, have the delta and theta come from the side and the rear. We're going to create a bottleneck," another agent shouts.

"Okay, handing back control to the network," Teagan announces as a black car speeds out from some part of the property.

Ariah's head whips in my direction. "They're getting away," she hisses, grabbing her stomach.

Dropping my laptop on the couch, I jump from my seat as a breaking news report appears on the television.

"Good evening, I'm Sondra Chen, reporting live from the Jacobi News Network chopper, and we have breaking news. Senator Matthew Baker and his wife and sister, Samantha Baker, have escaped." Sondra reports as they fly through the air.

"I'm fine. That one was just sharper," Ariah breathes.

Sebastian, Wes, Owen, and I surround her while Wyatt massages her lower back. "I don't like it, Riri," Wyatt grumbles.

Owen's gaze snaps to mine. "Call the doctor."

"Already done," Teagan yells from the computer speakers. "Dr. Jaffri is on her way to the house."

Ariah holds up her hand, trying to wave her off. "You guys are making a big deal out of. . . Fuuuuck!" Ariah screams.

"Senator Matthew Baker is racing down the George Washington Parkway at speeds of up to one hundred and ten miles per hour. On a rain-slick night like tonight, there's an increased chance—Holy shit," the new anchor swears. *"The senator and his wife's vehicle slammed into the guardrail before flipping over into the Delaware River."*

"Let's get her to the medical wing," Wes barks, scooping her up and running from the room. Owen and Sebastian are quick to follow suit.

I snap my laptop shut, knowing I don't need to tell Teagan we have to leave. I'm at the doorway when a loud boom blares through the TV. The news anchor speaks as I enter the hallway.

"There's been an explosion. The vehicle Senator Matthew Baker and his wife were driving went over the edge, and the car burst into flames before exploding."

73
WES

WES

Breathtaking. That's the only way to describe the scene before me.

"In through your nose, Angel," Owen coaxes, counting with her. The look she's giving him—all of us is priceless.

"I'm going to pretend I don't want to castrate you all for this p—" Ariah's words cut off, and her face twists in anguish.

Our daughter, Zoey, and our son, Aidan, are resting skin-to-skin on their mother's chest.

"Do you need anything?" Lev asks, pouring her a cup of water.

Ariah gazes in his direction. "Lev, I love you, but if you offer me another cup of water today, I might kick you," she grumbles, returning her attention to the babies.

Undeterred, Lev replies, "Water is great for you and the babies." Then, he picks up the container of fresh fruits, Greek yogurt, and soup. "You have to increase your caloric intake," he explains—their bickering triggering another memory.

"*Levi Nathaniel Washington. Stop giving me all the statistical analyses on* the best positions to deliver a baby in," Ariah seethes, breathing through her next contraction.

Dr. Jaffri stands, blocking Lev from Ariah's glare, the move probably saving his life. "Okay. You're almost there. Everything looks great. The first baby is head down, and you're eight centimeters dilated and about eighty percent effaced."

"Good, now tell this one," Ariah points at Lev. "To let you do your job and for him to do his, feeding me ice chips."

Ariah yawns, and I move to her side, picking up Zoey. "She looks so much like you." My gaze lifts to my mother's figure in the doorway. Ariah's eyes pop wide as she adjusts her top. "All that wavy black hair."

"That's it, one last push," Dr. Jaffri encourages as Owen runs a cool cloth across Ariah's flushed face.

"Gah... ahhh," Ariah groans, gripping my hand while she pushes. Moments later, a wail fills the room.

"It's a girl," Dr. Jaffri announces. "Who'd like to do the honors?" she asks, holding some type of scissors.

Wyatt steps forward, just like we agreed. Not that we would've argued if we hadn't decided before. Wyatt's been the lighthouse guiding us safely to our North Star. If anyone deserves to do the honors, it's him.

The nurses move about the room, taking our baby girl to be cleaned up. My attention centers back on Ariah as she prepares to push again.

"Holy shit, Wes," Wyatt blurts. "She looks just fucking like you." He's holding our daughter skin-to-skin.

I blink, refocusing on the present. None of us care who the babies look like or which one of us is the birth father.

"Mom, you're not supposed to be down here. We wanted time for it just to be us bonding for now," I admonish. But when have rules stopped Guliana Edgewood?

Strolling further into the room, my mother moves to Ariah's side. "I just want to see my daughter-in-law and ask her if she needs anything. People often forget the mothers after babies are born. Forget that we carried them into the world at the price of our bodies."

"The guys have all been very attentive, I promise," Ariah smiles, assuring her.

Squeezing her hand, my mother says. "I expect nothing less from my boys."

I shake my head, "I love you, Mom, but you have to go now. This is our time to bond. You can come back later."

My mother beams, her eyes filling with so much pride. "Of course, son." She's at the threshold of the door when she speaks again. "Always protect your family, and do so ruthlessly, without regard for anyone standing in your way." Then, she's gone.

"They're perfect," Sebastian murmurs as we watch Ariah, Zoey, and Aidan sleep peacefully. I look at our son. He has his mother's strawberry-blond hair and, like his sister, their mother's gray eyes—though Aidan's appear blue-gray while Zoey's are more silver. Aidan didn't wait long to follow behind his sister, joining the world thirteen minutes later.

"What are you thinking about so intensely over there?" Ariah questions, making me peer up.

The guys are all asleep in various spots throughout the room, much to the nurses' dismay. But there isn't a scenario in existence where we'd be anywhere else.

I've been lost in my head for hours since my mother left, her words playing on an endless loop. Now, even more than ever, the need to keep my family safe blares like an air horn sounding into my ears. And while I know Ariah will never allow us to treat her like a princess in the tower, protecting her from all dangers, I'll sacrifice myself to keep them from harm.

When I finally meet Ariah's eyes, I lower my walls, showing her the depths of all I hide—letting her see the strength of my love for her and our babies. I need her to understand that I will do something she hates if it means keeping them all safe.

Crossing the room, I stand beside her bed and lower my mouth to hers, then gently cup the back of her neck until our gazes connect before I declare, "I'll level universes known and unknown to ensure you're protected."

●

"How are you all enjoying fatherhood?" Ariah's uncle inquires while we wait for the Council to exit their chambers.

It's been almost three weeks since Ariah had Zoey and Aidan, and it's been quite the adjustment. Between feedings, diaper changes, and naps—each day brings a new adventure.

My gaze flits to where he's sitting, sizing him up. All of our previous interactions have been anything but pleasant. To put it frankly—*he's a dick.* One I begrudgingly respect.

Liam Bradford is a twenty-seven-year-old business mogul who didn't acquire his empire through old money. He did it with his fists, taking his earnings from underground mixed martial arts fights and flipping them into one of the world's largest and most successful MMA training programs.

"It's been more than we could've imagined," Sebastian replies, and Liam smiles.

"Good. Good. That's what I like to hear," Liam states before his grin melts into a scowl. "Don't fuck up, and I won't have to end you. For some dumbass reason, my niece has grown fond of you assholes."

I want to cut him off, but he's doing what we'd all do for her—looking out for her best interest. So I allow him to ramble on about how he knows over a dozen ways to *kill us.*

The door to the Council's private chambers opens, saving him from Owen, who is conveniently twirling one of his knives.

"Boys," my father greets as the Council members take their seats. "Let's get right to it. I'm sure you all would much rather be at home with your soon-to-be wife and babies."

Wyatt snorts, "I wouldn't go jumping the gun on calling her our wife just yet, Mr. Edgewood. We have to ask her first."

"And she'll have to say yes," Tobias adds. Like Ariah's uncle, her grandfather is still far from our biggest fans. To which I say, 'So the fuck what.'

Their opinions mean shit in the grand scheme of things. I'd

marry Ariah while she slept, taking a page out of Wyatt's book if she ever refuses to marry us.

I won't dignify him with a response, opting to do as my father aptly suggests—get on with it.

"We've heard no updates on the search and recovery efforts by the Coast Guard. There's no evidence they're alive, but there's no evidence that they aren't," my father begins. "Until then, it's time to finally clean house."

That captures my attention. "Do we have the names?" Lev inquires, pulling his laptop out.

"Already sent to your phones," Wyatt's dad replies. His unusually curt tone causes my gaze to narrow.

Rage. Each Council member's face is set in a stony mask. Their false calm would be convincing if I didn't know the signs.

"I don't think it needs to be said, but I want this problem dealt with without mercy," Ariah's father commands, clenching his jaw.

"What did you find out?" I demand. Something's up, and they're trying to hide it.

My father turns to me, and I see it—the solitary flare of his nostrils. "The presumed death of Senator Baker revealed their plan to take Ariah, Zoey, and Aidan. And their—"

I sit forward, my hackles rising as I watch the normally stoic facade of Donald Edgewood crack.

Clearing his throat, my father continues, "They planned to sell them." He's still not saying everything, but it's enough.

"To fucking who," Owen snarls. "Which dumb fuck is about to discover their beast is no match for our monsters?"

It doesn't matter what name is said. It won't exist when we're done.

The Council sees it—the sons they've been molding—the ones who'll assume the position of power. They see it and know we're ready. It's only then Ariah's father says, "Serge Volkov."

74
ARIAH

"How are my babies three months old already," Shay sighs, fawning over the twins while they sleep.

"Fourteen weeks, three days, and twelve hours. But who's counting?"

Whirling around, she whisper-yells, "You obviously, bitch."

I roll my eyes and tug her from their room, waving as I drag her past Reign and Elias while they guard the nursery.

Call me paranoid if you want to, but I won't chance my babies' lives on the false hope that we've seen the last of Samantha Davenport. That bitch is the definition of stage-five clinger, oblivious to the fact she lost.

"I miss you," I say as we sit on the couch in the den.

We're still staying at Wes's house, which I'm glad for. It would be nice to have our own space where we don't have to worry about a random unannounced drop-in from a grandparent. But for now, I'd decline if the offer to move out were on the table. This is the safest place for us to be.

"Didn't I offer to move in?" Shay quips, arching a brow.

Laughing, I retort, "I believe your exact words were, 'My suitcases are packed, and the movers are here. Just let me know when you're ready.'"

"You hehe, like you don't know I'm serious."

"That's exactly what makes it even funnier," I chuckle when my phone vibrates.

It lights up with three message notifications.

> **GW**
> Afternoon Ry! I have a few things I want to discuss with you.
>
> Can you meet me in my office, please?

"Oh, hold on," I tell Shay as I type out my reply to Mrs. Edgewood. "It's Wes's mom. Let me just shoot off a quick text."

> **ME**
> Afternoon! 😃
>
> Sure, I'm with Shay. Give me five, and I'll be right down.

"Everything okay?" Shay asks when I stand, sliding my cell back into my pocket.

"Yeah. She wants to talk to me. It probably has something to do with Aidan's and Zoey's birth announcement party," I answer, rising from the couch. "I shouldn't be very long if you want to wait."

Yet another weird Fraternitas tradition. Most people make a birthing announcement and are done with it. Not the Fraternitas. They make stupid rules about presenting any firstborn Heirs to society.

She nods. "I'm going to watch my niece and nephew to make sure I can see them breathing."

"Shay," I start but think better of it. The woman will only argue that Zoey and Aidan's chests don't move enough for her. Shaking my head, I head downstairs.

The conversation about the twin's announcement ceremony

reminds me of my fight with the Council. Initially, they said first-born son, but I told them to shove it. It was both or none.

After three weeks of back and forth, the Council suddenly relented. I might've considered it a surprise, but I think I have an idea as to why. However, the fact that the Council wasn't willing to budge until someone intervened still annoys me.

I'm in front of Wes's mother's office when I force myself to let it go temporarily.

"Ariah," Wes's mother greets, wrapping me in her embrace. The light floral notes of her perfume fill my nose, and I sink into her hug. "Come sit," she instructs, releasing me.

Another upside to living on the estate is spending time with all the guys' moms. At least one of them stops by daily, and we have lunch together once a week.

I sit, waiting for her to take her seat before greeting her. "Mrs. Edge—"

"Guliana. Please," she requests as always. "We're family. Save the mister and misses for the stuffy old suits."

I smile. She's always so welcoming, much like the other guys' moms. "Guliana," I correct.

"How are you?" she inquires. "Are my boys treating you and my lovely grand babies well?"

My face lights up at the mention of the guys and the twins. The guys. . . the guys have been amazing. Getting to watch them spend time with our babies is ovary melting. Not enough to want to have any more babies any time soon.

"Yes, we've found our groove. We finally were able to get the twins on a sleep schedule. At least until they tag-team us and change it around again," I joke, making her smile.

"I'm so glad to see you happy, Ariah. You deserve it in spades. I'm only sorry that it was at a great cost to you."

Guliana flicks a switch before opening the folder on her desk. I see the checklist we've been reviewing for the reception—every detail down to the napkin rings.

"Did we miss something?" I ask, pointing to the small stack of papers.

I watch as Guliana examines the list, flipping to what she's looking for, and stops. She studies the document for a moment longer before gazing at me.

"No, everything is as it should be. Whitley, our event manager for the estate, has been provided with clear objectives. The reception will be in the spring. Once that happens, Zoey will be the first female Heir now that the edicts have been revised."

I smirk. *My other win.* This time, a major one. Being able to strike the parts of the Fraternitas's bylaws that required the Selection made me feel proud of myself. So, while the idea of having my daughter and son part of an organization riddled with corruption and steeped in patriarchal bullshit appalls me, it's also important to ensure that the Fraternitas's archaic laws are changing.

"All thanks to you," I exclaim, still trying to wrap my head around the woman before.

Wes's mom is the Princep. . . The Princep of the Novus Ordo Seclorum is Wes's mom.

Guliana Edgewood heads a global organization responsible for every major power in the world. From governments to crime organizations, Guliana, all five-foot-nothing of her, oversees them, and she wants *me* to take her place once the time comes.

She shakes her head, "No. This is all you. It was your ability to rise to the challenge and ready yourself to assume the position of power."

I watch, in awe, as she moves the birth announcement reception plans to the side, replacing them with updates on the search for Senator Baker and Samantha. There's so much more I'll need to learn.

When we first met in person, I asked question after question.

How doesn't anyone know who you are?
Are any of the other guys' moms also part of Novus Ordo Seclorum?
What role did you play in my arrival to Edgewood?
Why did you pick me?

Guliana had to remind me to breathe because I nearly had a panic attack in my closet that day. I'm still uncertain that I'm not one piece of information away from having one.

"When can I tell the guys? I'm not a fan of keeping secrets," I state, addressing one of my most glaring concerns. It's not lost on me how much I harp on honesty and communication, but I'm being neither honest nor communicative.

The major downside is outside of Donald Edgewood and the highest ranks within Novus Ordo Seclorum—no one knows who the Princep is.

"Soon," she replies. "Right now, it's important to keep you safe. Until the Tribunal, your position isn't official. And even then, only those sworn to the highest ranks will ever know. It's how the Princep stays alive."

Huffing, I share my grievance. "Guliana, I don't like the idea of more secrets. There's been an endless amount of lies, and I'm sick of it."

"Part of being a leader is knowing when the information you withhold is life-altering. Would sharing this put the people you care about in harm's way?" she explains, pushing a report in front of me.

Her words play on a loop, making me question whether some of my anger toward the guys is warranted.

Smiling, she states, "I can feel the gears turning in your head. The answer is yes and no. No one ever wants to be lied to, Ariah. Especially not by the people you hold in high regard." Guliana stands before continuing, "But you have to ask yourself the why of someone's actions because whether we like it or not—*the why matters*. Think about this as more information begins to trickle out."

Guliana is around the desk before I speak, "Nothing is ever just black and white. I think I forgot that. My understanding of why and forgiving them doesn't mean my hurt is invalid."

"Exactly, but don't worry. I'm sure the boys will be in line soon enough. For now, focus on your training. When it's time to bring them in, they'll be brought in."

75
OWEN

Aidan's goofy grin grows at the raspberries his sister blows in my face.

"You think that's funny. . . you think that's funny." I tease, tickling his belly, only making him break into peels of laughter.

The apple of his round cheeks flushes even brighter pink when I scowl. "Zoey Bear, drooling in Daddy's mouth is on the nope list. We went over this," I say, trying to get my five-month-old twins to see reason.

"Mr. Jefferson." Lilah, our nanny, calls me from just inside the room. "It's time for the twins' naps."

"Looks like the club is being shut down early. The club owner said that they had to cut you two off. All those milk shots."

Chuckling as she approaches, Lilah says, "You've always had quite the imagination." I bend to kiss Aidan's forehead before she picks him up off of the bed, carrying him to the nursery.

"It's good to have you back, Lilah," I tell her. Lilah is one of the few nannies our families trust. She's gone through an extensive background check. With all the snakes still in our midst, we had to be sure she was safe to be around the babies.

Any mention of my childhood would normally send me into a tailspin that always leaves a trail of bloody destruction. I've had fewer urges over the last year. While I can't attribute all of my progress to Ariah or the twins, they've been motivators. They can't be the only reason. This is my journey, so I have to want it for myself first. That doesn't mean I won't turn someone into one of those fancy hedges cut into the Eiffel Tower.

"I'll take Zoey," Lilah remarks, prompting me to airplane fly her into Lilah's arms, and Zoey rewards me with more drool.

Lilah snickers as she exits the room, and I remind myself to skip her Christmas bonus this year.

I'm wiping the last of the baby dribble from my chest when I hear the bathroom door open, turning in time to see my angel.

"Baby drool looks great on you," Ariah jokes, stepping into the bedroom wrapped in a hunter-green towel.

I'm too busy admiring her to respond with a quip of my own.

"Keep it up, Angel, and you'll have three babies in you before the night is over."

"Ouch," I hiss, rubbing the spot on my arm where Ariah pinched me.

"Owen!"

Laughing, I reply, "What? Too soon?" Earning me another pinch. Then I grab her waist, scooping her up and pushing her against the wall. My dick is out and slamming inside her before she takes a full breath.

This time, when she calls my name, it's like a prayer, pleading for more. "Someone's in need of a good fuck," I growl into Ariah's ear as my hips thrust inside her.

Ariah's pussy wraps around my cock like a vice, enveloping me in its warmth as the sounds of her wetness fill the space between us.

"O-o-o. . . wen-n-n. . ." she screams when I pull out and then drive my shaft deep, groaning when her walls flutter.

"That's it, Angel. Feed me those fucking screams." I double my pace, sliding my fingers between our bodies, spreading her pussy lips, and flicking her clit.

Her legs wrap around my waist, urging me forward while her

nails dig into my back. "Fuck, harder," I demand, welcoming the sting when she breaks the skin. My grin grows at the thought of the crescent-shaped marks I'll wear like a badge of honor.

"I'm so fucking cl—" Ariah shouts as her back bows, her pussy spasms, clamping on my cock so hard my cum shoots out in one long spurt, but I fuck through it.

"I need you to come for me one more time, Angel," I instruct, lifting my hand from her clit to her neck, then squeeze.

Ariah's head begins to tip back. "Don't you fucking dare look away from me. I want to see the look in your eyes when I split this fucking tight pussy in half."

Gripping her throat, I set the pace, guiding her up and down my shaft, my balls slapping her ass with each stroke. My hips snap forward, then pull partially out, sitting at her entrance before slowly sliding back in. I repeat this two more times, then slam inside. Her shrill screams of pleasure almost deafen me as she topples over the edge, and I quickly follow.

●

"Do you know what pisses me off more than anything, Glen?" I ask the schmuck I should've killed that night, ignoring the Council's instructions to show mercy. *Fuck mercy.* That asshole can sit next to forgiveness at the 'no' table because that's what I'll be shoving down every fucker's throat who underestimates us from now on.

Glen being trussed up like a chicken next to his idiot uncle seems fitting since Byron Matthews and his nephew are a pivotal part of the shitstorm of the last two years.

"Imagine our surprise when we discovered how involved you were in Matthew Baker's plans, Byron," Lev confesses, his tone deceptively calm. Then, he turns up the temperature of the incinerator.

Glen tries to peer in his uncle's direction but is too weak to lift his head. They're both hanging face down from a beam in the warehouse—their hands bound to their feet, making a "U."

This is our fifth time working out here. The Jacobis never miss. The twenty-eight-thousand-foot, sleek, modern building is perfect. There are over two dozen rooms of pain with plenty of space for more. Today's room is aptly named, 'What you got cookin'.'

"Arms getting sore, there?" Sebastian taunts them. "Probably won't be too much longer before they fall entirely out of their sockets."

Wes strolls into the room with five one gallon-size bottles of cooking oil. "I hope I haven't missed out on all the fun," he says, placing four of the jugs on the table before uncapping the one still in his hands.

"I don't know what you're talking about. I already told you guys everything I knew," Glen rushes out. "I-I w-wouldn't lie. I don't know anything else."

"Shut up, you sniveling idiot," Byron wheezes.

A whirring sounds just before Sebastian swings the crowbar, striking Byron's side. "I'd save your breath if I were you—wouldn't want to trigger your asthma and suffocate."

Patting Glen's cheek, I add, "Your uncle here, Glenny boy, hung you out to fry—*literally*."

Wyatt grabs one of the oil containers and then moves to stand in front of Byron. "You see, Glen. Your uncle, here, tried to make it look like you were the one bankrolling the Senator."

"Ww-hat are you talking about?" Glen's words begin to slur.

"Would you sh-hut uhpp?" Byron garbles, choking on globs of oil.

Wes starts to pour his bottle over Byron while he responds. "Your uncle made a mess of a paper trail that stopped at your front door."

"But the jackass forgot two things—one, you're broke, and two, we have some of the best hackers working with us," I state, finishing Wes's explanation and grabbing my own bottle.

Lev opens the door to the incinerator, and the distinct smell of fire fills the room as a wave of heat wafts into it.

"But I-I—it wasn't me," Glen shouts. "Please let me go. I only did what he said, then I never did anything ever again."

Ready to go home, I pour oil over Glen's head, shutting off his whine. It's probably hard to cry when a thick liquid is falling into your mouth. "Lie with the dog and all that jazz," I sigh.

"Plur-rease," Glen pleads again.

"I could give you the whole fool me once line, but I think I'm good on being quirky today." I dump the last of the bottle down his back before chucking it.

Lev walks around Glen, emptying his container of oil. "I'm not—there isn't a cannibal's chance at being vegan that you or your uncle leave here today."

I throw my head back and cackle. I laugh so hard that I gasp for air while I grab my side.

Snickering, Wyatt says, "We need to see you like this more often, Lev."

Sebastian pushes the control, moving them to the conveyor belt. "I'm begging you," Glen croaks. "He was the one sleeping with that cunt Vivian, not me."

"I'm not your priest, and this is no confessional," Sebastian retorts, but there's no more vitriol at the mention of his cunt of an ex.

We're all in better places—far better than the first day of senior year when our lives changed in the best ways possible.

Glen's and Byron's screams pull me from my thoughts. Wes and Sebastian are cleaning up the tarp we wisely put down earlier. Lev and Wyatt join me to change.

"Never thought I'd see the day where I'm getting spit up and blood out of clothing in the same night," I quip, smiling.

"Can't say I'm mad about it," Wes murmurs, cleaning up.

We all grunt in agreement, then focus on finishing up so we can head back home to where our heart beats.

We're in the car on our way home when Lev exclaims, "Turn to the satellite news station. There's an update on the search for Baker."

"The remains of Senator Matthew Baker and his wife were discovered early this morning. Matthew Baker went from a presidential hopeful to a disgraced senator. Baker was among—"

I stop listening to the news report and peer over to the guys. "Are they sure she's dead?"

"We're waiting for confirmation, but some of her clothing and DNA were discovered," Lev responds as he continues to work.

Nodding, I refocus on the road before I mutter, "I wanted to be the one to gut the bitch, but a win is a win."

76
WES

"This reception is ridiculous," I mutter. "Zo, your grandmothers have zero chill."

Our daughter looks at me and laughs, and I wipe the drool running down her chin.

"This is not simple. I thought this was supposed to be a small event. This looks like the antithesis to simple" Owen groans, stepping into view. His mood shifts once he notices who I'm holding. "Hey there, Zoey Bear."

I twist, batting his hands away when he reaches, making her squeal. She and Aidan love this game.

In the three months since Matthew and Samantha's deaths were confirmed, we've been extremely busy. Between weeding out the last of the traitors working for Baker and parenthood, we've rarely had any time with our girl. That changes after tonight.

"With our mothers, we're lucky this is all they did," Sebastian chuckles.

The theme is the stork takes New York. The ballroom in my family home has been transformed into what I imagine birthdays for the twins will look like in the future. Gold stork statues stand at the entrance to a runway holding a sack filled with passports.

When Ariah discussed the idea of a travel-style announcement, I don't think she knew what she was signing up for with Guliana Edgewood. The woman, though I love her, loves throwing elaborate parties.

"You have to give them credit. This is pretty genius," Lev states, striding over to join us.

"I see your mother opened the extended ballroom for this," Owen observes.

Nodding, I reply, "Any opportunity my mother gets to go all out, she will."

We walk further inside, surveying the rest of the space. Stations, or should I say *gates* to different countries, are set up throughout the room. The goal is to visit each gate and get your passport stamped with a final destination of New York.

"I do love the vibrant colors," Sebastian says.

Zoey starts bouncing in my arms, squirming like she wants out, which only means one thing.

Turning, I take in Ariah as she approaches. *Fucking stunning*. She's wearing a hunter-green off-the-shoulder top with black leggings and some black knee-high combat boots. Her fuchsia-colored hair is loosely braided, hanging over her shoulder, showing off her lavender and raspberry highlights.

"Look at my babies," Ariah coos, kissing Aidan and his sister. Then she looks up, "Oh, you guys too."

Arching my brow, I lean down to kiss her, then whisper, "Hello to you too, beautiful."

Ariah smiles, peering into my eyes, "Hello, back at you." Then we each peck her on the lips. "I should go get my hair done more often if this is the welcome I get," she teases before taking in the ballroom. "This is amazing. Way more than I expected."

"This is our mothers being tame, which leads me to believe you gave them restrictions," Lev remarks.

She shrugs. "They found loopholes, obviously, but I think I'm happy they did. If we had to do an event, I'm grateful they made it special."

I see my parents out of the corner of my eye and instantly know what it means. "It's time to go socialize and pretend we like people," I grumble, making Ariah laugh.

We're heading for them when a server accidentally walks into me. "Oh, sorry, Mr. Edgewood," he blurts. Then, he adjusts the tray under his arms before brushing his hair out of his face.

Smiling, I pat him on the shoulder. "Don't worry about it."

His murky brown eyes widen in shock. I assume he's waiting for me to yell. Then he spins, murmuring more apologies as he strides away.

"Odd duck, that one," Wyatt says, and we both watch as he disappears into the crowd.

The room slowly fills over the next few hours, and we mingle amongst our guests. We're over by the gate to Jamaica with our families when the twins begin to get cranky.

Reaching for Aidan, Owen declares, "I think it's time for a nap."

"Nonsense. You all stay here and continue enjoying the party. I'll get them up to bed," Lilah urges, taking Zoey from Ariah.

"Are you sure, Lilah? I don't mind going up to put them to bed," I offer, and she shoos me.

Gathering Aidan in her arms, Tabitha announces, "I'll go with and help."

Lilah pauses momentarily, then scoops up Zoey's diaper bag while Ariah's grandmother grabs Aidan's before they exit the ballroom.

I'm speaking with some of my father's business associates when the lights go out.

"The twins," Ariah gasps. Then all I see is wild-colored hair darting in the direction of upstairs.

None of us skip a beat, running behind her as we shout for her to wait, but she's almost at the stairs when we catch up.

I hear orders being given before feet sound against the floor. "What the fuck is going on?" Wyatt hisses. "The backup lights should've kicked in by now."

"Wait," I exclaim, grabbing Ariah's arm. "You can't just rush the room, and you know that."

Ariah whirls around, peering into my eyes, and the anguish

seeping from her pores guts me. "I can't just do nothing, Wes," she snaps. "Those are our babies."

I look over her shoulder, watching as Owen, Lev, Sebastian, and Wyatt arrive with Elias, Reign, and Fernando on their heels. Refocusing my attention on Ariah, I assure her, "And we will. Let's make a pl—"

The lights flicker back on, cutting me off just as Reign speaks, "Someone shut off the power and destroyed the backup generators."

"How's that possible? Everyone here was vetted so thoroughly that we know if their great-great grandfather's third cousin, twice removed, who was adopted, ever jaywalked," Lev exclaims.

"I don't give a fuck about that right now," Ariah shouts. "We need to go check on Zoey and Aidan."

Reign dips his head in agreement. "I'd tell you to stay here while we make sure it's safe, but I already know none of you will agree to that. So, we'll go first."

Once we all agree, Elias and Reign take point as we work our way down the hallway. Whispered orders are given as each room is cleared. We're approaching the nursery door, and I know before we get there, something is very fucking wrong.

Reign enters the room first, but I dart past him, and the sight before me turns my blood to ice.

"No, no, no, no, no," Ariah mumbles, dashing to where her grandmother lies motionless on the floor in front of Aidan's crib—a wound bleeding from the back of her head where someone knocked her out.

Spinning, I rush toward Zoey's crib, already knowing a parent's worst nightmare is becoming true—the twins have been taken.

"This can't be fucking happening," Wyatt snarls, moving about the room, searching and hoping maybe, but I know they're gone.

Lilah's body is slumped on the ground, and her neck is turned at an unnatural angle. An angle no human can survive. My eyes shut as I roar in rage. Then, I push down my emotions, locking them into the place I always do when it's time to be calculated.

Lev is checking the security feed with Sebastian, and Owen is ripping the twins' room apart, desperately trying to find a clue when I snap my gaze open.

I don't acknowledge anyone who comes running into the room. "Teams of three or more." I hear Thomas order, but I'm already moving out the door.

Footsteps sound behind me as I continue down the hallway. I know who's with me without having to turn around. "You know who this is, don't you," Lev seethes.

Of course I do. We underestimated her from the beginning, and that is a cross I will always bear.

Lev and I enter the library, confirming my suspicions. The wall door in the bookshelf is wide open, and the server that bumped into me earlier lies dead on the floor, missing half his face.

"Lucky shit. You got off easy," he growls, stepping on his head.

"She's going to die, and I'm going to be the one to rip out her vocal cords after I chop off her hands for daring to take from me," I bark, running my fingers through my disheveled black hair.

My phone vibrates, and I don't bother to look. I know who it is.

Lifting my cell to my ear, I hiss, "You should've stayed dead, Samantha."

"I missed you too, Wesley," she singsongs, and I can hear the twins' wailing in the background.

I'm gripping my phone so hard it feels like it'll snap under the pressure. "Here's exactly how this is going to go," Samantha croons. "You're going to come outside and willingly come with me, or I'm taking these two spawns of a whore and—"

"Enough. Just tell me where you are, and I'll be there," I command.

"Aww, someone's broody today. Don't worry, I know exactly what you want when you're like this. I'll fix it f—"

At the end of my patience, I interject, "Listen, you dense cunt. Tell me where you are."

Samantha tsks, but replies, "The emergency road at the back of the estate. I'm at the end. You have five minutes. Oh, and Wes," she pauses, her heavy breaths heaving into the phone. "No funny shit, or I'll take off and drop these brats off the nearest bridge." Then the line goes dead.

"I won't talk you out of it, but let's devise a plan," Lev suggests, and that's precisely what we do before hopping into my truck.

We're nearly at the spot Samantha demanded I meet her when my phone buzzes for the millionth time, but I ignore it. I know it's either Ariah or the guys, and I need to keep the heroics down to a minimum.

"Remember the plan. We'll get you back," Lev declares as I step out of the car onto the road.

Samantha's exactly where she said she'd be. I glance at Lev and nod. "Once they're safe, Lev—*only* when they're safe," I order, then walk toward the waiting vehicle with my hands raised.

The window rolls down as I draw near. Samantha's pointing a gun at me when she instructs, "Stop. Turn around and empty your pockets."

I do as I'm told, ignoring the other dead waiter, and spin, showing her I'm not armed.

"Good. Now get in the car."

Once again, I do as instructed and slowly open the door to the car. I stare down at my son and daughter tied together on the floor of the passenger side. Tears flow down Zoey's and Aidan's red faces, and I can see bruises forming on their skin, but they look otherwise unharmed.

Samantha begins to point the barrel of the gun at them. "I'm here," I grit through clenched teeth. "Let them go."

"Drop the little shits out the door," she demands, training the gun on me as I pick them up. I begin to untie them. "No, just like they are, Wesley."

"Okay," I reply, looking over my kids for what I hope won't be the last time. Bending, I kiss both their foreheads and reassure them everything will be fine.

"Right now, Wesley," Samantha orders.

I give them one last hug, place them gently on the pavement outside, and close the door before the tires screech as Samantha speeds off.

My cell rings again. "Answer it. I know it's that bitch. Answer it and put it on speakerphone."

Nodding, I accept the call, and Ariah's voice fills the car. "Wes. . . Wes. Where the fuck did you go?"

"My forever girl," I breathe, pain lancing my chest that I so quickly have to keep a promise I made the night I told her I'd sacrifice myself for them without hesitation. I just wanted more time.

"Where he always belonged, you grubby man-stealing whore. He's where he should be," Samantha shouts over me.

The line is silent. "You don't listen very well, Samantha, do you?" Ariah's voice is subarctic. "I warned you on the first day of school. Do you remember?"

Samantha's face drains of all color before she snatches my cell phone, but before she throws it out the window, Ariah's lethal tone slices through the air. "I'm coming for you."

77
ARIAH

"We need to get Wes back now," I mutter, pulling up my cargo pants because fuck them if they think they can leave me behind.

"He's coming home, Ry," Shay says, trying to comfort me as I yank my black thermal over my head.

Pausing, I glance at her before I bend to zip up my boots. "He has no choice. Any other outcome, and I'll kill him." Then, I throw my hair into a bun.

When Lev walked in here with Zoey and Aidan, part of my heart started beating again. However, a large piece is still missing, and I intend to get him back. I wanted to kiss him and punch him. But the truth is, if it were me, I would've done the very same.

How do you fault someone for protecting their family?

"You can't," I grumble to myself as I stomp down the stairs. "Stupid idiot, going off half-cocked, trying to be heroic."

Tonight was supposed to go differently. Guliana finally gave me the green light to set up the meeting with the guys. I was planning on telling them everything tonight.

"We already know where he is," Lev announces as I walk into the room. Now that Zoey and Aidan are safely tucked in their beds with more guards than the President, and my grandmother is downstairs being treated, I get to kill a thirsty bitch.

I clench my fists at the reminder that my grandmother is downstairs fighting for her life, and my kids are upstairs with scrapes and bruises because of the cunt rag with a plastic face.

Samantha Davenport Baker, or whoever the fuck she is, will die with my hands wrapped around her throat as I gleefully watch her life be snuffed out.

"Where is he?" I demand, securing the hair sticks in my messy bun before I check my arm and thigh holsters to ensure I have all my blades before loading the magazine of my Walther PDP F-series 9mm semiautomatic pistol. Then I make my way over to the weapons table, perusing the other weapons before picking up a gun, pepper spray, and a cable saw.

"There's a tracker in his arm," Lev begins, bringing up an image on the screen. "He's at the part of our warehouse still under construction."

Twisting to face them, I cross my arms and arch my brow at this revelation. "You guys have a warehouse?" I ask.

Owen steps behind me, pressing a kiss to the side of my neck before he bends to slide his hunting knife into my other thigh holster. "We didn't want to bring work home," he explains.

Deciding now isn't the time to discuss this issue. I focus my attention on Thomas as he starts giving out orders.

"The building schematics show there are many points of entry, and based on where the signal from the chip is coming, Wes is being held near the loading dock." Thomas aims a laser pointer at the rear left corner of the warehouse.

Lev steps forward to speak next. "This part of the property sits four miles south of our new building." Then, he points to three different spots. "These are the best spots to enter so we can pin her down."

Thomas cuts back in, "We don't know how many people Samantha has with her, but she's far from sane. This means I don't think she'll hesitate to risk all our lives to win."

"That being said, no one puts Wes's life in danger," I command, and all the eyes in the room turn to me.

"You heard the woman. Now move," Thomas barks, and people begin to file out.

An arm wraps around my waist, holding me in place. "I want to make myself perfectly clear. I will handcuff you to me if you move too far out of our line of sight, Love." Wyatt demands.

"The same goes for all of you. I know more than three dozen ways to disarm and incapacitate a full-grown man," I retort.

We climb into the back of the armored truck, none of us speaking more than a few words the entire ride.

My leg bounces as I try not to let my thoughts suck me in. A hand rests on my knee, holding my thigh in place. "Wes's coming home with us tonight, Ry. We're going to make sure of it," Sebastian promises. I nod, letting his reassurance wash over me, fortifying my resolve.

"The drones are coming up with at least fifty heat signatures. The bulk of them are guarding the entire route to the warehouse," Lev announces as we draw nearer.

Shouting comes through the comms as the truck comes to a stop. Gunshots ring out moments later and we jump into action. I'm adding another knife to my ankle holster when a hand comes into view.

"Remember what I said, Ry," Wyatt reminds me, helping me stand. Then, he pulls his skull mask down over his face and heads for the back door.

I roll my eyes and follow, hopping out of the truck.

Fernando and Elias step into view. "Follow this way. Thomas and Reign are leading the Bravo and Gamma teams for the front assault. We're sneaking in through the side."

"Lead the way," Sebastian requests, and then the seven of us are running hidden under the dark of night.

We've been running for five minutes when the warehouse comes into view, and we stop. "At least a dozen men stayed behind to guard the building," Elias announces. "Thomas and the two teams are working their way to us, but they think they'll be at least another twenty minutes."

"No," I blurt. "Wes may not have twenty minutes. We need another pl—"

"Down," Lev yells, covering my body and spinning as we hit the ground with a thud seconds before shards of bark fly as bullets slam into it.

I roll out from his hold onto my stomach, pulling out my gun and returning fire. Two bodies drop before I shift my aim. Sebastian and Elias are battling four men while Owen and Fernando work as a team to handle the five men moving in. Lev unloads four rounds in quick succession, dropping a body with each shot.

A man slips from the darkness, and I fire without hesitation. He drops before he gets a chance to raise his weapon.

Popping up from my position, I reach for a knife and jump on the back of one of the men circling Fernando and Owen. He shouts, but I'm yanking his head back and slicing the blade across his throat.

I release him, stepping back before he drops to the ground while the last of our attackers are killed. Then, we move the last few hundred feet, taking out guards until our path inside is clear.

"He's down this way," Lev says, pointing to our left as we enter the building.

Nodding, Fernando takes the lead position, making signals to stay quiet and get into formation. We barely make it to the end of the hallway when at least a handful of men step into the path with their guns drawn, but we're ready.

I duck low and tuck myself behind a door, aiming for the legs of one of the shooters. He goes down first before the guys take out the rest of our opposition. I hear a grunt, and a body hits the floor near me.

"Fuck," Elias shouts, and I see him clutch his chest. I prepare to run toward him, but he holds up his palm. "It didn't pierce the vest. I just forgot how much it hurts when there's impact. Keep going. I'll be fine."

I sigh in relief. "Good. Now, let's go."

"Don't get yourself killed, Prescott. I only just started liking you assholes," Sebastian quips, and Fernando snorts.

We enter an open space when all hell breaks loose. Men pour out from all angles, and I prepare to fight.

A draft blows through the windowless building, and the hairs rise on the back of my neck seconds before I hear a shriek and I'm tackled to the ground.

"You stupid bitch." I hear someone wail as the wind is knocked out of me. The voice registers as she climbs on me.

Hands wrap around my neck as Brittany sneers. "You should've never come here. We had a plan, and you ruin—"

My dagger sinks into her side before she can finish. She screams, tipping off me. Then I'm on top of her, my arm rearing back and punching her in the face.

"Cry me a river. Your delusional skank friend needs to know when to take a loss," I hiss, then I rip the knife from her side and raise my hands above my head before slamming the blade into her chest.

"Why couldn't you just choose me? We are perfect together." I hear Samantha screech, and I don't think. I stand up and run in the direction of the voice.

I stop short, slowing my steps so my boots don't make too much noise. "Samantha, you have to know the only way this ends is with your death," Wes reasons.

Peeking into the room, I see Wes tied to a chair with a gun to his head.

"Don't hide gutter trash. I already know you're here," Samantha snarls.

Inhaling, I temper my anger. I need to be smart about this. It's just me, and I have no idea when the other guys will arrive. They'll raise hell that I didn't wait, but I'm not taking the chance with Wes's life.

"Drop your weapons at the door, bitch, and get in here," Samantha demands.

"Don't you come in here, Ariah," Wes counters, but I ignore

him. He can yell at me when he's home safely. Then, I'm going to torture him slowly until he promises not to do this shit again.

I step into the room, and she waves the pistol around in the air. "All the weapons." Then she aims it back at Wes's head. "Or half his face will be splattered on the floor."

"There's no need for the threats," I mutter, removing my thigh holsters first. As I bend, I meet Wes's gaze. He imperceptibly dips his head, understanding my plan.

Placing my knives and gun down, I stand and then walk further into the room.

"That's close enough," Samantha spits once I'm about five feet from them.

I stop. "Samantha, you don't—" Wes begins, but she presses the muzzle of the gun against his head.

"Shut up, Wesley." She sneers at his name with so much hatred.

"Hey," I exclaim, trying to get her attention back on me. It works, Samantha's glare fixes on me.

Lifting the firearm, she motions for me to get down. "On your knees, you dumb slut."

I fight back an eye roll, staring her in the face. "How about you put down that gun?"

"How about you get on the fucking ground where you've always belonged," Samantha snaps, training the pistol back on Wes. "Before I shoot him."

My hands shoot up. "Okay. . . okay," I breathe, slowly lowering to the floor.

"You should've heeded my messages to leave," Samantha declares. "I gave you so many chances to disappear!" She swings the handgun back at me when I'm nearly on the ground. "But you wouldn't fucking l—"

Samantha's words are cut off when Wes slams his head back, cracking her in the face. She screams, dropping the gun and grabbing her nose. Blood streams down as her weapon skitters away. I'm moving before she registers her mistake.

Springing off the ground, I charge forward. A snarl passes my lip as I pull back and jab her three times in the side of her head.

Samantha falls, and I hop on top of her, fisting her hair tight in my grip.

"You talk too damn much," I bark, landing blow after blow. She tries to protect herself, but I strike any spot she isn't covering. "You threatened me, tried to kill people I love, and took what was never yours."

"Ariah, watch out," Wes warns, but I'm so lost in my rage that I miss when she must have taken out a weapon.

I'm knocked off balance when I see something glint in the light.

Utilizing my momentary loss of focus, Samantha dives at me with a knife. I roll out of the way when the clank of metal hitting concrete sounds.

"I'm going gut you. Then make Wes fuck me in your blood before I sell those bastard twins on the black market," Samantha shrieks running at me again, but I'm already twisting up into a crouch.

Nope. Dead bitch on aisle one.

My foot swings out, kicking her in the side of her knee at full force. I hear the crack as she drops to the ground, losing the knife in the process.

Samantha shrieks, springing off the ground faster than expected, and tackles me to the ground.

"You stupid bitch. You never know when to quit," Samantha sneers as my back hits the floor. I grunt but manage to move my head before her nails can come into contact with my face. Before she can make another attempt to scratch me, I grab my hair sticks and swing, stabbing her in the shoulder.

She screams, clutching her arm as she falls off me. I'm up and straddling her chest and fisting her hair while I punch her repeatedly in her face. "No. You're the one who doesn't know when to take a hint. But don't worry, I'll happily teach you," I snap, landing another blow to her face. Then, I'm off the ground and kicking her side.

"You think you can threaten my kids," I shout, stomping on her fingers with the heel of my combat books. Samantha's choked sobs echo throughout the room, but it's nowhere near enough. "You think you can take from me and not lose the offending limb?" I snarl, slamming my boot down on her shoulder.

Samantha kicks out, and I accidentally go down. Then she belly crawls in the direction of the knife, but I've had enough.

Standing, I dart around her, whipping out the cable saw, locking the wire around her neck, and tugging.

Samantha's cries cease as she scrambles to find air. Her hands fly up, desperately trying to pry away the thin piece of metal cutting into her throat.

"You can call me karma, bitch, because I always come back swinging," I growl at her choked cries, but I refuse to let up until I know she's dead.

I hear footsteps and briefly look up to see the guys are finally here, but then return my attention to ending this cunt.

Somehow, she finds enough strength to speak. "Let me go, or Wes dies," Samantha croaks.

"Nice try bitch," I seethe. "Your reign of terror is fucking over." I pull the garrote tighter.

Samantha's fingers scratch at my hands, but I don't budge.

"It's true," she gurgles. "There's a chip in Wes, just like Owen's."

I hesitate. *There's no way*. Shaking my head, I exclaim, "You're full of shit. You'd say or do anything because you know you're dying tonight." Then, I pull the cord tight again, and her fingers desperately claw for freedom before she throws her arm up, displaying a watch.

"Check for yourself," she croaks. I peer down and freeze.

78
SAMANTHA

I gasp, precious air filling my lungs as Ariah slackens her grip a sliver.

"Talk fast, and don't waste my time. What do you mean 'like Owen's'?" the trashy bitch asks.

Rubbing at my throat, I rasp, "I mean, once he got here, I drugged his ass and had a chip put in."

"No," Ariah whispers, further loosening the chain around my neck. "You're lying."

My nostrils flare at the doubt in her tone, as if all I've done isn't evidence enough that I should never be trifled with. *Everyone always underestimates me.* "Does anything I've done so far strike you as a bluff?" I challenge.

"What do you want?" she demands as all the fucking Heirs step into view. I survey them one by one. They all stare down at me, their mouths twisting in disgust. Wyatt and Sebastian Grant, Levi Washington, Owen Jefferson, and—.

My gaze lands on the person that part of this was all for. Wesley Benjamin Edgewood stands tall. His imposing form towers over me even more from my place on the floor. It's not the vibe I get when he looks at *her*. He sees her as his equal—even more than that. Wesley regards her with so much respect, adoration, and *love*. Fucking love.

I never stood a chance. I knew it the minute he walked over on the first day of school and saw her.

Well, fuck them and their love.

Sneering, I hiss, "You let me leave, and I'll let him live."

"How stupid do you think we are?" Wes seethes.

"You haven't done shit to earn that kind of trust," Lev adds.

Rolling my eyes, I point to my watch and state, "Yet you'll have to chance it because if you don't, my last act will be to set this off."

I see it—the moment I know I've earned my freedom.

There's a pause, and then my face smacks against the concrete.

"Get the fuck out of here, and I better never see you again," Ariah shouts. "Or I'll kill you on sight."

Crawling, I slowly stagger to my feet. My vision doubles, causing me to miss a step when I nearly fall, but I hit a wall and keep my balance.

Their footsteps urge me on. I need to get the hell out of here.

Straightening, I limp down the stairs out into dewy air. I peer up into the sky, studying the orange and pink hues of the rising sun against the white clouds. A resolve sets in. I walk halfway to the fence and turn. They are all standing there, the six of them—unified.

Rage boils in my veins. They don't get to live happily ever after and walk off into their futures while I pick up my broken pieces. They stole my happiness, and I plan to destroy theirs.

Lifting my finger to my watch, I shout, "You're all fucking fools if you think I'd ever let you win." I take five more steps back before I continue, "Enjoy your *love* for the five seconds it'll last."

Wes runs outside, charging in my direction, but he's too fucking late. I press the button on my watch. Then, all I hear is a scream before the bang.

79
SEBASTIAN

"Look at them go," Wyatt says, smiling as Zoey and Aidan take turns tittering before they fall on each other.

It's been five months since the horrifying night, and it's been a mixture of anger, acceptance, and forgiveness, but all of it has led to a stronger bond.

We spent the first two focused on revenge—revenge for what was taken. The innocence that was nearly snatched from us before they had time to experience life. We turned over every stone until we eliminated every connection to the Filiae Bellonae, Matthew Baker, and Samantha.

I look to the spot where Wes should sit and rub the back of my neck as it remains empty.

Giggles pull me from my thoughts as Lev chases after them. The twins break into laughter, switching to crawling to get away faster. "I'm coming to get you." Lev lifts his hands like a mummy and slowly stomps toward them.

"Don't you scare them," Ariah mockingly scolds, striding into the living room. She's passing me when I wrap my arms around her thighs, holding her in place.

"Go, Lev. I'll hold her off," I joke, resting my head on her ass.

Owen play punches my side. "Unhand her, you twat. So, I may challenge you to a duel," he says in a horrible British accent.

Ariah's laughter comes to an abrupt stop. "Wait, look."

I turn in time to see Aidan ready to step.

"Someone grab a camera," Wyatt demands.

I release Ariah's legs and pull out my phone. "On it," I announce, hitting record just before he takes his first real steps without falling.

Ariah sits on my lap, leaning her head on my shoulder as we watch. Zoey stands and falls but doesn't let it phase her.

The Bradford and Edgewood stubbornness is alive and well.

"Wes should be here for this," she says wistfully as Zoey uses the couch to get up.

Humming my agreement, I kiss the side of her neck. "He should, and you know he would be if he could."

Zoey falls again before her face sets into a scowl that screams Wes, and I snort. Then she climbs back to her feet, holding on until she's sure.

"I think she's going to do it," Owen murmurs next to us.

"There's a package for you," Reign says, and Zoey plunks down on her butt. The look she gives him screams retributions.

Laughing, I stop recording, put my phone on my leg, and then take the envelope from him.

"Who's it from?" Lev asks, walking over with Aidan on his hip. Wyatt quickly follows with a sour-faced Zoey.

I flip it over and see a lavender-colored seal. It's a skull wearing a jewel-filled crown. Ariah stiffens at the sight.

"There's an inscription," I mutter, lifting the envelope closer to read it. "Per mortem vita nova regeneramur ex cineribus una ut."

"Through death comes new life. We are reborn out of the ashes as one," Ariah mumbles.

I look up at her. "What?"

"Call the nanny," is all Ariah says before standing.

Tearing it open, I pull out a written note along with an invitation. I open the note and then read it for everyone to hear.

The Heirs of Edgewood,

You have been tested and found fit to join. Your efforts have not gone unnoticed, but you must understand that if you agree to move forward, life for you all will take a drastic turn.

You all have until the end of the month to make your decision.

           Think wisely,
           The Princeps

"Angel?" Owen questions, his face matching mine with a look of confusion.

"The invitation is to the Tribunal six months from now," I read aloud.

Wyatt moves in front of her. "What's going on?"

Ariah spins to face us. She inhales a fortifying breath and then says, "It's time. I'll tell you everything."

80
ARIAH

"What do you mean you've been working with the Novus Ordo Seclorum?" Sebastian inquires.

This isn't going terribly, but I didn't think they'd repeatedly ask me the same questions.

Sighing, I repeat, "When I was in Colorado, I discovered my dad and grandfather were having meetings."

Wyatt and Owen are the only ones who find this amusing. The rest of them scrutinize my breath like it will give them insight into how we arrived here.

"So, how did you get in contact with a major secret organization?" Lev asks.

"They actually reached out to me."

It took almost half the day to get them to stop peppering me with questions. I smile at the memory of that conversation as I work to fix my hair. The loosely braided faux hawk shows my hair's vibrant midnight indigo, lavender, and violet colors.

Pausing, I stare at myself in the mirror. The woman before me is far different than the one who stood here nearly three years ago. Physically, I look the same, but mentally and emotionally, I've grown, and the guys have been part of that growth.

"When were you going to tell us that you were in charge of the Novus Ordo—"

Guliana interjects, interrupting Wyatt. "NOS is just fine. Wouldn't want you to have to keep saying the mouthful every time," she jokes, peering across the table at them while I'm sitting at her side, trying to hide my smirk.

"The goal was always to have you sit in these seats with Ariah at the helm," Guliana continues. "But you all needed to be tested. The Fraternitas has been in turmoil for too long. Between the resurgence of the Filiae Bellonae and then the disgraced Senator Baker and Miss Davenport, there's a need to revamp the leadership structure in Edgewood."

"Please be seated. We are about to begin." Tamara's voice booms through the room as I blink back into focus.

Owen snakes an arm around my waist. "You keep getting lost in your head, Angel," he murmurs before bending and kissing the top of my head.

"Just thinking back over the last year. Hell, the last two and a half years," I answer as we cross the room to take our seats around the table.

I slip my hand into Lev's and squeeze as we sit, grinning at how much he welcomes my touch. He's still the only one doing all the tying in the bedroom, but light touches are his favorite new thing outside of the bedroom. Having two almost toddlers whose love language is putting sticky hands on your face when you least expect it is definitely a form of immersion therapy.

Returning my affection with a squeeze, Lev rubs small circles with his thumb against the back of my hand. "How long do you think we have to be in the penguin suits?" Lev mutters, adjusting the collar of his crisp white button-up tuxedo shirt.

"You'd think members of such high society would be acclimated to such clothing. Some might even say it's the country club starter kit uniform," I tease, and they all laugh.

The next hour goes over all the requirements for the upcoming year. I survey the room, noticing all the factions that make up the NOS. Many faces are new to me, but a few aren't.

"Isn't that Azrael?" Sebastian nods his head to the space to the left of us.

My gaze shifts to where a giant man whose entire face is covered in a skull tattoo sits back in his suit. He's accompanied by three other men covered in tattoos as well. "Who are they?" I ask.

"The Lycéan."

I prepare to follow up with a tell me more, but Sebastian shakes his head, and Owen leans over and whispers, "A story for another day."

"You will each find a blindfold and earplugs in the box before you. When instructed, please put these on. Anyone caught trying to violate these rules will be dealt with," Tamara warns.

Picking up the case, I examine its contents. A silk blindfold and two black buds in a smaller container are inside. "I should bring these home," I joke.

Sebastian's gaze heats. "The things we could do with you while you can't hear or see—these *are* coming home."

My cheeks heat, and I clear my throat, refocusing on Tamara.

"You'll all be called down to the center of the room, where you'll be required to take the pledge. Once you've done that, you'll be tattooed with the symbol of the Novus Ordo Seclorum on your right index finger. This will also be where your ring will go, keeping the symbol hidden," she explains. Then she announces we're waiting on a few more members so we can talk amongst ourselves.

We're all laughing and talking while we wait for the induction ceremony to begin when Lev's jovial mood morphs, his smile melting into a snarl. I attempt to spin to see what could change his demeanor so quickly, but Owen holds me in place.

"Ah, if it isn't the beautiful Ariah Bradford." A thick Russian accent shouts, drawing Tamara's attention.

Gritting her teeth, Tamara's nostrils flare. "Mr. Volkov, you're late. Please take your seat so we can finally proceed," she commands.

Mr. Volkov hisses something in Russian before he says, "It's such a tragedy I wasn't able to make your acquaintance. Hopefully, that will change now that we'll see more of each other at these events."

"If you *hope* to keep your spine, I'd suggest you never try to *make her acquaintance again*," Owen seethes, gripping his knife.

There's another grunt, and then the noxious cologne assaulting my nose is gone. "Someone want to fill me in on what the fuck that was about?" I demand.

"After. Let's get through this first, Love. We don't want to taint the evening with the underbelly scum," Wyatt explains.

Tamara orders us to place our masks and earplugs in, halting any protests I would've made about waiting.

I feel the person before their cold fingers tap my shoulder before helping me rise. The walk doesn't last long before I hear the distinct sound of an elevator. I can feel the heat of other bodies, most of which belong to my guys.

The doors open and we file out, walking another ten steps before the smell of fire hits my nostrils. My blindfold is pulled off, and I look around the room. We're in the inner sanctum of the NOS. Guliana and I have had meetings here over the last few months.

At the front of the room is a stage where a man prepares the branding station. *That explains the smell of fire.*

A smiling Guliana signals for us to pull out the earplugs. "So glad to have you all here, finally." Then, she approaches and hugs each of us. "I want to explain how tonight will work, as you all will have a different induction ceremony than the rest of the NOS members."

Nodding, I move into Wyatt's side, needing his comfort for this part. It's bittersweet. We're finally here, but Wes isn't.

"You're all fucking fools if you think I'd ever let you win. Enjoy your love for the five seconds it'll last."

The words of the repulsive cunt still plague my nightmares. She's cost us so much.

"Stay with us, Dove. It's what Wes would've wanted," Lev encourages, but I want to tell him that if that's the case, he should be here to tell me.

My eyes bulge from my skull when Wes jumps from the platform, heading in Samantha's direction.

"Wes," I shout, but he's too focused to hear me.

A cry rips from my chest as I watch the scene unfold in slow motion.

Shaking my head clear, I focus on Guliana's instructions. "We've moved to the private portion of the ceremony. You'll each be called up one at a time and take the pledge."

It's time.

"Once you've done that, you will receive your brand. However, unlike the others, an invisible ink tattoo will circle it. Then the tattoo Tamara described earlier will be inked onto your finger before you receive your ring, which is only for appearance's sake," Guliana states.

Guliana moves to the podium, grabbing a gold metal box. Then she hands it to the man and continues. "In the meetings, no one in the room will ever know any of you are the Princeps or that Ariah is the true Princep. This is what allows for your identity to remain hidden. As we discussed, you'll fill some vacancies over the coming years. I will remain on until those spaces are filled."

Owen steps forward and speaks, "I, Owen Preston Jefferson, swear to uphold the tenets of the Novus Ordo Seclorum. I pledge my loyalty to the Novus Ordo Seclorum. I pledge my allegiance to the mission and swear to take all I know to my grave, never divulging its secrets to nonmembers. I pledge this of sound mind, body, and spirit." Then, the branding iron is pressed into the inside of his upper arm.

I have to cover my mouth to hide my snicker. Owen's face is gleeful, and the person branding him looks almost appalled.

Owen moves over, and then Sebastian's name is called. Wyatt quickly follows, leaving Lev and I standing at the bottom of the steps to the stage.

"Levi Washington, please step forward," Guliana orders, and he ascends the stairs, joining the others.

I sigh, staring at the empty space next to Lev. Wes's absence is glaringly apparent as only the four of them stand on the dais.

The echo of dress shoes reverberates off the hollowed-out walls of the once-quiet room, momentarily distracting me from watching Lev receive his brand.

Turning my head, I look toward the sound but no one appears. My nose scrunches in confusion before I return my gaze to the stage.

Lev is holding up his arm when the scent of spiced, smoked brandy fills my nostrils.

"There's my forever girl."

My eyes flick up, and I take my first real breath of the night. "Wes," I murmur, turning to level him with a glare.

"I can't believe you assholes didn't tell me you chipped Samantha," I yell, mostly in relief, but rage is mixed in. My heart stopped and started in the span of twenty seconds.

"In our defense, it would only work if she didn't get someone else to make the tech," Lev mumbles, and my pupils double in size.

I massage my temples before I glare at him. Between the ringing in my ears from an exploding Samantha and my loud shrieks, my head is throbbing.

Lev, at least, has the sense to look remorseful. Not Wes, though. That stupid fucker arches his brow in challenge, and I know what will come out of his stupid mouth before it opens.

"I did what I had to do." I mimic him as he speaks.

"That's right, asshat. I know your lines," I quip. "I'm going to tattoo it to your forehead in your sleep."

Throwing his hands up, Wes says, "I know. I know. I'm late. I was completing a very important mission."

My brow arches, "What could've been more important than this?"

Wes's lips curl into a Cheshire Cat smile. "You'll just have to wait and find out."

I huff, covering up my amused expression, but he's already seen it. I'm just so grateful he's here and not in the million pieces that cunt blew herself into. *I'm buying Karma a Christmas gift. That bitch came in clutch.*

His mother shakes her head. "Wesley Edgewood. Better late than never, son. Please step forward."

Wes takes his pledge, and I'm called on stage. I begin my pledge. It's the same as theirs except for one line. "I, Ariah Elaine Bradford, pledge to uphold the requirements as *the Princep* in the highest regard. I will do my due diligence to fulfill this position's roles and responsibilities until my time as Princep is complete."

I'm handed a towel, "Bite," the man grunts, and I do as instructed. I inhale, hoping to stem some of the pain, but nothing can prepare you for hot iron touching your skin. The towel muffles my shrill cries, and the initial pain is thankfully over nearly as quickly as it started.

The man immediately applies Aloe Vera on my arm and then covers it. "This is a non-stick bandage. You'll need to change this out and wear a bandage until your skin starts to crust over. No petroleum-based products, and don't pick any scabs."

I nod, then stand with the guys. "Did anyone see theirs before it was covered up?" I ask.

"It's the NOS emblem sans words. My guess is the tattoo will be the words," Wyatt replies.

"Makes sense," I hum. A lock snicks, and I turn to see we're alone. "Where did they go?"

I spin back around to see five men kneeling before me. My mouth drops open.

"Ariah Elaine Bradford," Wes begins, holding a perfectly simple, flawless princess-cut diamond engagement ring.

I feel tears prick my eyes. "What are you—" I can't even finish. I'm in complete shock.

"The day you stepped foot in Edgewood, our worlds changed in the best of ways," Lev adds, holding my hand.

"Some of us fought more than others, but our paths met at the time and spot they were meant to," Sebastian declares.

The tears I was holding fall, rolling down my cheeks.

Standing, Owen wipes my face, kissing them away. "We never want to exist in a world where you aren't."

"And we won't," Wyatt exclaims as the rest of them rise to their feet. "You know we won't say all the flowery things because no isn't an option here."

I snort. "You all are always so romantic."

Wes places the ring on my finger, pushing it on. "I thought we already established that you don't want roses and chocolates." He grips my neck, running his thumb along its column. "You want hand necklaces and dirty fucks."

A throat clears, but Wes doesn't move. "It's time for the meeting to begin," Tamara announces, and I want to stab the woman.

Releasing me, Wes bends and whispers. "And dirty fucks are what you'll get for the rest of your life." Then, he walks away, leaving me equal parts turned on and frustrated.

LEV

THREE YEARS LATER...

"I swear you two better get over here," Ariah groans, and I hear the joint laughter of the twins.

"Looks like packing for our honeymoon is going smashingly," I mutter, and the guys laugh.

Wes joins me, leaning against the wall as Zoey and Aidan come barreling through the hallway.

Sebastian and Wyatt scoop them up, then bring them to the couch. They're covered in chocolate, and I can guess what they've gotten into.

"What have you two been up to?" I inquire.

"I'll tell you what they've been up to." Ariah holds up the empty bag of Halloween candy.

Wes shoots off the wall and engulfs Ariah in a hug while I signal for Owen to bring a warm rag to Sebastian and Wyatt so they can get rid of the evidence.

Zoey and Aidan giggle, nearly sidelining our mission before it's even begun.

"Wesley Edgewood, you better move," Ariah begins to protest but stops once he kisses her.

I clear my throat once the coast is clear, and Wes releases her lips, holding her in place. "It's Bradford now, remember," he informs her.

"Only for a day, buddy, and if you keep this up, we won't make it to two."

"Five," Sebastian states, and Ariah flushes red.

All these years later, she still gets the best tint to her cheeks when faced with punishments.

"Oh no, Dove, that doesn't sound very nice," I tease. "Now, what could these two innocent angels have done?"

I have to fight back my snort because these two are anything but angelic when they team up.

"They ate all the candy after I told them it was for their costume party once we get back," Ariah huffs.

Oh, this is going to be glorious.

"I see no evidence that they've committed the crimes they're being accused of," Wes states with such seriousness even I question their known guilt.

Ariah's mouth opens and closes at least three times before she crosses her arms and utters, "Testing the limits of our vows already?"

That response catapults me back to yesterday.

"Today, we commit our lives to each other. We commit to the greatest of times and even more to the hardest of them. We commit to supporting each other in our triumphs and struggles." I hear Sebastian promise, but I'm too focused on our wife.

She's stunning. Ariah is wearing a white lace dress embellished with thousands of midnight blue Swarovski crystals along the train and in her veil. The mermaid-style dress has a strapless sweetheart neckline that looks painted on. I want to say screw the reception, throw her over my shoulder, and fuck her while she's tied with the white rope I bought just for this occasion.

Wyatt brushes the wisp of hair from her breathtaking face into the cascading curls falling over her right shoulder. "Our love story transcends the laws of fate because we stand here pledging before all present and absent that we are bound to each other through all of life's iterations."

"We'll honor our bond above all else and destroy all who try to oppose it. No objections will be heard today—or ever because I'll cut out the tongue of anyone who dares to."

I bend my head and pretend to be clearing my throat to cover up my amusement. Only Owen would find a way to threaten to cut someone in his vows.

Stepping forward, I capture Ariah's hand, peering down at the three slim diamond-encrusted bands adorning her left ring finger before gazing up at her.

She smiles through her tears as she mouths, 'I love you,' and my chest grows tight at the burst of the all-consuming love within our family.

"You are our North Star. We look to you and are home. You are the Ursa Major to our twins—fiercely protective and unconditionally loving. You pour support, passion, advice, and forgiveness into our lives, so we commit to ensuring that your cup is always full," I profess, sliding the band on her finger before placing her hand into Wes's.

"There aren't enough words in all lost and known languages that can ever encompass how deep our bond is and how much deeper it will grow. Even the totality of the words in our commitment to each other barely scratches the surface of what we have," Wes exclaims, pushing the ring higher. He pauses just before it's fully on, looking deep into her stormy gray eyes, and declares, "We will love you in this life and every reincarnation, Ariah Elaine Bradford, because you are our forever girl."

"Don't give me that the evidence speaks for itself," Ariah argues, pulling me from my thoughts.

Aidan and Zoey are sitting between Owen, Sebastian, and Wyatt as Wes begins his closing arguments. "At best, this is construed as—"

"Daddy, what's conchood?" Aidan asks.

"It's a train," Zoey blurts with the utmost confidence.

Wes shakes his head. "We'll go over the definition after I get these charges dropped."

Ariah is trying desperately to hide her smile, making this trial funnier. "They were caught with chocolate all over their faces and candy wrappers in their toy box," she retorts. "This is an open and shut case."

Owen stands. "I object. No evidence has been produced, and such inflaming allegations only serve to bias the jury. I motion for the statement to be stricken from the record."

I burst into laughter. "Sustained," I state.

Ariah throws her hands up in mock horror. "Justice will not be served in this kangaroo court. I motion for this matter to be addressed by impartial parties."

"Motion denied. This case is dismissed with prejudice," I instruct, knocking my fist on the wall just as Kylan, Kellan, and Jamie enter the room.

The twins shoot to their feet, excited to see their aunt and uncles. "Is it time to go?" Zoey squeals, and Jamie nods. Then, the twins dart out of the room without so much as a look back.

"Not even a thank you," Sebastian mutters, and Ariah cackles.

"That's what you all get for letting those cute faces fool you," she quips.

Lunging forward, I catch her off guard and throw her over my shoulder. I spin and wave goodbye to Ariah's laughing siblings. "Enjoy your honeymoon," Jamie shouts at my retreating form.

I'm upstairs, tossing Ariah onto the bed, when the guys come in.

"Someone's in need of being punished," Wyatt murmurs.

"How about you save the punishments for yourselves? I'm not the one defending two chocolate bandits," she retorts. "As a matter of fact, I should be the one planning ways to punish each of you."

"Is that right, Angel? You think we're the ones who should be punished?" Owen teases, cutting off her panties.

"You could've pulled them off, you know?" Ariah tries and fails to reprimand. The lust in her eyes and the wetness of her lacy black boyshorts say she's ready to play.

Sebastian yanks his sweatpants down, grips her hair, and orders, "Open." Ariah's lips part, and Sebastian slams inside. "You know better than to lie, Spitfire. This honeymoon is going to be filled with counting for you."

She groans when Owen slides under her, and Wyatt positions himself at her entrance as I pass him the lube. It's the one that Ariah loves because she comes so much harder.

"Fuck," she screams around Sebastian's dick, making him moan. Wyatt's dripping the gel onto his three fingers while he devours her pussy.

I stride over and drop my boxers, my cock painfully hard. "I need you," I grunt, and she's wrapping her hand around my shaft. Wyatt tosses the bottle to me, and I squirt it over my length and her fingers.

"This is going to be quick and dirty, Angel. We can slow fuck you when we get to our island in Matu Rauoro," Owen growls. Ariah mewls as he slowly works his way into her ass.

Once he's fully seated himself, Wyatt lifts her legs and slams into her pussy. "Holy fucking shit, this is. . . fuck—" Wyatt mumbles, barely coherent.

Wes climbs on the bed, straddling her chest. "I think that gorgeous mouth of yours runs enough that it can fit two of us. Why don't we test that theory?" Then, he pushes the head of his cock inside her mouth.

My dick stiffens at the scene before me. Owen and Wyatt feverishly piston in and out of her. Wyatt throws his head back, growling, before he looks down to where they're joined and doubles his pace.

Ariah's unintelligible words muffle as she grips my cock harder, making me want to stay in this moment.

"Turn her over," Wes commands, and we all quickly adjust, switching positions. Owen is now kneeling behind her, grinding back into her puckered hole. My cock is thrusting in and out of her mouth while Sebastian and Wyatt are getting jerked off.

"I'm never leaving this pussy," Wes snarls, snapping his hips up to match Owen's pace.

Ariah pulls back and demands, "Fucking harder!"

Challenge accepted.

Sebastian reaches between Wes and Ariah and massages her clit as he and Owen fuck her so hard she's gagging on my cock. "Keep doing that," I stammer, feeling the tingle low in my gut as my balls begin to draw tight.

Wyatt swirls one of her nipples between his fingers as Wes takes the other into his mouth.

"Fuck, grip me tighter. That's our dirty little slut," Wes grunts between thrusts.

"I'm going to die buried inside you, and I'll go out with a smile," Owen claims, slapping her left then right ass cheek before gripping her hips and pounding.

Ariah hums, and then her body begins to shake. The collective moans in the room, announcing they are quickly behind her.

"Fuckk," Wyatt shouts at the same time Owen does. Wyatt pulls from her hand and nuts all over her back.

"Your pussy grips me so—" Wes's words morph into a snarl of curses as he comes.

Sebastian lifts her as he sits on the bed. Wes rolls out of the way just as Sebastian rolls his hips up and pushes Ariah down. "Oh... my... fuck... I'm—"

She doesn't get to finish because I'm up and in her mouth, fisting her hair with both hands as I fuck her face. I hear Sebastian roar at the same time Ariah's release is triggered. Only then do I finally let go and shoot my load down her throat, then pull out of her mouth.

"I could do this every day," she mumbles as Sebastian lays her on the bed. She hums. "I can only imagine how great it would be to be woken out of my sleep to you guys fucking me."

We all exchange looks, but Wyatt answers, "That's something we'd gladly oblige." The sly fucker smirks. She's going to punch his nuts when she finally finds out he used to sneak into her room to get her off while she sleeps. But that's a future problem.

Now we get to celebrate our union together for three weeks, unplugged.

●

The SUV pulls to a stop, and we begin exiting the car. Ariah moves to grab her luggage when she's scooped into Sebastian's arms. "Nope. The flight crew will handle that. For the next three weeks, it's endless pampering and relaxation for you—for all of us. We've more than earned it."

I hum my agreement, looking forward to our first real vacation. The last few years have been a nonstop loop of bullshit. Couple that with all the responsibilities at NOS as we try to fill the remaining seats and work to oust members who have no place at our table—unplugging will be amazing.

Our security team gives the 'all clear' and we head for the jet. Sebastian is carrying Ariah up the stairs, and the guys follow behind.

Sebastian is crossing the threshold of the plane when my phone rings.

Everyone turns to me, scowling. "Sorry, I forgot to turn it off. Let me see who's calling, and then it's no electronics," I mutter sheepishly.

I slip the phone from my pants pocket as it begins to ring again. I notice King's name on the caller ID and pick up immediately. The phone is barely to my ear when he says, "It's time."

The End... for now.

Want an early sneak peek of what King needs the Heirs for?
Pre-order the <u>Violence & Virtues Anthology</u>

ACKNOWLEDGMENTS

We did it. It's been a hell of a journey, and there are so many I want to thank for all they've done along the way.

To my readers, thank you, thank you, thank you. You've fueled me in ways you can't begin to imagine!

Big ups to mi family, who have sacrificed so much to help me get my writing career off the ground. There aren't enough ways to show you my gratitude. Meg, momma's doing things!!

Raven! Spoons and knives to eat cake is still wild, but I love you for it. Thank you for always being there, not just for book stuff but for life stuff. From blanks to yelling at me to rest, you've been a pivotal part of my journey.

To my PA, Danielle, you came in at a difficult time and helped smooth out the transition. You run on hot Cheetos, caffeine, and popkern with nacho cheese. All of which helps make the magic happen.

My Alpha Team (Val, Teri, Jenna, Chayde & Lo)!! We might have people coming for us after this one, but we're going to keep bringing it. I can't wait to cause more chaos this year. *See you in The Tombs.*

To Jenn and C, thank you for being a constant source of encouragement, especially when I refused to give myself any grace. I love you heauxs.

To Tara and Ivy, half of the FAAFO chaos group, thank you for the sprints and laughter that helped me get through to the end.

Last but certainly not least, to my teams (TikTok, Street & Promo), y'all are still the best!

Made in the USA
Middletown, DE
24 January 2025